DRAGON'S ARK

A TALE OF THE SUPERNATURAL

by
Thomas
Burchfield

AMBLER HOUSE PUBLISHING
OAKLAND, CALIFORNIA
2011

DISCLAIMER

Monitor County, the setting of this story, is an imagined place with echoes of some very real parts of the California Eastern Sierra. As for the rest, all names, characters, and places are figments of the author's imagination and any resemblance to actual events or persons living and dead—especially the Dead—are purely coincidental.

ISBN 978-0-615-38547-1 print
ISBN 978-0-615-40322-9 ebook

Book Cover Design: Cathi Stevenson/Book Cover Express

Moon and cave image by Photosani; used under license from Shutterstock.com

Copyeditor: Bonnie Britt

Interior Design: Joel Friedlander
http://www.TheBookDesigner.com

Ambler House Publishing
584 Vernon St., #1
Oakland, CA 9410

http://amblerhouse.blogspot.com/

For Elizabeth
As night rose around us, you spoke the magic words.

CONTENTS

....

" …then he was no common man …he was spoken of as the cleverest and most cunning as well as the bravest of the sons of the 'land beyond the forest.' That mighty brain and that iron resolution went with him to his grave, and are even now arrayed against us."

—Dr. Abraham Van Helsing

"And reason's self shall bow the knee
To shadows and delusions here"

—Philip Freneau (1752–1832), "The Indian Burying Ground"

DRAGON'S ARK

The Hunter at Dusk

Jeff Potter was trying to text message the girl he'd left behind when he looked up and saw the mountain racing by. It felt to him like a signpost, its summit a knifepoint above the rim. When he looked back down, the bars on his iPhone had flat-lined. He fired an angry look out the van window.

Just a few miles back, a road sign announced:
"WELCOME TO MONITOR COUNTY!
LAND OF DREAMS!"

But that mountain was no dream, it was a waking, watching nightmare stabbing the innocent blue sky. More than ever, Jeff wanted to return to his old world of box buildings, sweeping power lines and neon lights. The lights most of all. There should be lights everywhere, in every corner, a safe and shadowless world.

Jeff tapped his iPhone once more, as though that would bring it back to life. "No service" was as good as "You're dead." He nearly threw the stupid thing out the van window.

As he stared at the mountain—and it stared back—he felt the urge to tell Mom and Dad to turn around and take him home. "I so wanna go home." But Mom and Dad would think he was a whining kid. It was so hard to say anything. Every time Jeff opened his mouth, stupid things tumbled out. He gazed at the mountain, as it grew taller behind them. "Be silent. Be safe" a voice inside said, a voice that didn't sound like his own.

They drove down into a valley shaped like a jagged-tooth mouth. The mountain watched them all the way. Jeff came to regret his silence and didn't feel safe at all.

"What's the name of that mountain, the pointy one to the west?" he asked the gorgeous chick, the knockout cougar at the resort check-in later that afternoon.

She answered with a gleaming smile that was tinged with sadness: "We call it Dragon's Ark."

By early evening, the Potters were in the resort's touristy pinewood restaurant waiting to order dinner. By now, Jeff's courage to speak his fears had swelled again: "I'll say it! Let's get out of here! Let's go back to L.A. now!"

"It's so beautiful here!" his mother Marsha blurted before he could speak, her papery face so flush, it looked like it would burst into flame. "I think we'll like it! It's like living inside a storybook!"

Now she'd done it. She'd all but committed them to staying. Jeff stared at his lap, concealed his horror-struck eyes behind black wings of hair. Moms always knew your thoughts, somehow—your eyes were open books that made your mind easy to read.

So Jeff closed them and saw the mountain, its unholy black shadow proudly painted across the red of his eyelids, burned in like a camera flash.

The strange eerie voice returned: "Every time you close your eyes, here I will be; you will never sleep again."

Finally, the server came. Andrew Potter, Jeff's dad, ordered a rib-eye steak. "Well done," he stressed, his once-booming voice strangled by recovery into a whine. Mom shook her head and pursed her lips. Dad shrugged off her disapproval as he shoved the menu at the server. He'd once been addicted to booze and power. Now he was addicted to food and unhappiness and people laughed behind the back of this much too fat and silly man.

Jeff hated being seen with Dad. As an act of rebellion, he'd starved himself to a beany thinness. But the contrast between them only inspired hushed jokes about how the two of them looked like a piccolo next to a tuba. Hopeless. Every word and every deed came back to bite somehow. All doors were locked, nothing but fire behind each one.

The server was a rope-muscled redheaded hippie whose t-shirt bragged "I'D RATHER BE CLIMBING" (and, considering his distracted manner, he meant it, too). The shirt was printed with another snowy mountain, but not like that weird sentinel to the west, that fuck-you finger in the sky.

Just as the server turned to take Mom's order, he looked across the dining room. His freckly face opened into a rubbery smile. "Mr. Bartok!" Then he took off, rudely abandoned the Potters to take care of another customer.

Wha the fuck …? Dad's eyes used to stare at the world with an eager ferocity that turned the air blue. Now they looked confused and helpless from within their fatty slits. Gone were the days when Dad was always seated and served before everyone else.

For a second, Jeff thought the server was talking to nobody. Was that a large white pair of hands tearing open a black slit in space? Was that someone stepping through as the space snapped shut behind with a cracking electric hum?

No. Only a trick of the dusky light. And it was just an old man. An old man in black, seated at a table by the window, watching the evening shadows crawl across the meadow and up the emerald hills.

The old man's face was the color of dirty milk and had an awesome number of wrinkles, in the millions, cross-hatching like thousands of tic-tac-toe games, or slashing up and down like razor cuts that should have been bleeding. Wiry hairs sprouted from his ears, bristled out his nose, and lined his wattles. The only things that saved his ugliness were his mustache and the black shades that covered his eyes like goggles. He wore a shiny black feathery suit from neck to toe. Silver hair frothed from his large head down to his shoulders. A hooked nose with flaring nostrils loomed over his sweeping mustache. An old tree stick leaned against the lacquered pine wall nearby.

While Jeff felt shame at his disgust, the server fussed over the old man like he was a cuddly grandpa. "How are ya, Mr. B!? Good seein' you! How was winter up in Alpine Canyon? Will Annie be joining you?"

The weird part about this conversation was that the old man didn't say boo, just smiled and nodded as the server yattered on, as though the old man had his hand up his back like a ventriloquist with his dummy. "What'll you have? Hungry? Just green tea? Comin' right up, sir!"

Jeff's Dad waved as the server zoomed past. The server snapped a look at them. "Oh! Sorry!" Not. "Be right with you!" Wouldn't. Got my own priorities! Dad's eyes sparked with some of that old temper, the anger that had once made the world go SNAP!

Mom anxiously patted Dad's arm. He was one beat away from stopping his overtaxed heart for good. "Andy, that might be the owner!"

Dad glared at the old man, who ignored him, content to watch the light turn to honey as the sun brushed the fir-covered hills and the blue sky turned violet. That was another thing Jeff didn't like. The colors here were so strong, thick and runny, like syrup or bright melting crayons; or like the insides of a freshly opened cadaver.

Dad sniffed, tapped Jeff on the knee and winked: "Now there's a face that wore out two bodies!"

The server slowed as he rushed by. The old man slightly turned his head, his huge ears almost perking like a cat's.

Daaaaaad! Jeff looked down in horror. Jeeez! What a thing to say!

Jeff's dad went on sincerely, "Don't ever get old like that." He patted his huge belly. "All this BS about staying in shape and living to a hundred is just the diet industry picking your pocket. Live fat! Die young! Eat life! That's my motto!" Dad shook with laughter. His face turned jolly red. "Live fat! Die young! Eat life! That's rich! If I was still in TV, I could sell that!" Then his sad look returned because he was not in TV nor much of anyplace anymore but here, in this nowhere.

The server returned, unfriendly and unapologetic for his poor service. He finished taking their orders: Mom, chicken salad; Jeff, tofu salad. Dad ordered another bottle of non-alcoholic Clausthaler. "This beer and wine list wouldn't get a cat drunk," he told the server. "Dog piss and grape juice," he carped when the server had gone.

As the Potters waited, Mom tried to break the strained silence with lame comments: "I'm sure we'll be fine once we move into the house Mr. Garner's got for us." Her eyes danced, feverish with a future only she could see. "You've never lived in the country before, Jeff. Give it a chance! You might like it!"

Dad checked his iPhone. No service here, not in this bottom of the world. He waved heavily out the window at the darkening hills and said, "I bet they'll put some cell towers up there," referring to his new employer. "Garner say the company owns most of the county now."

Jeff looked too. Then, as though on cue, the old man took off his sunglasses and turned his gaze on the Potters as though he had something to say.

His eyes were the worst thing about him. They shone from sunken caves, calm blue, ice cold, like a wolf's, relentless with hunger.

And they were fixed on Dad, as though they could see right inside.

A waking dream suddenly flooded Jeff's mind: The old man standing over Dad, pounding open a trench in Dad's head with his ugly stick—thunk thunk crunch—until skin and skull broke through Dad's thick gray hair, blood and brain oozing out gray and chunky, Dad staring up at the old man with slack dumb amazement, mouth open, the sour odor of blood. The old man's face wore a look of calm relentless brutality.

Jeff slapped his hand over his eyes to stop the dream. The image of the mountain flashed through his brain. When he looked again, Dad was staring at the floor with that same slack look. Their eyes met. Jeff understood. They'd both dreamed that daylight nightmare, dreamed it together.

But the old man had lost interest. His grave attention had returned to the evening sky, as if to say "I'm boss here. Just so you know."

"What's with you two?" Mom smiled nervously. She hadn't seen it, so the world remained wonderful and beautiful.

Dad shook his head: "It's been a long drive." Then he leaned over and whispered reassuringly to his son, "He's just an old man."

The server finally swept down with three plates balanced across his arms. Dad's steak lay half-sunk in a pool of bloody water.

"Hey!" Dad jabbed his finger at the plate. "What's this? When I said well done, I meant well done! What, do I look like a vampire?"

"Sorry Mr. Potty. I'll fix it right now."

The Potters rushed through dinner without another word. As they went out the door, Jeff glanced over in the old man's direction once more but saw only something like black air passing through the window.

A few hours later, Jeff had had enough of sitting with his parents in their tiny cabin. No TVs in this dump. No, not like the old days, Dad had sighed. Back then, he'd rent the whole goddamn resort. Hell, he'd own the place! Fire that server! Eighty-six that old black bird! Put some real booze on the menu!

Meanwhile, Mom painted a pretty future for them. Everyone they'd met so far seemed to love Monitor County. They would too! Jeff could make friends at the school down in the valley. It was a new start!

"New start for what?" Dad sipped his Clausthaler and belched. "They hired me for shit work. Me! The guy *Variety* use to call 'Captain Entertainment!' Is this what I went through recovery for? The guy who created the *Interpol International* franchise! Five top-rated separate series, bigger than *CSI!*"

He'd go on all night like this, scratching at his failure until he bled tears. It was so much more fun when Dad was bellowing from the top of the world. That Jeff could respect, even when Dad was on a binge. Now the only thing left was embarrassment.

Jeff blurted out he wanted to explore the resort. Dad understood the fib and tried to hide his hurt feelings. Mom nagged Jeff to wear his jacket and take the flashlight with him. "And watch out for bears!"

Bears? Shit. Attacked by a bear. That'd be good news. They'd have to take me back to L.A. for sure.

Outside, it was total dark. Even with the flashlight as a guide, Jeff tripped over rock after root as he hiked up the path through the resort. L.A. nights showed only a few stars in a soft blue sky. Here, zillions of icy stars glittered, embedded in a coal black uncaring sky above black treetops that swayed and moaned in sad windy chorus as though this were all one big funeral. Everything was too much here: the mountains too high and jagged, the valleys too deep and blue.

At trail's end, Jeff found a wooden gazebo built at the bottom of a rocky slope. From inside he could see far back down the hill to where cabin lights dotted the darkness. Windblown branches made the lights flicker. Jeff zipped up his jacket tight around his throat against the late spring cold.

He didn't want to think about being stuck here, so he made memories of his old junior high and the girl he'd left behind: the impossibly beautiful, blond hottie Karen, the only thing that made fourth-hour American History not-boring. On his last day at school, he gave her a poem he'd half-written from a rap song—he loved her, she was beautiful and it broke his heart that he'd never see her ever again, but all she had to do was call and there he'd be! ("Forever!" it ended with triumphant tragedy.)

Stooooopid! Instead of jumping into his arms as she had in his dreams, Karen only blushed and giggled. From there, Jeff's poem was passed down the lunch table. Jeff felt as bad as if his fly had split open and his junk had fallen out. Soon all he heard was merciless laughter and all he had was a ruthless lifelong memory. Did no one but Jeff have feelings like these? No, they didn't. Everyone else was *Cool*. Except him.

Still, there were other memories, memories of fantasies. His hand slipped into the roomy pocket of his low-riders and found his cock.

He stroked it back and forth against his thigh and aroused a favorite pillow dream: Karen ripping her blouse open, her full tits leaping out into his face while words poured like honey out from her mouth.

But suddenly, as he felt himself pouring over the brink, a huge vibrating hum rose from behind, mixing itself in with Karen's whispered words.

A ball of liquid cold struck the back of his head. It felt soft like a water balloon. It blew through his skull, soaking his brain. He saw arctic blue as he felt his feet briefly lift off the gazebo floor. His cranium buzzed and his eardrums swelled. Then the balloon blasted out through his forehead, taking Karen's image, leaving behind creamy pools of chill floating in his brain.

Jeff's hard-on shrank, his balls rolled up and he slumped against the gazebo frame. The watery blue balloon, shaped like a blood cell, floated away down the hill. It split into two shimmering orbs as it weaved among the pines. The orbs drifted back and forth in tandem. One of them blinked off and on, once. Like a winking eye.

Holy shit, those are eyes! They had no head, no body, but they were *eyes* alright, seeing eyes, flying by themselves on invisible wings, gaily sweeping and weaving down the hill among the trees. And then they vanished, into the rear wall of …the cabin where he would sleep.

Then, from up the hill behind him, branches snapped and footsteps fell. Huge black shadows slipped around the boulders, headed for the gazebo and the meal standing inside, waiting to be devoured.

Jeff fled the gazebo. The flashlight slipped from his numb fingers. His low-riders fell down and so did he. He clutched his belt, bumping from tree to tree, nearly impaling himself on sharp broken branches.

He reached the rear of the cabin. Nothing behind him now. He looked for the blue-eyed whatz-it, but it was gone in the dead quiet night. Jeff began to doubt himself. Maybe it was just his imagination. Like he'd imagined that Karen Hale had loved him. Like that old man beating his father. Just another crazy thing flitting in his mind.

Exhausted, Jeff stepped around the corner of the cabin to see a boy standing on the porch. A boy who looked just like Jeff. No. A boy who *almost* looked like Jeff.

Jeff almost didn't recognize this mirror-reverse image of himself. His watch was on his right wrist instead of his left, like in his reflection in the three-way mirror at Macy's. But this wasn't Macy's. There were no mirrors here, in the forest.

Jeff's eyes were brown. The boy's were blue. Wolf blue. Blue like the thing that had flown through his head while he was daydreaming on the hill above.

Jeff understood immediately. The thing had sucked out everything Jeff knew about himself and remade himself as Jeff. From his mirror image to his dreams of Karen. No wonder he felt so weak.

Then the Jeff Potter on the porch grinned at the Jeff Potter who watched from the shadows like an orphan. The Jeff Potter on the porch wore a bully's confident grin: Go on! Stop me! Dare ya! Dare ya double! Dare ya triple!

"Jeff!" Mom's voice called from inside. "Don't stand out there—"

No! Don't say it, Mom! Don't let him in!

"— in the cold! Get in here! Now!"

The hologram Jeff winked, waved an impudent bye-bye with the fingers of his left hand and strolled inside exactly like he belonged.

The real Jeff, who had no idea where he belonged, stumbled into the kitchen seconds later, but the only monsters there were his parents smiling wanly from the kitchen table. Dad waved. "What's wrong, Jeff?" Mom asked.

"Oh nothin'." Just me again. They hadn't seen the Other Jeff, that impossible, blue-eyed Jeff. Never tell your dreams, he warned himself. Asleep or awake, never tell your dreams.

"Why doncha sit with us?" Dad asked. "Huh," Jeff grunted as he fought to conceal his fear as a new dark idea dawned—anything that could fly through his head and so easily disguise itself could hide any damned place it pleased, hungry and sniggering.

And so he set off in frantic search for the Other Jeff in the little bedroom—nothing there. The closet—nothing there. Under the bed—nothing there.

In the itty-bitty bathroom, he ripped back the shower curtain and jumped, half-remembering creepy Vince Vaughn in that *Psycho* movie. Nothing there but a bar of soap that Mom would steal. Even peeing seemed perilous. As the water funneled away, he wondered: Was that a blue light shining from the depths of the toilet? Maybe. Maybe not.

He joined Mom and Dad in the kitchen just long enough to be polite. As he pretended to listen to Mom's happy talk and Dad's grumping, it slowly dawned on Jeff what had really happened out there. In the woods. In the dark.

The truth hit him like a triple Tony Jaa punch to the gut. There was no flying thing in the forest! That was no Other Jeff Potter standing out there on the porch!

It was all stuff happening inside his brain! Hallucinations!

That could mean only one of two things, both of them dreadful: First, he might be going crazy. His brain was frying and popping with weirdness as it roared into schizophrenic overdrive. The same thing happened to his Mom's cousin Teddy. They put Teddy in the hospital where he now sat and stared all day, every day, for the rest of his life while his brain circuits melted into a white buzz.

Or maybe it was a brain tumor! A fiendish cancer monster that would suck his life away until he was a hallucinating, helpless husk! He would die in slow agony! Young and all alone! Never to know a girl's touch! Oh, Karen!

Either way, it was shit, it was bad. Tortured by those two possibilities, Jeff said goodnight to Mom and Dad with zombie kisses as though he were already dying. Fighting off tears, he stripped and slid into his sleeping bag in his little corner. (Dying of cancer and still I have to sleep on the floor!)

His feet pushed into something soft at the bottom of the bag. Probably old smelly socks he'd peeled off with his feet during a long-ago camping trip. Fuck it. Jeff pulled the bag over his head, alone with his aching heart, and swooned between fantasies of impending insanity and implacable death, both of them melting into awful doom.

Finally, Jeff's parents went to bed. Jeff pretended to be asleep. His parents' shuffling, their bathroom business, Dad's muttering at the burden of his body, his Mom's humming: the world carelessly went on as he lay there suffering.

Just wait 'til I'm dead, then ...

Then Dad started snoring like a cartoony file, every snore sending a puff of near-beery breath wafting across the room. Jeff fantasized what it would be like—to die so young in a hospital bed, while Dad, who really did love him, would insist on sleeping next to him. Pathetic! Jeff would die alone with nothing but the odor of Clausthaler and the sound of—

—suddenly, the wad of socks under Jeff's feet moved. They wiggled like plump wooly worms across his feet. They crawled up his legs, pulled themselves along with tiny claws. Jeff poked his head out into darkness darker than the one under the covers.

What the fuck? He remembered the animals who'd chased him down the hill. They'd gotten in here, too! A mouse? A rat? Rodents were everywhere, carried fleas, spread the plague! This new fear crowded out the other two. Jeff braced himself up on his elbows as tiny claws gripped his tender skin. The mouse-thing crawled over his groin, up his belly, toward his chest.

He lifted the mouth of the sleeping bag and peered inside to find two tiny points of wolf-eye blue light looking back. The weird creature crawled out on his chest. It sprouted wings, grew bigger, launched itself into the air and hovered inches above his face.

"Always in the last place you look," a calm voice smiled inside his head.

"Dad!"

"SQOOONK!" said Dad.

It looked like an insect, but not like any bug Jeff had ever seen in biology class. Something like a mosquito or moth, but big as a bird with two large wings that spun and hummed in the air. A long proboscis stuck out from its mouth like a hypodermic needle that could puncture steel. It had to be a—

"No. I'm not a dream!" the insect laughed, its clear voice making a cheerful echo.

It hovered in front of the boy's face as though trying to kill him with its ugliness. Jeff felt frozen into silent fear. But he still could think. What are—what do you?

"I am hungry," the insect told him matter-of-factly, like a man sitting down to dinner. Then it buzzed away. Over to where Dad slept. Jeff could sit up now, but that was all. He watched paralyzed as the insect cast a blue light on Dad's sleeping face and inside his open mouth. Dad awoke with a snort and saw what Jeff saw. And, like Jeff, he couldn't believe it. This had to be a dream. Another waking dream.

The dream dove down into Dad's mouth. The blue light briefly glowed from within as Dad pawed at his throat and tore away the glittering crucifix grandma had given him. The blue light vanished. Perfect night fell again.

Jeff saw nothing, but heard everything. He tried to scream, but he had no voice. Mom slept away like a rock—or, she was being kept asleep, like Jeff was being forced to listen alone to the horror. The Dream was strong. It could multitask: control their minds while it viciously rummaged around inside Dad's body.

"Wake up! Wake up!" Jeff's mind screamed. But he was awake. Awake in a malevolence where he could do nothing but listen to Dad's death struggles as the bedsprings creaked and the mattress jumped in its frame. Soon, the bed slats snapped. The mattress crashed to the floor. Mom slept on. The whole world slept on.

"STOP IT! STOP IT! LEAVE MY DAD ALONE!"

But the insect perversely, defiantly, doubled down on its torture:

"The less you want, the more I give," it laughed.

Suddenly, finally, the gurgling and thrashing stopped, so abruptly, Jeff thought maybe it had been only a nightmare after all. He'd wake up to a bright morning and there'd be Dad and, this time, Jeff would hug him and say "I love you!" And that was more true than any bad dream.

But that second passed. The blue light reappeared, a beacon from inside Dad's mouth that lit up the room. The insect crawled out the way it went in, struggled like a butterfly from a cocoon. Bigger now, it hovered in the air, admiring its handiwork. Dad's face was flat, his eyes open but empty. The insect looked full, bright and hungry no more.

Then it flew back for Jeff.

Jeff lay down, closed his eyes and gritted his teeth shut, so it couldn't get in. (But it would. It would drill its needle through his teeth, if it had to. It was a Powerful Thing and did what it pleased.)

Jeff waited to die. But when death didn't come, he opened his eyes.

There the insect hovered, teasing, a foot away, its mothy wings spinning and humming, grinning blue eyes ringed by a pulsating circle that was red with Dad's blood.

The boy could keep his life. The boy could keep his blood. It only wanted to show its strength and power. It wanted the boy to know how clever it was:

"Look at me. Know that I am real. Whenever you close your eyes, whenever you sleep, whenever you dream, you will find me there. You will know that I am real."

"Who are you!?"

It laughed again, a light, airy chuckle. What looked like two long fingers slowly rose up and pressed down on Jeff's eyelids, pulling them down like window shades.

"Just an old man," the insect whispered.

....

CHAPTER 1

Dragon at Dawn

Ever since the day she learned that she was dying and would have to move back to the city, Carla Sutton started out each morning thinking about all the things she would miss about her life in Monitor County: the long weekend hikes and camping trips through the splendid mountain scenery with her husband, Dave; her part-time job—already lost—driving the county public bus on the scenic mountain highway to and from Lake Tahoe; her other job working the front desk at the St. Ives resort; her monthly Saturday afternoon movie program at the little Byrneville public library; the people she knew and, of those, the ones who had become friends; she would miss the sure, comforting rhythm of the seasons.

But most of all, she thought as she awoke again in night's closing minutes and shook another flying dream out of her mind, she'd miss these sweet moments just before sunrise. After she and Dave were told the terrible news, instead of rushing into her warm robe, she'd been taking her time putting it on because of how she'd miss the cold slap of morning air on her body. As she sat at the foot of the bed and looked out into the fading darkness, she thought about how she would never see the scraggily little side yard outside the bedroom window again, where, after another long but heroic winter, green grass and wild flowers would soon blaze in springtime to deliver a sweet shock through long-wintered souls. As her body was slowly dimming, she would be taken away from a world that was growing ever more beautiful, the closer she drew to death.

Most of all, she'd miss this ritual that had drawn her from sleep every morning before the sun came up, ever since she and her husband had moved here two years ago.

She looked west out the bedroom window, waiting and watching, breathing with a soft gentle rhythm like meditation. As always, Kat, the Sutton's pretty tabby, snuggled in next to her with her steady purr, as loyal as a dog.

As morning light spread over from the eastern mountains behind her, the mountain seem to float into view as though from the depths of a black pool, its outline teasing and tantalizing. The sky passed through all its shades of blue, the stars were washed away until there was only a smattering left around the distinctive peak that loomed over their world.

Where it got its name no one knew, but Dragon's Ark was Monitor County's most stunning feature. The mountain rose like the prow of a sinking ship as though defying the gray and white waves of the Sierra Crest that rose behind it. It lorded over a plateau that dropped off to the north into a hidden crack in the earth that was known as Alpine Canyon.

The Ark may not have had the altitude of the Sierra Crest, but it had plenty of attitude, a personality, confident it would remain standing while all the other mountains around it would erode to nothing. Some visitors were put off by how it seemed to stab the sky. A fundamentalist preacher was heard to declare the mountain "a vicious knife to the heart of God's Heaven." Others though were happily swept away by its Gothic glamour. Some folks were even enchanted into moving into its shadow, folks like Carla and Dave.

The Suttons lived in a old rented bungalow on Walsh Springs Road, a mile west of the village of Byrneville (pop. 150). From here, they could see the top third of the Ark rising from behind the Samson Hills. The Samsons' altitude was low and their pine green contours pleasingly soft, but those contours concealed some of the toughest hiking in California. They'd defeated—and occasionally swallowed—their share of overconfident backpackers and high-stepping day hikers. Few ever returned to try again, describing their experiences as disorienting and draining. Dave had treated some of these hikers for injuries, altitude sickness, and exhaustion.

"The Samsons give me bad dreams," said a distinguished outdoor photographer who never explained why he never published any of the photos he took there.

As the edge of morning pushed across the sky, Carla started breathing faster as she awaited the last fantastic touch to another perfect Sierra dawn. "Here he comes!" she whispered, her long fingers stroking Kat's fluffy coat. The cat stretched her head forward, her purr swelling with the coming dawn.

This morning the raptor flew from the east over the Samsons, as though chasing the stars, big and black against the bluing sky, its great black wings driving it toward the Ark in a race against the sun. Though the bird was miles away, Carla felt certain that its nightly hunt had been successful, that a marmot, a fox pup, or maybe even a doe hung helplessly from its talons.

She fought back a sob as the great bird plunged down out of sight behind the hills to its nest, located, she thought, near the base of Dragon's Ark. "The dragon of Dragon's Ark," she whispered, as she wiped her eyes.

Seconds later, the Ark's snowy peak flared like a candle flame. The birdsong rose like a flood, sweet and carefree, unleashed by the rising sun.

I don't want to go. I don't want to go. Why do I have to go?

It had been Dave's idea to move here so he could live his dream of being a country doctor. Carla, a city girl, had followed out of her love and faith in him, all the while fighting her worries that the boredom of country life would kill both her and their marriage.

It hadn't. On their very first morning here, she found a new religion with its own heroic ritual. She never missed a sunrise and the big bird was always there, flying home, as though just for her. Even in a blizzard, she glimpsed its shadow sweeping by the bungalow, a promise always kept. Not even Dave was that reliable.

Even so, after two years, she had no idea what species it belonged to. It moved too fast for binoculars, which failed to reveal enough detail, no matter how close it flew and it resembled nothing in the Sibley guide. She mused that the animal knew it was being watched and was teasing her with its *mysterioso*. Even Dave, the more experienced birder, couldn't name it the few times he'd seen it. A golden eagle, he said the first time. A bald eagle, the second. A great owl, he shrugged the third. "Hawk," he muttered the fourth time and lost interest—

Dave's bedside phone broke the spell with a sudden cold flutter that made Carla jump and swear through her tears. The noise reminded her of the world of horns, bells and whistles, the world of engine blasts and bitter smog that she'd be returning to, the sounds she would hear as she lay dying.

Dave sprang out of bed. Oh well. This morning's show was over. The sky was now all blue and empty. The only trace of night left was the Ark's lofty black face.

"You sure?" Dave rasped. "Gotcha, Tim. Twenty minutes."

Kat padded across the bed to greet Dave who scratched her sweet spot before he leaned over to plant a kiss on Carla's cheek and swirl his tongue in her ear: "Morning."

Someone had died up at St. Ives, he said. They wanted him there. Tim didn't say why. Maybe someone didn't show for the EMT shift.

Uh-oh. Carla recalled the morbidly obese man she'd checked in to St. Ives yesterday afternoon: Andrew Potty—*Potter*—and his morbidly miserable wife and son. The only cabin available was the little Piñon. "Like packing a hippo in a shoe box," she'd snickered to Sean Temkin, St. Ives's Cafe server. Crowded together in that tight space, the Potters might easily have turned on each other like crazed caged rats.

"Anyone hurt?"

"Sounds like a heart attack."

Of course. Potter's strained heart plus high-altitude oxygen levels equaled potential trouble. Even a walk across the room could kill a man in his condition. But why would the sheriff's department call Dave in for a simple heart attack?

She'd mentioned the Potters to Dave last night, but now felt too guilty to say anything. Anyway, who said married couples had to tell each other everything? While Dave had previously seen her practicing her morning ritual, he had no idea that it was a ritual, that it had meaning. He loved this world as much as she did, but mysticism was not in his medical kit. "It's returning to feed its young after hunting all night, sweetie. That's all."

Carla dressed and went down the dark hallway to their funky kitchen at the back of the house. She carefully made coffee without dropping anything. Dave effusively thanked and kissed her as he took his cup. She slapped his bush hat on his head and followed him to the door.

"I shouldn't be too long, but Henry West is scheduled for a ten o'clock. If I'm not here, he can come down to the Osgood clinic this afternoon."

"Dave? We have to decide."

He heaved a painful sigh. After the shock of the news, they'd spent nearly three weeks staring at the wall, weighing their options through their tears, until they made the only decision left to them: move back to San Francisco.

"End of June, okay?" He gave an endearing manly nod, his black-bearded chin up. "I'll start giving notice today."

"I'll call Papa. He can start an apartment search for us. I'll call the landlord, too."

He tried to shrug it away. "This place is changing anyway." He embraced her, kissing her head through her jet-black hair.

"The time you spend not thinking about me, use it well."

She turned from watching his truck drive away down Walsh Springs Road and headed into their combination living and waiting room with her coffee. Kat joined her on the couch, leaning against her thigh in dopey wonder, as Carla stroked and cooed to her while looking out the picture window at the Ark.

What was it about that mountain? she wondered. With each passing day, its beauty seemed to intensify toward some transformation. But into what? How could something become more beautiful with each passing day? It had to either stop becoming beautiful, and become mere scenery, or it had to turn into something else. What did a mountain, even one as magnificent as Dragon's Ark, have to reveal but a granite soul?

"Trees don't return your hugs," Papa Caminetti had warned her when she and Dave had left San Francisco for this faraway wilderness. Papa had a point, a big one. Nature created life and beauty. It also took it away. It created that magnificent dragon of Dragon's Ark. But the bird was a predator that killed, sometimes with enthusiasm, always with hunger and without pity. And now Nature, the realm where Life and Death rolled entwined together, had cast its cruel eye on her. Everything seemed to circle around back down into that dreadful hole into which all life vanished, including hers.

"Fuck!" She buried her face in her hands. When she'd finished crying, she called her father and he started in: old Jake Caminetti was so happy that his beloved youngest daughter would soon be home. He was still weeping when they hung up.

After drying her tears, Carla called their landlord, Barb Albanese. Her fingers fumbled over the keypad twice before she heard Barb's cold chirp floating out of her message machine. God help us if that woman comes back as a ghost with that voice, Carla thought. She left a message suggesting Barb stop by for a chat, around ten.

She carefully ate a breakfast of eggs and muffins then opened the Netflix envelopes for the final Saturday monthly movie matinee. "Oh Christ!" Her last program would be *I Want to Live!* and *Pride of the Yankees*, the one about Lou Gehrig. "God, I'm going stupid too! I should've checked the queue!" She imagined herself announcing: "Good afternoon everyone! Because I'm moving away to die, I thought for my last program, I'd share two *really* depressing movies!"

But that joke would fall flat. It would have to be another Hopalong Cassidy movie from Dave's western DVD collection.

Carla booted up Dave's office computer and pecked at the keyboard, no longer able to wing her fingers like she used to. One good thing about moving back to the World Below was that they'd have DSL or wireless instead of dialup, not that she had any use for the Internet except for the latest ALS news. Today, it was the discovery of a new gene that *could* lead to the new development of model systems that *might* someday open the door to new treatments.

"I can't fucking wait for someday." Someday she'd be only a brain trapped in a drooling sack of bones, her voice replaced by a computer chip, her thoughts her only friends, the only view out her window a block of grey sky. She now stayed off the message boards. Only last week, her gallows humor had gotten her into trouble (again) after she'd mischievously proposed holding a Stephen Hawking impersonation contest as a fundraiser. Instead of a wave of laughter, she found herself overwhelmed by a fiery wall of indignant rage.

"It's the ALS community board," Dave had drily pointed out, "not open mike night at the comedy club."

Suddenly, there came a knock at the door. Ten o'clock already! Stop Time! Stop, you villain! Where's my husband? The sand grains fall like ticking seconds!

Carla could smell Henry West long before she reached the door. She found him standing on the stoop, clinging to the newel post as though afraid he'd be carried off by the cool gentle wind.

Until her diagnosis, Carla believed Henry West to be the most miserable soul she'd ever met. His flat green eyes squinted warily from under the bill of the San Francisco Giants ballcap he kept pulled tightly down on his brow (to relieve his acrophobia, which Dave suspected was related to vertigo). His long black hair stuck out like weeds from under the cap. He hadn't bathed in awhile, but he hadn't drawn his first drink of the day either—that was why he was here. Henry needed Dave to certify him again as eligible for his disability check so he could continue his slow suicide by alcohol.

(Though, with the county's famously strict beverage laws, he seemed to have picked the wrong neighborhood in which to drink himself to death.)

Henry's chronic combative nature put Carla on her guard. She said a polite good morning and informed him that Dr. Sutton was out on an emergency.

Henry carefully leaned his lollipop body out from the stoop and peered into Dave's office window as though he suspected that the Doc was avoiding him, like everyone else did.

"Folks always got somethin' better to do." He spoke with a whiff of whine. Still, he wouldn't dare pick a fight with the Doc's wife, not if he wanted his medicine.

"He'll be down at the Osgood clinic this afternoon. He'll see you there."

"Too far to walk." Henry gave a fidgety shrug. "Gotta get that check. I get bad dreams if don't get my medicine." He was hinting for a handout, instead of flat out demanding it, as he usually did with stunning coarseness. He turned away, taking the steps one by one, like Carla had to now.

She felt a surprising pang of empathy. "Maybe you can get a ride. I'd take you myself, but I can't drive either."

Henry stopped, lifted his leg and dug his fingers into his ass in reply. Carla rolled her eyes: Oh. Right. I get it. *I* want to live. *You* don't.

He slowed as Barb Albanese came sashaying up the path. Barb wrinkled her pert nose and shook her blond poodle-hair in a gesture of revulsion as she passed by Henry who, of course, lavished her with a long blatant leer.

As Henry headed down the road toward the village, Barb gave Carla a puzzled smile like a white crescent moon on the red plate of her lips. Yeah, the situation did look peculiar: Henry West leaving the house while Dave was away. Carla fought down another burst of her antic humor: Yeah, he smells bad, but WOW! What a STUD!

But Barb was only another audience that wouldn't get it. If anything, she'd turn the joke to gossip and the Suttons could wind up fleeing Monitor County under a cloud of farce, not the sad shadow of a fatal disease. Discretion was the better part of humor.

Carla now regretted even inviting Barb over, and not just because Barb's breasts were bigger than hers. Barb owned and operated Sierra Real Estate and Property Management in the village and was all real estate, twenty-four seven. She was as dull as old winter snow and arrogantly shallow. As her bra lifted her huge knockers, they, in turn, undoubtedly lifted her profit margin, at least where male buyers were concerned. They were the balcony she stood on, the jiggling front stoop to every house she sold and she sold plenty.

Carla came out, closing the door behind her: "I was on my way to clean out the car. I forgot you were coming by."

"Oh, that's okay. I can't stay long."

So, Barb didn't like her either, Carla thought. Great! That meant a short visit. As they walked to the dumpy three-car garage, Carla told her the news but not the reason, though Barb, like many, probably knew the facts by now. Carla wanted to know her plans. Would she sell the property to the Sierra Future development project, like others in the western reaches of the county had? Sierra's pockets, sewed into those of the multinational resort consortium Getgo, were deeper than space. Few had the nerve to refuse their fantastic (though secret) offers.

And just what part was Barb playing in all this? Among her management clients were Monitor County's two remaining old families—the Byrnes and the Bartoks. Of the Bartoks, only frail old Klaus, who'd lived on the land around Dragon's Ark for a century, remained. Sierra Future could crush him without him knowing it. Would Barb guard his interests? Or did she already have a warehouse picked out to put him away in?

The questions remained unanswered. Barb departed in her shiny Mercedes. Carla ended her charade of cleaning out the Volvo she was no longer allowed to drive.

At one o'clock, the screen door banged and the nail polish slipped from her fingers into the sink. Her blush looked smeared under left eye because she couldn't quite feel her cheekbone. Her right eyelash looked like a loose feather. "I used to be an artist," she murmured. The smallest losses loomed like tragedies.

She buttoned her shirt to cover her cleavage and forced a smile when she found Sean Temkin waiting in the hall, here to drive them both to work at St. Ives. She grabbed her purse and the gleaming metal cane, a thoughtless gift from Sean after she'd told him about the ALS. Carla used it to be polite, though she still didn't need it. She refused his hand as she climbed into his old yellow Jeep, which reeked of weed and jangled with climbing gear.

Sean had arrived in Monitor County last fall and from there eagerly dug his roots into country life. Like the Suttons, he only wanted to make a decent living in a beautiful place. Climbing was one of Sean's three passions. He was happy to work for minimum wage just to be close to the county's pointed peaks, sheer cliffs, and deep canyons.

His second passion was politics. As he drove through the village—Carla glimpsed Henry West sitting alone on the sidewalk, probably rudely begging for change while waiting for the Byrneville Tap & Grill to open—Sean awkwardly launched into another rant against the Sierra Future project.

Sean was a veteran of both Berkeley politics and a lost war to stop the construction of a gondola across Yosemite Valley. He'd hoped Monitor County would stay pristine in the twenty-first century, but after only six months that dream also seemed doomed. This magic land would be refashioned into a luxury suburb of both Tahoe and Reno "unless someone stands up to these bastards!" he declared in his scratchy voice. "I didn't come here to crowd this place and you didn't either!"

Carla played devil's advocate: Good intentions were irrelevant. Everybody had a right to live in the Sierra, not just tree huggers. Sean countered that private property rights were not an ideology, but a general and flexible principal. If "public" was a fungible legalism, so was "private." It deserved consideration, not dominance.

As they made the left onto Osgood Canyon Road, Sean made another point: Barb Albanese, who also owned Sean's tiny place on the south side of Byrneville Creek, was doubling his rent, starting July. "You get what's happening? Poor and working people like us are being kicked out. I work here, but I won't be allowed to live here. Not by law, just by manipulating the marketplace. She's your landlord too, so get ready!"

"It doesn't make any difference." Carla looked out the window as she told him the news and blinked back tears. She couldn't let him see her cry.

Sean swore. She knew this was coming because Sean had a third great passion: his unrequited love for Carla, a love that had bloomed like dandelions the second he saw her on his first day at St. Ives Café last fall. She'd all but slashed his face with her wedding ring—"Yoo-hoo! Older Married Lady!"—but no matter how much she gushed over her happy marriage to Dreamboat Dave, Sean wouldn't stop bouncing around her like a puppy, sure that she would someday, somehow, dump her husband and turn to him.

"Well, if that's how it's gonna be, I'll move back to the Bay Area too!"

Carla sighed: "No, Sean don't do that." She turned to see him glancing at her as she fought back tears. "You belong here. The county needs you more than anyone. It's bad Dave and I are leaving, but they'd win for sure if you left."

"It's not fair," Sean's voice was breaking. "You have to leave. If you could stay, you'd fight them. I'd bet my life you would."

Carla quickly changed the subject: "Someone passed away at the resort last night. They called my husband in."

"You think it might be Mr. Potty—Potter?"

"If so, no surprise there. He was not a well man."

"By the way, I'm still mad at you! I wouldn't have called him Mr. Potty to his face if you hadn't said it first!"

"Sorry, Sean. I should keep my mouth shut. I apologize."

"I don't know what to think. I mean if it is Potter. He's one of *them*."

Carla agreed. Andrew Potter had given her one of his business cards like it was a party favor: "Andrew Potter, Executive Assistant, Sierra Future" blah blah blah. She'd fired it into the recycling bin without reading the rest of it.

Sean wondered what role Potter was meant play in Sierra Future. Carla replied that maybe they hired him to be Sierra's 800-pound gorilla—sit on reluctant sellers until they suffocated or sold out, a joke that Sean's PC sensibility did not find one bit funny. But maybe that suited Carla: the more he saw her as a glib insensitive bitch, the less likely he'd be to follow her back to the Bay Area. He belonged here. There were only a few like him scattered across the globe, it seemed. Most people were only fearful; only a few were as angry and courageous as Sean. These mountains needed him.

"Speaking of Potter, did you see Mr. Bartok leave last night?"

"Mm-mm. Maybe I was in the back."

"He left me a twenty for a cup of tea! Forgot his walking stick too. I hope he got home okay."

"I think he grabs his walking sticks right off the forest floor. I'm sure Annie Goodman picked him up."

"Potter insulted him right to his face. I thought Mr. B. was gonna beat him with his stick." Sean's rubbery grin stretched across his freckled face. "Mr. Bartok's such a cool dude, living alone up in Alpine Canyon for so long. I'd give a week's pay for permission to climb around up there."

"He can only say no. I'm sure he'll like your money."

They emerged from Osgood Canyon. Up ahead, St. Ives huddled at the eastern foot of the Samsons. Cherry lights flashed and spun in the parking lot: county police cars, an ambulance. Dave's call had taken longer than expected.

"Uh-oh," Sean murmured. "Memorial Day weekend's next week. I hope this doesn't crimp our business."

"It's nothing. People die at hotels and resorts a lot. I'm surprised it doesn't happen more often. We'll do fine." Carla narrowed her eyes and grinned impishly.

"So long as we don't put up a big flashing sign that says 'GUY DIED HERE!'"

"Car-la!"

....

CHAPTER 2

Like a Cougar Walking By

It wasn't until Dave Sutton rolled down the truck window and felt the freezing mountain air splash on his face that he finally woke up to the message behind Under Sheriff Tim King's unusual six a.m. phone call. The message was one simple word that was stronger than the coldest air.

Plague.

Dr. David Sutton had worked with Tim and the Monitor County Sheriff's Department many times before. As a county search and rescue volunteer, supervised by the Sheriff's Office, Dave had saved his share of hikers, skiers, fishers, and climbers, alive and dead alike, from all the trouble a body can encounter in the wilderness. During Dave's part-time stints with the Osgood Memorial Hospital Emergency Room, Tim or his deputies often accompanied accident victims brought in from the west county.

But as Monitor County's public health officer, Dave hardly dealt with Tim at all. In fact, this was only the second time since he took the oath of office that something like this had happened and that case, too, had been a suspected case of hantavirus plague.

Tim had said "maybe" a heart attack on the phone only to avoid panic. Panic would have to start with Dave who sorted his thoughts while ignoring the scenic beauty racing over his windshield. If it was hantavirus, where did it start? A bite from a flea that hopped over from a camp dog? Some kid playing with a sick or dead squirrel? Whoever it was had probably picked up the contagion more than a week ago. Whatever the vector, how far had the virus burrowed into the population? By the time Dave arrived at St. Ives, he was at full alert and ticking off his list of things to do: call county supervisors; call state health officials …

Tim King greeted Dave with a loose handshake and led him into the Piñon Cabin's little bedroom. The room was cozy for two but the body on a mattress on the floor made it smothering and tiny. "Whoa," Dave murmured as he looked down at one of the worst cases of morbid obesity he'd ever seen.

The deceased's name was Andrew Potter, the name Carla had mentioned last night. He looked to be well over 300 pounds and must have been a source of endless grief to both family and physician. And he'd died in terrible pain. His convulsions had collapsed the bed, splintering one of the sideboards. His upper body lay twisted and his mouth hung open as though he'd died with a scream on his lips. His eyes stared through slits from within his sunken facial features. His arms stretched out, the right hand open like a claw, while the left hand clutched a small diamond cross.

Dave was still thinking about the plague. Had Mr. Potter shown any signs or symptoms of illness in the last few days? Nope, Tim said. According to the deceased's wife and son, he died suddenly.

"So, it's not plague?"

Tim asked, "What do you think?"

Both Sheriff Parker and Under Sheriff King, along with their deputies, were licensed coroners, able to pronounce death in all circumstances. But, like coroners in most small, rural counties, they were political appointees, not trained pathologists. Most of the time it's easy to tell when a body's dead. How the person died would be a question for someone in a larger, wealthier county like El Dorado to determine. Further questions would bring in the state's pathologists.

Dave felt put on the spot. Forensic pathology wasn't his field. He'd shown potential for forensics while in pre-med, but had no passion for it and dove right into family care. Regardless, he'd do his best. Slipping on rubber gloves, he knelt down and opened up the pajamas to examine the front of the body. The folds of flesh were massive and deep; the surface was hard, gray-white, and cold. The tissue had sagged and settled into the mattress making the body like a clay mold. It was nearly impossible to probe under the back. Dave found no visible marks, animal bites, or wounds of any kind.

Dave examined two medicine bottles lying on the floor by the nightstand. They were generics: enalapril, for high blood pressure; orlistat, for obesity.

"Just looking at him, I'd say you what said on the phone: heart attack. Myocardial infarction with coronary heart disease as the mechanism. With his weight problem and no visible trauma, that's the best call I can make."

He cocked a skeptical eye from under his hat brim at Tim who carefully watched from under his gray Stetson: You got me out of bed at 6 a.m. for this?

"Could you estimate time of death?"

"Not too close. He went into spasms as he was dying. Even if he hadn't, someone of his weight in this cold air might never reach rigor mortis. We'd have to get his pajamas off and lift him up to check for lividity on his back, but again—you know this—it's like a refrigerator up here: Death processes slow down. All that subcutaneous fat will keep the blood from pooling. So my answer is, maybe as far back as twelve hours or more, but I can't be precise. You want more accurate information? You'll have to go higher up the food chain. Sorry Tim, I'm just a sawbones on this."

Tim nodded and gave an unhappy grunt, though it was clear that he wasn't mad at Dave. Instead, he invited him outside. Once they were away from the cabin, the two fidgeting deputies, and the EMTs from Osgood Memorial, it looked like the first of a long string of perfect spring mornings in Monitor County, a world where no one ever died. But, of course, they did. While county residents had far and away the best health stats in the state—some wags called it "Wholesome County" to Dave's economic frustration—death rates for visitors ran above average. Andrew Potter was only the latest and only stood out because he'd died indoors, in bed, not in a campsite, on the trail, in a stream, or at the bottom of a cliff.

"I think you're right, but I wanted to hear it from you," Tim said quietly. "So it could've happened last night, right? You see, there's a timin' issue."

Tim had been a deputy all over Nevada for some years before he brought his family across the state line to take one of the two Under Sheriff jobs with Monitor County under the popular Sheriff Parker. For ten years, Tim had been running everyday law enforcement in the high west section of the county. "My dream patrol," he called it—except for mornings like this one.

"I got the call about four-thirty, arrived here just before five. Jim and Sarah Chapman were both on the premises. They told me the man's son woke 'em up about four, sayin' his dad was really sick—not dead, just really sick. Ambulance from Osgood arrived thirty minutes later, just after me and Deputy Berman, and found what you saw in there, except the headboard had fallen on his face."

"And so?"

"I'd say that busted bed and the look on his face means that he made a racket while dyin'. But nobody outside his cabin heard a sound." He paused. "Not at four o'clock, anyway."

"You mean there was an earlier disturbance?"

"Jim Chapman got woke up by somethin' around midnight. So did one of the guests at Alpine Cabin about fifty feet away from the Piñon. Most of the other cabins are still empty. Jim and the guest said they heard a whole lot of thumpin' and yellin', like someone was knockin' down a barn. Jim tells me he spent half an hour pokin' around in case a bear was tryin' to break in somewhere. Found one, too, but it took off without doin' any damage. There were other critters around here about the same time: deer, fox, coyote, hawks, owls, like they was throwin' a jamboree. I see it myself sometimes. Jim just figured that's all it was and went back to bed."

Dave wasn't up for playing detective but Tim did like talking shop with him when they got together. Sheriff Parker was away too much these days in Sacramento in an often fruitless fight for dwindling state and federal funds. Of his deputies, Paul Berman was green and awkward and Sam Colbert was hasty and lacked discretion. (As Tim once said, "Sam would arrest his own mama for fishin' with an out-of-date license.")

"If Potter was dyin' at around midnight, then Mrs. Potter and her son—his name's Jeff—seemed to have slept right through it. Orrrr. …"

"They let him die." Dave felt another kind of chill under the morning cold. "Carla checked them in here yesterday. She told me the Potters looked seriously dysfunctional. Where's the mom and boy?"

"Sarah's got Mrs. Potter in the office tryin' to calm her. She's upset, like she should be. But so far, she insists she woke up the same time her son says he did to find him that way. Already gone."

"And the boy?"

Tim pointed at a big blue Ford van that sat in the middle of the lot, its rear door open. A tall, skinny male in black t-shirt and low-rider jeans slumped in the back seat.

"I'm too much the big bad sheriff to him. Paul Berman's a good deputy, but he's young and doesn't know how to ask the right questions. Sam'll just spook him into really clammin' up. You've had some experience with these situations. Maybe you can relax him a little. I'll go chat with Mrs. Potter some more—ah, here he comes."

An old rusted brown Dodge pickup rolled into the resort, a mid-size engine hoist in its rear bed. "Jerry Monaghan's Automotive" was stenciled on its doors. They'd use the hoist to lift Andrew Potter onto the stretcher, only because the county's small hoist couldn't handle the job. The work was just beginning. The other bed, where the wife had slept, would have to go, along with the other furniture and the bedroom and kitchen doors. Maybe the cabin front door, too. And the porch rails.

Tim waved and smiled at Jerry Monaghan, then bellowed for Sam Colbert who came out on the porch carrying an electric screwdriver. "Try to snip those PJs off the body as much as you can," Tim told him. "And when you get him in the air, let us know, okay? I want the Doc to check him for lividity." Tim jabbed his finger in the air for emphasis. "Don't lay him on the stretcher yet! Comprende!? Let the body hang until we look at him."

Sam saluted and rushed back inside. Tim turned to Dave: "Can you hang around a piece? Good. You're deputized for this mornin'."

When Dave leaned in the van, Jeff Potter jumped, almost hitting his head on the ceiling. His hazel eyes glared fearfully from between wings of messy black hair. His face was pitted with mild acne and eerily white. He looked malnourished.

"Sorry, I didn't mean to scare you." Dave introduced himself and gently offered his condolences. His easy manner, as Tim predicted, seemed to relax Jeff a little. The boy mistook him for a court pathologist, like those on TV. Dave decided not to correct him.

Beyond hello, Dave could get nothing, no matter how gently he tugged. He assured Jeff that disliking his parents was neither a crime nor unusual, an idea that Jeff fiercely resisted.

"I liked my dad! I mean, we had fun, went lots of places. He wasn't always like that."

Jeff nodded in hesitant agreement when Dave asked whether his mom had a problem with sleeping pills or alcohol. "Maybe I don't see everything that happens," he added, showing a remarkable perception about how the world worked that Dave admired and sympathized with.

So, Dave decided to risk sharing a story about the time he got in trouble with the law when he was Jeff's age. He told how he'd became ensnared in an elaborate con by a "trusted adult." While he sensed something was wrong, he didn't want to betray his "friend—a guy who could make you think white is black, up is down and the moon is made of gold. He just kind of took over my mind."

When finally the cops did come to arrest everyone, young Dave kept his mouth shut for three weeks, torn with guilt about how stupid he'd been, how he should have seen what was coming and feeling terrified at being called a snitch. Most of all, he figured "no one would believe my story."

"But in the end I did tell everything and it all worked out for me. I didn't have to go to jail. All I had to do was tell the truth."

He turned from gazing at the powdery half-moon that floated peacefully above the Samsons, amazed at how far away his awful youth was now and how lucky he was to be here, of all places, where he'd always dreamed of being—

But Jeff Potter was staring at him, his pupils shrunk to black points of fathomless horror, his thin frame starting to tremble like a leaf.

"Yeah, you wouldn't believe me," he whispered, as the shaking increased.

Dave reached for Jeff's arm. Jeff violently pulled away.

"No! I thought it was a nightmare! I didn't believe it was happening! I thought it was a bad dream! It looked too weird to be real! I went back to sleep!"

He buried his face in his arms, violently shuddering, his voice raw like tearing flesh. "I thought I was having a nightmare, so I went back to sleep! That's what happened! Leave me alone!"

Later, Dave approached Sarah Chapman and Tim as they walked with chalk-faced Mrs. Potter from the office. Dave hung back and listened in: She didn't know what more an autopsy could tell them. His doctor had warned her husband a million times to lose weight. They even tried to get him in for an intestinal bypass. His AA group told him quitting drinking wasn't enough. Now she only wanted to take him back to L.A.

"He was a bad man in some ways," she said as she turned away, "but he was a good man, too. I hoped we'd see his good side again."

She gazed up at the moon in the sky and the mountains all around. "I thought living here for awhile would help. You're lucky to live in such a beautiful world. The colors are so bright and strong! I'm so sorry we won't be staying."

She slowly walked toward the van, her head held high.

Dave told Tim about his interview with Jeff. Tim pulled his hat brim down and shook his head. Despite the questions, it was as far as they would get with this for now.

Their attention was drawn away by the sound of a fast engine. An apple-red Jag shot out of Osgood Canyon and zipped neatly into the parking lot. It slowed abruptly as though the driver feared he'd driven into a speed trap. Dave knew the car and the passenger and his driver: Bob Garner, boss of the Sierra Future project and his scowly number two, Peter Schlesinger. They parked at the far end of the lot. While striding toward the main buildings, they saw Mrs. Potter with her son and bee-lined to her.

Like most everyone, Dave disliked glad-handing, red-headed, red-bearded Bob Garner. Although both Garner and Schlesinger were clearly disturbed by the sudden death of their brand new employee, Dave grimly enjoyed watching Mrs. Potter wave away Garner's condolences in the same way that Dave and Carla had once dismissed the developer's efforts to win their support. He recalled the time Garner came by Dave's home office—ostensibly about his migraines, but actually to pump Dave and Carla for information and offer a bribe. Dave winced at the memory of taking the money. Though he'd given no favors, he'd been craving atonement ever since.

"Why yore just a humble lil' country boy tryin' to put a li'l ole' two-hunnert story buildin' on this here property and make ever'body happy!" Carla had mocked Garner right to his face. He left with a bigger headache than he had walking in.

"Hey! Tim!" Sam Colbert trotted down the sidewalk behind them, happy as a little boy who'd just painted a whole barn by himself. "We got him on the stretcher!"

Tim King looked deceptively big and slow, but he could move

fast when his hair caught fire. "I swear I'm shippin' that boy back down to Osgood," he growled as he marched up the sidewalk. "Sam, I said wait."

While Sam pouted, Dave politely turned away to hide his smile. The lividity question didn't matter now. Jeff Potter was still a good kid and there'd be no erasing the guilt that would haunt him all his life about the dream that wasn't.

As they waited for the deputies to finish clearing the cabin, Dave told Tim that he and Carla were leaving. With a stoic nod, Tim dug a stone from the ground with his boot and kicked it away: "Feels like you just got here. Guess it's back to Dr. Durant for us."

Dave helped remove the body. It was fortunate that Potter's widow and son stayed by the van—it wasn't a pretty sight. They had to wrap two extra cords of rope around the stretcher. Tim strained a back muscle; Sam's fingers almost got crushed as they forced the stretcher through the doorway, which at one point wound up on Deputy Berman's left foot. Fortunately, Dave quickly determined, it was only bruised. It took six of them, including Dave and the two Osgood EMTs, to lift the stretcher off the porch. The stretcher wheels groaned and squeaked as they rolled it down the sidewalk. The double-sheeted body sagged over both sides as the supports almost snapped under the weight.

Dave stepped back when they reached the ambulance. The red Jag had gone but a battered yellow Jeep was rumbling in: Carla, and Sean Temkin, arriving for work. Dave checked his watch: one-thirty. He was late for clinic duty!

But his lateness faded from his thoughts as Carla stepped gingerly from the jeep. A dark swoon rose in him. Here was another reminder of how things worked their grim course. It seemed like only yesterday when she would have leapt out like a deer. In the early days of their love, she would sometimes greet with him by doing cartwheels or handsprings, her long shapely body flipping through the air, before falling cleanly into his arms, their mouths meeting in a perfect wet kiss. Carla's spirit had shined its light into the darkest corners of Dave's already dark life, a light that he'd once believed did not exist. How could that light be going out so soon?

He swallowed his surging grief as he waved at Sean's nervous "Howdy." He embraced his beloved in the middle of the parking lot. Her smile faded when she saw the struggle to load Andrew Potter into the ambulance. The stretcher slipped from Tim and Sam's grip and thudded on the ground. The sheeted body shook like pudding.

Carla looked away, her hand over her mouth: "God, I said such terrible things about him." Mortality was no longer so abstract to her. Dave held her while she murmured about the landlord's visit and how cranky, smelly Henry West scratched his ass at her. He probably wouldn't come down to the clinic out of sheer spite and …

"Wow, look who's here."

It was Annie Goodman's huge Chevy Suburban. Big as a Hummer, snow white in the afternoon sun, it rolled slowly past the resort heading east, silent and smooth, like a cougar walking by. Though the windows were tinted black and their faces rarely seen, every local knew of both the driver and her passenger.

Klaus Bartok and Annie Goodman were rubbernecking, and maybe that was natural, but it was the wrong thing to do. An angry shout came from behind Dave and Carla. A rock flew by, arcing over the SUV. Jeff Potter charged past, his black hair flying, his fists punching an invisible, unreachable opponent as he screeched with rage: "Go away! Get the fuck outta here!"

Jeff scooped up another rock, threw it at the voyeurs. That one missed too. He fell into the grassy ditch, dug around in the weeds and poppies until he found another stone to cast. Amazingly, this one missed too, curving away as though it had bounced off a force field. He threw one more before realizing his target was pulling out of range. His thin shoulders bowed as he buried his face in his hands. Dave started toward him, but Mrs. Potter got there first. Meanwhile, the SUV calmly vanished around the bend, out of sight, into Osgood Canyon's shadows, as though uncaring of what it had left behind.

CHAPTER 3

A Meeting of Two Honest Men

Henry West, who hated everyone, especially himself most of all, had been waiting for just the right moment to let loose the blimp-sized fart that had been ballooning in his lower gut for nearly half an hour.

The target of this favored expression of disdain was toothless, hairy, lazy-ass Alvie Simpson who was sitting two short feet away with his two equally useless dumbfuck hippie buddies. Alvie had been blowing his pompous pie-hole about all the "bad karma" sweeping through Monitor County, whining about how they (the latest wave of wealthy Big Shots) were gonna despoil this "great heaven with their greed," especially for him and his shitty friends.

"It's all gonna be about money for them that got it," Alvie drawled. Right then, the afternoon wind shifted in the right speed and direction, allowing Henry to lean left and lift his right ass-cheek off the raised sidewalk. "These mountains'll no longer be a holy sanctuary for free spirits, no longer be the temple of John Muir. And the Great Spirit of Nature'll be driven away and no longer—aww for chrissakes, Henry!" Alvie jumped up, waving away the cloud floating past his swollen red nose. "Not again! God-Jesus-damn it!"

It was a big smoky brown one all right, strong enough to drop a dog at twenty yards and more than enough to set Alvie and his shaggy-ass friends scurrying like ragged chickens back to their shitty little shack up on Byrneville Creek.

"How's that for a whiff of Nature's Great Spirit!" Henry laughed. When they were gone, he sighed contentedly. Once again, rudeness had scored him what he wanted: the sidewalk in front of the Byrneville Tap & Grill all to himself. Any jack he'd mooched would be all his, no sharing. And when the bar opened, he could drink enough beer and wine to pass another blessed dreamless night. If he cadged enough, that is.

I know more than I see, Henry thought as he pulled his ballcap down over his eyes. I know more than those assholes can see with their fuckin' hats off.

Thanks to his vertigo, Henry West saw life through an exceedingly narrow slot. His life had already been hard, and it made for even harder living among Monitor County's crazy big skies and gut-rolling heights, but he had no choice. Though born in the Carson Valley below, he'd long ago worn out his welcome there, even before his ten-year sentence in Folsom on a trumped-up drug charge.

After his release in September of last year, he tried living on the west slopes of the Sierra, but the first night he woke up to find himself face to face with a tarantula marching up his bare chest, its forelegs waving as though asking for a kiss. The very next day, he fled here to Byrneville, where the spiders were small and stayed out of sight. He tearfully prevailed on soft-hearted Cousin Danny East-of-the-Moon to let him stay in the second-floor attic of the garage out back. Danny was a spineless shit with a nagging bitch-wife, two spoiled kids and a new squawking baby, but it would have to do.

Henry shifted and sighed, worried with boredom. Nearly noon and Byrneville stood empty. No real tourists until next weekend. What if he couldn't beg enough change? What if he had to go to bed sober? Ever since he'd come to this hellhole, he'd been suffering nightmares. Nightmares only alcohol could drown.

His anxiety turned to anger and he aimed his bitter thoughts at

Doc Sutton: It's his fault, fuckin' quack. I'm on my ass 'cause of him and his cunt wife. Fuckin' pussy was hidin' under his desk from me, I know it! I oughta shove his stethoscope up his ass! I ain't hoofin' down to Osgood, no fuckin' way. Nobody, white or Washoe, gives a ride to a half-breed, and I don't take none! That lyin' big titty bitch was just tryin' to ease her own guilt. What could I do? 'Cept scratch my ass at her.

No, Henry couldn't do much about anything, not with all his problems, the "AAVs" as he called them: Alcoholism, Arachnophobia and Vertigo. And then there was that fourth "A" that Cousin Danny and those other do-gooders were always nagging him about. Namely, Attitude, as in Anti-Social Ass-*hole*.

But who could blame Henry for his proud nihilism? His vertigo made him nearly unemployable. He couldn't eat normally and had to dine in small dark rooms. If he went outside, where the sky crashed through his brain, he'd barf, though one time, he got a kick when a dumb tourist saw him and got her skirt in a twist about it—"What? You never puked in public before?" Henry laughed scornfully as he wiped his drooling mouth. "Fuckin' snob!"—

A-ha! Here's some distraction action! Barb Albanese's Mercedes suddenly drove through the bright white space between his ballcap brim and his nose and parked across the two-lane highway to his left. Barb climbed out and click-clacked in her pink stilettos and painted-on jeans toward her realty office. With a grin, Henry lifted his cap a tiny bit: Get a load of them grand-o bazzoongas! Miss Boobalicious! He sighed. Another stuck-up cunt I'd like to see run outta here!

Henry lowered his cap again and relaxed against the awning post. At least the Underpants Sheriff and his dope-i-ties weren't around to bother him, he thought as he slipped into a doze. Not long after though, the doze was interrupted by the hum of a fast engine. He had to shut his eyes against the nauseating flash of whirling hubcaps. He knew that car. When the engine fell silent, he lifted up his cap. The sun had rolled to the west behind him. The afternoon shadows allowed him to handle a bigger field of vision.

The two developers got out of their red Jag and headed up the other side of the road. Bob Garner, in his Joe Cool sunglasses, looked pissed, his mouth sunk into his beard. Schlesinger, his buddy, wore the same pissed-off look he always did. They were talking hard. They'd got bad news. Petey spread his arms and shook his head: "What the fuck do we do now, Boss?"

Bob Garner slowed and pointed right at Henry as he replied. Petey swayed in disbelief, like he'd been beaned by a fastball. Incredulity sucked his face into a little puckery asshole.

"You're kidding! Him?" Schlesinger's yappy voice cracked across the road. Garner nodded down the street. Dismissed, Petey shrugged and walked on, sneering at Henry. Henry bared his teeth, crossed his left arm over his right and jerked up his middle finger: "Cocksucker!" he mouthed. "C'mere and blow me!"

Meanwhile, Garner was a-striding across the highway right toward Henry, long arms a-swinging, in his yellow and brown-striped shirt, pre-washed jeans and Nikes fresh off the shelf. His pearly teeth gleamed through his beard. He propped up his ultra-black sunglasses onto his reddish-blond surfer hair as he entered the afternoon shade. His light green eyes were squinty and lined with crow's-feet.

"Hey, Henry, how's it hangin'?"

"Outta your ass," Henry sniffed and looked away.

Bob Garner chuckled, like Henry was the funniest dude in the county, and then whipped out his wallet from his back pocket. Henry's heart fluttered.

When Henry moved to Byrneville last fall, Bob Garner was already here, one of them new big shots in the county that Alvie had been whining about. Since then, he'd become even bigger. Garner made a point of swinging by the Tap & Grill at least once a week and buying rounds of wine and beer for everybody at the bar. He even bought rounds for Alvie and his buddies, though it was clear he wouldn't let them hippies drink his own piss if he didn't have to. It was also clear from his hick talk that he was running to be the Guy You Most Wanna Have a Beer With. Plenty of dumbasses fell for this shit and a lot of losers didn't, but the ones who bought it, Garner wound up buying them out. The Sierra Future group now owned big chunks of both sides of Byrneville Creek, which ran right through the village. They'd even bought most all the land the state and feds had been selling off. Most all the older families grabbed the money and skipped out, leaving only their soon-forgotten names on road signs, rivers, and mountains.

Much as Henry hated the hippies, the changes that Garner seemed to have in mind worried him just as much as it worried them. How long would it be before Cousin Danny folded like a towel for Garner's bribes and leave his hard-luck cousin homeless again? Danny, a full-blooded Washoe, talked a shit-streak about sticking with the tiny number of the tribe still scratching out a hopeless living up here, but he had his price. Everyone did. Who would look after Henry once that price had been met?

But right now, Garner was okey-doke with Henry, because every week or so, especially around the time the money from Henry's disability was running out, Garner would stroll by and lay a twenty on him. And, unlike most everyone else, no matter how much shit Henry dished out, he always came back with more.

But today was different. For one thing, Garner was holding not one, but two twenties in his big pink hand: forty fucking bucks! He held the bills slightly apart, just out of reach, next to his grinning face.

"Guess two'll stick easier up your ass than one, huh?"

Garner rocked with laughter: "Henry, that's your best comeback yet! You're one heckuva funny varmint!"

But Henry had been playing along with Garner's phony compliments for too long. It didn't do to look a gift horse too closely, but goddamn, this oily asshole wanted something and Henry was bound to find out. Better know now!

"I don't know if I wanna take your money anymore, man. You're gonna kick guys like me outta here. What's your fuckin' game? Nobody ever dropped nothin' on me, they didn't want somethin'. You don't need to pay me to leave. You're wearin' the boot."

Bob Garner straightened up, pulling the money away. Henry's wings of rebellion sagged.

"You got me, Henry. I didn't get where I am just givin' away the farm. Damn right, I want somethin'."

"Yeah, Mr. Big Shot. Like me outta town."

"No, not that. Actually, I have a little proposition for ya: A new employee of ours has suddenly skipped out. Things didn't work out like we figured."

Henry rocked back on his butt, like he did when he blew away the hippies, but all he had to let go was a disbelieving laugh. Yeah, I get it. How stupid is this guy?

A wave of dizziness washed over him; he sat still to make it go away. As the world steadied, Garner leaned down and slipped the twenties into the pocket of Henry's soiled blue work shirt. Henry felt the money press against his nipple.

"Look Garner, you're either the biggest fuckin' fool or the biggest asshole I ever met and I've met plenty. If you're lookin' for a blow job from rough trade, you're kneelin' at the wrong glory hole."

Bob Garner grinned and dropped his black sunglasses over his green eyes.

"Henry, you and I have one thing in common—we're pissed-off dudes. There's a million people standin' between us and what we're entitled to. I started out exactly where you're sittin', a bum on a bench, eatin' plates and plates of shit until I got lucky and met someone who thought he could use me. So, I let him use me and he showed me how to take the breaks I found …and so here I am." He shrugged spreading his hands. "Now I'm thinkin' it's time to give a little back to someone who's where I used to be. Everybody in this postcard shithole thinks you're a useless bum and I happen to agree. Except," he held up his finger, "for the useless part. 'Cause I've been there. You're angry and an angry man's a hungry man. I need an angry man workin' for me."

He nodded at the world around. "They're the real losers. They don't see how things'll change for the better, so they stand in the way, try to keep it all the same, frozen in a jar forever. That means keepin' guys like us in the gutter. But you and me, we've seen lots of change in our lives, right? You either get run over or you find a way to get on and ride that horse." He started to turn away, then stopped. "Oh, one more thing, Henry my man: You called me an asshole." He paused again. Uh-oh, Henry thought. Here comes the kiss-off.

"You nailed it. I am an asshole. I can tell you, 'cause you know what I mean. You're right about the world."

Garner flicked a salute and strode back across the highway. Henry pulled the twenties out for a look, shaking with confused excitement. Goddamn, when's the bar gonna open? With the tight-ass liquor laws around here, he had to drink twice as much to put himself out, but Garner's gift—bribe—guaranteed a dreamless night; a night of deep empty sleep, freedom from this awful life.

Blow my fuckin' lantern out! I've met an honest man! The last time Henry was this impressed was in Folsom: Teddy Nerbacke. Twenty-five-to-life for murder and drugs; so big, so impressive, Henry was on his face, pants down, before he knew it—

Henry shook away the ugly memory and tucked the money away with disbelief and fear. Teddy got his jack for his "protection." What would Bob Garner get?

Forget it. Stay in the now. I got money. I'll sleep without nightmares; no black lightning on a white sky, or spiders at my throat. God, bein' sober's a fuckin' sin.

But just when he thought he was feeling better, the big white SUV came rolling down the hill with unnatural silence into the village, its windshield like cold black eyes. Inside that car was the one cocksucker Henry West hated most of all, the Numero Uno Asshole of Monitor County.

The SUV parked near the real estate office. Annie, the big Lesbo, got out on the driver's side, went around the front and opened the passenger door. A long, thin, black leg stepped down, feeling for the earth. Then came the other. Then a thin walking stick.

Vile! Old Klaus Bartok, one of the last of the old timers. The only one in these mountains who acted like Henry didn't exist. Evil! He never came close enough to hear Henry's insults. Never looked at Henry. Never spoke to Henry. Too good to even walk on the same side of the street. Mr. Fuckin' High-falutin all by hisself up in his mountain castle, with the world linin' up to wipe his wicked ass. Wicked! He was one of the losers Garner was talkin' about! Old fucks like him need puttin' down. Be easy. A little push. Bam! That ugly old head would crack like an egg on the rocks.

The old man tottered in his direction. Leaning on Annie's thick arm, he reached out with his walking stick, like a spider. A spider like the one in a cable nature documentary Henry had mistakenly seen once. One of them motherfucking giant jungle bird spiders, chewing on a little mouse, chomping with fangs so shiny and black, that Henry imagined the mouse could see its own face reflected in them as the spider ate. The monster turned its prey under its black mouth like a rotisserie chicken, its eyes hungry black holes. It stared at Henry as it munched away: Yoo-hoo! I see you! I'll want dessert when I'm finished I am hungry—

Frightened, Henry got up too fast. The image vanished, but his stomach turned and the world spun. In tears, he grabbed on to the post and hung there until the world steadied. He stepped up on the sidewalk, pulled his cap even lower over his eyes. There: nothing but safe, flat, dull ground. He let his feet guide him toward home. Suddenly, the pungent odor of his unwashed body smothered him. I smell like ass! I need a bath!

But the spider was gone. It was almost like the old fuck had made him remember so Henry would get out of his way. Another of the world's endless tricks to get rid of him. Henry now needed a drink more than ever or else that spider would return, enter his dreams and make him see his face in its moonlit fangs ...

CHAPTER 4

Stone Hand In Mine

In the two years they'd been living here, Dave and Carla Sutton had driven over every single road in Monitor County, paved and unpaved. Now there was only one road left, the one called Alpine Canyon Road.

They'd avoided touring it until now, mostly because Tim King had warned them off it. "Folks get lost up around there," he'd told them one moonlit evening in his slow sleepy voice as they ate together on his back porch. Alpine Canyon Road was mostly unpaved, treacherous, and twisting. It was also posted private property at the last rise before it entered Alpine Canyon.

But now, with their days here drawing to a close, Carla insisted, saying "It's the last road we haven't taken." And Dave agreed. He couldn't save her life, but he would give her everything else she wanted. There's no spoiling the dying.

They took Dave's big GMC truck up the Monitor County Highway, past St. Ives and across Mystic Valley, driving between rows of "No Trespassing" signs that lined the fenced-off meadow. The valley was afire with springtime green and blazing orange poppies (though, strangely, no purple lupine, a common flower throughout the Sierra). Miles to the west, the meadow ended in a forest of red firs. Above the forest rose a barren slope. On the other side lay mysterious Alpine Canyon.

Finally, topping the plateau to the south, above the canyon, Dragon's Ark stood against the sky, taunting, daring the world to knock the snow off its shoulders.

"I'll miss that mountain," Carla said. "I'd preferred dying seeing that over my bed instead of a stupid ceiling."

"I'm gonna miss every pine needle around here," Dave agreed.

Eons ago, Mystic Valley was a broad lake carved by a glacier. Over time, the glacier melted away and the lake it had fed slowly dried. Grasses moved in and soon there was the trail made by the Washoe people, along with herds of elk, deer, and other critters that migrated to and from the high country with the seasons. A section of the Emigrant Trail ran through here in the mid-1800s; then, for several decades, cattle grazed the valley floor. Fifty years ago, after the bottom dropped out of the cattle ranching business, Mystic Valley became a state park.

That relatively short lifespan ended late last fall when the state sold the land to pay off its deficit. The buyer, Sierra Future (aka Bob Garner, and a division of Getgo) spun the purchase as a "progressive evolution." The campground was closed with no sign that promised "Reopening under new management" or even "So long! Thanks for camping." Without the homey sight of khaki-clad park rangers, the county felt emptier.

The emptiness wouldn't last, but what would come in its place, no one seemed to know. Except, of course, for Bob Garner who had cleverly blown so much angel dust about his plans for Byrneville, the two ski resorts, and other parts of the county that the news about Mystic Valley knocked everyone else off their pins. He'd played a good head fake and, once again, pranced away down the field with the ball.

As they reached the north side of the valley, Dave slowed down, looking for the turnoff. A little ways on, Monitor County Highway became Sierra Crest Highway and climbed northwest up the ridge, past Dr. Leo Durant's house on the north slope above Alpine Canyon before it crossed Jackson Pass at eight thousand feet. A month from now, the Suttons would take that same road back to San Francisco, but Carla didn't want to think about that, not until she had to.

The entrance to Alpine Canyon Road sat so far back from the highway, it was nearly invisible, which partially explained why they'd never driven here. It had been last paved decades ago. Barely two lanes wide, it wound lazily through green pine and gray boulders. Tim told them to expect a relentless string of hairpins. A couple of miles later, the Suttons learned how right he was.

"You might get carsick," Tim warned while pointedly guiding the Suttons down other trails, some of which led to his favorite fishing holes. The weather in the upper reaches of the road was more erratic and stormy than other parts. In spots, the road skirted the edge of sheer cliffs.

"Only the Lord'll know if you go over," Tim advised. They'd be forever lost in the forest below unless Annie Goodman and Klaus Bartok, the only residents up that way, happened by. "Ain't a bet I'd care to make."

Yeah, well, I'm willing to make it, Carla thought. If I'm gonna die, I'd just as soon die there.

The switchbacks curled up the north slope above the valley floor. The road hugged the slopes, snaked into deep ravines then whipped out over the ridges in a series of dizzying fifty-plus degree hairpin turns as the valley ran below like a giant green river.

It was about then that Carla recalled one final comment of Tim's that now made no sense at all: "The scenery's not as great as you might think."

Surely, he meant not as great as other parts of the county. They shouldn't expect to be wowed, he was saying. Maybe he'd lied out of concern for their safety, but goddamn it, was he ever wrong.

"I don't believe this," Carla said to Dave. "What the heck was he thinking? This is the most beautiful drive we've been on!"

"You're right. We should've come here first," Dave agreed.

"Maybe Tim wants to keep it for himself."

Again and again, they swept from gloomy ravines out over the valley into bright sun, through a stunning, ever-changing vista of green hills and blue and white mountains. Over and over came cries of "Oh my God!" "Wow!" "Holy shit!" and more clichés of wonder. When the superlatives ran out, leaving them both in dumbfounded silence, Carla felt a creeping sense that reminded her of religion. This though, she kept to herself.

"It's not beautiful for us, dear," Dave would have argued like a party pooper.

They stopped often. Dave took digital photos. Like everywhere else in the county, the colors here were unusually vivid. Carla's eyes, so saturated with blues, greens, and yellows, started to tear up. As her life faded away, memories of this day would be her last pleasure.

I'll sit crumpled and silent and won't be able to tell anyone what I've seen. She squeezed Dave's arm as they stood on the edge of a cliff, far above the valley floor. Only he'll know.

The conifers gave way to chaparral, other kinds of scrub, and the occasional tough and stumpy mountain juniper: "Ernie Borgnine Trees" as Dave affectionately called them. Blinding pockets of snow gleamed here and there. The air turned colder, drier, and thinner. Soon, only chunks of tarmac were left, but Dave's high truck cleared every rut and rock.

Then suddenly, on yet another outward turn, Dave hit the brakes again and pointed to the right. "Get a load of that." It was the first time Carla had looked out the passenger window since they'd started. Her neck felt stiff.

A dirt driveway shot up to the right, ending in an empty sky. The cut was deep, its steep sides fenced by large boulders to guard against erosion.

"That's gotta lead to the Bartok place."

On the left, the road seemed to drop away into nothing. Miles away, the Samsons stretched east to west. The Sierra Crest rumbled off south. Dragon's Ark loomed close by. Dave smiled enviously: "This is their view every time they come down there."

"I thought the old man lived in the canyon."

Dave shrugged. "That may be the legend, but I'm sure he lives up there with Annie." He shuddered. "Coming down that driveway every day without going over the cliff would give me a myocardial in-farc-shun. Cook the hell out of the brakes, too."

There were no utility wires up here at all, so they must have been living off the grid. How could they manage so many miles away from anything? Carla wondered. What did they use for a power source? It would have to be a small generator, but getting even that up there would have been a nightmare. Maybe they lived off solar.

On they drove. Every time they circled around the ridge and into another ravine, the Ark passed like a hand across their windshield. A few outward curves later, the west end of Mystic Valley came into view. White water gushed through a deep notch in the rim and then spread out into a silvery cascade as it splashed down into the valley, so perfect, it looked like a handmade fan.

But the air was turning dark and Dave was slowing down. "Storm's coming."

Tim was right about the weather up here—it changed fast. Just minutes ago, there were clear skies everywhere. Now they were headed toward a bruiser of a storm that was prowling the west rim and blanketing the plateau around the Ark, making the mountain look like a massive sky ship floating in space.

"Keep going," Carla urged. "We'll be okay. We'll find a place to turn around somewhere." She sighed and looked at her hands, wondering if she was really hoping that something would happen and that she would die up here after all, like she wanted. In the last few days, she'd lost more feeling but hadn't told Dave.

On they went, more bends in, more bends out, higher and higher.

With frightening suddenness, the storm plunged down upon them. The world turned gray and purple. Powerful winds shook the truck cab. Sleet hissed against the windshield as the wipers pathetically squeaked and grunted. Excited by beauty and by peril, Carla smiled. She and Dave both loved big, bad weather; loved to get it on during thunderstorms and blizzards, when they could scream as loud as they could, their raucous voices joining the tempest in a howling chorus.

But right now, instead of looking horny, Dave's face looked a little tight with grinning fear. Tch, Carla thought. Such a wuss.

"Close to time, sweetheart. I'm feeling a little edgy."

"Just a little further, puh-lease?" Carla winked, her tongue slipping out of her mouth, a dirty trick she played to get her way, but it worked, sometimes.

Dave rolled his eyes, his caution at war with lurking lust: "I hope we don't run into anyone. Too bad we didn't bring the Wagner CD."

"*Götterdammerung* would be—" Carla started to laugh as the wind rose to a roar.

But no, she suddenly realized, that was not a Wagnerian wind thundering from above. It was something else. Something familiar everywhere, but not familiar here. It started out as a steady hum, then grew louder. Something not natural. An engine's roar, a growl from the world below, but coming from around the bend up ahead.

A massive shadow, like a black-eyed white bear, streaked in front of them only a few feet away. Dave slammed the brakes as the bear stormed past with a whining bellow, then vanished behind them, into the storm.

The truck went into the ditch to the right, inches from the slope. Rocks and dirt crumbled loudly across the hood. Carla threw up her arms against the dashboard. The impact rocked her back and forth.

Then it fell quiet, but for the wind. The gray sky cleared. To their right, the gray clouds parted to reveal the grim visage of the Ark.

"You okay? You alright?" Dave reached for Carla and pulled her close. She was fine as far as she could tell. The impact hadn't been enough to even pop the airbags.

"You okay?" he insisted until she found the voice to answer that she was fine. Dave asked her to move each one of her limbs, to turn and then raise and lower her head. Everything worked. He held up his fingers and she counted them. She knew her name and location: "Carla Sutton. I'm in a GMC truck on Alpine Canyon Road in a snowstorm with my hysterical hubby. Achtung, Herr Doktor Sutton! Move ze left leg! Move ze right leg! Mach schnell! Mach schnell!"

Dave laughed, but quickly turned serious. "That was an SUV." He immediately got on the CB to contact Byrneville, but got nothing. Then he tried to reach Osgood, but another storm gust tore the signal apart; regardless, they would be first responders.

Dave turned on the emergency lights, rolled down his window and glanced out behind him. He ordered Carla to stay as he jumped out and pulled on his red down jacket from the back seat. Carla listened to him fetching his medical bag from inside the truck shell. The shell also contained a stretcher, a portable respirator, two oxygen tanks with masks, a defibrillator, and a small medicine cabinet: a bare-bones backup ambulance that Monitor County Search and Rescue had made good use of and would hate to lose.

Carla dragged herself across the driver's seat just in time to glimpse Dave disappearing around the bend into a gust of snow, into gray mist, into nothing.

She now felt alone. From there, it didn't take long to feel scared. She dragged herself over the gear box and exit into hard-driving sleet. She grabbed her blue down jacket and a walking stick from the back. Patches of ice and snow covered the muddy road. Fucking stupid SUVs, she thought. They tricked drivers into feeling as safe as babies, but like big ships, they took longer to stop and responded slowly to important commands like "DON'T DRIVE OFF THE STUPID CLIFF, STUPID!"

She checked for oncoming traffic before crossing to the edge. She shuddered as the wind almost lifted her from behind to carry her back down the road. She had little confidence in her footing and balance now. Finally though, she found where the tire tracks disappeared at the edge and looked down.

Annie Goodman's white SUV—it couldn't be anyone else's—sat about twenty feet below on a shallow slope of rock, gravel, and dead grass. It had spun around on the slope and now faced back the way it had come. With its tinted windshield, it looked like a sleeping bear.

Dave approached the SUV, looking like a diffident ghost as his feet skidded over the wet grass. The sleet lifted enough to reveal a huge gray rock. In this light, it looked exactly like the hand of God, and it was this holy-looking stone that had stopped the SUV from plunging down into the valley. So, the situation wasn't so bad. Maybe Mr. Bartok and Annie were all right. Maybe they'd be able to walk out. Annie for sure.

Dave reached the truck and set his bag down. The doors were locked, so he picked up a rock from the ground and smashed through the rear passenger window. Carla jumped as the car alarm screamed, the most absurd clamor she'd ever heard in this part of the world. Dave reached inside, unlocked the front door and slowly opened it to reveal a slender but dark and misty figure reclining in the front passenger seat.

Carla carefully picked her way down the slope. The scars left by the SUV tires made for decent traction and her walking stick made a good third leg. She came up behind Dave while he was leaning deep inside the cab. Finally, he stepped down, shaking his head, frowning, his mouth grim through his beard.

"Is he—?"

Dave jumped and snapped at her: "Hey! I told you to stay put!"

"I'm alright," she insisted. They continued shouting at each other over the noise of the alarm.

"I can't be worrying about you!"

"I'm alright, alright? What about them?"

Dave glanced inside. "The old man's still breathing."

"You're kidding! What about Annie—"

He leaned close to her, speaking carefully: "That rock stopped them from going down into the valley but part of it went through the driver's window. Blunt force trauma. She's gone."

Dave turned back to examining Klaus Bartok, feeling for fractures and internal injuries under the old man's black coat. As he checked the pulse, Dave's eyebrows shot up. He put a stethoscope to the old man's chest, confusion darkening his face. Then he shook his head and murmured something about a hammer.

Mr. Bartok's neck wattles folded in as Dave carefully fitted him with a blue cervical collar. Though the headrest looked custom fitted, Dave would take no chances.

He grabbed Carla's arm and leaned in again, wincing at the car alarm. "Wish we could shut that off. Look, I'm gonna try to get the dispatcher again on the CB. I hope I don't have to drive back down." He gave her the fish-eye: "If you'd stayed up there, you could've made the call."

"I'm sorry, Dave."

"I'm sorry I bit your head off. Now that you're here, stay with him in case he wakes up while I'm gone. Keep him calm." He hesitated. "Try not to look at the rest of it," he added, alluding to the reason why Carla had dropped out of medical school. "Can you—"

"I've got it. Get going!"

Dave shook his head: "I don't think he'll make it either."

Carla felt a sweet thrill as she watched Dave sprint up the slope with long-legged grace. Then the car alarm finally stopped, and Nature's sounds took back their realm. The storm was fading to the east now. The air was returning to its chilly blue and gold hue.

Carla stepped carefully up on the running board and braced herself inside the truck. Both air bags drooped like white scrotums. When they exploded, they'd blown white powder all over the interior, even dusting Mr. Bartok's feathery suit, an insult to such a dapper, elegant gentleman.

His seat was a hi-tech safety marvel, an expensive, custom-made, bucket. He fit inside it like a jigsaw puzzle piece, safe and snug in an elaborate rig suited for a test pilot. All he needed was a crash helmet, though the headrest filled that function well, molded almost to his large ears. If he made it, he'd have a large team of safety engineers to thank.

She'd never been so close to him before. His skin had more wrinkles than skin, a sight that made her queasy. The only thing that compromised his old man's ugliness was the fine white mustache that swept over his upper lip under a hawk nose that jutted like granite from a cliff face. His ears were huge and sprouted thick tufts of hair. He probably could have a heard a pin drop from a mile away when he was younger, but now he was just ...*old*. He even smelled old, with the slight perfume of a forgotten corpse in an abandoned morgue. For him to live through this might not be such a great outcome.

His chest gently rose and fell beneath his black shirt. Carla breathed along with him and, without thinking, placed her hand over his hand. It felt like hard cold stone. Like her mother's hand as she lay in her coffin. Carla squeezed Mr. Bartok's hand, hoping he'd feel her warmth.

Then, before she could stop herself, she looked up at Annie. "Don't look," Dave had warned. He'd been right.

Like Mr. Bartok, Annie Goodman had also been pretty much a stranger. The last time Carla recalled seeing her was at her Saturday film program last fall, maybe September or October. She'd brought along a friend—not Mr. Bartok but some woman—and neither of them seemed to like the movie Carla had shown that day.

The huge stone that had saved the SUV had smashed through the driver's window alright. Blood was spattered across the crushed glass, making a crimson halo around Annie's curly hair. Annie was staring straight ahead, blue eyes and red mouth wide open, lips drawn back, teeth bared, her whole face frozen in a scream—a vicious angry scream, as though she were enraged at dying such a stupid death on this lonesome road.

Another violent wind gust shook the cab. With a sickening wet squelch, Annie's head peeled away from the window and the rock that had killed her, tipped sideways and flopped down. Her screaming face was now staring at where Carla Sutton's and Klaus Bartok's hands were joined together.

"Right ...shouldn't have looked." Shaking badly, Carla looked away. The storm was far to the east over Nevada now. Still, somehow, even the sun itself felt cold. A voice called from the road above, but now other strange things had come to claim her attention:

Carla found a bright red fox staring at her from behind the left rear tire, its brown eyes direct and knowing. A herd of mule deer, led by a pair of proudly antlered bucks, was coming up the slope from behind. A coyote calmly watched from the road above. Where had they all come from? It was like they'd been summoned. The wind roared again from the west. She felt a shadow drag across her face like a cold sheet. Directly overhead, a black hawk circled a patch of sky, staring down as though it too had been called to this place.

Then a sudden blue shock raced through Carla's body. Her nerves surged like a switch had been thrown. Every one of their endings sparkled and tingled with a sweet fire. The creeping numbness retreated. She felt alive. She felt impossibly younger, impossibly stronger.

She looked down to find Klaus Bartok's birdlike white hand suddenly gripping hers and squeezing it hard. His hand shook desperately, as though he were hanging over an abyss and Carla, only Carla, could save him from falling.

The old man's blue eyes shined up at her from under his massive brow, flaring with the same fire she felt coursing through her. Carla met them fearlessly. Yet, despite all the new feelings, she barely noticed her own smile, barely heard her own voice whisper under the howling wind:

"Don't worry. I've got you."

....

CHAPTER 5

When The Colors Fade

Dave watched Carla rub and flex the fingers of her right hand as they sat together in the corridor outside the tiny emergency room at Osgood Memorial Hospital. According to her, Bartok had "a grip like Superman." In fact, the EMT crew had to pry Bartok's clawed fingers from Carla's hand one by one while the old man stared desperately into space. It wasn't until they freed the last digit, that his eyelids closed, and his head tipped forward. For a minute, they thought he had died, as Dave figured he would.

Carla's fidgeting made Dave fidget, but just as he reached over to stop it, Ted Knowland, chief ER physician and hospital co-director (with Dr. Leo Durant) popped through the door, his fleshy head shaved, beaded, and glistening. He wore a tight smile that seemed about to spill over with uncomfortable news.

"Are you the patient's primary?"

"No, first responders. We saw the accident."

Ted nodded. "He's made it past the golden hour"—the critical time frame following any trauma—"but considering his age, I'm not optimistic. He's a really interesting case. The heart appears larger than normal and it's working extremely hard. The blood sample we took indicates anemia."

"Anemia? No internal bleeding?"

"No sign. We can't seem to determine his blood group."

"His pulse and heart seemed stronger than usual when I checked them. I wouldn't have said anemia. How about fractures? I detected a rib fracture, third or fourth rib, right side."

"We're still waiting for X-rays. There seems to be no skull fracture or brain injury. Head and neck seem fine, too. Considering what happened to the other passenger, he's very lucky. That passenger seat you described might explain it. Still, considering his age, I'm surprised the shock didn't finish him. He has an unusual bone structure, too. Very light and thin, almost like a …"

"A bird?" Carla held her hand up to the light, as though to check it for translucence.

"Kind of. Very low density. I doubt he weighs more than a hundred pounds. Anyway, we'll review the X-rays and take it from there. We'll keep him in our ER bed for now and if he improves we can put him in the observation unit, but if he doesn't …" Ted blushed and stammered, "Maybe you noticed that he's not carrying insurance."

Klaus Bartok didn't even carry a billfold, but a search of Annie Goodman's purse turned up a thousand dollars in cash in hundred dollar bills and an old state ID issued to Klaus Bartok in the 1960s, long before they started attaching photos. It gave his birthdate as 1906. The ID seemed to be the only record of him. No insurance put tiny, strapped Osgood Memorial in an uncomfortable dilemma.

"Tim King's looking for his next of kin now," Dave said. "Except for Annie, I don't know of anyone. But he's a big landowner, so he's gotta be wealthy."

"Land rich maybe, but he could be cash poor." Ted lived in El Dorado County to the north and knew little of the legendary Klaus Bartok, so he was not reassured. "I don't know how long we can keep him."

"Could be Dr. Durant's his primary." Dave grimaced. The old doc lived above the north rim of Alpine Canyon. The two old men were distant neighbors. "I'll call him."

"If he lingers too long, we'll have to transfer him out. Maybe to Tahoe or Reno, to some elder facility." Ted seemed in mourning for a lost world where no patient was sent away until cured. Osgood Memorial was hanging by a suture and likely to close soon. As cities like South Lake Tahoe and Reno modernized their own facilities, small rural hospitals like Monitor County's were being zeroed out.

Ted started back inside, then braked. "One more thing, I don't know how often he changes his clothes, but we had to peel them off. It was like skinning a squirrel. Whoever becomes his caregiver should be sure to change his clothes more often."

"Call Dr. Durant." Dave clenched inside as he hunted down a clear signal out in the reception area. He found Durant's number and paused before pressing autodial.

Dr. Sutton's relationship with Dr. Durant had been strained almost from the day the Suttons arrived in Monitor County. In addition to being co-director of Osgood Memorial, the old doc was both an advisor to the county commission and had been Dave's predecessor as county health officer for almost thirty years. He'd been agreeable about stepping down from his position and handing the reins to Dr. Sutton, but once faced with actually losing power, he sprouted horns, especially when he realized Dave was also a competitor. He was stingy with information and advice and had left the county health service in less than shipshape condition.

"Hardly anyone gets sick here anyway," he groused on his way out the door. In a last effort to defend his turf, he tried, but failed, to keep Ted Knowland from taking on Dave part-time at the ER. The old bull never called the young bull by his first name. The young bull returned the favor.

"And," Carla had encouraged her confused husband, "you're George-Clooney young and handsome and will eventually steal away all his patients until there's nothing left for him to tend but cattle."

Durant took his time picking up the phone and probably only because Dave had told Tammy Verneuil, Durant's physician assistant and nurse, that he was calling from a block away; Durant had fixed it so that the hospital was built right near his main office.

"Dr. Durant? Dr. Sutton at the Osgood ER. How are ya?" Meaningless greeting, but at least Dr. Durant couldn't accuse him of being rude.

"All right."

Meaningless response meaning what do you care? I'm still here and you're not getting your paws on any more of my patients.

"We have Klaus Bartok here. Car accident." Just the facts.

"Yeah." Whoop-de-doo. Like I'm supposed to drop everything?

"Is he, uh, your patient?"

"Hmm. No. Not him." Great job, Dr. Sutton. You've asked another dumb question. No, he's not one of those *other* wealthy patients of mine that aren't yours, ha ha.

"His primary might be up in Tahoe. Call around there. Wait. What's his condition?"

"Unconscious, vital signs stable. He's also a hundred years old. I'd say touch and go."

"Wow." Dr. Durant suddenly sounded interested. "That'll be the end of an era."

Dave then told him about Annie Goodman. Durant answered with a long pause. "She hasn't been my patient in years. Well, we all gotta go sometime and that includes me."

Dave snapped the phone shut. He was still seething when Carla found him.

"Fuck you very much?" Carla asked.

"Not his patient, not his problem. We'll have to hope he regains consciousness, or Tim scares some family out of the woodwork."

"I told the staff to call us if anything happens. You can call tomorrow."

Dave winced: "Dear, I can't be accepting new patients."

Carla pursed her lips like an indignant aunt, her eyes rolled toward the ceiling. "Ohhhhh, I see! Not my patient, not my problem! Uh-huh!"

"This is different. We're moving away, remember?"

She hooked his arm and dragged him toward the door: "Look at it like this: If he lives, you ride out of town like the Lone Stranger

Who Saved Klaus Bartok, the Old Man of the Mountains. He'll be soooo thankful, he'll shower us with his gold. Count on it!"

"If he's got any gold." One thing was true: Klaus Bartok was desperately hungry to stay alive, and if he could back his gratitude with a little extra….

Then he stopped: "I almost forgot. X-rays."

Carla laughed. "A-ha! I knew you'd turn! It's okay, they told me they weren't ready. Some problem with the machine. They called the tech." She shrugged. "Monitor County, dear. It ain't San Francisco."

Dave tried to call Tim King, but couldn't get through. Still, he wasn't worried. Somewhere, someone had some information on the old guy. There was always a character or two who managed to stay off the grid for most of their lives. While a pre-med student in Pittsburgh, he'd spent a couple of summers chauffeuring Mennonites around the northern Pennsylvania countryside as part of his rural training program. But sooner or later, even those folks had to open their doors to modernism. Everyone left traces in the world, and the days when you could hide your tracks were over.

Later, as they drove west out of Osgood back toward the mountains in the early evening, Dave realized a funny feeling had come over him, a kind of strange depression. For one, things didn't look right. Usually, at dusk, the mountains formed a romantic blue wall and the sunset painted the western sky with a crimson wash, while houselights twinkled warmly along the lower slopes.

Not this evening, though. The mountains looked gray-black, like a warehouse wall. The sky was wrong, too. At first, Dave thought a haze had settled over everything, until he saw the sun floating clear in the sky just over the rim, a distasteful blob the color of dishwater. The sky had simply turned gray, flat, and featureless. He couldn't, he realized, see one speck of color anywhere.

Dave blinked and rubbed his eyes under his sunglasses. What was wrong? In his two years here, there hadn't been a single day or night, rain, snow, or shine that he hadn't thought: This is great. I'm so glad I came here! Even when times were tough, even after Carla's first symptoms appeared. No one could ever be sorry to live here. He had completely forgotten what it was like to be depressed, a state he once knew too well.

Now that leaden state of mind seemed to have returned, so strongly that it had drained Monitor County's unique and wonderful colors and light completely from his vision. It was like an artist had decided to strip all the color out of the canvas. That's a stupid notion, he laughed to himself. The colors hadn't gone anywhere. He just wasn't seeing them, that was all.

But what if something were wrong with his eyesight? What if he were going color blind? Maybe it was a symptom of temporary depression, a letdown after all the excitement with the accident and rescue. In fact, all his senses felt depressed. Even his tongue tasted like a wad of wool. He always felt a little exhaustion after a shift with EMT or at the Osgood ER. But even then, the world hadn't suddenly gone black and white like this, like an especially dull, dry old movie.

He glanced at Carla, who was still flexing her right hand, looking like an infant who had just discovered she had limbs and could use them. He had to ask her how she was feeling twice before she snapped out of her reverie. "Oh fine." Had Bartok hurt her? Maybe a little, she shrugged, but it would be okay. At least she still has feeling, Dave thought. Maybe the disease was slowing down a little. He tried to remember how ALS progressed exactly.

A few miles later, they were in the mountains and still everything looked gray and dreary. In the middle of long, winding Osgood Canyon Road, they made the left for Byrneville. The evening sky was now turning a cardboard black. The first stars appeared like white holes that had been poked through construction paper, with no sparkle to them at all. The pine trees looked like tuffs, the meadows like colorless sand, and the rocks like the ruins of an abandoned city. Concerned he might be losing his night vision, Dave slowed down.

Byrneville looked dead. Mercifully, it had never made any attempt to make itself look "rustic cute," like a lot of rural towns did nowadays, to bad effect. Still, never had it looked so forlorn and dumpy, a ghost town without even a ghost. There seemed to be no one around at all, until they reached the intersection of Walsh Springs Road.

Suddenly, Deputy Berman sprinted across the highway from left to right, toward the Tap & Grill, right into the middle of a fight. Sam Colbert was restraining Henry West. Alvie Simpson was backing away down the street, waving for Henry to come on and fight. Way out of character for peace-loving Alvie. But Henry was sagging forward on his knees, almost pulling Sam down on top of him. The fight had gone out of him already. That's how it went for someone suffering from vertigo, but Henry seemed determined not to learn to stop swinging haymakers at the world whenever it got him mad. Poor guy loves his suffering, Dave thought as he turned right toward home.

It was clean dark when Dave and Carla pulled in the driveway. They went inside, arm-in-arm, in silence. Dave wondered how the sky could look so impossibly black, like a tar pit, the stars like ugly white specks of dust glued to its surface.

Twinkle, twinkle little star, please? Okay, maybe I need sleep. I'll feel better in the morning.

For the first time in a long time that night, he decided to have a drink, a shot of golden brown, cherry-sweet Macallan. He chuckled when he saw how much dust had gathered on the bottle. How long had it been? Right after they moved here, both he and Carla had cut back on their alcohol consumption, not just because good booze was hard to find around here, but because there was a magic about these mountains that made them both want to stay clear headed and sober. He had started dreaming more, too, wonderful dreams of flying over the treetops and up mountain slopes under golden stars, dreams so bright and vivid, he swore he could feel the wind racing over his body, as the fabric of his blue pajamas fluttered like wings. He had these dreams—and that's all they were of course—maybe once or twice a month, mostly during the winter. Every time, he awoke with the sense of the mattress bouncing under him as though he'd been dropped into bed and always felt a little exhausted and drained, as though he'd come down with a touch of anemia. But he was still happy. When he did drink, he woke up not only feeling hung over, but also felt a deep stab of abandonment and neglect, like he had felt when his father had finally rejected him. And that was why the dust covering the Macallan bottle was almost as thick as Kat's fur.

The Macallan tasted delicious as he sat in his reading chair in the living room with Kat curled and purring in his lap, so good, he wondered why he'd ever stopped. But his sleep was light and restless, his consciousness slopping muddily in and out of slumber. Toward morning, he thought he saw Carla standing at the window, her hands braced against the window frame, her forehead pressed against the glass as she wept and pleaded to the emptied night: "Please don't die. Please don't die." But he could do nothing for her, because the world was dark, a blackness so heavy, it was like he had no free will left, maybe never had any at all.

....

CHAPTER 6

The Bloom Off the Rose

From the moment Klaus Bartok was brought down from the mountains with the expectation that he would die, all of western Monitor County seemed to be dying along with him. An acrid inertia settled over every rugged square mile, like a woolen fog, moist and stinging. Weather reports claimed that an unusual high-pressure system had settled over this pocket of the Sierra landscape. It was the only explanation for the humid stillness in the air, the sudden shriveled droop of the spring buds and blossoms, and the mysterious way in which the uniquely vibrant colors faded, as though they'd been sucked away. Somehow, the explanation, though feasible enough to the sensible ones like Dave Sutton, wasn't enough for many others.

Even the sheen off the lakes, streams, and rivers had disappeared. Lakes sat like pewter-colored pools of oil and the spring melt ran with mud. The famous, fearsome, but gorgeous afternoon thunderstorms stopped as though for good. The sky seemed to have emptied forever.

The people turned pale, their postures sagging with their spirits. Arguments and fights broke out all over the western county, taxing the Sheriff's department, which found itself dealing with increased incidents of public drunkenness and disorder. Tim King was called to the Byrne residence, a half-mile up the south side of Byrneville Creek, to break up a fight between Chloe, who was more than ninety years old, and her frustrated niece Virginia. Virginia probably had no business living in the boondocks but, as Chloe's only surviving relation, she had an estate to consider.

By the second day, the mood affected Tim and his deputies, to the point where they felt like sitting back and letting the whole county go to hell, if that's where it wanted to go. For a time, no one thought of Monitor County as a good place to live.

Except for Henry West, who, sitting in the tiny single cell at the Byrneville station after decorating both Tim King and Deputy Colbert with royally purple and fat bruises, felt a grandly smug satisfaction that everyone around had sunk into the same wretched hole he'd lived in all his life.

There also came an increased incidence of road kill: deer, fox, coyotes, and possibly hundreds of rodents. Drivers reported increased numbers of goldfinches, mountain jays, Clark's nutcrackers, and crows deliberately flying into their cars; one trucker claimed a black bear had leapt in front of his rig "like on purpose, like something that wanted to die."

It was as if all life in Monitor County was committing suicide.

At the Sutton house, even Kat, their cat, was affected. She slept all the time, as her fur lost its color and became stiff and dry. Dave walked about like a zombie.

But no one was as affected by the change in atmosphere, by Monitor County's sudden loss of its bewitching beauty, as Carla. When she awoke the first morning, her right hand, which had so throbbed with restored life the night before, had returned to its previous numbed state.

That morning, the first morning ever, the dragon of the Ark, failed to return home.

He's dead too, she thought and howled with despair. Dave, caught in the same miasma as everyone else, failed to offer little beyond feeble words and a lame touch. Even after he called the hospital and told her that Mr. Bartok had stabilized during the night, she remained distraught, folded over on the couch in front of the picture window, through which Dragon's Ark looked only like a ruined castle in the white cloudless sky.

This is it, he thought. She's finally facing up to what's happening to her. She knows she's going to die. All it took was a spot of bad weather. Funny.

He left her for his afternoon shift at the County Search and Rescue with a kiss that felt like an accidental bump to Carla. Later, when Sean Temkin picked up her up for work, she snapped at him about the messy condition of his Jeep. Sean flinched and asked, "What the hell's wrong with everybody?" He'd found out about Klaus Bartok and claimed that a "funny vision" came to him while he was working lunch yesterday afternoon: He just knew that Mr. Bartok had been hurt somehow. And then Tim and Marissa King stopped by for dinner that evening, almost in tears, with the news of the accident; it was as if the world had come to an end. Sean even started comparing Klaus Bartok to John Muir.

Oh, puh-lease, Carla thought, her uncharitable thoughts feeling like hardboiled truth. She was about to take him apart for being a sap when he started whining about Sierra Future again: It seemed as though Bob Garner and his gang were putting on some kind of presentation at the county commission meeting in two weeks about their glorious future plans for Monitor County. The final vote for approval would come the following week. And no one was doing a damn thing to stand up.

"Stay and fight then," Carla snapped, her voice edged with sarcasm. She imagined the county commissioners rolling their eyes as Sean whined and stumbled about spouting sappy puerile rhetoric about nature, environmentalism, and "what about spiritual values versus money values?"

Carla took the devil's side with a relish that stunned her: "You know what it is about money values? People can see money, people can feel it, hold in their hands, read it on their computer screens, see it on their bank statements. Money values build houses and put food on the table. What the hell do you mean by 'spiritual values' anyway? I was brought up Catholic and I still don't know what that means."

Then she really nailed him by calling him the worst thing in the world: an Elitist. No, it didn't matter that he didn't have any money. What he had was a minority set of beliefs that he believed made him better than the majority of people who needed and wanted things like Sierra Future to happen—ipso facto, Sean Temkin was an Elitist with a capital E, a bigger snob than the richest millionaire.

As they approached St. Ives, Sean slowed down. The Jeep started to weave and Sean's voice welled with frustration and grief: "For chrissakes, will you lay off? You're starting to sound like that Henry West guy, just biting and pissing at everybody."

"I'm just trying to show you what you're up against," Carla said with prim insincerity as they pulled into the parking lot. "Someday, your body will starting going on you and you'll look in the mirror and it'll be just you, the world around, and nothing else."

To this grim wisdom, Sean had no reply and Carla felt like she'd won something, but the victorious feeling passed quickly under the sour sky and still air.

St. Ives was packed with the first tourist season rush and Carla hit the ground running. She could barely keep up. Her focus was off, and more obviously, her coordination was bad: Pens and pencils, credit cards and paper, kept slipping from her hands.

Everyone seemed lost, and with the weather so oddly depressing, for the first time ever no one seemed happy to be here, not just the urban malcontents. The questions the guests asked seemed spectacularly stupid. ("There's no fish in the river? Where did they all go?" "Where are all the flowers?" "Is this a vegan restaurant?" "Where's the swimming pool?" "Where are the TVs?" "Can I have another lock on my door so the bears don't get in?")

Things didn't slow down until around four. Then desperation and helplessness returned with a sudden violence. More terror struck when Sean wouldn't even look at her as he ran back and forth between the refrigerator and the dining room. She didn't mean to be so cruel to him, really. She felt him slipping away; the thought of him no longer being smitten with her seemed frightening. She was feeling sick of everything again, most of all herself. She had to do something.

So she called Dave. He'd been so cruel, doing nothing while she suffered. He owed her a favor.

He answered the phone out of breath. Search and Rescue had just come back from taking in a guy who sat down on his open tackle box and got up with his butt bristling with fish hooks.

"Dave, would you look in on Mr. Bartok after your shift?"

"Matt Gordon's called in sick for the five-to-nine. I gotta fill the slot. I'll be late to pick you up as it is. Hey, have you given notice—"

"Look in on him afterward, then. You're only a short drive away. What if they've stuck him in a corner to die? I don't want that to happen and I know you don't either. Sean'll drive me home after work. Puh-lease?"

At last, she felt better. When Sean rushed by to fetch drinks from the refrigerator, she told him the news. His stricken lover's smile returned. I should've kept my fat mouth shut, she thought, but at least I did *something*.

CHAPTER 7

Into A Sudden Sleep

Nine o'clock came none too soon. After they'd rescued a child who had wandered away from a campsite in the southern part of the county, Dave and his partners, Mike Einsohn and Bettina Munson, returned to Search and Rescue headquarters just after seven o'clock. Search and Rescue occupied a big old garage in Woodfield, a village at the entrance to Osgood Canyon, a few miles to the west above Osgood. Minutes after they collapsed in their metal chairs and shared a large microwave pizza, an argument broke out.

The subject was Sierra Future versus Monitor County's future. Mike, an assistant county surveyor and a recent ambivalent transplant from Los Angeles, was pro-Sierra Future. Tina, a lifelong Sierra resident, was opposed. Their debate was fraught with mutual resentment. Dave tried not to pay attention. By giving notice of his departure that afternoon, he felt he'd dealt himself out of the game. Mike and Tina seemed to agree and argued as if he wasn't there, Tina especially; she made him feel like a traitor.

Finally, the next shift arrived and Dave fled the chilly garage for the fifteen-minute drive to Osgood.

Thirty years ago, Osgood was only a road house, but the huge 1965 fire that destroyed most of the then-county seat of Byrneville inspired county officials to relocate the county seat to the valley and build a new gateway to the mountains to draw vacationing Nevadans—some in the county claimed a closer historical kinship with that state than they did with California.

Osgood went up in a twentieth-century rush. Once the road-house was gone, nothing remained that was more than thirty years old—only a strip mall that housed the county offices, including Dave's clinic, the main library, a shopping center, and two hotels, all built of the same dull sandstone, surrounded by developments built over ranch land. It looked like a block of warehouses. Osgood had destroyed what identity it had for a prosperity that never came.

The single-story hospital was laid out like a three-fingered fan on the eastern edge, unrecognizable except for the signs. Dave found a parking place next to the front and, down here where most of Monitor County's poor now had to live, locked up his truck.

As he got out, he saw red and blue lights in the distance and thought maybe his color vision was returning. Even the red traffic lights looked new. His mood lifted. How different it was to be able to see color.

Dave entered the lobby, his tired brain musing over Klaus Bartok's outrageous luck. Though he didn't share Carla's concerns, he wondered if they were justified. Not because anyone who worked here was necessarily a slacker, but because Osgood Memorial was underfunded and understaffed.

He waved and murmured hello to the receptionist but she looked lost in her work. When he called earlier, they said they'd moved the old man to the north observation wing. He yawned as he pushed through the double doors. The lights in the hallway were dimmed. A nurse was standing by the nursing desk, very still, staring like a manikin. He said hello, but she didn't respond.

He saw something floating toward him. It was flat and it rippled like a black sheet in a wind. From beneath this sheet, hung two blue lights and a big open hole and Dave thought, Someone's sure hungry.

Dave felt the big hole close over his head. His mind shut down.

When his mind re-opened, he didn't know where he was. He

didn't who he was. He didn't even know *what* he was. Every object he saw had no name and no content. He saw a silver pool of light, surrounded by pure black. Through the middle of the light pool weaved a broad, black ribbon, with another thin, white double ribbon weaving down inside it. His hands—two objects that were also strange to him—were gripping a hard circular object that moved whenever he moved his hands.

Then, ahead, two bright white blobs of light flew at him from the darkness, moving inside the black ribbon. They grew bigger until they hurt his eyes and they made a loud blaring noise. He turned the wheel in his hand.

His mind stammered out thoughts: steering wheel—road— driving—SHIT—I'm driving!

He swerved. The two bright lights zipped past, the car horn swelled to a crescendo, then quickly faded. He felt panic, pressed a floor peddle. The vehicle he was driving skidded across the gravel and stopped inches away from a gray metal fence.

He climbed out into a cold wind. He'd been driving a truck. Truck. He looked around and up into a blackness that was full of tiny white lights. Sky and stars. Those were hills, cliffs, and mountains. He walked around the truck, heard his footsteps crunch, a river roaring under the wind. Where am I? Who, what am I? His mind worked like a baby's: soft as it slowly assembled a relationship with physical reality.

The license plate read MTNDOC 720. My truck, he thought. My name's …He found his wallet and looked at the card inside: "Dr. David Sutton," he said aloud.

Now he remembered who he was, and recognized where he was—on Osgood Canyon Road. He'd been driving as if unconscious on narrow, winding Osgood Canyon Road. His watch read almost eleven.

Dave started shaking with fear. Then he threw up and cried. Afterward, he leaned against his truck and tried to think straight. He ran his hands over his body, flexed his limbs. No sign of trauma or bleeding, except for a sore on the left side of his throat, over the jugular. He found the BP cuff in the back of the truck. Blood pressure 70 over 100. Heart was racing, maybe to compensate for blood loss. But where was he bleeding? Inside? No symptoms.

Dave sat in the truck and tried to reconstruct his memory. I left hospital garage at nine. After that, he could remember nothing. Almost two hours gone, snap, like that. A piece of time, snipped, edited out and thrown away, like a piece of movie.

I was driving while …He didn't want to say *sleeping*. He could've been killed.

When more of his thinking skills returned, he decided to go home. It was a slow and shaky trip. He had the feeling that he was seeing his house for the first time as he pulled in the driveway. He struggled to remember who else lived there with him. He dreaded seeing a human face and not know how to relate to it.

Carla, that's her name. The lights were out. She had to be asleep. It seemed very far from the truck to the house. Dave felt afraid as though he might float away forever, freeze and die, all alone in the cold black sky.

This is the earth. The earth. Stop thinking like a child, he thought.

A familiar animal waited by the door. "Hello cat." The cat purred. Its fierce affection comforted him. The sound of Carla's breathing from the bedroom comforted him, too. He opened the kitchen cupboard and stared at the amber-colored bottle: "Better not, pilgrim." Instead, he went into the office to check his blood pressure again. Still low. He took a sample of his own blood. The blood looked black as it spouted weakly into the barrel. He stored the sample in the fridge.

All he wanted was the safety of sleep. But as he was lying down, Carla stirred.

"Dave?" Her head rose in the darkness as though from a pool. "Dave?"

"Yeah. Here."

"You alright?"

"Mm-mm. Fine." Big sigh, pretending he was only tired.

"Mr. Bartok okay?"

Dave took a deep breath: Bartok? "Oh, yeah. He's alright. He was asleep, resting."

That's why I was there. How is it that I know what I don't remember?

Her head sank down out of sight, as though to drown in darkness. Oddly, he didn't care that she didn't say thank you and was relieved, as though she'd gone away.

Toward morning, his empty mind finally dozed. Somewhere in his sleep, he remembered what happened, just before he lost consciousness. That black sheet, like a cape, a leaf calmly sailing on a clear stream down the hallway right for him. He saw it more clearly now. Those two lights were eyes and they shone above a gaping black hole. That hole was a mouth. The mouth was so big, it crushed the rest of the face into gray folds, except for the eyes—bulging blue insect eyes. The mouth was a wide-open suction cup that closed over his face—

Dave awoke to another dismal morning. Gray light poured through the window to reveal Carla's silhouette, bent in sorrow. She was crying again for herself, for the dead sad world outside.

Dave could still feel that mouth from the dream closing around his head, could smell its moist sweet breath. His heart pounded. Sweating, he gripped the sheets and lay there shaking, too frightened to reach for Carla. It was no good. She had her own unknown sorrow to bear. They were both completely alone, all alone.

....

The Fourth Man In The Room

Dave said nothing to Carla about what happened that night; there were too many health issues in this house already. In the morning, while she was in the shower, he rang up Jim Schaefer, a fellow med school grad at UC–San Francisco. Jim now worked in Neurology at the Renown Hospital, south of Reno. Jim squeezed him in for early that afternoon.

Dave slipped his blood sample into his pocket. In the hallway, he found Carla in her rust-brown robe, scouring her wet hair with a towel, her face dull and uncaring. Her skin was tasteless and dry when he kissed her, not even pursing his lips.

"I'm gonna call in sick at St. Ives today," she sniffed. She was all right, just a hint of spring cold creeping in. Dave said he had to go into the clinic to catch up on work. Then she smiled in a strange way, up one side of her mouth.

Light-headed and ravenous, Dave devoured a barely microwaved pile of sausages, (he was tempted to eat them raw, the blood-red meat looked so sweet and mouthwatering), four scrambled eggs, a mound of hash browns and a mango juice chaser. He still felt famished. He furtively checked his pulse; its rate was slower than last night, but still too fast.

Carla picked up the phone as he flew out the door: "Sean? Good morning."

The weather in the mountains remained dismal, gauzy, dreary, and colorless. But once Dave drove down into the valley, the colors bled back into reality and his mood lightened. He felt less concerned about his eyesight. Even Osgood looked cozy. So, it was bad weather and a damn good thing that it was staying up in the mountains.

There were no cop cars or emergency vehicles parked outside Osgood Memorial as he drove by. Nothing seemed to have gone wrong during the night. Had he even gone there in the first place?

Dave arrived at Renown Hospital just before noon. During the initial exam, he mentioned the blackout, but said it happened at home. The initial findings were negative but for some signs of anemia. The hemoglobin in the sample he brought was down by ten percent, a whole pint. No, he hadn't given blood yesterday, but his current hemo levels were higher now, more than half. No bleeding, externally or internally. The throat rash probably wasn't involved. It had to be his diet. Breakfast sat like a lead ball in his gut as he talked to the woman ER doc.

Then Jim rolled him into the CT donut. Two hours later, Dave and the ER physician were waved into the viewing room. Dave and the doctor stood behind Jim and the radiologist, all of them focused on the screen on the wall. Though a family physician, Dave marveled at how little he knew about his own body.

"As far as we can see," Jim grinned, "you have the healthy brain of a thirty-four-year-old male."

"Yep," Dave grinned back. "I keep it in a jar on my desk!"

"HA! HA!" Dave and Jim slapped five. *I must be feeling better.*

The outpatient doc rolled her eyes: "Tch! Jokers!" while the CT tech scowled, failing to get the old med school joke.

From there, Jim was all brisk business: Nothing wrong. No indications of stroke, tumor, or trauma. Negative for Alzheimer's, Parkinson's, *et cetera.*

"We could do an MRI if you wanted, but you'd be waiting awhile for the results. How are you feeling now?"

"Draggy, like I have anemia. But I don't think it's related to the blackout."

"What happened exactly?"

Dave told a story about getting up from his reading chair in the living room to get a glass of Macallan in the kitchen and coming to in his chair two hours later. It was the only story he had that didn't sound embarrassingly freakish. The rest was factual enough: It was as if someone had closed his eyes, shut down his brain, and then booted it back up again. "I didn't know where I was or what I was. I even forgot my name. It was like experiencing the world through the mind of a lizard."

How hard had Dave been working? Jim wanted to know. Eating right? Enough sleep and exercise?

Yeah, he'd been unusually depressed the last couple of days.

"It could be a stress reaction with everything you're going through with Carla and all. What about your drinking?"

"Hardly touch it anymore. I'm almost a teetotaler, and Carla's off wine completely now. I'm not gonna have to quit the scotch altogether, am I?"

"I hope not. That might leave environmental factors."

And that was when Dave thought about Osgood Memorial. He had blacked out while he was there. He remembered the receptionist and station nurse, how they were still and staring at nothing, as though hypnotized.

As he drove home through the suburbs, box stores, and strip malls that spread south of Reno, Dave considered the possibility of a gas leaks. He didn't recall any telltale blue odor. Did some prankster pumped anesthetic gases into the air system as a joke? That would be a crime, a major scandal, and mean the closing of Osgood Memorial. It didn't feel like an accident: a *person* had done this. He wished now he'd stopped by the hospital earlier. He'd be a witness. It would be his duty to report his version of events.

He arrived at the hospital at four-thirty to find the lot almost full and a county police car by the front curb. But the kind of disaster Dave was envisioning would have brought authorities in from all over. As he went in, he noticed the sun still looked like a 40-watt bulb above the gray mountains and unpolished silver sky. He stopped by the front desk to see if Terry, the receptionist, knew anything.

"Someone broke into the blood bank last night."

Dave's scalp tightened and grew itchy. "Damn. My wife and I are in their database too. Identity theft comes to Monitor County."

"Don't know about that," Terry shrugged.

The blood bank was right off the lobby and connected directly to the ER. As he walked past the open door, he glimpsed Sam Colbert inside talking to someone. Dave laughed. Tim had made good on his threat to get Deputy Sam transferred down here.

The north wing was smaller than the other two as it had six rooms, two of them private. It seemed sunk in brown gloom, doors closed, curtains pulled, even at the end of the hallway.

Jeannie Sally jumped when Dave leaned over the nursing station counter. She was one of the best nurses around, usually brimming with bustling energy, but today, she looked frazzled, her black hair like a woolen rag, her brown eyes red-rimmed, her mouth turned down, tight and wary. She hastily turned over some papers she was looking at. Dave recognized this behavior from his work as county health officer; whenever he sprang a surprise inspection on a restaurant, an action like this meant a troubled kitchen.

Dave leaned his elbows on the counter and licked his lips.

Hey, I walked in here last night and blacked out—no, um, did anybody see me here last night? I don't remember being here, but I was—no, that's not good either. No, circle around it, start with something unrelated.

"Klaus Bartok was checked in here the other day. I thought I'd see how he's doing."

She rolled her eyes and gave a short laugh. "He's ready for discharge and," she whispered, "I'd like to discharge him out of a cannon!"

Dave laughed softly. "That bad, huh? Can I peek at his chart?"

Jeannie waved her hand at the wheeled cart on which green binders slumped across the top row. She made a point of busying herself as he crossed behind the counter. He opened Bartok's binder.

According to records, this was Klaus Bartok's first admittance ever to Osgood Memorial. His age was given as 100. No medical history, no report of previous medical encounters with anyone in Monitor County.

Dave paged back through the notes. The last, at 12:30 that afternoon, by Ted Knowland, today's attending, said simply, "Patient still uncooperative; severe B.O.; resistant to bathing; refuses lunch; refuses to allow taking of BP. Manual exam: no indication of earlier fractures; pulse very strong and rapid, as is heart; skin unusually flush; again, patient would not allow further taking of blood samples. No stool or urine samples since admission; no discharge pending contact with family, caregivers."

The note before that, at 7:30 a.m., said: "Patient passed night peacefully; refused breakfast, not hungry; severe B.O." He wouldn't even let them take his temperature: "Threw thermometer on floor."

The pen tip had practically ripped a hole in the paper.

Then there was a startling gap. Yesterday's final note, made at 6:37 p.m. read: "Patient alert, responsive, unpleasant. Ordered RN out of room. T.K."

That would be Tanya Kyme, who was a little scattered, but always eager to please. Between that time and midnight, when the night nurse came on, she should have rounded by Bartok's room at least twice, every two or three hours. But if she did, she didn't note it. The night nurse didn't round by at all, not until after dawn.

Dave looked at the 7:30 a.m. note again: "P.A." was Paul Anderson. He'd never heard any complaints about him. What had he been doing all night? There was no excuse for ignoring any patient. The old goat would likely have been asleep anyway, so how hard would it have been for Paul to check on him?

There were no patient notes for Wednesday night, either, the day Klaus Bartok was admitted.

Dave asked Jeannie if Paul was going to be on tonight. She kept her back to him as she replied that Paul had called in sick.

"All three night nurses called in sick," she added. "Last night's attending, too."

"Liz Grayson?"

"Yeah, somethin's goin' around. We had to call all the way up to Reno to get someone to fill in. I'm gonna be here all night." She spun around in her chair, poised to say something, but then turned back around with a resigned sigh.

Dave wondered, Gee, why didn't ask for my help? His feelings were hurt but he knew why he hadn't been called—because Leo Durant would kick up righteous dust about it, like last time. That's why.

Dave reviewed Klaus Bartok's test results: The boxes indicating blood type were not checked off; after that, the old man refused to let a needle near him and wouldn't give a urine sample either. You'd think the guy never went to the bathroom. But they weren't keeping track, that was all.

Dave quickly scanned the other charts. Six other patients on this wing. He winced when he saw Miranda East-of-the-Moon's name. She'd been a regular at the county clinic. The jolly Washoe matriarch always brought her immediate family with her when she visited, like she had two weeks ago, when Dave pronounced her as healthy as could be for an eighty-five-year old who wouldn't cut out the junk food. Then a week later came the stroke. Dave decided he would look in on her before he left.

No notes in her chart for last night or the night before. No notes for the fisherman from Yerington who'd suffered a heart attack at his campsite south of Byrneville on Sunday afternoon. Dave had seen him at the ER.

What the hell was going on? For two nights in a row, the patients in this wing appear to have lain in their beds unattended. Fighting off panic, Dave glanced over at the X-ray shelf: Klaus Bartok's slot was empty. Dave got up from the desk chair a little too fast. The room spun. Jeannie looked up wanly as he leaned over the counter.

"Didn't anybody do any patient rounds the last couple of nights?"

Jeannie shuddered and glanced around before whispering: "I know. I asked, too. I think Paul was sick, but he said he didn't know what happened. He said he must've fallen asleep, but that's not like him!"

"Didn't anything else go wrong? What about the patients?"

"I checked everyone. They took some waking up, but they were fine, even old Mr. Grouchy down at the end there. Paul couldn't explain what happened. He said he blinked and then it was morning and he felt lousy."

"No sign of a gas leak? That might have caused fainting."

"No, nothing like that. Both Dr. Knowland and Dr. Durant are really P.O.'d, if you know what I mean. I hope Paul doesn't get fired." She dropped her voice down lower. "I hear it happened on the other wings, too. No chart notes from the last two nights, like there was no one on duty."

Or, they blacked out like I did, Dave thought. He felt helpless. He was a witness, but to what? It was so much like a dream, he might not have been here at all. Would anyone even remember seeing him? He couldn't pursue the issue with Jeannie, so he changed the subject.

"Where are Klaus Bartok's X-rays?"

"There aren't any. Radiology said they didn't turn out."

"Don't tell me radiology has been down for the last two days."

Jeannie emphatically shook her head: "No, the machine's been working. We have up-to-date films for everyone who needs them." She paused. "Except him."

Then she added: "I don't know what the problem is, but it looks like he's gonna be discharged soon anyway and that's great with me. If I have to do a double, I'd rather not even walk past that room. Oh no, he's going all right. He's found someone to look after him" her eyes rolled "finally!"

As Dave drew near the room at the end of the hall, he heard whispers pouring softly from within. There came a woman's laugh, high, sharp, and familiar, and his heart instinctively gladdened even as his mind grew static with a new confusion.

The room was almost as dark as night, lit only by a slit of light through the curtains. A man had just finished making the bed. He sat down on it, cheerfully bounced up and down, his back to Dave.

It took Dave almost a minute to recognize Carla sitting there in the dark. She looked nearly invisible against the curtains as she leaned against the windowsill. She wore tight jeans, a blue blouse unbuttoned at the top, and a big grin. Her arms were folded underneath her breasts, lifting them. Turquoise earrings dangled from her ears (a gift for their second anniversary). Her hair looked wind-blown. Even in the dark, the blush on her cheeks was intense and her eyeliner made her eyes looks wild, like a visionary's.

"Well! Look who's here!" she sang out, as buoyant as she'd ever been.

The man on the bed looked over his shoulder—Sean Temkin.

Sean's rusty eyebrows flexed as he smiled slyly: "Hey Doc!" He turned to gesture at the third man in the room, his voice full of admiration: "God, you guessed it right!"

Klaus Bartok seemed to melt into the room out of nowhere. His blue eyes shined at Dave from a chair in the darkest corner by the window. He seem absurdly relaxed in his shiny suit. His thin crooked smile, not quite a snicker, exposed teeth that were too white for someone so old. His long-fingered, birdlike hands lay casually folded in his lap. All that was left for him to do was say, "I've been expecting you."

Because he had been. They'd all been waiting for Dave. They knew he'd be there.

"Hello." Bartok spoke in a ragged but tough voice.

Dave knew he should walk out, but he couldn't. He'd made some kind of mistake coming here, one whose effects would run downstream forever. Too many other mistakes had already been made to take this one back.

"We are all here now," Klaus Bartok said with wry cheerfulness. "Time to take me home."

CHAPTER 9

Mr. Bartok's Ride Home

Dave tried to delay what followed as much as he could, but his efforts were fruitless. "Mr. Bartok was in such good shape," Sean Temkin said, waving the hospital gown like a summit flag. "He'd even dressed himself before we got here!"

Dave was about to suggest a consultation with Dr. Knowland when Ted materialized at his elbow, with Jeannie behind him, a wheelchair at the ready.

Ted stated that he couldn't find a thing wrong with Bartok, adding, "Not that he let us look too closely."

"After a hundred years of precious sweet privacy," Bartok laughed heartily, "I'm now supposed to surrender my dignity to the fingering of children in white coats? My secrets shall remain *my* secrets. I've lived long enough to see how everyone comes to know more about everyone else. It's a wonder you all don't hold each other in greater contempt."

He turned his large, spidery hands palms up. "If I can walk out of here, what more do you need to know?"

Ted waved the clipboard. "But you will sign this release, sir. We don't want you coming back here." Then he added, "To sue us, that is."

Klaus Bartok nodded curtly. Sean sprang to his feet, produced a Bic from his t-shirt pocket, and presented it to Bartok with a bow.

Carla cast her beautiful eyes on Dave. "Dave, be a sweetheart! Bring your truck around!" She pretended the idea had just occurred to her, even though they'd clearly been waiting, for him and him alone.

"I can—" Sean moved toward the door, but Carla cut him off.

"Noooo you can't. He's not going anywhere in that deathtrap."

Sean blushed and shrank away as Bartok laughed. True, his Jeep was barely safe for Carla, but Sean had missed the point she seemed to be making: *He is mine.*

Carla pulled back her shoulders and batted her eyes. Her tongue tip poked pink and wet through her teeth: "Dave?" She winked.

This time, her come-on made him stubborn. Dave retreated to his original agenda and turned to Ted: "I need to talk to you."

"Sorry, I'm busy. We've got a situation."

"I know. I was here last night."

Ted's eyes shivered: "We've got *another* situation. But call me later."

"Dave! Puh-lease! We're ready to *gooooo*!"

Dave defiantly sauntered out. He looked in on Miranda East-of-the-Moon. She was slumped in her wheelchair facing the door, her face sagging on one side. Muddy words poured out of her mouth. She raised her remaining good hand and pointed.

"Blooooo! Was m' blooo? Yoo! Yoooooo!"

"Hi, Miranda, how are ya? Yeah, that's a nice blue dress!" Dave agreed, though her dress wasn't blue, but a green and yellow print. Poor woman's eyes were going, too.

Her son Danny East-of-the-Moon stood behind her with a wan smile, one-year-old Hannah in his arms, the only baby Dave had ever delivered in the county. They talked briefly. Danny said he'd be moving down here from Byrneville to take care of his mother. He'd be selling his place on Byrneville Creek.

"Dave!" Carla's voice thunked into his back like an arrow.

86

He turned to see her leading a royal parade. Behind her, Jeannie pushed the Emperor in Black in his chariot. Sean shuffled behind. Ted Knowland hurried around them and rushed past with a nervous whatever shrug-and-smile: not my patient, not my problem!

When he reached the lobby, Dave discovered why Ted was in a rush: Deputy Colbert, tall, thin, his black-and-bruised eyes earnest behind his silver wire-rimmed glasses, was interrogating the hematologist in charge of the hospital's blood bank.

"Are you one hundred percent sure you didn't go in there last night or the night before and remove any blood product for any reason whatsoever? Maybe you forgot!"

"What?" the hematologist sputtered. "How could I forget something like that?"

"It could happen," Sam insisted earnestly. "I forget lots of stuff."

Dave was shaking with quietly laughter as the door banged open behind him and Carla barked: "Dave!"

When he drove his truck around, he found a tableaux waiting for him at the curb: Klaus Bartok sat regally in his wheelchair. Carla stood over him, shielding him from the pale sun. Sean squatted earnestly at his feet, as though he'd just kissed his hand. Jeannie paced impatiently behind them.

Dave marched stiff-legged around the front of the truck with his arms out, a parody of a monster in some Abbott and Costello movie: "Yes, Master! Must. Walk. Over. Cliff."

Carla shot him a dirty look. "Shsssh!"

He dropped the act. He didn't find her sexy. She didn't find him funny. Was he even married to this woman? How'd she ever get so rudely serious? And look how she kneeled down, her legs strong and steady. She couldn't do that anymore—

The old man was delivering a speech. Even with his sunglasses on, it was clear that Bartok's eyes were blazing with noble passion at the distant mountains, where home waited. Dave felt a surprising surge of sympathy for his yearning.

" …and protected by a thousand miracles in the very home and brooding-places of storms. Only the unimaginative can fail to feel the enchantment of these mountains."

Dave was trying to remember where he'd heard those words when Sean broke in: "So you'll help?"

"Of course!" the old man boomed, smiling and nodding. "In every way, I'm with you! Whatever I can do, whenever, you'll find my shadow coming up behind!"

Sean rose, trembling, his freckles darkening with fighting fury. "We'll bury Sierra Future! We won't let 'em put up a privy in their own backyard!" Then he added, "Chloe Byrne arranged a memorial service for Annie Goodman tonight at the Alpine Church in Byrneville. A lot of folks'll be there. Maybe we can talk more afterward!"

The old man laughed. "Oh yes, Miss Byrne. Been a long time ...!"

Sean offered Mr. Bartok his hand. Bartok casually squeezed it, looking away, his fast mind already on other things.

"We'll see you there!" Sean and Carla exchanged fist jabs and Sean trotted off without saying good-bye to Dave, running his victory lap before the race had even started.

Klaus Bartok stared up at Dave's truck and slumped angrily in the chair, turning into the gloomy, grumpy old man he actually was: "So: another death chariot! Come to kill me for sure this time, have you?"

Carla opened the back door: "C'mon! We'll help you in!"

"Does your husband know how to drive?"

To hell with you too and let's saddle someone else with—

Carla hurried to reassure him: "We're sorry this isn't what you're used to, but Dave's been driving these roads for years *and* he's a physician."

"And that's equal to possessing a chauffeur's license? I suppose it's convenient having a doctor around in case of another accident."

Dave related his experiences as an ambulance driver and as a chauffeur to the Mennonites. This was felling like an employment interview.

The old man shrugged. "You're taking me *from* the hospital, not to it. Keep your foot soft on the pedal. I'm not impatient to die at your hands or anyone else's."

"I guessed that already," Dave swatted back. "We all love life."

"You take it for granted like all the young. It's wasted on you."

Carla patted Bartok on his thin shoulder: "Dave and I'll get you home safe. I promise." She drew her fingers across her breast and made a promise that Dave found horrifying. "Cross my heart and hope to die."

"What about you?" Bartok gestured at Carla. "Can you drive?"

"Perfect record. Not even a speeding ticket. But this is Dave's truck."

Bartok wasn't asking that. Why not tell the truth? You can't drive anymore!

But Dave didn't want to argue. So long as he felt ensnared in this obligation, the only thing to do was to get it over with before day's end.

Bartok's bones creaked as he pushed himself to his feet. As Jeannie swept the wheelchair away, Dave reluctantly guided Mr. Bartok into the back seat. His long lustrous coat felt like a weave of soft fur and fine feathers of several species, or a creature from some evolutionary crossroad. Bartok felt light as a bird, his bones thin, soft, and flexible. The old man stared ahead as Dave buckled him in, not even saying thank you. After all, what lord thanks his servant?

They almost had an accident right out of the parking lot. As Dave turned left onto Osgood Canyon Road, they narrowly missed being hit by a pink Corvette zooming carelessly down from the canyon. Dave pulled over to see if Carla was okay, but she was more concerned about their passenger. Bartok wore a look that could've killed, even from behind his shades. As he raised a knotty fist, Dave felt a familiar but long-forgotten dread that pushed him even closer to hating this man.

"Sorry about that." Dave felt ashamed of his quavering voice as he his shoulders automatically bow, like they used to long ago, just before the beatings started.

Bartok punched his shaking fist back in his lap: "Perhaps you should have arrived at that spot a little later. Or a little sooner."

"I apologize for my lack of control over time and space. If I'd been able to predict that car was coming, maybe I wouldn't have taken this job at all."

"Dave. That's not called for."

"It wasn't my fault."

"I don't care whose fault it was," which was bullshit, but the more he argued, the longer he'd be stuck with this job. His resentment went down his throat like a barrel of tacks but Klaus Bartok made no more violent threats.

But Bartok remained an awful passenger. Driving him was like driving Hitler. He grumbled and whimpered and with each passing mile, the grumbling and whimpering increased. He seemed to be watching Dave's every move, as though his eyes had popped out of his sockets on two long stalks. He saw every tiny mini-variation in speed. Dave was always either driving too fast or too slow.

Carla, however, seemed perfectly happy. From the corner of his eye, Dave watched her hand snake into the back seat to pat Bartok's hand. It was such a privilege to meet him after hearing so much about him, she told him.

Klaus Bartok kept his eyes on Dave. Dave could make out the angry crescent of his wrinkled face in the speedometer glass. Clearly, he was ...

"Amaxophobic?" the old man barked suddenly.

Carla said "Huh?" She looked offended. Bartok hadn't been listening to her at all.

"Fear of riding in cars," Dave said. "So you're a telepathist, eh?"

"I memorize all the latest dictionaries."

When Dave slowed and signaled at the left turn for Byrneville, Bartok ordered him to keep going straight: "Straight home. Now."

"Don't you feel well?" Carla asked. "You'll miss Annie's—"

"I'm just out of the hospital. Why should the world see its grief mirrored in my tears? Public mourning is for the lonely. Home, please."

That was only a rationalization. His detachment only concealed another phobia: "Thanatophobia?" Dave winked in the rearview mirror, but Bartok said nothing. Fear of death: It would account for his lousy attitude toward riding in cars and attending funerals.

When they finally started the long drive up Alpine Canyon Road, Klaus Bartok turned from angry to nearly hysterical. He wailed as they swerved out again and again over the valley, as though the truck were an unsecured roller coaster.

"Careful! Careful! Watch where you're going, moron!"

He acted as if every second might be his last. Why did he live all the way the hell up here if he hated the ride so much?

Finally, they reached the driveway. "No, no! Not here!" Klaus Bartok bellowed. "Keep going!"

When they passed the scene of the accident, Dave glanced in the mirror to see Bartok had put his hands over his sunglasses! It was almost funny and definitely pathetic. Poor little man without his child's safety seat! Klaus Bartok hissed like a cobra just as Dave finished the thought.

Finally, after what felt like forever, the road ran straight for a while then appeared to shoot straight up to a deep granite notch, a nearly perfect V cut in the western summit of Mystic Valley. Hundreds of feet to the left, the waterfall cascaded down.

A broken wooden sign warned "Trespassers W—." Far beyond the notch was the misty shadow of the Sierra. The upper half of Dragon's Ark loomed above, to the left.

Dave shifted down. As they went up the hill, the old man sobbed as a dry sky filled the windshield. At the top, in the middle of the notch, Dave stopped again. The road beyond seemed to run straight down into a granite wall, then it curved sharply to the left. The wall was an outcropping. Another outcropping jutted out behind the first one and after that, another, like books pulled halfway out of a bookcase. The other side dropped off into vertiginous nothingness. There was no place to turn around either.

"I hope we don't run into anyone." At last, Carla looked scared.

Dave carefully let the truck roll its way down. It felt like the sour weather of the past couple days had concentrated here. There wasn't any color anywhere. The escarpment cast shadows like city skyscrapers. No wonder hardly anyone came up here. If this had been his first sight of Monitor County, Dave would have turned right around.

Meanwhile, the old man kept crying and moaning. Whoever was the first to offer a toast to long life, Dave thought, had no idea what he was wishing for.

Finally, they made it to the canyon floor where an amazing thing happened: Klaus Bartok stopped crying. Dave looked in the mirror to see Bartok calmly wiping away his tears. The old saw was true: Old people really did revert to their childhood.

The dirt road rose and fell across the canyon bottom. The walls towered over one thousand feet on both sides, tightly framing a crack of colorless sky. Dave lowered his visor against the sun. He only needed to see the road ahead.

"How far?"

"Until we get there."

"When will we get there?"

"When we arrive."

If we were in the city, Dave thought, I'd put you on a bus.

"I wouldn't let you," the old man muttered.

"What?" Carla asked.

"Nothing," Dave said. Lucky guess. He's only pretending to read my mind.

The road ran through granite boulders the color of chewed gum. To the left, down the middle of the canyon floor, a low grove of wind-flattened conifers, looking to be only waist high, spread east to west. They drew their meager nourishment from a mound of detritus that had accumulated over the centuries of floods. Dave estimated they were at eight thousand feet. No spring flowers bloomed; only the hardiest grasses, scrub, and those sad trees, bowed by hard storms and high winds, would survive for long. It was hardly fit for people.

A hard west wind rose, the first in days. Dust devils drilled into ground, sending twirls of dust into the air. Dave drove across several sturdy old granite bridges that arched over the wide and roaring canyon stream. Mining companies had probably built them over a century ago.

It was quiet in the truck; Dave felt alone, even with Carla there. He'd been in the backcountry before, in many faraway places, but this was past the end of the world, a bleak and barren Universe.

Carla, on the other land, looked wide-eyed and wonder-struck, with her hand still reaching into the back seat to comfort Bartok, who seemed not to be there at all.

"Do you live up somewhere on that mound?" she asked.

He grunted.

Dave envisioned Bartok's house as a crumbling old cabin where he kept his money stuffed in a moldy mattress. Every day, he counted out every cent, thought himself the luckiest man alive and mocked everyone else as a fool.

Soon, they drove into the canyon's west shadows. Dave kept the visor down. Up ahead, a thin grove of small white pines curved around the end in a horseshoe and thinned out on the north side. Through them, a small tar-black lake was visible.

"Here. Stop here."

Dave turned the truck around to face east. He shut off the engine and set the brake. Except for the howling wind, it was quiet. Before he could say a word, Carla got out, ignoring his warning that the wind was strong enough to knock her down.

"Come on!" She pulled on a brown sweater from the floor of the back.

Before Dave reached the other side, Carla was already helping Klaus Bartok down. She looked around the canyon floor and cried "A-ha!" She found a long bent tree branch, flipped it in the air and handed it to him like sword, adding a ladylike bow: "Your walking stick, Mr. Bartok? Sir!"

"That's over," he muttered with cynical relief. He took the stick from her, plunked its tip into the ground and strolled away along a trail that led across a redwood bridge and rose up onto the boulder-strewn mound.

"Can we walk you home?" Carla called.

He halted, slowly turned, and took off his glasses, showing smiling blue eyes. "I am home!"

He waved at the mountains where gray clouds billowed up into a suddenly bluing sky. "I'd fly out of here soon, if I were you. Before dark." Then he smiled hugely and winked. "But of course, I am *not* you!" He neatly pocketed his glasses and tottered on.

That you aren't, Dave agreed and sneered a loud "You're welcome!" before turning away to stomp back around the truck.

The old man laughed in reply, as though crowing, I'm a hundred years old. Go screw yourself.

"Wait!" Carla said as she watched him go, fascinated.

"He said good-bye!" What the hell difference did it make now what *he* wanted? He was *home*.

Bartok's walking stick thumped as strolled across the sturdy pine bridge over the lively stream. Water from the spring snow-melt frothed above the banks. Above the mound, the canyon walls loomed, cracked in places and streaked with a distinctive large waterfall. Another crack ran diagonally up the cliff face, from east to west. Probably an old mine trail. At the top, Dragon's Ark sneered down from behind the rim.

Dave shuddered but took a moment to look around. The canyon was maybe a half-mile wide at this point. The south rim stood higher than the north rim. The snow on the Ark's flanks melded with the white sky, making its rocky patches look like they were floating in space. Then he noticed a very odd thing: the sky was turning blue, the vegetation green. The colors were returning. Nature was coming back to life.

"Goodbye!" Carla waved. At the top of the mound, Bartok became lost among the boulders. A column of debris swirled in the air. The wind blew strong and cold. Plum-colored clouds boiled up from the west.

"Carla!" Dave jumped into the truck, and pawed at the passenger door handle. Carla climbed in, slowly, reluctantly, distracted. Dave reminded her to buckle up and then said: "What's the big idea? What gives you the right to force a commitment like this on me without asking?"

Carla averted her eyes: "You weren't at the clinic this afternoon when I called. That's why I didn't ask. So Sean and I just went on ahead." She spoke with steely calm. "So." Her lips kissed the air. "What have you got to say for yourself?" She broke the sentence like a stick into its separate words, and jammed the pieces in the ground between them, one by one.

Dave confessed about his blackout and his visit to the clinic. He hadn't told her because he only wanted to protect her. "It's probably stress." He tried to be nice. "Stuff like this doesn't help."

As he drove, Carla watched the canyon go by. She looked happy and seemed to be drinking in every detail. But even though the changing weather improved it a little, Alpine Canyon seemed a grim, depressing place to Dave: I'll never come here again.

The storm rose quickly from behind, as a blue night fell. The storm seemed to shoo them out through the gap with bolts of lightning, blasts of thunder, and torrents of rain. Dave drove slowly, aching with alertness.

"This is so cool."

If you think so, dear, he thought, too tense to argue. It was a terrible drive. Every bend seemed to end in black space, ripped apart by lightening. The rain turned to snow, the world to blue and gray dusk.

"Oh my God!" Carla shrieked. "Look! It's the dragon! He's alive! He's back! He'll get us down safe!"

It was too dangerous for bird watching but Dave did glimpse something out there, a shadow sweeping by, heedless of the storm.

When they reached the highway below, the storm died out and Monitor County was its old self again, indescribably beautiful in the golden gloaming.

Carla laughed as she looked out west into the night. "There he goes! Look at him fly! So free and graceful! And so lonesome! I wonder if he has a mate."

Dave saw only a speck melting in the mist as he fought his temper: "It's a bird, Carla! It's hunting. It's looking for a mate. Whatever it's up to, it's not a dragon and it wasn't leading us to safety! *I* got us down off that road!"

She kept staring out into the dark: "O-kay!" she sang. "Mis-ter Party-Pooping Science Man! It was *your* idea we move up here and get close to nature."

"That doesn't mean I think birds control the weather!"

"He's all alone up there now. The old man, I mean. Who's gonna look after him with Annie gone?"

Dave gave a guilty sigh. "It's not our problem, Carla. It really isn't. We've got—I mean—you've got …you know what I mean."

She looked at him now. Her eyes were huge. At first, she looked so childlike it broke his heart; then she raised her right hand and closed it in a fist. He swallowed as he tapped his watch. "We might make it in time to say good-bye to Annie Goodman."

....

CHAPTER 10

Comes the Clear Dawn

As a cold rain fell, Carla grew impatient watching Dave push against the sagging church door. She reached out and the door gave way like butter. She slipped in past him.

Only a dozen or so had gathered in the candle-lit chapel to say good-bye to Annie Goodman. Did any of them really know Annie? Carla sure didn't. The few times she'd talked to her at St. Ives, the grocery store, and elsewhere, Annie seemed awkward and Carla always had to re-introduce herself. She had the impression of someone who wasn't a people-person.

A few heads turned to glance at the Suttons. She recognized Sean from his orange flame of hair blazing from the front row, next to Chloe and Virginia Byrne. He saw her and waved, but stayed seated.

Carla followed Dave as he sidestepped down the rear pew where Tim King sat with his wife, Marissa, and their two sons, Timbo and Brendan. All three waved. Carla waggled her fingers toward them. Normally, she would have sat with Marissa and gossiped, but this time, she sat a little apart flexing her hands, until Dave, with an astonished smile, nudged her and pointed toward the front of the chapel.

Bob Garner stood at the podium in all his J. Crew glory. His lazy, hard-to-place country drawl—it could have come from anywhere, from Arizona to South Florida, all the way north to Kentucky—

twanged around the chapel like a steel guitar sweetened with just enough arrogance so you didn't notice it: Ah don't care if y'all believe me or not: I got yore pecker in m' pocket!

Dave nudged Tim and jabbed his thumb at Garner. Tim winked a doughy eye and waved his Stetson under his small thin nose as Garner finished his homily, which despite its drizzle of sentiment, essentially thanked Annie for removing another obstacle to Sierra Future by getting herself killed.

Carla realized with painful suddenness just how alone Klaus Bartok was in the fight with Sierra Future. It was working out so neat for them, they might even have killed Annie themselves.

Garner flashed a grin and smartly left the podium, his boring but necessary task done. Chloe Byrne stood up, still straight and strong at ninety years. With her reedy voice and old-fashioned politesse, she thanked Garner and everyone else for coming.

Then she finished by gazing at the ceiling as though Annie were watching. "I wish I knew how to say good-bye to you, Annie. For many years you carried a shadow none of us could ever know, one that almost caught me. I'm so glad you've escaped. I'm so glad you're free and I pray there is peace for you in the end."

Lightning flashed and thunder rumbled after this baffling farewell (as though Chloe was also somewhat glad that Annie had died). Pebbles of hail rattled on the roof. A boy and girl popped up from in front and scampered down the aisle, out the door, running heedlessly into the storm. A tall, cadaverous blond, probably their mother, hurried after them, followed by Bob Garner and Peter Schlesinger. It was unclear who belonged to whom. The woman and her kids seemed like accessories.

As Carla stood up, she glimpsed someone familiar standing with Chloe and Virginia Byrne. She couldn't see the woman's face, but she knew that hair, worn in a stiff page-boy style.

Suddenly, Sean appeared at her side, asking about Mr. Bartok. His face fell when she told him the old man was still recovering from his accident. Her impatience grew as he shrank away in embarrassment at his stupid question. Behind her, Tim said to Dave: "No immediate family, just distant cousins." So, Annie was alone.

Carla saw Lindsay Carlson, one of the county supervisors standing with another supervisor, big gnarly Edie Ferrand. Lindsay owned Byrneville's only market while Edie ran a fishing camp south of the village; they could be counted on to oppose Sierra Future.

"Look!" cried someone, pointing at the skylight. It must have been a great owl scratching at the skylight and fluttering its wings over the shingles. Chloe laughed and waved at whatever it was: "Oh, that's just Annie's spirit saying good-bye!"

The woman with the page boy hair hurried away from the crowd, moving with small, timid steps, her head bowed. Meanwhile, Chloe started talking to Lindsay and Edie. Virginia Byrne, tall, bony, and stiff as a bristle brush, stood back from the group. Carla gave Sean a hard poke: "Don't let your meeting start without you."

Sean looked like he wanted her to take him by the hand. She shook her head: "Later." He heaved a little sigh and went down the aisle.

"A cousin in Bakersfield claimed the body for cremation," Tim was saying. "She also had a friend. There, that's her." He waved at the woman coming down the aisle. "Claudia Prentice. She's from over in Carson City. She stayed with Annie awhile last fall, says most of the stuff at the cabin is her property. Looks like Annie didn't leave much."

Claudia Prentice looked to be in her mid-forties with a soft homely pug face and a thin-lipped mouth that seemed permanently set in grim anger. She wore shapeless, modest clothes, as though she were determined to be ignored.

Right as she drew even, Carla finally remembered where'd she seen her: one of the last times she'd seen Annie Goodman alive, seven months ago.

It was a brisk, windy Saturday afternoon last October. Instead of being outside enjoying the fall light and fiery aspens, Carla was at the Byrneville branch of the county library, screening the old Bela

Lugosi *Dracula* in the main meeting room. Only about seven people came—three of them had been Marissa King, with Brandon and Timbo. It was a much smaller audience than had shown up for *Gone with the Wind* the week before.

Dave had passed on the movie this time to go deer hunting with Tim. He frankly turned his nose up at this kind of movie. "I like reality," he said archly.

"*Daaave*, you like Roy *Rogers*," Carla replied.

"Trigger doesn't grow wings and fly," Dave countered, brushing the argument away as he shouldered the scoped hunting rifle Tim had loaned him.

Chloe and Virginia Byrne, who were regular filmgoers, didn't show, either. Chloe had nervously declined: "Oh, no, I've seen enough of that," meaning she'd seen *Dracula* when it first came out. Maybe it scared her so much as a young girl that she didn't want to repeat the experience.

Why Chloe would have found this movie scary nearly ninety years later was a mystery. Carla watched with amusement and wistfulness as *Dracula* drifted along. Maybe it was scary back in the 1930s when movies were new and took audiences into worlds only feebly imagined by books. Decades later, the movie looked stiffer than the celluloid that preserved its ghost. If they'd adapted it from that fever-dreamed novel instead of that stupid, awful stage play, they might have had something.

"Not the greatest movie," she admitted after it was over. "The first twenty minutes promised a lot, and so did dear Bela. It's too bad that the rest fails to deliver."

The audience seemed less than interested and unwilling to comment until Timbo King, who'd squirmed throughout, finally sighed: "I don't get it. What's it about?"

"Well …" Suddenly, an idea flapped into Carla's mind: "There's another dude who also wears a cape. You know him as Superman. Maybe Dracula is Superman's dark side, his Evil Twin." The idea suddenly set her mind and mouth running off into a lecture: "To me, he's *waaay* cooler than Superman. He can turn himself into stuff and you never catch him prancing around in underpants!" Finally, when she felt herself running out of ideas, a voice that sounded like a badly blown flute piped from the back:

"I think this is dangerous nonsense. This movie is the worst kind of garbage. I'm offended we're even having this discussion."

It was the woman who sat with Annie, the one she'd later learn was Claudia. She looked frail and tiny next to Annie and they had both sat so quietly, Carla almost forgot they were there. Claudia stood up, shaking with indignation. Carla graciously invited her to go on: "All opinions are welcome."

"It's about things that don't exist and shouldn't exist in any world!" Claudia said. "It's a rape instruction documentary, just like the novel is a rape manual! It promotes the subjugation of women by men! What more do we need to know? Why do we need to see it? It's nothing but a naked act of pure, unadulterated gynocide." The woman folded her arms and sat down, lips pursed, chin up, her gauntlet thrown: Are you on the side of women and the oppressed or are you not? Answer now!

The Kings looked embarrassed. Carla fought down a laugh. Claudia's rhetorical style was, in its way, as quaint and overblown as Dracula's. Gynocide? Sheesh! Carla had taken a course or two with a couple of academic feminist instructors as a Berkeley freshman. Like Claudia, they seemed frozen in 1970s amber, a decade Carla was too young to give much thought to, even with her own Old Left father.

Dracula sexist? Well, duh! Sure! But it was that and a lot more somehow, despite its artlessness. Driving the blunt stake of moralism through its heart, like Ms. Van Helsing wanted, revealed more about her than it did the movie: I am wounded, weak and lonely. It would be cruel and easy to ridicule her academic faith in how the tail of culture wagged the dog of the world's injustice.

Anyway, it was too late in the day for nuanced debate. Carla pretended to glance at the clock: "Well, that's *verrry* interesting, but that's all the time we have. Next month, I'll show *Going My Way*."

Then she lifted her chin and smiled at Claudia: "If that's okay with you!" God knew what she'd have to say about the Church.

Claudia huffed out, all porcupine quills. Annie gave Carla an enigmatic sneer that seemed to convey a different message than Claudia's. Carla heard later that Claudia was staying at Annie's place. They must have had an interesting talk that night, with cries of "how could you!" shaking the walls.

Now here she was, over six months later, looking sadder and more disappointed in the world than ever, too closed off to recognize Carla. Sean followed his group out the door, absorbed in their excited talk. For once, he didn't look at her. She jumped when Dave nudged her in the spine, letting her know that it was time to go.

As Tim locked the chapel door behind them, Dave asked, "What did old Bartok say?"

Tim turned around, jangling the keys: "He said he was nappin'. Says he always napped while she drove, like an old man does. Woke up when the vehicle went off the road, then didn't remember anything more until"—he nodded at Carla—"he saw you."

Marissa and the boys ran ahead to their van. Carla, Dave, and Tim bent against the chill as they walked to their vehicles. "That SUV had enough safety features and armor plating to survive a crash all the way down into the valley and he still might have come out. Annie too, if they hadn't hit that rock like they did. The engine still runs. It's just smashed in along the driver's side and torn up a little underneath. Barb Albanese had it sent over to Sacramento for repairs."

"You think it was an accident?"

"You saw it shoot right past you, right?"

"Like a bullet. She took that turn too fast."

"There were no skid marks, but the tire tracks ran straight and deep, like she gunned it."

"It was snowing heavy. Maybe she missed the curve."

Tim shook his head: "She'd been driving that road for years. She had to know every foot. You might be right though. It happens sometimes. The expert gets a little too confident."

A nervous silence passed. Dave's next question hinted at an unpleasant possibility: "Did you find a note at her place?" No one wanted to say that word yet.

Tim shook his head: "Nope. No note."

"Claudia what's-her-name might know how things were with her."

"If she does, she's not sayin'." At his van, Tim stopped to stretch, stood on his toes, looked at the sky, and yawned. The fluctuating temperatures had been turning the rain to sleet and back again. Now the squall was fading. "She said it got boring and lonely up there after a couple days. She left behind most of her belongings. She says it's all her property, even the furniture."

"She left in a hurry."

"She says she'll pick up the rest soon, but I've got a hunch she'd just as soon leave it all there. Wonder what old Mr. B's gonna do for help now."

"They must have had a big fight. She didn't indicate that Annie was suicidal?"

"Nope." Tim's face crumpled with mild disdain. "Just that living up there wasn't as wonderful as she thought it would be. Lord knows, I hear that a million times. Folks think it's a lazy man's paradise up here." A snowflake snagged his thick eyebrow; he blinked and let it melt and drip down his cheek. He looked content. To him, this was paradise. The stars above glittered for the first time in days.

"That's more like it." Tim smiled. "Say, you're comin' fishing one more time before you go, right? We got Westerns to catch up on."

"I gotta get your rifle back to you."

As they made a date for Saturday morning, Carla looked sadly at her hands, flexing them: We can't leave now. Something's happening!

On the drive home, Dave started arguing, unable to let go of his resentment over having to drive Klaus Bartok home.

"I did notice you took an immediate dislike to him," Carla said archly.

"Sure. Why waste time? What? You get to let fly with the wit and I don't?"

"Face it, you're the straight man in this marriage. What was that Frankenstein monster act?"

"I was feeling a little pushed-around."

"You don't like being a caregiver anymore?"

"I didn't say that. Just 'cause I'm a doctor doesn't mean I let the patients bully me. He might look like Mr. Hipster down in the city, but it doesn't pay to be rude like that up here." As he gnawed on his lip, his teeth rasped over his whiskers. She wanted to scream at him to stop it. She could see and hear everything and it hurt.

"Oh, that little homily he delivered in the parking lot when I drove up?"

"What about it? It was a nice speech."

"Right out of John Muir, word-for-word."

"So? People recite Shakespeare all the time—or they used to. Whether they're his words or not, they're true. It's nice someone bothers to memorize poetry these days."

His petty argument deflated, Dave changed the subject: "I'm sorry, but we're both under a lot of stress. We need to lower our stress levels, not raise them."

Spare me the jargon, she thought. "Okay, he's crabby, but we won't be any better at his age—at least, you won't. He's got such a quick mind for such an old man."

"Yeah, I'll give him that. He's got all his marbles, all shiny and sorted. It's almost unnatural to be as sharp as he is at his age."

When they pulled into their driveway, they glimpsed a black bear lumbering up the bank behind the house. Then a deer sprang away behind the garage. Other shapes and shadows, names unknown, dispersed into the night; a gigantic owl, its back glistening with starlight, perched on the peaked roof of the garage before flapping away with an eerie, resonant hoot. "There he goes again! Hello and good night!" Carla laughed, but Dave stormed inside. She was needling him. Oh, well. He was only trying to numb himself about having to move away, demystifying paradise to ease the pain of saying good-bye. Science-minded people could do that.

Carla was feeling great, but she said nothing to Dave. Oddly enough, she felt no desire for her husband that night like she normally would have and let him go to sleep mad.

She lay through the night, waiting for the dawn as every nerve of her body shimmered with an incredible awareness. She could feel her cells dividing, morphing, dying, and being born again. She felt and heard her heart thump, her pulse beat, and her blood gurgle and rush through her veins and arteries. Best of all was the hum of her body's electricity in her brain. It felt as though she could turn it on and off, at will, increase, and decrease her power, like a well that could fill and empty itself, at will.

She looked at her right hand, the hand into which the healing power seemed to have flowed. Was it glowing in the dark?

These were new senses. She'd never felt so completely powerful. She'd heard of total awareness before and it had always seemed like New-Age nonsense. But there were no "seems" in this fresh, sweet, shimmer and surge. If there were a cliff nearby, she'd jump right off it, without a thought. Who was to say she wouldn't fly? This mountain world had moved inside and given her soul its sense of sweep, its windblown spaces, and towering freedom. The mountains were now in her.

"I will now sleep," she whispered in the darkness.

She blinked and awoke to a clear wonderful dawn. This time, she put the cat, who'd never understand, out of the room. She stripped off her pajamas, sat naked on the bed and wept with happiness as the dragon flew home once again, as always, just ahead of rising sun. It was enough to make her wish that it would stay night forever, the stars always shining, the moon always bright, always full.

CHAPTER 11

Turn of Fortune

Within a day, Monitor County's splashing colors and broad smile returned as if the land had never known a bleak day. Alpine Spring coursed along as waves of pink dawns and red and violet sunsets rolled in and out like tides of light. Plum-colored afternoon storms sailed through proud and purple. As the storms broke apart, shafts of golden sun drilled down into the earth. The orange, yellow, and purple flowers blanketed the valleys and foothills. Each haunting, soul-stirring moment was a little sweeter and a little warmer than the one before. The fields were flush with poppies that seemed to turn orange before a flower lover's eyes.

Yes, it was a grim scene that greeted Henry West upon his release from the Byrneville jail. As seen through his sooty, desolate vision, Monitor County and its citizens exuded their usual infuriating odor of smug: "We live in the most beautiful place in the world and you don't!" He wanted to slap every one of those cocksuckers, "Slap 'em until their mouths bleed!" as his Irish old man used to bellow.

To add to Henry's misery, he'd been 86'd from the Tap & Grill; the Byrneville Market wouldn't even sell him near-beer, and if he wanted to get drunk like he needed to, it meant taking the long, winding road to Carson Valley where everyone still sang their same old warrior chant: "Henry West Go Away!"

Not surprisingly, his vicious nightmares returned.

On the third morning, a giant spider sporting a huge stalk from which grew his mother's ever-gentle face, scrambled hungrily into the garage attic and tore his mother's rabbit skin robe from Henry's shivering, sweating body. "Henry! Henry! Gotta talk to you!" it called to him in Cousin Danny's smoky voice.

Henry woke up to realize it really was Cousin Danny calling to him from the garage below. Sweating and shaking, he carefully made the sickening climb down the ladder. When he finally reached safe ground, it dawned on him exactly why Danny wanted to talk. Henry spun around, ready for combat, even though it made him dizzy:

"You sold your house, didn't you?"

"Wow. Guess you're psychic," Danny sighed and the argument deteriorated from there. No matter how many accusations Henry spit at Danny (sell-out to the white man; breaker of the tribal promise to Mama that they'd look after half-white Henry just as though he were a full Washoe; his B.O. wouldn't be so bad if Danny's wife let him in the house to shower; so what if he talked dirty in front of the kids? They knew those words anyway.)

"Yeah, it's always about you, isn't it?" Danny bared his perfect teeth like a dog.

"Who the fuck else is it gonna be about?" Henry sneered back.

Danny went on making excuses about his mother's stroke and how he was the only one with the resources to look after her, blah blah blah.

But Henry punched in the last word, his finger jabbing in Danny's face: "You're only movin' in with your mama to make sure you don't get cut out of her estate, ya fuckin' vulture!"

Boom! Victory! Danny threw up his hands and retreated to the house. But Henry only got madder. No sonuvabitch turns his back on Henry West! His fists clenched and the air turned bloody red as he marched toward the back steps.

But the second he reached for the door, a familiar grinning presence rounded the corner of the house and called out his name. It was Bob Garner.

"Howdy, Henry! Been lookin'—whoa there! Easy! I ain't here to hurt you. Chill, buddy. Chill."

Henry stopped two feet away, shuddering. He leaned against the house to keep from falling down, shaking his head as Bob Garner asked if was okay. Henry said he was just pissed off, that was all: His cousin had made Henry homeless again by selling his house. "To *you*," he shouted and started shaking again. "You're fucking me up the ass!"

"Yeah, Henry, I know," Bob nodded with phony affability. "I don't want to be pullin' the rug out from under anyone. Everyone deserves somethin' for their trouble." He winked. "Even you."

Henry asked what he meant and, this time, instead of hinting around, Bob Garner offered a job if Henry wanted it. Henry shrugged, pretending to be cool, because that was what everyone expected of an ex-con. Then Garner said: "It'll put more in your pocket than you can guess. Interested? Come along with me."

Henry obediently followed Bob Garner to where a green Hummer sat with its nose in Danny's former driveway. Bob Garner opened the door for him and as he crossed around to his side, Henry very carefully climbed in without looking down, tightly buckled himself in, and pulled his ballcap down so only the hood and a sliver of the road ahead was visible.

As Garner drove, Henry asked what he had in mind, because any conversation would distract him from the sway and roll of the Hummer.

"Folks here think I'm just a rich bastard moving in to throw everybody out and bring in other rich people," Bob Garner said, his hick accent starting to turn into another accent Henry didn't recognize. "I want them to think I'm here to help everybody, rich and poor. White, black, Mexican, Indian, it's all people to me."

Henry rolled his eyes: another racist trick—pretending not to be racist so he could shit on you and call it something else. Henry snickered: "Whatever you say."

Instead of getting mad, Bob Garner laughed. The truck swayed as it crossed a bridge over Byrneville Creek. Henry's stomach yawed a little.

"You alright, Henry?"

"Mmm? Yeah, I'm cool."

A mile later on Walsh Hot Springs Road, Bob Garner turned left, into a new tarmac driveway; the red Jag was parked next to a Rav-4. Henry let Garner start getting out first, so he wouldn't see how carefully Henry climbed down from his side.

Bob Garner had built himself a brand new, butt-ugly, three-story manse, big enough to house four families. The first floor was smaller than the second, which was smaller than the third, like an upside down pyramid. It was painted a sunshiny yellow.

The sight of this monstrosity revealed something about Bob Garner. He was all about standing out—as in standing out in his front yard and giving the finger to the pussies with their cutesy craftsmen cabins and houses. He didn't give a fuck what anybody thought so long as he was on top, which was how a man should always be.

Instead of taking Henry into his house, Garner led him around the back to a skinny bungalow that was once the property's main house. Whoever was the pretentious fuck who'd lived here before, he'd shit to see his precious cottage reduced to an outhouse.

The interior was shotgun style: simple, clean, and neat, almost bright. The kitchen was in the front. It opened into a comfortable living room, which led to a bedroom and bath in the back. There was a used green sofa and a flat screen TV with a DVD player. Outside, Byrneville Creek burbled nearby, while the wind moaned through the pines.

"Kinda nice!" Henry meant it too and winced at his enthusiastic sincerity.

Garner waved Henry to a seat at the Formica kitchen table. The window faced to the north, up toward the Samsons. From here, Dragon's Ark was invisible. Bob Garner pulled the curtains closed and took off his sunglasses. He asked Henry if he would like anything to drink.

Henry grinned, patted his stomach: "Beer! Tequila?"

"Don't have that. Not now. Maybe later. After work."

He sat across from Henry and leaned forward, spreading out his long, freckled arms and picked up where he left off: Bob Garner and Sierra Future really did care about the folks around here, all of them, especially "the little guy."

Henry agreed: He was the littlest guy in the whole territory.

"That's why I picked you."

Henry put on his gangsta face; it was a dangerous tactic because Garner might call his bluff and Henry would crack like an egg: "That's a nice pile of bullshit you're shovelin' there, Mr. Garner. You're usin' me to make you look like a nice guy. You're a nice guy like I fart French perfume."

Henry stood up with pretend dignity and walked to the kitchen door, but Bob Garner laughed again and sat back, spreading his arms:

"Bang! Got me! Yeah, I'm definitely using you!"

"To con everyone around here."

"Like you give a fuck? You think folks around here will treat you any better because you do the honorable thing, like refuse my job offer? If folks don't think you're stupid now, how stupid will you look when word gets around that you turned down a good job with the biggest employer in Monitor County?" He paused. "Especially when the county and the state find out and cut off your checks?"

Whoa, Henry thought. The world's changed that fast already. I wasn't even lookin'.

"Wow, you really are a son of a bitch." Henry returned to his seat.

"I know you a little, Henry. There's some stuff out there on the Internet about you. You been low man on the totem pole your whole life: Youngest of eight, got pulled out of tribal school so you could go to work, developed a drinking problem real early. Then that cocaine deal went bust. Your two partners got off light, while you didn't. You have that prison look in your eyes. I can use that, too. I bet you can be scary when you want to. At least prison taught you to be tough."

Henry laughed to himself. Most of that story was either half-true or complete bullshit; for one, Henry was the only child from Mama's second marriage. Garner had dug, but not deep enough to find out about Henry's vertigo. He thought Henry was a lazy Indian welfare cheat. He didn't know about Henry's white blood and wasn't about to, either. In his way, Bob Garner was as big a sucker as the suckers he was rolling. Sucker versus Sucker, that's the real game here.

"It'll take more than beer money to buy my loyal labor."

"Like a thousand a week?" Garner spread his arms to embrace the bungalow. "And a clean place to live, all your meals, free."

"Free, my ass. Even breathin' costs somethin'." Henry again braced himself to get up and walk out.

"Oh, yeah, I have definite expectations. C'mon, sit down. I'll give you the scoop. It could gross you a hundred thousand when it's over. But only if you start by listening."

Henry sat again and nodded for Bob Garner to show his cards.

"It's called *noblesse oblige*. Yeah, it's a smart-ass phrase. It means guys like me looking like we're helping guys like you and we're going to do that by remaking you—or rather remaking your image. That means clean clothes, a haircut, and regular baths. Next week, for example, there's going to be a public meeting about Sierra Future, and you're gonna deliver a little talk to everyone that shows you as an example of what the future will look like around here from now on. You don't have to be smooth. In fact, it's better if you're not. All you have to do is make 'em think you mean every word of what you say. It's called acting."

"Kinda like what you do?"

Bob Garner laughed. Henry felt the itch for a drink. He couldn't stand the thought of another sober night.

"Sure gettin' thirsty." Henry rubbed his belly, working on his innocent act.

Bob Garner got a bottle of apple juice from the fridge and poured it into two small plastic cups. He set one right in front of Henry. Henry looked away smacking his lips in disappointment. Bob Garner took his seat and raised his cup to Henry.

"Fuck me, you sayin' I gotta stay clean and sober?"

Garner clacked the cup on the table: "Clean, yes. As a whistle. You're going to shower, use mouthwash and deodorant, and wear clean clothes every day and we'll be checking. As for sober, well sure, there's a limit to what I can ask. I don't want you getting the DTs in public, but we're putting down hard rules."

His face turned serious as a storm. He started pounding out words like a jackhammer. The friendly twang completely vanished as Bob Garner revealed his true face.

"No drinking outside of this cottage, not one drop, from the second you wake up in the morning until I'm through with you for the day, and the days'll be long. Then you come right back here. No stopping at the Tap & Grill, or anywhere ever. You'll find enough in the fridge to keep you happy. But no one's gonna see you out on the porch with even a beer. Do you understand? Is that clear?"

He paused: "Don't even think you can sneak around. I'll take away every penny I pay you and welfare will cut you dead. The day will come when there won't be *any* welfare at all. They used to cut off the hands of beggars. If I can, I'll bring that world back. There won't even be a corner for your lazy ass, not in Byrneville, Osgood, or anywhere. It's a long walk to the next county, especially in winter. You might not make it. Who knows? Wherever you go, when you get there, I may own that too."

Bob Garner closed his eyes and rubbed his temples as if he'd given himself a headache. Then he put his friendly mask back on.

"Agree?"

Henry felt cornered and hated himself for it. But he agreed. At least the fucker wasn't demanding a blow job. But he had to know the rest, the part called "The Catch."

"The catch is, when it's over, when I'm through using you, you leave Monitor County and don't ever show your face here again. Ever."

"So you're throwin' me out anyway."

"But you leave a rich man with maybe a bonus if I'm extra pleased."

Garner pulled open a kitchen drawer and threw an official-looking envelope on the table. Inside was a bank statement from over in Carson City in Henry's name: a savings account with a thousand dollars in it: "Your first week's pay, and a thousand every week after, as long as it takes, with that bonus at the end."

They raised their cups of apple juice.

"To business," Garner smiled and winked, "and to lying and deception."

"To reality," Henry said as their cups clicked together.

Right then, the kitchen door flew open and Garner's scrappy partner strode in with his ever pissed-off look, wearing a tight burgundy Izod shirt, cargo pants, and carrying a pile of clothes with towels and washcloths on top.

"Peter Schlesinger, meet our poster boy for Sierra Future, Henry West. Peter will drive you over to Tahoe to get you some new clothes. We'll also get you a driver's permit and maybe later a license. You have to show folks you can get around and take care of yourself now."

"Thanks to you?" Henry suddenly shook his head to conceal the new wave of fear that rolled through him. Driver's license? Drive? I gotta drive? Ohhhh fuck me!

"Of course, we don't say that. They'll get that idea themselves."

"Guess they'll have to, now that you own the whole county."

Bob Garner laughed. "There's a few holdouts, like the Byrne family. And Leo Durant. He's got that great property up below Jackson Pass. You know them at all?"

"Assholes, all of 'em," Henry said. "They don't know I exist, except for dickhead Durant." He grinned. Not too long in the future, the name Henry West would be on everyone's lips, not as the town drunk, but a man whose ass you needed a ladder to kiss. If he could survive driving, that is.

"And old Klaus Bartok. What do you know of him?"

Henry shuddered. "He gives me the heebie-jeebies. Look, I ain't exactly in the loop around here."

Bob Garner rose to his feet: "No problem. Your first task is to take a shower. Peter'll take it from there. I need a nap."

He nodded at Schlesinger, who dumped the towels on the table in front of Henry and pointed toward the rear of the cottage. No pretense from him; he hated this job; he hated Henry. Henry couldn't wait to tweak his ugly little nose.

That chance came on the drive back from shopping in Tahoe in Petey's red Jag, when Henry ripped out another big smelly one. As the stench filled the little car, Petey pulled over without a word and pulled a .45 automatic from under his seat. He sprung the magazine open, then snapped it shut. He held the pistol up. His little turd eyes smoldered.

"Two things: The boss acts like you're funny, but I won't. Not ever. Second thing: the boss says I can't hurt you." He paused. "At least, not now."

What an asshole, Henry thought. Bet he's never fired a gun his life. But Henry would wait to test this theory. Just as they pulled into Byrneville, he asked to stop by his old place to pick up the one thing he wanted from his old terrible life—Mama's rabbit skin robe.

Back at the cottage, he found microwave dinners, two six packs of Coors, and a pint of Cuervo Gold. He ate, then drank until he was numb. Then he checked the house for spiders. He found two and crushed them dead, all the while brooding that no matter what he did, he always wound up with that screwed-into-the-floor feeling.

That night, drunk, he wept as he lay wrapped in Mama's rabbit skin robe, but at least the dreams stayed away. He passed the night in plain, unadorned sleep.

....

CHAPTER 12

Trick of the Light

"Oh God, now what do I do?" Carla cried out as she sank into the living room couch, staring at her hands. Within a couple days after Mr. Bartok's trip home, her nerve endings had started failing once again, the sensations a forgotten dream.

Outside the living room window, the Ark stood in snowy silence. Had the healing been an illusion conjured by her mind? Mr. Bartok seemed unaware of the effect it had on her: "Oh, you want to hold my hand? Go ahead." If he didn't think anything happened, then nothing had.

Now he was faraway in Alpine Canyon, and she had sunk back to dying, again without hope. She cried hours of raging tears. But rage at what? At him? At herself for being fooled, for projecting her own needs onto him? He was just an old man! Nothing more.

Later that night, unable to sleep, she opened her eyes to see the starry night sky over the bed, as though the bedroom ceiling had turned to glass or disappeared. When she reached over for Dave, her hand found a wet, cold fog. Next to her floated a roiling black cloud from where a pair of smiling blue eyes looked up. A dry voice said: "Tomorrow around one o'clock. In the canyon. That is," the voice added, with a taunting edge, "if you *can*."

The eyes sank back down into the cloud. Carla fell back to sleep. Just before dawn, she threw Kat out of the bedroom. The cat was stupid. To her, the dragon of Dragon's Ark was a tempting meal, not a Holy Sacred Thing.

Dave woke up feeling weak and looking pale. He'd had another flying dream. They always left him a little out of sorts. Still, she agreed with them that they needed the money when he insisted on leaving for the clinic and another shift at the ER. "Did you give notice at St. Ives?" he asked. "Yes," she lied.

She waited until she was sure he had gone before she went out to the garage. No call to Sean this time. She'd go alone. The garage door felt so much heavier now. She watched her hand to make sure she had a good grip on it. Of the two remaining vehicles, the white Volvo would handle easier on the long slow drive than the green Jeep.

But what if Tim King or someone else saw her? ("What are you doing, Carla? I thought you weren't supposed to drive.") She remembered reading about how successful party crashers worked by thinking themselves invisible. So, she thought of herself invisible, thought *hard* about it, like she had once believed in Santa. It seemed to work. No one saw her drive through the village. A county sheriff Explorer driven by Deputy Colbert flew by on Monitor County Highway without even slowing.

Driving with ALS meant she had to keep three things in mind: hands on wheel, feet on gas and brake, and eyes on road. At Alpine Canyon Road, she stopped to rest. Now, she didn't have to look out for anyone else. Now she could really focus. She only paused to wonder if she was going too far. But what did that voice with that taunting tone in the night want of her? She had to know.

She stayed under fifteen miles an hour and completely ignored the scenery. There were few bad moments, and she made it around every rock and rut. The engine coughed and gasped for air, but never quit. At the bottom of the rise leading up to the notch into the canyon, Carla was gasping too. She rested again for awhile, slumped against the steering wheel. Her weakened muscles shook with exhaustion.

Carla turned the engine off and let gravity pull her down into Alpine Canyon. The braking and steering tired her again, so she rested once more at the bottom. From here on it would be relatively easy, unless floods had washed away the old road.

At least she could enjoy the scenery. The canyon had the same lofty sparkle it had before and her grumpy spouse wasn't here to spoil the hope.

But at the end of the road, she could drive no farther. She could hardly turn the key to shut of the engine. She took in the mountains in front of her, the dark blue lake through the trees, and the glittering cliffs towering on both sides. A wind shook the car like a warning. "How am I gonna get out of here?" she asked out loud. The dashboard clock said she was an hour early. If she was going to make it out, she would need more rest. But now her left hand was too weak to even press the lever to recline her seat. She slumped against the door, her head against the window, closed her eyes and fell into fluttering sleep. Red flashes swirled and spilled across her eyelids, making rolling balls of fire.

Then the red suddenly turned deep black and she jerked awake to find Klaus Bartok sitting in the passenger seat in his flawless black, his face immobile behind his sunglasses, holding a walking staff.

"God! You almost gave me a heart attack! Why didn't you knock or say something? Oh, I'm sorry! Good morning," she babbled. "Or afternoon."

He said nothing, didn't even ask if she'd been waiting long. He looked terrible too, his skin a chitinous red, as though it had been cooked to a crust. It turned her stomach. Again, she regretted coming here. What if he suddenly died right there, or on the drive out? If anything happened to him, she was screwed.

He nodded silently at the road ahead: Drive.

But she couldn't. Carla's hands, number and weaker than ever, slide uselessly off the steering wheel and flopped at her sides. She broke down sobbing.

"I'm sorry! I don't understand what I'm doing here. I didn't tell

you this, but I'm sick. I have ALS, Lou Gehrig's disease. I'm not supposed to drive at all. I can't take you where you want to go. I can't
even get myself home! I'm so sorry!"

But Klaus Bartok was unperturbed. A soft smile cracking his
cracked lips, he held out his strange hands.

"Give me your hands."

She did as he commanded. His hands, bony and cold, wrapped
around hers and gave a little squeeze. Her body jumped as if she'd
stuck her finger in a socket.

The third time, it's true. It has to be true. I'm alive again.

She could grab the steering wheel now, firmly and completely.
Klaus Bartok looked around the interior of the little Volvo with a
bleary smile, rumbling in his tattered voice. "Unfortunately, I don't
have the power to change this thing into something more secure.
But I've been informed my regular conveyance will return soon." He
nodded at Carla as if this news would also matter to her.

"The sun saps my energy and is bad for my skin and the trip is
dangerous, but I must face the day to protect my interests, especially
now. Drive slowly and stay to the left, away from the edge. I might
spare you my tears." He chuckled, a sound like boiling mud. The
shriveled skin around his right eye shivered in a wink. "Think of me
as the most precious cargo. Life is a diamond, every second a precious jewel. You understand or you wouldn't be here." He nodded at
the road ahead. "Now: to the village, ma'am."

The drive in had been hell, but the drive out was heaven. With
Carla's strength fully restored by Mr. Bartok's healing touch, the car
responded obediently to her every move and handled beautifully.
Fully alert now and ordered to take her time, she found Alpine Canyon's glittering walls and the blue slash of sky above more heart-
stopping than before. Driving him home would be an equal joy.

She stopped at the crest of the notch, not to rest, but to take in
the valley below, the Samsons to the south and the Carson Valley, far
to the east, a plain of sun-splashed gold, spreading below dusky blue
and gold mountains.

"Isn't this …" But when she looked at him, his head had tipped forward and he was breathing gently. He'd fallen asleep.

He feels safe with me. He gives me life because he trusts me.

Driving down Alpine Canyon Road gave her a rush, like paddling a fine canoe down a slow easy river. Eagles and hawks swooped and sailed alongside. Normally, they were solitary birds, but she remembered how they had gathered around them the day of the accident and realized that she carried a special passenger. Her responsibility was a grave one, but one to take pride and pleasure in.

Carla paused at the mysterious driveway. Annie had undoubtedly lived up there. She made a note to herself to explore it sometime. Mr. Bartok's intentions toward her were clear now. This was a test, an audition. Her husband had flunked the first one. She had to succeed. The stakes were high. If she didn't, death would start its course again.

When they arrived in Byrneville, Klaus Bartok awoke smoothly to hand her his first compliment: "So. I'm alive." He directed her to park in front of Sierra Realty, facing back the way they came. She jumped out and trotted around to his side, no longer caring who saw her. She gently guided the old man to his feet, delighting in the soft delicate touch of his feathery coat. Where, she asked, could she get one like it? He answered with mild chuckle.

Gripping his right arm gently but firmly, she led Mr. Bartok to the sidewalk. She glanced right and was startled to see Dr. Leo Durant striding away toward the center of the village, his shoulders hunched up around his big jug ears and white horseshoe of hair as he swung his fists at the air, delivering roundhouse punches at an unseen opponent. He was cursing almost at the top of his lungs.

"Bastards bastards, think they can get me! Goddamn sonsabitches …!"

Klaus Bartok tugged on her to draw her attention. "Your neighbor kind of, isn't he?" she asked. He shrugged and nodded toward the realty office.

As she reached for the doorknob, he told her, "This is as far as I need you. I'll be awhile." He saw her confusion. "You'll know when."

Carla's heart sank as he pushed the door open. She could make out the frizzy halo of Barb Albanese's hair. Barb's voice chirped from behind her desk: "Mr. Bartok! Good afternoon!" Someone behind the door closed it in Carla's face.

She felt humiliated, as if she'd been dumped at the door to the prom, but what could she do? Up to now, it had been a perfect day, and it would be a shame to spoil these miracle moments by throwing a baby fit. If he didn't want to share the details of his business life, that was fine. Maybe that was how it had been with Annie. She probably hadn't cared, either. Business? Yawn.

Carla's stomach growled and whined. She felt hungrier than she had since before her illness. So, her appetite had returned too, completely. Lots of eating to catch up on. She walked to the little deli down the road. She was looking at the menu when she noticed Vera, the Russian owner, slicing slabs off the juicy pink center of a fat roast beef. Saliva squirted into Carla's mouth, so much, she had to swallow it to stop from drooling.

"I'll take a half pound of that."

"You vant sandvich?"

"No. Just the meat." Carla felt impatient and angry. "Right from the center."

She responded with irritated grunts to Vera's small talk ("How vas Carla? How vas Dave? Is he still handsome?"). What did this old cow care? She only wanted Carla's money. People complained that family businesses were being driven out by impersonal chains with interchangeable employees. But what was the difference? If Carla did die after all, Vera would only weep cold brief tears. Then, "Next customer!"

As Carla hurried back to the car, she noticed for the first time how mean and dumpy Byrneville looked under the white glare of the afternoon sun. Once in the car, she pushed her seat back down to make herself invisible and ate the red meat, lowering the chunks into her mouth like a Roman emperor eating grapes. She chewed every salty sweet fiber, sucked out every drop of blood until only a gray saliva-soaked mash remained. Her body flushed with protein energy: To think I almost became a vegetarian. Ha.

She looked up through the roof window at a cloudless pale blue sky. She held up her hand. Against the blue sky, it looked like a black rent in space. She rubbed her fingers together, feeling every single ridge in her skin. Simple solid flesh, but flesh now infused with a new and strange energy. Where did the energy come from? She recalled a science theory about another energy in the Universe, a force stronger than gravity that seemed to be pulling the galaxies and the Universe itself apart. They called it "dark energy."

Had Klaus Bartok's touch infused her with this dark energy? But where did he get it? How did he tap into it? Only he knew. She would ask him. She had a right to know. Not only had he brought her back from the brink, he had remade her.

"I'm different now," she said, her burgundy voice sounding simple and strong in the silence of the car. "I'm new."

Then she felt her self, her soul, expand to encounter and connect with another sense in that dark space made by her own hand. In that darkness, she sensed another mind, his mind, though he was nowhere to be seen.

She sat up, crying out: "I'm on my way!"

She got there just as the door closed behind him. She asked how it went as she led him to the car, but he only shrugged. She buckled him into the Volvo, as tenderly as she would a crystal doll. As she got behind the wheel, he offered her a thick roll of twenty dollar bills.

"Five hundred a week?"

"Oh. Thank you. I should pay you." She tucked the money in her blouse pocket. This is too easy!

Then, as she turned the ignition—like unlocking a door—she invited him to her house for tea. He accepted the invite with the grace of an Old World gentleman, with a quiet bow of his large head. Maybe he could stay for dinner, too. She would ask him everything.

She didn't realize how late it was until they got home. A marmalade sun hung in a honey milk sky behind the Sierra, southwest of the Ark. How would she get him home before dark? she wondered.

Shaking, she asked him to wait on the stoop. "The house—the living room—it's a mess." Normally, she didn't care, but the thought of Klaus Bartok sitting in his elegant clothes surrounded by a dirty house repelled her.

She shooed Kat into the kitchen and frantically cleaned the living room. The Osgood throwaway paper; the *Sacramento Bee*; the *People* magazines Dave insisted on displaying for his few patients; the copy of *In These Times*, a gift from her father; all of it stuffed under the couch. The sun coming through the window made the room an oven that would cook the old man to a black flaking crust. She pulled the dingy muslin curtains shut, but a slice of sunlight still slashed the pinewood floor. She took some safety pins from her sewing box and pinned the curtains closed. There. Cool, dark, and safe.

Klaus Bartok was waiting on the stoop, patient and still as an old tree. She opened the door and waved: "Come on in!" She closely watched his left foot, encased in soft pebbly black leather, almost like a bird's foot, step over the threshold. She felt the house close snugly around them, shutting the world way.

She led him into the living room and sat him in Dave's reading chair between the two bookshelves. Her husband wouldn't mind (or he'd better not): "Make yourself comfy! You like green tea, right? I'll be right back!"

She saw the phone's message light blinking. She fidgeted at the sound of Dave's voice. He'd be late. A meeting with the county commission tonight to tender his resignation. Wouldn't be home until late. His voice sounded like a nerd's nasal whine, but she clapped her hands and skipped to the kitchen. Plenty of time remained to get Mr. Bartok safely home. He wouldn't be the wiser.

She returned to the living room to find Kat had snuck back in. The little tabby sat before Klaus Bartok full of wide-eyed wonder, like a penitent in front of the Pope, her paws tucked neatly under her little body, the perfect tchotchke. Klaus Bartok had removed his sunglasses and was beaming benevolently down at her.

Carla's hands shook as she set the tea on the table next to Mr. Bartok. She clapped her hands. "You! Out!" Kat ran away. Klaus Bartok watched her go, then looked up at Carla, his bushy eyebrows arcing.

"She's a nuisance. I brought her home, but she's more my husband's cat. She's needy and drools a lot." Carla anxiously pulled at her hair and rubbed her neck. "I can see you're good with animals. You live among wild things. She's domesticated." Then she said something she knew to be amazingly stupid the second she said it: "I'm so much smarter than she is."

Mortified at this display of jealousy and insecurity, Carla retreated to the arm of the couch, hugging herself: "Maybe I should shut up!" she laughed. Her house felt tiny and ugly now. She'd made a terrible mistake bringing Mr. Bartok into her boring world.

Still, he didn't seem bored. His blue eyes smiled up at her from the deep pits of his ragged sockets. From behind those marvelous eyes, his mind reached for hers, as it had when she was waiting for him in the car: Bored? With you? Of course not!

Their minds met in space. It was as though he'd clicked on a hyperlink. As Carla opened her mouth, a hole opened in the floor of her skull. Her life story rushed out.

Carla told all about her fractious but happy life with her Catholic-Atheist, left-wing family among the hills of North Beach; about the schools she'd attended, her stormy teenage years and how they ended with her mother's slow, painful passing; about her discovery of sex, her frustration with college, and her aborted medical career. "The blood was too much for me, yeah, that's lame, but that's how I felt."

Then she met Dave. Here, she backed up to tell Dave's story, a tale both grim and heroic. His father had been a professional criminal, a con man, a swindler. He'd actually used his own teenage son as a front in a scheme that almost put them both in jail. Eventually, the father got out to continue along his criminal path until he was finally caught for murder. "In Texas. Maybe you know what that means. Lethal injection. It was some years ago. Apparently, he'd left children all over the country, but I guess Dave's the only one to escape his shadow."

It was one of Dave's uncles, an Episcopalian minister, on Dave's alcoholic mother's side, who took the boy in and proved to him that not everyone was a scheming crook. "He gave Dave his values," she murmured. "But the religious part didn't take. Instead of healing souls, Dave decided to heal bodies. He's a wonderful man, but he can be a stick in the mud about some things." Then she giggled and blushed: "But sometimes not. I mean in bed. Well, you're beyond all that now, aren't you? When you live long enough, you leave that sex stuff behind, right?"

Without realizing it, she found herself sitting at Mr. Bartok's feet, legs crossed, her hands in her lap. Her mouth ran completely on automatic. She told him about it hard it had been to live up here. She touched on the Leo Durant problem: "If it wasn't for him, we could stay." She almost forgot to tell him about her ALS: "Then I noticed I was dropping things. My limbs went numb. I was told I had maybe a few years to live."

Finally, she stopped. Not because she'd run out of things to say, but because it was time to ask the questions and get the answers she'd been craving from the moment that Klaus Bartok had taken her hand that day on Alpine Canyon Road.

But then she glanced behind her. The orange glow behind the muslin curtains was fading away. Night was on its way.

"Omma God!" Carla sprang up. Already past eight! Where did the time go? No way could she drive Mr. Bartok home and get back before Dave! Should she invite him to stay for the night? ("He followed me home, sweetheart. Can he stay? Huh?")

Mr. Bartok's green tea had gone cold. As she picked up the cup and saucer, she turned on the reading lamp on the table.

"I'll warm up the tea and we'll decide what to do."

She came out into the hallway to find Kat eagerly scurrying toward the door, determined to interfere. Carla stopped to close the sliding doors: "You stay out!" Kat threw herself at the door as Carla rushed to the kitchen.

As she waited for the tea to heat up, she stared through the glass doors out into their concrete slab patio. Only blue twilight remained. She felt like she was being turned upside down. Something was happening out there. It started when she noticed how dark it had become, when she turned on the reading lamp.

Mr. Bartok looked different in the dusk's light. For one, his face seemed to have lost some wrinkles, as though his skin were smoothing itself. Well, that was just a trick of the light …but his hair was also changing color, white turning gray, black streaks inking through it. *That* was impossible. And there was a blue glow in the room that seemed to come from …from his blue eyes. They were *shining in the dark*.

Shining like the eyes that looked over at her from Dave's side of the bed in last night's dream. The dream of the voice that challenged her to make the drive into Alpine Canyon. And then Dave woke up feeling weak again, like that night when he blacked out when …he visited Mr. Bartok at the hospital …where blood had been disappearing from the blood bank.

They'd both been having episodes of early morning lassitude and mild rashes ever since they'd moved here. They always followed a night of wonderful dreams, dreams of flying over and among the very mountains they lived among. The dreams, in fact, had started the very first night they camped up the road at Walsh Springs. And then they'd moved here, almost right away.

Not for the scenery. Not for the wonderful people who lived here.

But for the dreams.

The dreams didn't come every night. Sometimes only once a month. But they came. And as she watched her dragon fly home and the day begin, she always had the sense that the dreams somehow came to her from the mountain beyond.

They came from the man sitting in her living room, the man who had driven away the disease that had tried to kill her, to take her away from here. He was both a healer and a Dream Master who softly, secretly sowed dreams in the sleep of those he wanted near him. He was why they felt a little sick in the morning, because of what he took in exchange. He was also what made this land so—

Ding! went the microwave. Carla jumped. Night had fully arrived, blanketing everything. She forgot the tea and rushed down the dark hallway, her mind reeling: Who are you? What are you? What have you done? What are you doing?

The doors split open without a sound. "Mr. Bartok?" The walls, the floors, the ceiling all seemed to have disappeared, leaving a palpable woolen darkness. A perfect nothingness. But when she looked up, she saw that wasn't true. Because there he was above her, his merry eyes like blue stars, his face now handsome, rugged, and years younger, sporting a raffish grin. His large white hands reached down to her, their palms open with generosity. She reached up and felt her feet leave the earth.

....

CHAPTER 13

Fly Along With Me

How did he do it? Carla wondered as the little house sank away into the darkness below. How could Klaus Bartok, the Dream Master, fix the world so that he could fly into the air, through the ceiling, through the roof as if they weren't there? And how was it that he could he turn her body to weightless vapor and take her with him into the sky?

It had to be another of the wonderful flying dreams. It just had to. And like any great dream, you didn't ask. You rode with it. You let it takes its course. So, Carla let herself be carried. She felt perfectly safe. If something did happen, she'd wake up. And if it were real—and the wind chill she felt indicated it was—she knew that the Dream Master would not let her fall. She already knew that he trusted her. So she had to trust him.

The world below raced by in a blur of rocks, trees and a road that snaked in a swooping, unfinished line. She heard the wind whistling over the rustle of strong wings. The air was the color of blue silver, but there was no moon, only the stars above.

Up ahead, jagged, snow-capped mountains raced toward them. She realized he was showing her the night and his world, through his eyes, in ways she could never see from the sorry earth below. She felt a soaring detachment and an exhilarating clarity.

Soon they reached the tops of the snowy peaks. The Dream Master took her south close above the ragged summits. To their right, a flat plain stretched to meet another, smaller mountain range, where the fallen sun had left a trail of orange. Beyond that gleamed a flat pane of green that was the ocean. She used to know the names of these places, but now their names registered like tiny unreadable print. From where she flew, what did it matter really?

Then he made a quick sweeping circle to the east, making her go "Whoooo-hoooo!" and took her back the way they came. The snowy peaks below looked like anonymous little bumps but for the singular mountain that stood alone and apart from the others.

He made a circle around its sheer flanks. If birds had brains, they'd be fools not to be happy, she thought, as they raced inches away from rock walls thousands of feet high.

Then he turned away from the mountain and took her down over the rocky plateau on which it proudly stood. The animals that lived there looked up at them as they passed over and then followed along behind. The plateau stopped in a brutal, familiar cut in the earth. "Whoa! Whoa!" she cried. The wind shrieked as they plummeted down into the narrow canyon and zoomed over the canyon floor, inches away from its massive walls. To her left, she could count the feathers of the hawks and eagles who struggled to fly alongside, until they rapidly fell behind.

Up the Dream Master took her, up out of the canyon, to wheel up over the scrubby slopes on the other side. Below them ran another narrow black band with lines down the middle that curled away west above the canyon rim. A road. And down this road a little shiny-eyed bug wandered innocently in the darkness. She recognized it as a car.

The Dream Master flew right for it, picking up speed until the wind nearly burned. Seconds later, they shot right over the hood, missed the glass by inches, flew close enough to glimpse two startled faces, mouths opens, eyes bulging, dumb with disbelief. She looked behind them, but the car was gone. They probably had to pull over and stop, they were so stunned. If only she could have seen herself and the Dream Master from their point of view! How dream-like it must have been! The Dream Master laughed and she laughed right along. Those people now had a strange wonderful memory that would last a lifetime.

But on to the next thing. Up ahead, at the top of the shrubby slope sat three little boxes, like pieces of wrapped candy, waiting to be opened. The Dream Master swooped down to the biggest one. They flew around it once, then stopped to swim back and forth in front of a window that faced the canyon rim. The Dream Master brushed his wingtips against dusty, warped glass and made a great, booming hoot.

Then the Dream Master spoke to Carla for the first time since they broke free of gravity, his voice now clear and young: "Call to him. Say hello!"

"Okay!" Carla laughed in the darkness. "Hello in there! Hello!"

"Who's there?" She was startled to hear a human voice calling back, male, crusty, and small, like that of a strange animal.

The Dream Master brushed his black wings over the window-pane again. Again, that lame question. Eager with mischief, she giggled. A light came on, hurting her eyes. She heard bare feet sticking to the wood floor they walked across. There came a wet coughing and grumbling.

"Hello!" Carla called again, this time without prompting from the one who had brought her here. "Come out, come out wherever you are! Olli olli incomefree!"

He would come out for sure now.

As the house's occupant cursed around inside, they flew away from the window and up to the roof. With great talons, the Dream Master reached down and grabbed onto the roof's peak. He gave a great sigh and she felt a rush of warmth as he gathered in his great black wings. Somewhere below by the house and out of sight came the desperate bark and howl of caged dogs. They knew something was there. They knew something was wrong. She giggled.

Now they waited. She looked down a wide, scrubby slope, out over the canyon to the ship-like mountain on the other side. It was amazing she could see so well in the dark now. Everything was a deep beautiful blue. She felt impatient to return to the starry sky.

"Why are we here? What are we waiting for?" she asked plaintively.

"I am hungry," he answered calmly.

Of course, she laughed. Stupid me!

He scraped his talons across the old shingles. Looking closely, Carla could see her face reflected in the polished surfaces of his claws, whose tips shined with starlight: Her eyes and mouth were wide with astonishment, joy, wonder. And why not? The rules had not only been broken, they had simply crumbled and fallen uselessly away.

The dogs' barking grew increasingly frantic, their frightened little brains telling them that something insane and awful waited above. The other animal snuffled around within its shelter. She felt its excitement. She felt the Dream Master's trembling hunger.

"Come out, come out wherever you are!" she cried again.

Finally he did. He was an old man with big jug ears and almost no hair, in a bathrobe. He came up on the side toward the road. He shined a feeble cone of light at his feet and carried a small stick, a gun. She felt a brief prick of fear but no harm would come from this either. As they could fly through walls, the gun's fire would pass harmlessly through them, like light through glass.

She smirked as the fool circled the house, waving his flashlight, croaking his silly question, "Who's there?" like a parrot begging for a cracker. He didn't see them at all, even when he shined his light right at them: That meant Carla and the Dream Master must have been invisible, too! Flying and invisible! Wow! The best of both worlds!

Then the others birds arrived to join the hunt, hundreds of them, nighthawks and owls circling the house in a swirling cloud. The old guy ducked and stumbled, crying out: "What the hell is this? Who's there?" His world had gone crazy wrong and he didn't get it. So great was the gulf between him and those who watched in secret. They were a leopard in a tree, a spider in its web waiting for its prey to pluck the right string. And it was so much fun!

The old man disappeared around the house on his pathetic hunt for the invisible thing that watched. Seconds later, he appeared on the down slope side.

"Go on," her pilot whispered. "Call to him. Let him know we're here."

"Up here!" Carla called out. "Yoo-hoo!"

They flapped their great wings, leaped up and down and hooted together: "Up here!"

The Dream Master must have made them visible again, because this time the old man screamed: "Oh hell, oh shit!" Pop went his little gun. Just as I figured, thought Carla as the little red ball of warmth passed through them. Can't touch us! Can't kill us!

The Dream Master leapt off the roof, up into the air, with a great laugh. "Let's go!" cried Carla. "Woo-hoo!"

Her eyes zoomed in on the old man's like binoculars. His huge pupils shrank to pinholes as he tried to deny what was coming for him. He thought he was going crazy. He knew he was going to die.

He ran. They gave chase, made him run for his animal life. This was sport, too. Feeding was fun! Down the slope they chased him, through the brush, toward the canyon rim, letting him run just out of reach. The old man dropped his flashlight. He stumbled, now too blind to see where he was going. He clung to his gun. The howling of the dogs faded away. Soon there was only the roar of the wind and the old man's desperate gasping.

This was a strange thing that she was a part of, she knew, but it didn't occur to her to try and stop it. Things had gone too far. His hunger was hers now. She understood. This was where the dark energy came from, the same energy that made her strong again.

She sensed the Dream Master was getting bored with his play. She watched his feathered legs reached down, his talons unsheathed, glinting with starlight and there, her face again, watching.

The old man tripped and fell to his knees. He cried out as the talons plunged through his robe and pajamas down into his shoulders, making a "pup" sound as they ripped through the flesh and subsurface tissues. Blood welled up around the talons. The predator's flesh soaked up every drop of it. He grew stronger. She grew stronger. The blood gave power.

Predator lifted prey into the air, gripping the victim by its shoulder bones. The old man cried, kicked and flailed at them with his silly gun. The Predator carried him down the scrubby slope, toward the yawing canyon. A needle-like beak came down and made another "pup" noise as it punctured the old man's neck. Then came a liquid sound like water slurring through a straw.

The prey weakened and soon became a dead, swaying husk. They circled down into the canyon where they rode along on a powerful river of wind. They glided over the wide, frothing creek that dashed across the floor alongside the black canyon wall. She glimpsed a vehicle and a tent. Someone was here. Maybe he saw them and asked Is this a dream? like those people in the car, like their prey before he died.

Animals ran along the canyon floor below, all following him. Because he, their Master, their Shepherd, fed them. They all wanted to be with him, but he had chosen her.

They released the empty husk into the creek. As it fell, the gun came loose from the dead man's hand and spun away in the darkness. The creek swallowed the husk and she forgot all about it.

On to the next thing. Back up to the mountain top where they spiraled down to the summit, until they hovered only inches above a small hollow at its peak, where lay a bright pocket of snow.

"Souvenir?" he chuckled. "Sure!" Carla laughed. She watched her hand reach down and grab a handful of crusty snow—cold, heavy and absolutely real.

And then the Dream Master flew Carla toward tiny white lights in the little valley below. She knew this meant the wonderful night was over and she wept like a child at the end of a long happy trip. Like before, he turned them both into a mist so they could pass together down through the roof and the ceiling of her house.

She came to slumped in the reading chair. Klaus Bartok stood over her, tall, handsome, and strong, with capering smile and playful eyes. He was drawing a long sharp fingernail over his left wrist. As his blood, an incredibly rich red tinged with a hint of blue, welled out, he grinned down at her and winked:

"A little something to remember me by, until next time," he said as he offered his wrist to her. "No no! Not too much! Just a little now. Ahh, there you go …"

She placed her mouth over the wound. The blood tasted wonderful, like a rich chocolate, as she felt the snow melting in her hand.

....

CHAPTER 14

Stranger at Morning

Dave staggered in close to midnight, feeling guilty, tired, and haunted. His guilt resulted from having left Carla alone all day again. (He could have called Marissa King or Sean Temkin to look in on her, but he forgot). The exhaustion resulted from a long shift at the ER, followed by a long wait until eight-thirty before the county commission would see him to accept his resignation and discuss a successor. The haunting came from the memory of a dead man's eyes.

His talk with Ted Knowland about Thursday night's weirdness also left him unsatisfied. Ted was evasive: "We still don't know what happened. No one seems to have been hurt"—Dave winced inside: Ohhhh whatever, the whole hospital fell asleep, just one of those things—"except we found signs of anemia in some patients and packets of red cell blood were missing from the bank." Then Ted winked: "An unauthorized withdrawal."

Finally, Ted did address Dave's concern. "I know we should be on top of this thing." He leaned to murmur: "I'm not sure we'll be here for long. They're stonewalling us on the budget."

Later that evening, Dave got what he meant. But just before he went in to the commission meeting, he bumped into Bob Garner coming out. Garner clumsily grabbed Dave's hand before Dave could back away. He heard a tiny click as an icy electric aura flashed around his eyes. It came from Peter Schlesinger, standing nearby with his flash camera. Dave was too tired to openly protest, but it was an ominous development.

Commissioners Chris Mooney and Hugh Lanham were polite but expressed no particular sorrow at Dave's resignation. The three others commissioners were distracted, even loud and loquacious Edie Ferrand. They shrugged away the question about his successor: "We'll worry about it later."

Just as Dave was getting into his truck, Deputy Berman pulled up next to him. There'd been an accident up on Sierra Crest Highway, near the summit. The Osgood EMT was out on another call. Would he come?

Two fatalities: an older couple from San Jose, according to their IDs. Their silver Honda was equipped with crash bags, but they did little good once they deflated and the car bounced another twenty feet from boulder-to-boulder down the chaparral slope. It looked like a crumpled beer can. The wife appeared to have died instantly; the husband was still conscious.

Tim asked the husband what had happened, but he didn't seem to understand. Then his eyes fixed wildly on Dave, and he choked out his last words: Something about a "big fat fly." Then the blood gushed from his mouth and the light faded from his mad-eyed stare, as if he had died insane.

The dead man's stare followed Dave home, remaining fixed and vivid until Dave saw the Volvo in his driveway. Maybe, his thoughts stuttered, Sean Temkin—or someone—had come by and taken Carla out for a drive. Sure, most likely Sean. She hated riding around in that rat trap of his, so she insisted they take the Volvo. Then he dropped her off and left in his Jeep, leaving the car outside.

Despite his weariness, Dave didn't feel like going in. The house looked small and stuffy, while the gorgeous night sky remained welcoming. Still, Carla might be up waiting for him. In some ways, he couldn't wait to get back to San Francisco where he wouldn't feel like he was carrying their shared miseries all by himself. It broke his heart to leave, but he had to live with it, as he'd learned to live with much else. Life was hard and he considered himself lucky to have even been able to live in Monitor County at all.

As he approached the front door, he heard a noise to his left. A black shadow sailed slowly away west into the darkness. From where Dave stood, it looked like it had flown out the living room window. It was too big to be an owl and swam through the air like a swimmer pulling himself through water. He had the weird feeling that it saw him too, because it slowed briefly and tipped its wings as though saying hello.

After Dave wiped the stinging sand from his eyes, the odd creature had vanished. Then he saw a young doe springing away in the darkness. A bear lumbered out from behind the garage and up the bank behind the house. Black wings flapped overhead. He remembered Jim Chapman's story about the night Andrew Potter died and his funk deepened, not because of what he'd witness just now, but because he'd never see a spectacle like this again. That was the wonderful thing about this world—even the bears moved like they could fly.

Kat murped and scampered around his feet as he tottered in the door. He felt so tired, he barely noticed that the lights were off. The house felt empty, already abandoned.

Kat was normally quiet as a mouse, but now she chirped anxiously and her goofy eyes were pleading. "Kat hungry?" Dave knelt down and knuckled her sweet spot. She marked his hand in purring reply: "Mine mine mine!" "Feed the kitty?" But instead of trotting toward the kitchen, she turned away and slipped into the living room through the half-open doors.

Dave followed her to find Carla sound asleep in his reading chair. "His" chair, they'd joked, where he read the latest JAMAs. He'd never seen her sitting there before. Maybe she was trying to ease her loneliness the same way Kat eased hers by sleeping on his side of the bed when he wasn't home.

Carla's head hung down, to the right, and her right arm lay curled in her lap. Her left arm lay stretched out, palm up and open like a blood donor's. Dave shook her shoulder and whispered her name.

No response. Alarmed, he knelt to examine her. Her breathing was normal. The pulse of her carotid artery felt a little weak, but nothing serious. He started to lift her into his arms, like the prince he hoped she still believed him to be.

Then he saw the water on the floor by the chair. "Shit." Her bladder muscles had deteriorated and incontinence had begun. She'd seemed to be at least holding steady the last few weeks, even perking up now and then. But in the last couple of days, she seemed to shrink back down into her cautious posture.

But her khakis around her groin were dry. So was the chair cushion. As he grabbed her left wrist, ice cold water spilled from her palm and streamed down the underside of his arm. A tiny ball of slush plopped on the floor.

His mind fumbled: She'd fallen asleep while eating a snow cone? She and Sean must have gone out for snow cones, but this wasn't yet the weather for that—oh, the hell with it, ask her tomorrow. Sean must have forgotten his sunglasses, too.

He set her down on her side of the bed by the window and turned on the light. As he unbuttoned her blouse, a wad of twenty dollars bills emerged suggestively from her shirt pocket. Five hundred dollars in twenties. Where would she get that kind of money? "I thought you were kidding about opening the brothel," he murmured sleepily as he laid the roll on the bedside table. That question could wait, too.

Despite his exhaustion, Dave felt a little thirsty. From behind his fog of fatigue, that crash victim still stared out. Maybe, he told himself, a couple fingers of Macallan would be just the thing to drown that vision, to put him into soft gold sleep.

Instead, for the first time since he moved to Monitor County, instead of those astounding dreams of flying to the stars, he was attacked by nightmares.

The first was stark, brutal, simple: Just the dead man staring. His soft blue irises turned black, then widened until his eyes became screaming black holes that sucked in silver streaks of light from all around. He spoke through the gouts of blood that geysered from his mouth: "Big fat fly big fat fly big fat fly ..." Over and over he chanted his last words, even after Dave screamed for him to stop.

The second dream was more subtle, but somehow worse: Carla slowly materializing in the blue dawn light, standing naked at their bedroom window. Past her bare shoulder, Dragon's Ark loomed like a king as that whatever bird flew past. Carla's head was thrown back, her face bathed in fading starlight as she sang an achingly sad wordless melody, a mourning morning song of someone sad to see the night go away and the day rise.

•

"GET OUT OF MY WAY!"

Carla's sudden fury broke the peaceful morning air. Startled, Dave dropped his coffee cup on the counter and glanced down the dark hall while frantically wiping the hot spill with paper towels. Kat shot into the kitchen as though pursued by a pack of dogs and scampered under the table by the sliding patio doors.

He saw a shadow coming down the hallway. He saw feet swinging up in the air, upside down. He heard them thump as they landed on the old plank floor. A woman's head, hair flying, flashed into view, back lit by the light from the other end of the hall. The feet appeared again, then the head and arms, repeatedly, spinning toward the kitchen, thump, thump, thump.

It was Carla. She landed in the doorway on her hands, legs bent, feet dangling down her back. She pushed into the air, her hair brushing the ceiling, and struck a perfect, open-armed landing on the kitchen floor.

"Ta-Daaaaa!"

She threw herself at Dave, knocked him into the corner, and punched him in the mouth with a hard, dry, kiss and a big "MWAH!" Then she spun a dancing doll's pirouette: "Good morn-ing! Good morn-ing!" She danced over to the sliding doors and closed the curtains, darkening the kitchen.

Kat shot out from under the table and scurried back down the hallway, her four legs becoming a million. Can't say I blame you, Dave thought. I don't know this woman either. The overloaded wires connecting his brain to his mouth pulsed feebly: "Wha-wha."

"What's what, sweetie-poo?" Carla threw her head back and laughed, her teeth gleaming, her mouth a hot, healthy pink. Her uvula swung like a Christmas ornament. She hadn't laughed like this since—

"Why the long face, loverboy?"

Dave leaned against the counter for support. He looked away, the only way he knew how to form an intelligible question: "What's with the gymnastics? You're not really in shape—"

She laughed again. "Who's not in shape? Watch this!" She cartwheeled gracefully over to the fridge and opened the freezer. She took out a package of ground beef, tossed it in the microwave and hit defrost. She stared at her hand, rubbing her sharp fingernails into the palm. At last, she was doing something familiar.

"Carla, you have ALS."

"Oh, do I? If so, how come I can feel my fingernails in my palm now?"

A long uncomfortable pause passed before the microwave dinged. Carla yanked out the meat, ripped off the cellophane and forked a huge chunk of soft, pink meat into her mouth with her fingers.

"Carla!"

"Huh? Sorry!" She opened the kitchen drawer and took out a fork. "You're right, it's rude to eat with my hands. Yumm!"

"You can't eat that raw. You could get *e. coli* poisoning."

"Don't patronize me. I can look after myself."

As her eyes blazed with surprising energy and her mouth turned bloody, Dave remembered the Volvo sitting in the driveway and felt a growing terror.

"Don't tell me you went driving yesterday."

"I went driving yesterday." She grinned, waiting for him to retort with that old *Get Smart* line, "I *asked* you not to tell me that!" but

Dave, unamused, slammed his fist on the counter.

"I've been feeling better for the last week," Carla shrugged. "I didn't want to say anything until I was sure. Yeah, I went driving. I did fine. I went out. I came back. Nothing happened. It was easy." She paused. "I drove up to Klaus Bartok's and took him for a drive. Poor man, stuck up there. We both needed to get out."

"You drove up all the way up to Alpine Canyon without telling me?"

"I wanted to be a billion percent sure. And now I am." She shrugged and pouted. "A ba-jillion ka-billion percent. Gee, I thought you'd be pleased."

Dave held up his hands to stop her: "Whoa! Listen, this doesn't make sense. We saw all the best specialists. We ran every test, two, even three times. You were definitely losing coordination and muscle mass. I could see it! ALS doesn't go into remission. Ever. It might slow, it might stop, but it doesn't run backward. There's no cure!"

Carla kept on chowing down raw hamburger with an infuriating insolence that made him feel stupid. So Dave decided to get really mad, took her hand, and dragged her to his office. She was strong all right. She pulled hard, but he was still stronger.

As Dave searched for the rubber hammer, Carla closed the blinds, killing a white square of morning sun that lay on the examining room floor. He sat her on the examining table and bopped her on the tendon below the left kneecap. Sometimes, she'd respond with that old gag of raising the opposite leg, but not today. The left leg responded normally. So did the right. He pulled and pushed both her arms, had her raise them over her head and then tried to push them down. He felt up and down her legs, squeezed her arms and shoulders, calves, thighs and buttocks. She accepted all this with grand haughtiness.

But it was true. Her muscle tissue seemed to be regenerating at an unbelievably fast rate, almost overnight.

This would constitute a miracle, but Dr. David Sutton stubbornly held to a foot-stomping disbelief in miracles. He kept asking questions—about eyesight, taste, touch, and smell; had she changed her diet? Was she sleeping well? While he asked and Carla answered, he was furtively unwrapping a sterile needle.

"OW! Hey! Goddamnit, that's not fair!"

Pain response, normal. She furiously shook her hand, then stuck her blood-beading finger in her mouth, her cheeks going concave as she sucked. Then she pulled her finger out and pouted, making saucers with her huge gray eyes: "Aren't you happy that wifey's getting better? Huhhh?"

She stuck her finger back in her mouth, still pouting, kicking her legs in the air. Most of the time, this little girl act was adorable. But not today. Dave threw the needle in the basket: "Carla, from a medical standpoint, this is a completely unexpected development."

"Paging Dr. Killjoy, paging Dr. Killjoy. 'From a medical standpoint, this is a completely unexpected development!'" she mimicked. Before he could protest, she cut him off: "I don't think it's anything weird at all." She spread her hands, palms up and shrugged. "In fact, it's easy: I never had ALS at all. It was a misdiagnosis. We were warned early on; ALS is frequently misdiagnosed!"

"After five specialists?"

"Every one of them with a built-in bias toward finding what they specialize in. That's how they stay in business."

"That's not fair! It's not like they want you to have ALS!" She was nattering like a talk radio crackpot. He tried to turn the dial back to the reality station.

"There's a valid explanation for this. Whatever you had, it was serious. As your doctor, I don't think we ought to be popping corks yet. I'm calling Dr. Martinez in Sacramento for another battery of tests so we'll know what's going on." He paused. It was an awful thing to puncture someone's hope. "It could come back. Maybe it's multiple sclerosis."

She snorted. "Even MS doesn't work like that, dear Dr. Sutton. Maybe it was inflammation or some virus that burned itself out. Maybe I had something new."

"All the more reason to get you checked out ASAP." He looked away with a long sigh. "I'm tired of seeing our hopes dashed."

"So this is about what you want. Why do you always have to look a gift horse—"

That was when the house phone rang. Dave let it ring twice, hoping it would stop.

"Answer that. It might be the case of your life."

It was Deputy Sam Colbert: "Tim asked me to call ya. We got a body up in Alpine Canyon. Tim was wondering if you'd come and lend a hand."

"You don't need me to pronounce it. Did you call Leo Durant? He lives up on the north rim."

"Can't raise him. I'm calling from St. Ives. Can you meet me here? Tim would really like you to take a look."

Sam sounded stressed and confused and Dave hated refusing Tim a favor. Tim was trying to keep him in the loop, as though there might be a way to keep Dave here after all.

"Twenty minutes." He hung up. He looked in the office, but Carla had gone. He found her on the living room couch, still sucking on her finger in the dark with the curtains closed. She took her finger out of her mouth: "I heard."

"Alpine Canyon." As he remembered her story about driving up there, he also remembered the five hundred bucks he'd found in her pocket. That too was an argument for later.

"Be careful up there," she murmured as he kissed her forehead. "Maybe we can stay here after all."

BS, he thought as he drove away. Heartbreak was sure to follow, as death, weaving its sly determined path, found a way to raise its head again. There had to be a rational medical answer and he did not see how it could ever be good news. The answer to this mystery had to be a cruel one.

....

CHAPTER 15

Death in the Canyon

Dave drove down into Alpine Canyon, straight into a blinding dust storm so fierce, he had to delicately apply the gas or he would have been stopped dead as though by a great hand. A couple of times he nearly rear-ended Deputy Sam's Explorer. The road seemed unfamiliar from the day he drove Klaus Bartok home, as though the canyon walls been remodeled by that same giant hand.

Dave reached the canyon floor as tired as if he'd been fighting city traffic. Ahead, Sam's vehicle faded in and out through clouds of hissing dust. He drove through dust devils that shook the truck as though in retaliation. The canyon walls seemed inches away. Dave unhappily recalled the promised he'd made to never return to this open-air dungeon.

Finally, Sam's brake lights flashed. Dave stopped right behind him. To his right he saw a man half buried in the earth, frantically waving his arms, as though he were sinking into quicksand.

Dave pulled on a heavy down jacket and found a pair of goggles he'd purchased for these conditions. He tied his bush hat down tight and let the wind close the door for him. Tim King's Explorer and the S&R wagon materialized ten feet away.

The man who looked like he was caught in quicksand turned out to be Tim himself, wading across the swift-flowing stream running next to the canyon's north wall. Hatless and in waders, he was roped to the bumper of the S&R wagon. Two S&R guys Dave couldn't recognize at first were guiding him across, like swinging a pendulum against the strong current.

"Over there," Sam yelled in Dave's ear, pointing across the creek.

The body lay face down on the other side on a narrow bank under the canyon wall. It looked to be male. The upper half sprawled up the bank at an angle, the arms stretched over the head as though he had died while clawing his way ashore.

Dave stepped back and looked up. A huge overhang jutted out above the creek. Above that, nothing but dust-blown sky. The deceased couldn't have fallen straight from the rim—he would have hit the overhang and bounced, maybe hard enough to break into pieces and scatter all over the canyon floor. He had to be a careless hiker—a trespasser as far as the canyon's owner was concerned. Klaus Bartok should have been forced to repair that feeble broken "No Trespassing" sign that stood at the canyon notch—Bartok's kind of warning invited being ignored.

Tim finally made it up the opposite bank. He took off his gloves, slipped on rubber ones, knelt by the body and reached down to feel for the pulse on the neck. He jerked his hand away and reached for the left wrist instead. He nodded: The deceased was indeed officially deceased. Then he lifted the body up. It was stiff. He peered down into the face and gave a start. His mouth made words shaped in the name of God.

He stood up, wiping his hands on his pants. He searched through the blowing dust until he saw Dave and Sam. He cupped his hands around his mouth, but he might as well have been in the next county: Dave could only hear one syllable: "ant."

"A-ha! I knew it!" Sam, who was definitely not in the next county, hollered in Dave's ear. He eagerly led Dave to Tim's vehicle. Dave waved hello to Bill Martin, Joe Stengel and Betty Tomlinson. Bill and Joe turned to setting up a pulley system and a Stokes' basket to retrieve the body from across the creek while Tim busily tied his end of the rope around a spire of rock on the other side.

There was a stranger here too: a slight African-American wearing a brown down jacket and ballcap, maybe the dead man's camping buddy, probably feeling sorry that they'd ever set foot in these parts.

Sam dramatically pulled out an old 12-gauge Remington shotgun from Tim's vehicle and held it up like a trophy. He pointed toward the west end of the canyon: "The witness says he found it a piece up that way! Look at that!"

A name was clumsily carved in the unpolished wooden stock of the shotgun:

L. DURANT

Dave bristled with goose bumps as Sam's eyes gaped from behind the goggles he wore over his glasses: "It's been fired! Here! Smell it!"

Dave shook his head: How did Dr. Durant get all the way down here? From his guess, Leo's house was two, three miles to the west and a ways up from the canyon rim. "Did you find his car down here?"

Sam shook his head broadly back and forth: "*Ve-ry* sus-pi-cious! The witness says he's a naturalist from the DNR; he was campin' down here last night. C'mon, you can talk to him."

The wind herded them back to where the group was watching Tim wrestle Leo inside the nylon body bag they'd sent over with the basket. Leo was still in rigor mortis. With his arms sticking above his head, closing the bag completely was a grim struggle.

Dave shook hands with the stranger who was leaning against the hood of the S&R vehicle; he looked to be a man who was always close to a smile, even on bad days.

His name was Emile de Grasse, a naturalist with the state Department of Natural Resources. He'd driven into Alpine Canyon yesterday afternoon. He'd received Klaus Bartok's permission via Barb Albanese to perform a biological survey of the area's flora and fauna. As he explained it, Alpine Canyon and its environs were one of the last pockets in the Sierra to undergo a study of the effects of climate change that had been underway for the last several years.

Emile had set up camp late yesterday about three miles to the west, where the road ended, on the northern slope, out of the reach—he'd hoped—of flash floods. He'd started following some track—"a lot of track," as he put it—he'd found early that morning. The track led east. He found the body at 8:17 A.M. (He pointed at his wristwatch as he said this.) He drove all the way down to St. Ives to report it. "Ugly drive," he shuddered. "The scenery's best ever, but I thought was I gonna die. Wicked, wicked curves."

Fifteen minutes later, the body was pulleyed across the stream. Bill and Joe set it in front of their vehicle, out of the wind. Sam and Betty swung Tim back across the creek downstream. Tim staggered ashore soaked, exhausted, his short wavy hair plastered on his large head, his face red, white and cold. He told Dave who it was. Dave replied that he'd seen the shotgun.

They gathered in a semicircle around the Stokes' basket. Tim nodded at Sam. Sam knelt and ripped the zipper down fast and hard.

Leo Durant sprang out of the bag like a jack-in-the-box with his arms over his head. The right half of his face had been destroyed. The left was frozen in a wide-eyed scream.

"Oh my, oh my, oh my, oh my." Emile deGrasse staggered away right into the pitiless wind and tumbled to the ground. Betty Tomlinson rushed to help him up and get him in front of Tim's vehicle, out of both the wind and the sight of Leo Durant.

"A little fast with the zipper there, Sam," growled Tim.

Dave slipped on a pair of latex gloves. As with Andrew Potter, they'd need a pathologist, but he could provide a few initial findings. Tim knelt beside him, notebook and pen in hand. Dave ran his hands over the corpse:

"Are you sure his car isn't parked here somewhere?" Tim shook his head firmly. "Okay. Well, this body is too intact. Especially if he fell in from up canyon and got washed down here. He still has his drawers on."

"They're pajama bottoms."

"They're buttoned wrong, too. Compound fractures in both his legs and a fracture in his lower right arm though it's hard to be sure until rigor mortis passes."

"Any idea how long he's been dead?"

"Maybe late last night, early this morning," Dave shrugged. "Was the ground under him dry?"

Tim shook his head: "No, it looks like he washed ashore."

"So where did he fall in? Let's look at his back."

Gouges and bite marks covered Leo's back and shoulders. There were no massive splinters and fractures that would indicate a thousand-foot fall. Most of his buttocks appear to have been chewed away. The scavengers had struck fast: considering how barren the landscape, that wasn't surprising. The corpse of any large animal would be a feast for thousands of smaller ones.

There were also two sets of puncture wounds, raised around the edges, five on each side, ten of them in all, spread across Leo's upper shoulders. Each group was about five to six inches across, each puncture circled with pale pink. Dave changed his gloves and inserted a finger into the biggest, deepest-looking wound, on the right shoulder. The hard flesh parted reluctantly. The hole curved around and down into flesh and muscle, about four inches. When he pulled the finger out, there was only a film of blood. An image of Carla on the couch sucking her finger flashed into his brain; he shook it out as though it were a spider in a blanket.

"Not much blood. Those are talon marks. Whatever made these wounds was big, maybe an eagle or an owl. You see how they're raised around the edges? It must have tried to pick him off the ground post mortem."

A large gash lay open on the left side of the neck. The left common carotid artery poked up, looking like a drinking straw. Bite marks covered the neck and upper body, all of them smaller than the talon wounds, some no more than punctures. Rats, mice, squirrels, maybe a fox.

"Cause of death?"

"That, as you know, is for the pathologist in Tahoe to determine.

If he was down around here and fell in upstream, then was washed down here—that would explain the broken bones and that head and facial damage. He could have bled out from the all these cutaneous injuries. But most of the wounds appear to be post-mortem." He shrugged. "That's all I got."

"So," Sam Colbert declared dramatically, "Leo was hunting along the creek here when he slipped and fell in." He looked upstream and shook his head. "The wind's probably scoured away all the track by now."

Tim coughed politely: "But where's his vehicle? What's he doing in his PJs?"

"The quarter moon rose around one last night. Maybe that was when…" Sam trailed off as Tim gave him a don't-be-stupid scowl.

"Don't get me wrong, Sam, but there's no other vehicle down here except for the DNR fella's, and Leo couldn't have climbed down in the dark, moon or no moon, and it really don't look like he fell from up there."

"What about that DNR guy?" Sam jabbed his thumb over his shoulder.

Dave followed Tim and Sam over to where Emile de Grasse huddled unhappily in front of Tim's vehicle. He haltingly told them the rest of his story:

Barb Albanese had warned Emile about the winds of Alpine Canyon. She was right. It took him an hour to find a camping spot that was out of the wind and safe from flooding. Last night he couldn't sleep. The ground was rocky; the tent poles rattled like bones and the wind keened "like a crazy woman."

He got up to piss at 10:59 P.M. "I forgot to take a bottle to bed." When he finished, he'd shined his flashlight south over the canyon floor to see dozens of pairs of eyes glowing right at back at him from among the debris and matted trees piled in the middle of the canyon. "It made me feel like a meal," he laughed nervously.

They were too far away and it was too dark to identify them. "I get it why most everyone once believed in ghosts and spirits. It creeped me out. Add to that the track I saw this morning, it could've been every species that inhabits this elevation which, considering how little food there seems to be around here, is pretty amazing."

He was just about to start back to his tent when he heard a huge hoot and howl, the weirdest he'd ever heard in all his years of field-work. He couldn't tell from which direction it came from in the dark. "Right then all those eyes in the rocks snapped off like a light. I heard hoofbeats, footsteps, wings flapping, like they all took off in one big herd."

"I looked up and saw ...something, a shadow against the stars, flying east along the north wall. The largest nocturnal flyer around here's the great owl, so I thought it was that. It looked like it was carrying a big rodent, maybe a squirrel. But the proportions didn't seem right, somehow. It was too dark to tell much." He shrugged, looking embarrassed, his scientist's pride in his clarity and precision wounded.

Emile decided he'd feel safer spending the night in his truck. "That was at 11:20 P.M. I woke up at 5:18 A.M. and heard 'em coming back this way. A deer herd ran by below and I saw bear, but I wasn't about to get out and look. I got up at 6:01 A.M. The wind had blown my tent across the canyon floor into that bottom scrabble. It took me an hour to put my camp up again. Then I hiked down here looking for track to see if I could figure out what happened. I've never seen so many species running together like that before, and there that poor gentleman was—just like you found him."

"You saw no one else down here?" Tim asked. "No other vehicles?"

"Nobody and no one. I had the whole place to myself, from what I can tell. I tell you, I've spent years hiking in Desolation and the Emigrant Wilderness. But this place, God, it's the loneliest I've ever seen. It's tweaked somehow."

"Does the name Leo Durant mean anything to you?" Sam Colbert asked slowly and carefully.

"Is that the poor man's name? Sorry, no." Emile shuddered

from the cold and from what he'd seen. "I'll tell you something else strange." The scientist came back to life. "Species at this elevation always live on the edge, hand-to-mouth, day-to-day. Food's scarce, so their numbers are low and thinly spread. I can't tell you the number of critters I've found dead from starvation, especially in early spring. But this place is unique. It supports more life than it should be able to. The biologist in me would love to come back here, but I'm human too and this place doesn't seem human or nat—"

"Guys, we gotta get out of here!"

Betty Tomlinson was pointing to the west where indigo clouds were boiling on the rim. Dragon's Ark seemed to be drawing them around its base at the top of the canyon, like a king swirling his robes about him. The storm would come like a flood.

They loaded the body into the S&R vehicle. Tim ordered Sam to help Emile break down his camp lickety-split; Emile would spend the night down below.

"A-OK, Chief!" Sam said with a broad, almost comical, wink.

Dave followed Tim and the S&R wagon out of the canyon. This time, Dave hardly had to touch the gas at all as the wind hurried them along and lifted them out. When they reached the intersection with the Sierra Crest Highway, Tim signaled he was pulling over and waved for Dave to follow suit. He was on his cellphone when he got out of his vehicle and came over.

"Yeah, I'm sure he'll come by." He put the phone away and leaned in Dave's window. "I'm goin' up to Leo's to have a look. Just struck me, he might have some patients in his waiting room. Somebody oughta look in. Sorry to throw that at ya—"

"No problem. I'll do it." Dave sighed. He wanted to go home and look in on Carla, maybe talk some more about what happened, figure out what to do next and ask her why she insisted on sitting in the dark.

"Fishing Saturday?" Tim asked.

"Huh? Yeah, sure." He nearly added, "One more time before I go" but didn't.

Filling in for Leo just this once wouldn't be a problem. It was the least he could do. Focus on the urgent care needs, send the rest home, and close the office early.

Leo's parking lot was full. His office was another one of those faceless ultra-modern boxes embraced by Osgood. Dave parked in Leo's space—its extra large sign warned that violators would be towed. But Leo wasn't here to do anything about it now.

The waiting room was also full. Unlike the county office, most of these folks were middle-aged or older, well dressed, with no children. As Dave walked in, some looked up hopefully while others looked put out. They'd not been told the news.

Sheila Wilson, Leo's receptionist, threw open the door to the back, her face drawn and pale. Tammy Vernueil, the nursing assistant, joined her, her eyes swollen red. Sheila closed the door and burst into tears. Tammy, who was older, around forty-five, stayed calm, but she embraced Dave tightly: "We're so glad you're here." Dave started to feel overwhelmed, but he carried on.

Everything else came easily, as though it were meant to be.

CHAPTER 16

In the Shadow
of the Ark

When the blood stopped oozing, Carla returned to Dave's office, found a clean needle and popped a new hole in her finger. On her way back to the living room, humming with her finger in her mouth, she heard the phone ring again. She let it go to the machine.

Sean Temkin's needy, reedy voice burbled out: There'd be a meeting of the Committee to Stop Sierra Future—really, Sean is that the best name you could come up with?—at the Byrneville library tonight. "Please come! And bring Mr. Bartok! Hope to see you there! Really! I mean it!" As if she doubted his sincerity. He hesitated before hanging up. Yeah, just in case I rush to the phone. "Oh Sean!"

She returned to the darkness of the living room. Kat came up and sat at her feet, stupidly begging for attention with her round green eyes. Carla bared her teeth at the cat until she went away in confusion, too stupid to even sulk.

As she savored the cocoa flavor of her new blood, she realized that it wasn't being flown back from the brink that made her feel so wonderful. No, she was a new person, free and strong. When she walked, she couldn't feel the floor under feet. This wasn't the creeping banality of ALS, but the liberation of weightlessness.

What caused it? What was so special about the blood that he offered her with such amused, easy flair? Some sugar substance, an energy-packed, super-fission molecule that sped like light through her body? Something he'd found in that Dark Energy and turned to his own use?

Whatever it was, it had changed her undoubtedly for the better; unquestionably.

Dave, naturally, didn't believe it because he didn't understand it; and if he did, he wouldn't accept it. So out with the wet blanket and the cold water. That man would scrub the twinkle out of the stars. To him, the world was dead, except for people in it.

But then a sudden worry flooded in. What *if* Dave turned out to be right? Not about the miracle, but about its transience? The power had already faded away twice. What if this restoration and renewal, this glorious glow that made her feel like she could grow wings with a simple wish—wings like the ones that took her on last night's glorious adventure—were only temporary? What if her life started fading again? What if she needed more? To be refilled?

As the doubts kept tumbling through her mind, she stared at her wounded weeping fingertip: "You sir, have not answered any of my questions."

Just before she walked out the door, she returned to the bedroom and opened her memento box in her dresser drawer. "Luck on the road," she murmured, as she grabbed her mother's rosary and dropped it into her blouse pocket. She paused to push the crucifix away from where it leaned against her nipple.

She stood before the garage door, pointed her finger at it: "Open Ses-a-meeee!" she intoned with mock drama. The command didn't work, but her little finger got the job done. This time, she'd take the green Jeep.

Once she was on the road, though, she noticed how strong the sun shined, how it made her squint and stung her exposed skin. She pulled over, found the floppy straw hat in the back, then the sunglasses and sun block in the glove compartment. She slopped half a tube of the sun block on her face, neck, and arms.

She passed Deputy Colbert just as he turned onto Sierra Crest Highway from Alpine Canyon Road. A Dodge camper followed right behind, both of them chased by the storm that was breaking up over head, that seemed to be clearing the way for her.

The storm had scoured Alpine Canyon clean, revealing its haunting, glittering chiaroscuro majesty, an epic play of light and shadow. Even the juniper and cypress that lay on the alluvial pile had a stubborn mystery about them. The great walls glittered with white mica. The big stream tossed its froth into the air. Sean was right: Klaus Bartok's kingdom, his place in the world, needed to be protected at all costs.

She imagined Mr. Bartok living in a cozy cabin somewhere in that alluvial pile, high up enough to protect him from floods. The cabin would be of sturdy granite or big logs, and furnished in comfortable mahogany chairs. She imagined Persian carpets across the flagstone floor, large mahogany bookshelves along the walls and a big warm fire in a handsome stone hearth. There, they would huddle together, their minds meeting again to weave and flow in fine conversation—and this time, he'd reveal his secrets.

When she reached the end of the canyon, she slathered on the remaining sun block while looking up at the high south rim. The Ark's summit peered over the south rim, gray and snowy. Maybe he lived far on the other side of the debris, she thought, as she walked over the redwood bridge. The bridge, though caked in mud, was still sturdy. She stopped to look down into the stream, until the water became a snow-white blur. Not so long ago, she used to play Poohsticks with her husband in such places. But this stream ran too fast for Poohsticks and that was a kid's game anyway.

She climbed the slope to the island. Not much here but boulders and flattened clusters of cypress, still wet from the storm. Blue puddles of rainwater lay about, already lightly buzzing with insect life, small lives whose only destiny was to devoured by the arachnid denizens of the hundreds of cobwebs that had re-jeweled the many

cypress mats that lay along the path after the storm. That these pred-
ators still lived here thrilled Carla. Their diet appeared to be more
than adequate. From within one spider bed, a squirrel's paw reached
out, open and desperate. Another web-wrapped trophy looked to be
in the shape of a bird. Another resembled an old woman's silk muff,
probably a marmot. The biggest of all was a fly-covered ornament
shaped like a fox, frozen in midair, caught by death as it ran for its
life.

Unlike him, she mused, it was Klaus Bartok who had outfoxed
death. A memory of last night flitted breezily in her mind. Not what
happened, but how it felt.

But while there were plenty of signs of life, there was no sign that
he or anyone lived along the winding trail, except for one small spot.
Here, sheltered by stones, lay the mossy remains of a little cabin buried in spider webs; it had probably been empty for a hundred years.
One wall was gone and the remaining three sagged inward.

No, he couldn't be living here. This barren environment was too
exposed to rain, wind, and especially sun, for Klaus Bartok, or anyone else. On the other side of the pile, she found herself looking
down on a small park-like area of pines and boulders. The south cliff
rose about a hundred yards away, its face streaked with runoff. To
the left, a huge waterfall thundered down all the way from the top.
A trail ran up at a low angle across the cliff face, from east to west
and disappeared at the rim, right under from where the Ark's summit
looked down.

From here, there was no sign that anyone lived down here within
the walls of Alpine Canyon. Then she looked up at the Ark again and
thought, Of course. A man like him would have to play hard to get
to, wouldn't he?

She had maybe less than an hour of direct sun left. She quickly
followed the trail down to a pair of faded wagon ruts that ran straight
ahead before making a sharp left where it met the stream created
by the falls. Then it went east along the stream, then south again,
straight to the cliff wall. The trail up seemed to start there.

So! He lives all the way up there! It was obvious how he made it too, once he'd been dropped off. All he had to do was wait in the canyon's cool shadows for night to fall. Then zoooooom! Ha! On his daylight business days, he must've either flown down here before dawn to wait to be picked up by his driver or else walked all the way down that trail. That's a long walk, she thought. Hope it's a wide one.

Carla ran along the trail to the falls. The falls were actually two falls. The upper falls went down to a shelf three hundred feet above the floor where it re-gathered its force before thundering down the rest of the way. From its base, it seemed to pour from the empty sky. She stared for awhile into the white froth until she could see every single drop rising and falling like music notes. His blood did wonders for the eyesight, too.

From here, she followed the trail as it curved slightly to the right between boulders, then up into a cave behind the falls. The thunder of the falls shook her to her marrow as she hiked around behind them, her hands over her ears. She brushed around the jagged corner of the wall and set her sunglasses firmly on her face, shocked by the stinging power of the afternoon sun over the mountains. Gunmetal shadows were already spreading across the canyon floor. The stream below flowed north from the falls, then turned west to curve around between the alluvial heap and the end of the canyon, just missing the glacier lake. It then rushed east, threading across the floor, its ribbon weaving with the simple thread of the road. The Jeep looked like a toy.

It was an easy climb. Over a hundred years ago, silver miners, smart boys, had blasted the cliff away, carving a road wide enough for their ore carts. With every step she took, Carla felt stronger. She reached the top with amazing speed to gaze down the thousand-foot drop into the canyon. I am Queen of Everything. She wasn't even gasping and felt she could have climbed another thousand feet without breaking a sweat. With a shriek of triumph, her fists in the air, she looked out over the same view she'd seen last night, except now it was daylight. Proof once again that last night had been no dream, but as real as the ground under her feet, the flesh on her bones and the quiet wind blowing through her hair.

Alpine Canyon's narrow gauge made it appear unfathomably deep, almost bottomless. The north rim looked close enough to reach with a single hop. The scrubby slope ran up to some buildings at the top: Leo …Leo Durant's place. Mr. Bartok had taken her there last night on their little starry jaunt. It was Leo who came out to stare at them, stupefied, wide eyes, wide mouth, and his white hair stuck out in shock. (What he was thinking now? Carla wondered. Just another dream? Oh, if you only knew Dr. Durant!)

The clarity and precision of her eyesight amazed her. She could see the house, a garage, and a Quonset hut to the left. She could read the Alpine County Sheriff's insignia on the Ford Explorer parked by the house word-for-word, count the feathers of the eagle logo. What were they doing there? She held her hand up, so it looked like she could wipe it all away, like a child sweeping his toys from a table. Whoosh! Gone!

Then she turned around to look behind her and promptly stopped feeling big and suddenly felt very small as she craned her neck up to see the dark monolith of Dragon's Ark.

The Ark's shadow was already creeping toward Carla and would hold her within its cold grip within minutes. Maybe I should turn around, get out of here, she thought. For here, its stark grandeur brought to mind a massive castle rather than a sinking ship. The afternoon sun bathed its pointed peak in chilly white light while a west wind blew wispy curtains of sterile snow from its flanks. Its proud tower made Carla felt like an ant on its desolate plain of granite boulders, weary whitebarks and lodge poles, and a nearby little grove of fallen aspen. A few mountain junipers with their thick trunks and stubby branches lay flat like praying peasants. There were no flowers anywhere. Springtime never touched this place.

Carla was profoundly afraid and didn't feel powerful and strong anymore. She'd been careless, made an awful mistake climbing all the way up here so late in the day. She hadn't told anyone where she was going. If she didn't find Mr. Bartok, if she didn't turn back, it would mean long hours of miserable death from exposure. Even her bones might be long gone before anyone thought to search for here.

Only days ago, she was telling herself that she wouldn't have minded dying up here. But that was when she was dying. Now she didn't want to die, not ever. She hadn't come here for that. She'd come here to ask, Why? And what next?

Survival: just one more reason she had to find Klaus Bartok.

Her shoulders slumped as she bowed her head. She walked with small steps into the shadow of Dragon's Ark.

The old mining trail wound through the rubble toward the base of the mountain. Coal-black vultures wheeled about drawing interlocking circles with hawks and eagles, all of them hoping she would die so they could eat.

"I am hungry," he'd said last night. "We are hungry," they were saying.

As she walked, she looked to the east. If she hadn't been so scared, she would have been awestruck by how the Samsons rolled down and away, dropping out of sight. Beyond them, the vista stretched hundreds of white-gold miles across the Carson Valley to other mountains beyond. The storm had broken into fat, gray-bellied cotton balls that dragged dark tails of rain behind them. Gray shadows contrasted eerily with silver shafts of sun. Except for the oddly muted colors, this had to be the best view in all of Monitor County, maybe in all of the Sierra. And Klaus Bartok had it all to himself.

She passed by the grove of dead aspens. One fallen tree still had a large patch of white bark that had survived years of a violent climate. On it, someone, a miner or sheepherder, had carved a face. All that remained was a pair of huge eyes, black and hard; the carver had etched a few words in what might have been Spanish or Basque underneath, along with a date:

08 JUNIO, 1906

A vulture flew over her shoulder. Its wings made an eerie whoosh, its clammy shadow made her shudder. It flew straight to where the trail ended at the mountain's base. On each large boulder along the trail, a vulture perched, waiting. They coolly watched her, waiting for her to make a mistake. She tried to pull her shoulders back, to walk straight and fearless, but try was all she could do. There was no way this vulnerable morsel of life would ever fool them.

It was nearly night-dark where the trail met the foot of the massif. There, stood another two boulders, perfectly placed, each with its own vulture. Between them was what looked like an entrance. As Carla approached, the birds took off in opposite directions, like a gate opening. "Guess I passed," Carla laughed nervously.

Carla walked to the mountain's base, and there, set into the granite, she found a door. It was carved from heavy mahogany that had long ago been turned black by the elements. It had no knocker and no bell, only a door handle made of tarnished brass.

She told herself to turn around and go back, but she thought hopelessly, back to what?

"Hello!" She grew desperate, grabbed the door handle and pressed the button.

The door flew open, pulled her inside with enough force to spin her around into a greater, deeper darkness.

As Carla struggled to keep her feet, the door slammed behind her like a hammer. She found herself in an utter blackness that stripped her down to nothing but stuttering panicked breathing and pounding heart. She couldn't even feel the floor beneath her shoes. She felt poised forever on the edge of death, a mote of thought on the shore of a terrible sea.

She forced herself to stay still. For all she knew, she might have been standing on a point of rock surrounded by a bottomless pit. She ran her hands over her body to reconfirm her existence. Yes, alive. Nausea churned nefariously within and her bladder muscles contracted. Her face muscles shrunk with revulsion, but the scream stayed in her mind. Whatever was out there was just waiting for her to scream …

Slowly though, her eyes adjusted. At daybreak pace, a blue light, cool and subtle, filtered in to cast a spotlight around her feet. She saw her cringing shadow stretching behind to her right.

The light came from a pair of shining blue eyes looking down from above.

Klaus Bartok's voice echoed with weary amusement:

"Why can't they ever stay away?"

By now, Carla could tell she was inside a huge mountain cave, likely an old abandoned mine. Klaus Bartok appeared to be hanging head down from a wall, almost like a sconce. His body spread upward like a swash of black paint behind him. His long hair hung in a curtain around his tough and rocky face, which was, as it would be in darkness, completely free of wrinkles. He wore the same sly grin he wore last night, just before he allowed her a sip of his blood.

Klaus Bartok floated off the cave wall and drifted down to her, his shadow fluttering like a black velvet sheet behind him. He was making himself look more human, something she could understand. He was both fiercely centered and marvelously fluid.

"They always come to my door sooner or later with their questions."

He landed gracefully on what looked like a cushion of air that turned into a chair. Once settled, he raised his right hand. Carla felt herself being pushed backward into a chair that hadn't been there before. He was treating her with tolerant contempt. She grew extremely angry and it was then, at last, she remembered her mother's rosary, nestled in her shirt pocket.

But the pocket was empty.

She looked up angrily. Klaus Bartok was impishly swinging it around with his left hand like a key chain, the crucifix like a rabbit's foot. He winked impudently and tossed it to her. It floated slowly through the darkness.

"I might have guessed you'd bring that too," he said, as the rosary drifted through the blue air like a deep sea creature. "Some people still wave those symbols they only half believe in, betting their faith will crawl from the grave where they let it die. But you're only experimenting like a curious child. You had an idea about me and decided to test it. You're a better sport than some. I'd stopped being scared of those things by the time I arrived here. Once upon a time, I too believed Christian tchotchke could harm me. The rebel secretly trembles before the power he rebels against. But no more. Those who fought me then are all dead now. And I alone remain."

He laughed as the rosary dropped into her shirt pocket with a soft chink. More light rose in the cave. The room they sat in was large, mostly empty and remarkably clean. Granite walls disappeared into darkness above, creating the impression that the whole mountain interior had been hollowed out. From the books she had read, and the movies she had seen, she had expected a world of cobwebs and ruins. Of shadows, there were plenty, but otherwise Klaus Bartok lived in cool, ascetic luxury.

The floor, she was somehow pleased to note, was made of obsidian flagstone, but the only visible piece of functional furniture was a giant four-poster bed, its mahogany frame draped with a pearly canopy. Carved into the left side foot panel was what looked to be an old family crest: a circle, around the inside edge of which was engraved writing, in an indecipherable language. Inside the circle, crudely embossed busts of two crowned figures stared at one another over a little tree. On the right side of the panel was a graceful calligraphic initial:

D

Behind him, tall bookcases marched endlessly away in the dark. She wondered if he had really read—

"Yes, every one of them," he cut off her thought. "And I am who you think, but not *quite* what you think. I keep the bed mostly for nostalgia." He lazily waved a hand upward. "I spend most of the day as black smoke under the ceiling. No, no box of dirt." He sniffed. "Another of those erroneous details. Why would I struggle for the life freedom I have for the privilege of sleeping in a box of *dirt*?"

Though his lips didn't move, each word of this rhetorical question made a distinctive musical note. He was communicating to her telepathically! It gave her no pleasure. The man whom the world called Klaus Bartok was injecting his thoughts into her mind, like a ventriloquist puts words in his dummy's mouth. She could only sit where he made her sit and listen. She wouldn't even have to bother asking questions; he knew those already, too.

"You're here, in part, because you're curious. What's happened to you? Why did I make it so? Who am I? Why am I here? I haven't told that story in awhile." Klaus Bartok's eyes glittered with pleasure. "Fifteen years, in fact. A long time to you and to the poor girl who was here before you, but to me, time is putty I pull apart and squeeze together. Yes, I'd love to tell my story again. I'm sure you'll be fascinated.

"Sit back. Relax. You're not going anywhere. Not now."

....

CHAPTER 17

The Emigrant's Tale

Klaus Bartok may have been a stiff wizened corpse by day, but inside his sunless but comfortable mountain cave, Carla found him to be a compelling charming raconteur, a thing of grace and substance. His every word boomed and echoed with gusto inside Carla's skull, weaving together into a hypnotic, rhythmic melody spun by his large expressive hands. He laughed, he smirked, and his eyebrows rose and fell with amazement at every turn of his story. Once in awhile, he'd simply bare large, snow-white teeth in an impish grin. Carla had never seen such happiness in such darkness.

"Yes, a hundred years ago, they knew me as Dracula. Good thing that silly book is remembered as a 'novel.'" He drew quote marks in the air, as he would often. "Or I might never have made it here. Stoker was a dullard who cobbled his story from original sources to plump up a teary pillow of lies and half-truths meant to comfort, not enlighten. 'Good will triumph!' Pfui! A tale for a kitten who sees itself a lion when it looks in the mirror."

"The ending was a total fabrication! Why would I scamper all the way back to *Mitteleuropa*? It wasn't even my 'native land'! Oh no, I'd burned through many nations over the millennia before I landed there and I remember all of them. And then that contrived, silly race they ran against sundown and the 'sacrifice' of that idiot Morris. He actually died much earlier. I'd made him a vampire, but left him to fend for himself. Once his friends discovered what he'd become—he was the one they caught forcing Mina Harker to drink his blood as I made him drink mine—they killed him with his own Bowie knife.

"So, they say, they bravely knifed my heart, cut my head off and wept with triumph as I turned to dust, before trundling home to boo-hoo again upon their fainting couches. It's a wonder their tears didn't wash England into the sea.

"The real reason I never flew back to Transylvania was because I had nothing to fly back to. I left it in the first place because I'd made it a desert, stripped it down to dead rock. I was still 'young' and impetuous and had already spent centuries eating myself out of one house after another. I picked London because I'd finally gleaned a simple truth: I had to cease exterminating my prey if I wanted to live. I moved to London to live and feed peacefully but invisibly among that city's teeming millions. I'd never run out of food there.

"Or so I thought. I turned out to be wrong, but it wasn't those pasty Victorians who sent me packing, but England itself. London was the first large city I'd ever seen and I was completely unprepared for the amount of filth. Their industrial revolution had turned human blood into a poisonous soup of soot, alcohol, opiates, and disease microorganisms beyond number and name. Even the blood of the supposedly dominant classes was often indigestible. Oh yes, ma'am, I'm as finicky about my food as you are about yours. I'd no more eat poison than you would.

"In short, I failed to adapt. I would have died and my kind would have become extinct—I was among the last by then. There were no great battles. I simply fled and let Van Helsing's vigilantes believe they'd won the final victory in the 'war against evil.' Some of them must have lived to witness the next century's mass slaughters. I suppose the joke was really on them, wasn't it?

"But now they are all dead." Klaus Bartok rocked back, spreading his hands with a pleased, almost daffy grin. "And here I am!"

"What I did do was hop a passenger ship bound for New York—by the way, without dragging along boxes of dirt. By then I'd also gotten over my superstition about resting in 'the soil of my native homeland.' If anything, London taught me that my continued existence boiled down to a few simple needs: reliable darkness during daylight, a clean natural environment, and a clean, reliable source of high-quality blood.

"On the voyage over, I further honed my craft of silence and disguise. I killed no one. I stayed in my berth as much possible, appearing only as a querulous, psoriatic, frail elder, sensitive to sunlight. The first night out, I filled the ship's steward with the 'Voice of God' and inspired him to dump the ship's supply of recreational alcohol over for everyone's 'Christian salvation.' The next morning, God's voice was gone, the steward dismissed, and I had what I needed: good blood. From there, I slipped from berth to berth, sleeping brain to sleeping brain, like a bee from flower to flower, pollinating them with dreams, sometimes outright nightmares, to sweeten my supper.

"I missed the orgies of violence and bizarre public spectacle of my 'youth' at first, but I learned to play in the landscape of dreams. I laughed as I watched the people weave about in anemic confusion the next morning. A couple of them almost fell overboard. 'I have snakes slithering my head! Ahhhhhh!' Ha! One passenger actually accused his fellows of being vampires. Never was a man so right for the wrong reasons! No one cast an eye on poor, helpless old me! The distance between what they believed and what I knew opened like a vista! The ship's population was large so I fed well and enjoyed the voyage."

He sat back. "But then we disembarked in New York City." He shook his head. "It was even fouler than London and this time, I also nearly starved. I fled west in hungry despair as soon as I could, flying by night, sleeping in abandoned houses, barns and caves by day, often feeding off livestock and wildlife. That was when my new education began. As the sky cleared and the clamor of the eastern cities faded, I was happy to find America to be an almost infinite land. I quickly fell in love, a love that inspired a restlessness to see as much of this new world and its peoples as I could. Somewhere I would find a place for me.

"Peoples! You Americans are not one tribe of provincial peasants, but many tribes, amazingly diverse, down to tribes of one. You don't mindlessly moo like cattle, but sing of yourselves as 'free men.' Every man a king! Like me! I admired their freewheeling talent for deceit, how they moved across great distances, secretly shed their pasts like snakeskins all the while crowing about 'manifest destiny.' Meaning, whatever stands in the way better get out of the way. Truly, this country is a large glove and my hand fits it perfectly. By the time I reached here, I truly felt ...American!"

Then he sighed with charming ruefulness:

"But it took awhile, quite some time in fact, to find a home, a stable community with reasonably healthy inhabitants. The teetotaling Quakers seemed a good fit at first, but they were so sober and conformist that I stood out like the full moon. The dreams I gave them they knew to be a sign that danger was near. Luckily, the sun was setting when they arrived with their torches, clubs, and pitchforks." He shuddered at the memory of his narrow escape. "I can still feel the fire. Ho-ho! That I inspired even that pacifist hive to violence amuses me still! How those deluded hypocrites must have wept with guilt when they saw themselves in the light of day.

"I kept on my westward journey. There were so many choices and it was difficult for even my mind to choose. The Midwest was healthier than the East, but too many were too superstitiously sober like the Quakers. Too much sun and not enough shadows in the dreary flatness for me hide in. The Rocky Mountains were lovely and would have been perfect, but they were thinly populated by alcoholics. I was like Goldilocks! Ha! The soup was always too hot or too cold!

"It took me ten of your years, but eventually ..." He looked around pleased, raising his hands to the dark ceiling. "I found my paradise! Here, the 'soup' was just right and little stood in my way. The Indian gods were weak and left quickly, leaving only the godless, who were less inclined to poison their blood, especially the wealthy. Many visitors come and go, some industrious and sober, some not so, but overall, the quality of blood is good enough, often excellent! Pure, bright tasting, and clean! (You're right about the sugar molecule by the way!)

"By the time I arrived, I'd taken this Hungarian name, and for the next half-century, I lived in what seemed a cozy obscurity. Then one night, while drinking from a girl who'd fallen asleep in front of the television, I saw a moving image of a human creature feeding on another in a similar fashion. At first, I thought Oh no! Competition! I thought I was the last vampire, with the whole world to myself, and now here was this unexpected contest! After awhile, I realized that it was all playacting. Actors pretending to be me. I'd become a myth! Amazing! Still, I'm not impressed. The movies are anemic mirrors of what I really am. These days, I see I'm portrayed as suffering from addiction, but that's absurd! Blood is food to me as chicken is to you! It's the same! Blood is only the key to the treasure and the treasure is life!"

"Yes, in these great mountains, I am master and gloriously happy. From the top of these peaks to the far corners of sleep, *Ich habe genug*. A hundred years of sad, sweet red dawns and golden sunsets like a curtain rising on the night. I weep when darkness fades and I must return home. Sometimes, on mornings when I must go to the village, I stroll down that canyon trail to bathe in the sweet pool of darkness of the canyon below where I wait—waited—for Miss Goodman. A few more minutes of daylight's sting kept at bay in the sweet blue shadows."

"Here's another advantage! The hunting here is better than it was in ravaged old Europe. To the wild life, I'm both one of their own and their master. You saw how my dear pets gathered that day on the mountain road, how they flew with us last night, and now wait for me outside? I call, they come, and they guide me home at dawn.

"They also willingly offer their blood, especially in winter, when the tourists are mostly gone and people are few and they drink more alcohol, even those that normally don't. Animal blood is bland and animal minds are tiny playgrounds, but they get me through the winter. I rarely kill my victims, but when spring comes I am like a bear emerging from hibernation." He leaned forward raising a broad hand: "Allow me to say here, that I'm very sorry about poor Mr. Potter, but it had been a long winter and I was famished. While feeding on him, I detected signs of an imminent major stroke, so I'd say I did the poor man a favor. Wouldn't you? Most importantly, he was one of *them*. I'll make clear my meaning in a bit.

"I keep the human population low to keep things clean. Most everyone lives here because I want them to. Dear Dr. Durant kept my people healthy for years—ohh, yes, now you remember last night. Don't let it bother you. Durant was ill and his mind was failing. Immortality would have been lost on him, as youth is on the young. At least he died experiencing something miraculous and strange.

"Besides, to keep you by my side, I need to keep your dull spouse employed, too. He'll be a fine doctor. The enchantment of this land will always keep you here. I take your blood and I give you the sweetest dreams. That is the bargain. Those I don't wish to stay or return get nightmares. Most of them do leave. Those that won't—the addicted, the lost, the wounded and the stubborn—usually turn to heavy drinking or drugs and I can't touch them, but they are few. My allies on the commission see that the county stays relatively dry, except for a few beer and wine licenses. A county populated only by fanatical teetotalers would set tongues wagging with difficult questions. It needs a nuanced veneer of normality to hide behind."

"Yes, isn't it funny? A dream creature fretting over prosaic matters of liquor licenses, health care, and real estate! And so it goes: the world I depend on for nourishment must remain orderly and incurious, in a waking sleep.

"But while my powers are many and vast, I only have them when night falls and so I compromise with the day. I've struck a fine balance here and I don't do it alone. Miss Albanese handles my finances, real estate transactions, and leasing; you hate her, but she is helpful. Others assist me in other areas; but only one has ever known my true identity." He sighed. "But suddenly, one day, like that"—he snapped his fingers—"she was gone."

He lowered his eyes and wept pearly tears that splashed down his stone face. He wiped them way, a gesture that touched Carla more than the tears themselves.

"Oh, yes, Mrs. Sutton. One shortcoming to eternal life is how it's sharpened my terror of death. I am close to few and when those loyal souls die, well …Miss Goodman was more than a chauffeur. She was both my best ally in the world at day and my protégé. She'd nearly completed her evolution and was ready to join me in endless life. So many years, so much hard work. And then that day …I'll never understand!"

Frustration twisted his face, as he gnawed his lip and punched his hand into his fist with a loud smack. "Maybe she got lost in a fantasy of her future life and forgot the mortal clay within which she was still trapped. Where was I? Asleep, as I usually am during the day, as you've seen. That vehicle was built to my specifications to keep us both alive on those deadly roads, but I lost her anyway! For all my worries about my death, I forgot her mortality!

"But now I have you, ma'am." He laughed. "I'm a lucky soul that it was you who took my hand that day! You've received both my welcoming gifts. One, the promise of a long life; the other, the promise of a life worth living. This is only the beginning, but it will take time as evolution will. We are rare for a reason, Mrs. Sutton, rare for a reason."

His mood changed as his face sank into a furrow, like a cliff wall folding together. For the first time, the master of the night revealed a trembling fear.

"Her death came at a terrible time, because I face great danger. A hundred years ago, I fled the poisoned cities, but now they're spreading toward me like a cancer. Look to the east and west at night and see how the city lights flood the sky and dim the stars. I no longer seek to conquer the world. I have learned my limits, but human civilization remains passionately blind its own and maybe always will. Its lights spoil every pocket of darkness, brightens every corner, scours out every secret, leaving only soulless 'facts' in a fruitless attempt to drain every last speck of mystery from Being, as if somehow will stave off the end. But there's only one way that could ever happen and only I know it.

"The precious balance I've fought for will be destroyed. Sierra Future is an evil power, greater than I could ever be. Where I bring people dreams of starlight, Garner bribes them out of their dreams not with greater dreams, but with money." He exploded into an angry sneer. "Oh, we're only being reasonable and rational,' the bastards say with their reasoned lies! 'Cities of boxes and parking lots only make sense! We're only bringing freedom and making it efficient!' Of course, my extinction is only fair and rational! How selfish of me to want to stay alive!

"Sorry, I'm ranting again. But my obstacle is this: Garner and his minions are heavily medicated drunkards so I can't bend their minds to my will. Thousands will follow them, their veins running with poison. They'll dirty the skies, dim the stars forever and I'll die, eons of life dwindling to a whimpering end. Sure, I can fly away again but where to? Wherever I go, civilization's poisoned glare will follow or be there waiting in ambush.

"I must make my stand here even at the risk of my life." He smiled directly at her, his gorgeous eyes urgent with pleading. "Please stand with me! This is our fight now, yours and mine. And Sean's and your husband's and all those whose sleep is steeped in perfect dreams. You don't want me to die! You don't want your dreams to die! The lines are drawn and they must be drawn to the quick. Everyone has their part and must play it!"

"What do I want you to do? Glad to hear you thinking! I want you out of my home. Now! You erred in coming here—no, no apologies, you meant well. In the future, understand that I need you only when I specifically call for you. Miss Albanese will contact you or I may simply drop a hint in your dream as I did the other night. You'll always find me waiting by the stream below. Never come this way again! The trail is dangerous and the roads you drive are risky enough!

"If you leave now, you may just make it to the meeting to which

Mr. Temkin invited you and where you should be now. (Yes, I read that in your mind, too.) He needs our help. His marijuana smoking is a prophylactic against my direct influence. How such bright talented people fog themselves on drugs frustrates me no end! But he's a sensitive soul and he rightly adores everything about you." Mr. Bartok wagged his finger and winked. "Inspire him for the battle ahead and report back to me on how the day goes, so I know what actions I can take. The way they are, it's difficult to strike at them as I'd like. But, we will find a way! And we will win and this land shall remain free!"

Suddenly, Klaus Bartok was in Carla's face with his blue-fire eyes, his hands close to her ears. He pressed both thumbs and middle fingers together—

"And now off with you!"

SNAP!

Everything changed like a dream: Carla was flung out of the cave to find herself dashing across the dark plateau on the balls of her feet, lifted along by a powerful wind. His pets, the hawks and vultures, flew about, as though herding her along, as she tripped over rocks and boulders, fell into pockets of snow, got up, and kept going.

But it was night when she reached the rim and a powerful wind howled down into the black pit of Alpine Canyon. The trail vanished down the cliff to the right.

I shouldn't be here. I shouldn't be here

She thought of Sean. His meeting might be falling apart, the fight for the life of Klaus Bartok and the soul of these mountains over before it started. Sean needed her to be there, by his side, at his back. Who loved or didn't love who didn't matter, not when so much as was stake—the night soul of the world!

Carla started down the cliff. Only a few steps later, her foot hit slick wet granite and slipped out over black space. A gust of wind gave her a final shove, and she toppled down into the pit.

It didn't feel like she was falling. Mother's rosary drifted out of her pocket and fell alongside, glittering feebly, Jesus a forlorn abstraction. Then she began to faint as her blood pressure dropped. The rosary fell into the darkness below.

That was when she realized she wasn't falling anymore. Something had caught her. She was being flown, again. Mr. Bartok was there to catch her once more, save her life again, this time from her stupidity. They made their exchange: blood for blood.

Laughing gaily, Mr. Bartok took her over the meadow, the debris mound, and the rushing creek. She glimpsed the redwood bridge beneath them, saw the dark outline of the Jeep rushing toward her.

Mr. Bartok gently set Carla down by the vehicle. Stunned, exhausted, she sprawled across the hood, then pushed herself up and spun around to look behind her, hoping it was all a dream, because it was simply too much, too insane, for any human mind to tolerate. Somewhere deep inside, she wanted to awaken and find herself in the sturdy realities of daylight and gravity, not this fantastic no-gravity absurdity.

But there Klaus Bartok stood, defiantly real, tall and elegant, his eyes aglow, in the liquid black cloak that he spun from darkness.

"Apologies for not taking you all the way there, but I'm sure you understand. My sudden loss of years would be hard to explain. Hurry safely! Remember, I value your life as I value my own. Life is the only real treasure!"

He bowed with a showman's smile, then spread his arms and leapt into the air with a shout, like a boy bouncing off a trampoline, his face joyful with starlight. He drew his body up like a curtain that was its own revelation and turned from black to fire red to blue flame. His white face sharpened and shrank until it became hawk-like.

With wings rippling, the hawk flew a perfect circle around Carla. He tipped his wings in farewell and sailed up the rocky hill with a whoosh. He sank down out of sight, on the other side, then appeared once more and shot straight up the canyon walls, night's angel at play among the stars.

CHAPTER 18

Fly on the Wall

Just when things were falling apart, Carla appeared to save it all.

Until that turn of the wheel, Sean Temkin was ready to once more crumble in defeat and despair. First, late that afternoon, came word of the death of Leo Durant. Sean had been counting on the old doctor's support and presence on the Committee to Stop Sierra Future. His mind reeled thinking about how he'd only seen Leo alive and cranky a few days before, when he'd came spluttering into the St. Ives Cafe during lunch, his beety face bursting with rage. He'd just come from a brutal encounter with "Garner and his thugs" who'd tried to squeeze him into selling his place on the north rim above Alpine Canyon.

The diners, all tourists, got an earful along with their meals: about how Barb Albanese "shook her big tits at me;" about how one of Garner's hired thugs had glowered menacingly at him and how they tried to stop him from leaving until he agreed to sell the land he'd always sworn would stay in his family.

"I'll never sell!" he bellowed as he rose from the table, his lunch half-finished. "Not to the government, not to the tree huggers and definitely not those sonsabitches! You goddamn bet I'm comin' to your meeting!" he promised Sean, as he stormed out, leaving an embarrassed silence and no tip. "Local character!" Sean laughed to everyone.

Leo's death was only the first of Sean's problems. From the time everyone started showing up at the library meeting room at seven-thirty, the only topics were Leo and how someone had been arrested for his killing and what they would do for health care now that he was gone. ("Dave Sutton?" Chloe Byrne suggested hopefully. "He's leaving," her niece Virginia rasped, baring her teeth in irritation at this apparent sign of her aunt's senility.)

No sooner had Sean tried to get the meeting underway at eight, than Edie Ferrand immediately ripped the proceedings out of his hands, first by trying to make herself chair. She attacked Sean's leadership qualifications—in the third person—regarding any issue involving Monitor County ("My people on my mother's side were here long before the Europeans; my father's side was among the first white settlers! When did Sean say he moved here? Last fall?") Alan Frederickson offered backhanded support for Sean by saying he didn't think length of residency mattered so much, but then touted his own great age and experience as owner-operator of the Foxwood Ski Resort. Whether either of them should have even been attending this meeting, since they were commissioners, was another issue that Sean felt too intimidated to bring forward.

Though on the same side of the Sierra Future issue, Edie and Allan were mortal enemies, and the meeting quickly fractured along those lines, as each drew supporters around them like iron filings to a magnet. Edie's clique advocated uncompromising war against Sierra Future; Alan's, good faith negotiation and compromise. No one seemed interested in what Sean had to say.

Sean actually agreed with Edie, but after the way she'd treated him, any gesture in her favor would make him look spineless. Fighting off tears of rage and frustration, he shrunk into his shell like a turtle as he so often had before. Between occasional glances at the door in the hope that Carla would appear with Mr. B at her side, he grieved about how he'd been overwhelmed, outflanked, and intimidated once again, like he'd been in Berkeley and everywhere else. Maybe it was time to face the fact that he wasn't cut out for political life. He could barely deliver an intelligible speech. He didn't have the savvy, the guts, and the easy willingness to make enemies that politics required. He was too kind, too honest, and maybe too gutless.

What would he do now that this paradise was about to be destroyed by disunity on the one hand and mindless greed on the other? Is there no wild place on this earth left for me? As Edie and Alan snarled at each other and some of the others looked ready to get up and leave, Sean himself prepared to flee through the empty doorway.

But just as braced himself to stand, he looked again and there Carla stood, tall and lovely, as though she'd stepped through an invisible wall. He couldn't see her face because it was lit from behind, but he knew her raven, windblown hair, and her sharp, graceful frame and the way she stood leaning slightly, her hand on the doorframe. His breath caught and his heart actually slowed, as he felt a calmness steal over him even though every cell in his body hummed with fearsome desire.

As she stepped into the light, she saw her khakis were torn and scuffed and her eyes were wild. She slid gracefully along the wall, as a large black fly buzzed after her. She swiftly took the chair he'd saved for her. She was breathing heavily.

"How's it going?" she mouthed.

"You hear about Dr. Durant?" She nodded impatiently—that could wait. What about now? Sean rolled his eyes and waved his hand at the bullshit steaming behind him as Edie openly accused Alan Frederickson of being naïve. "They'll tear into you like a bear!" she sneered, clearly enjoying the idea. Even her clique looked embarrassed.

"We're screwed!" Sean whispered to Carla.

"Go all in!" she hissed. "Lose big now, win bigger later."

He jabbed his thumb at Edie making a face: Who's gonna follow her?

"Sean, they'll follow you!" Carla said this right out loud, her gray eyes sultry from under her jet black brows. She tapped his arm. A delicious shock ran through him.

"Excuse me!" Edie cut in. "Do you have something you'd like to share?"

Edie's and Carla's eyes locked together across the room, lightning swords clashing in space. Oh-oh, Sean thought. Cat fight!

But it was Edie who blinked as her dark face actually seemed to pale. Carla had made the space for Sean, and he jumped right in.

"Y-yeah, yeah, I do." He stood up again. "I got a lot to say."

Edie attempted to recover her authority by shoving a spiral notebook at him: "You can be secretary."

Sean tossed it back to her: "No, that's your job."

"Edie, let him speak," Chloe Byrne's voice crackled like wind-blown fall leaves. "He's done the hauling so far."

Sean looked into Carla's eyes one more time for the fire he needed. He loved her and now that she was here, that love would inspire him. He turned back to his audience, his head cool and clear as if he were poised to fly from the rim of a great cliff.

"Edie's basically right." Speak from the diaphragm! "Because as things stand now, our chances of winning this fight are zip."

The more he stumbled on, the more he relaxed. His voice caught, cracked and squeaked, but he kept going, telling of one battle he'd won and another one he'd lost. Sure, Edie and Alan knew how things worked around here, but he knew the Enemy. Sierra Future and Getgo had no good faith to negotiate with. Getgo had been privatizing the West for years. They were like gangsters who'd taken over the government to legalize their crimes. Their favorite tactic was to negotiate to buy time while they destroyed their opponents by other means. They'd already been secretly at work in Monitor County for awhile; those "new families" moving in the last few years were Getgo moles, hired to buy property cheap, then flip it to Getgo's front, Sierra Future, and drive up prices.

Getgo had invaded other places: Yellowstone, Yosemite and Grand Teton. Their defeats were few, their victories absolute, thanks to smartly purchased politicians in Sacramento and Washington, D.C. They were out for every blade of grass, every flower, rock, stream, canyon, valley, and mountain. They were totalists, monopolists, visionary empire builders who played winner take all. What weapons did Monitor County's citizens have to fight with? Only their voices, their hearts, their love for this land, and for these mountains.

"Our only chance is to throw every rock and stick we got!"

They couldn't expect much from the outside world; definitely not the very government that was selling off public lands to corporations like Getgo to pay the public debt that had been run up with the connivance of those very corporations. "They drowned the baby by bankrupting it, all for their vision of freedom, the freedom of the bully, the liberty of the tyrant."

Even the NGOs couldn't help much. Next to Getgo, they had no pockets and a zillion other fires to stamp out all over this overheating world. This little band in this small room in a tiny mountain village stood alone.

"Think of it like John Wayne at the Alamo! Our only real chance is to fight harder and louder than anyone else. Lose with a bang, not a whimper. Go down with our flags flying. We'll inspire other communities to fight on. They may win, but it'll be so costly, so public, that the next community they try to bully and bribe will be ready for 'em and may be the one that stop's 'em dead. We'll inspire others to fight on for what's wild in America and in the world …that's uh, thank you."

He collapsed in his chair, shaking, exhausted. He saw that sweet tasting spliff waiting for him by his futon in his little house, like a faithful dog.

Everyone clapped, even Edie Ferrand who banged her hands together like two boards, her eyes ablaze. Carla gave him a tasty wink and for the first time ever, a smile that didn't look forced. This triumph was as sweet as the first time he climbed El Capitan. Even the fly sitting on the wall next to Carla hopped in the air as if going "Woo-hoo! Go Sean!"

A fine speech was only the start. He heaved a big sigh and gave a nervous laugh:

"Okay, everybody, time for a big heaping bowl of nuts and bolts."

"The sausage making part," Alan chuckled. He pointed out that Sean's viewpoint regarding outside help wasn't entirely bleak. There were a handful of sympathizers he knew in Sacramento and Washington. Chloe Byrne said she'd get in touch with a few former residents, descendants of Monitor County's first families, who might be willing to return to fight for the old homestead. Edie grumpily offered the use of her desktop Macs and media contacts, while Alan seconded with his own list. While coordinating their efforts, Sean would contact an old college buddy, fellow climber, and former government investigator, Johnny Pyle, who was now an attorney specializing in white-collar crime and corporate fraud and worked on the side as a private snoop: "He'll dig up the nasty stuff about Getgo and Bob Garner. Garner especially. Guys like him leave slime everywhere. Maybe we'll send him out in handcuffs! And we've got Klaus Bartok, too."

Nobody reacted to this name drop, except for Chloe who stiffened in her chair as though chilled. Uh-oh. Buzz kill. He hurried on, hoping everyone would forget whatever faux pas he'd made.

"I lied in there," he later told Carla as they stood together by Sean's Jeep. Carla seemed different from how she'd been just a few days ago, when she was sinking slowly into frailty. Tonight, she was strong and full of life. He'd never wanted her—or any woman—so much as this one. She was the perfection that always seemed be hiding just beyond the face of the common world.

"Ab-bout my political experience. I've just been a sideliner until now."

"You've united them. You've got them believing in themselves and fighting back. That's everything."

She turned away toward her Jeep parked nearby. "Say, are you alright? I mean, I thought you quit driving. You look like you'd just hiked over from Sacramento."

"I'm fine."

"But—"

"It was a misdiagnosis. Whatever it was, it's gone away."

"Oh." Sean didn't know much about her disease, but it sounded funny. "Does that mean you're staying? I mean you and Dave?"

"Mr. Bartok wants us both here. He's sorry he couldn't make it but he has our back. He's happy with your efforts. He wants to win."

"That's great! That's so cool!"

Then another miracle happened, the kind that the shy, lonely and insecure believe will never come true and when it does, it still feels like a dream.

Carla came back and kissed him tenderly, wrapping his lanky body in her arms. He felt the fullness of her breasts, like a message, her cool lips sweet, gentle but swelling with promise. She smelled of fresh pine air and high mountains.

"You were right," she said. "I'm staying and fighting. We're gonna win, aren't we?" She smiled as she brushed his cheek and then turned away.

"Oh yeah, we're so gonna win." Trying to hide his shaking only made Sean shake harder.

With deer-like grace, her hips swinging, Carla strode to her Jeep, looking off to the right. Sean followed her gaze to where a large bat was hanging from the dead branch of a cottonwood. At least that's what it looked at first because instantly, the creature swung up like a gymnast on a parallel bar to a standing position and—well, seemed to melt into the night.

Whatever. It was late. He was tired and prone to see things, especially around here. You could see wonderful, weird things every day and every night in this part of the world—especially at night. That was Monitor County. That's what made it so worth fighting for.

He licked his lips, sweet with Carla's perfume, on the drive home, the swell of her breasts still palpable. When he got home, he glanced at the joint by his bed, thought about how ugly it looked and how it would cloud this ecstatic moment, turn his joy into a fuzzy dream that he might wake up not believing in.

That night, for the first time in many weeks, Sean went to bed sober. And he dreamed. In the dream, the fly at the meeting morphed into the bat in the parking lot; and the bat became an owl who guided his Jeep safely home. In his room, it transformed into a dapper, striped-jacketed bee that landed lightly on his forearm, waved one of its tiny forelegs, and actually winked at him with one of its many eyes, a tiny blue flash.

Hey there, clever, handsome bee! Sean thought sleepily as it gently inserted its stinger; and then he dreamed that he was a pollen-dusted flower, his petals opening and blooming with unstoppable joy.

CHAPTER 19

Here Comes Mr. Wrinkles

Henry West leapt from his chair and punched the air when word of Leo Durant's death came over Bob Garner's speakerphone, delivered by Booby Alban-easy's rasping chirp as they sat in the basement of Bob Garner's manse. He couldn't help it; bad news for others was often good news to Henry, especially when it concerned the deaths of cocksucking assholes like Leo Durant.

"Yes!" As a wave of dizziness swept over him, Henry sat back down and put his arm on Garner's desk to steady his spinning brain. But he was still happy. Dr. Durant, or "Dr. Turdhead," was high on Henry's lovingly kept Hate List. He'd tended Henry's extended family when he first arrived in the area thirty years ago. He played the Good Wise White Coat at first, all tender touch and soft words. But once more and more outsiders, outsiders packing big wallets, moved in and both Henry's Mama and Irish-German Papa had died, well, the old fuck knew Henry and his Washoe relatives no more: I got real patients, white patients, paying patients and well, I'm only gonna see you tree niggers at my cheap-ass county health service. Of course, Turdhead didn't say that, but his attitude was as obvious as runny shit in a glass.

Henry looked up to see stern shadows darkening Mr. Garner's and Petey's faces. Petey, seated at one of the computers, darted another poisoned look at him. Henry retorted by pointing at his groin with his left hand and moving the right toward his mouth in a sucking motion. Bob Garner heaved a pissed-off sigh and pawed at the pile of paper containing the speech that Henry was supposed to deliver next Tuesday night at the commission meeting. Then he massaged his forehead: another of his headaches was smoldering. Soon, he'd be painting his noggin with HeadOn or popping his pills. Or maybe call naptime, which meant work would end a little early and Henry could start drinking.

Petey had been working on the PowerPoint presentation for one of the main portions of the Sierra Future Project. Henry had never seen a PowerPoint presentation before; its zooming, sweeping images made his head whirl and stomach yaw, but he managed to hide his discomfort by looking at an empty space a foot or so to the right of the screen. Among other stuff, the presentation featured a complete teardown and rebuild of Byrneville village into what looked like an old cowboy movie set, except it'd be all "green" with solar and wind power, electric cars and stuff. These guys thought big.

So what was their problem? Just yesterday, Monday, they treated Dr. Turdhead like he was the only thing that was standing in the way of everything. He had something they wanted: that fine house on that fine piece of land up near the crest for their fancy hotel. Now he was out of the way, but their faces said they'd lost the whole fucking thing.

Hell, they all but ran the bastard's ass up the flagpole and spun him on it. They probably gave him a stroke, pissed him off enough to kill him!

The Sierra Real Estate office had been dark and stuffy that morning. Henry was alright with hanging there because he could sneak peeks at Booby's big boobies while she yakked business with Bob and Petey. Business, especially real estate business, bored Henry shitless, even with what Bob Garner was paying him. While they talked, his mind wandered between dreams of Booby's tits swinging free of her barely-there bra and the beer and tequila waiting like good dogs at the cottage. Fuck all the boring business shit.

Just before eleven, Bob Garner gave Henry a poke and pointed at the aqua plastic chair to the right of the door: "Just sit right there." Five minutes later in walked Dr. Turdhead, slipping off his A's ball cap, his gray hair sticking out like a raggedy halo around his shiny scalp. He didn't see Henry sitting behind the door. Henry started getting an idea of what Bob Garner was up to, placing him by the exit like that.

Bob Garner greeted Turdhead with his phony drawl and waved him into a seat at the rear left corner of the desk, right next to Booby, who strategically set her spectacular balcony right on the desk like she was the star of a beer commercial: "If you give us your property, I'll let you play with my titties!"

Bob Garner sat directly between Henry and Durant, so they couldn't see each other. Henry could only see the old man's brown checkered slacks, skinny white ankles, sagging white socks, and brown loafers. Petey leaned against the other side of the door from Henry, his muscular arms folded. Henry recognized the setup from his brief criminal career: "You're goin' nowhere asshole, 'til we hear 'yes'!"

By noon, they'd gotten exactly to nowhere. Bob Garner offered Durant more money than God, but the old quack sneered at every offer, saying "no" a dozen different ways. The property was his; he was hanging on to it, gonna leave it to his three children. He used show-off words like "legacy." No way would he sell his "legacy" to "outsiders" who didn't appreciate the land and what it meant to those who'd lived here.

Fuckin' hi-lar-ee-us. Durant himself was an outsider, one of them who'd made Henry and his mother's people outsiders on their own land, just like the Byrnes, the Sulzbergers, and the Bartoks before him.

Durant's place up above Alpine Canyon had been sacred Washoe ground since Creation before the whites stole it. Henry's Washoe Gramma told stories about how the whites came in the 1850s, with their mines, their cattle, and finally the Basque sheepherders and how all of 'em wound up fighting over it. A hundred years ago, as Gramma told it, the battle ended when some white-faced, blue-eyed demon swept in with a curse that finally chased away everyone, including the last of the nearly forgotten Washoe spirits.

That was a myth, a sideways story of telling about the white man's crimes. It all boiled down to white Eur-o-pee-ons with their bigger guns, saying "It ain't yours no more." You didn't need no bullshit ghost stories to get that!

Leo Durant was just another racist asshole who thought himself a god, living up there on the crest while the thin air sucked the sense out his brain cells. He was finally getting his, but he was too old and stubborn to know it.

The more the old man dug in, the more Bob Garner sweetened the pot. The doc was getting up there in years; the commute on that mountain road down to his Osgood office must be getting hard. Sierra would not only pay him a good price, they'd give him the down payment on any property in the Carson Valley he wanted; he could walk to his office every day and with the price of gas and all.

They would "respect" the land, Garner said. Turdhead's house and the Quonset hut where he'd been seeing patients from the ski resorts and remote parts of the county for thirty years would remain. They simply wanted to attach a small, exclusive hotel onto the house and open a restaurant in the hut, all with the latest "green" technology. It'd be an experiment for the future. They'd even name it after him, a monument to his years of service to the county; to his role in its history. Sheesh! Henry thought. These guys'll say anything.

Durant batted every idea away. He seemed to enjoy coming up with new cracker-barrel ways to say "no." "Like a hen in a butcher shop, I'll say yes" was one. Both men were competing to see who could come up with new ways to "talk country," though the both of them were city boys down to their ass hairs.

"Doc, it's not gonna be Six Flags! I warn ya, the guvmint ain't in the buyin' market no more, with the deficit and all. In fact," Bob jabbed his finger, "they've started unloadin' their property to us, cheap. We already got most of it up here." He spread his long arms: "A big wave's comin', Doc. You'd better hop on your board now."

It was getting late. The afternoon sun burned through the window. Bob Garner's shoulders sagged and he started rubbing his temples.

He had one more gag: just when Henry thought Garner was going to give it up, the boss shuffled his plastic chair a little to the right and Henry West and Leo Durant found themselves face-to-face, man-to-man.

Henry understood then what he had to do. It wasn't in the job description, but what the fuck. He leaned forward, hunched his shoulders, narrowed his brown eyes, curled his hands on his big thighs into fists, and lifted a corner of his thin mouth, showing a sliver of yellow teeth. All that was missing was a nice fat bad guy's mustache.

Mr. Garner glanced behind him at Henry, a smile lifting his beard. But wouldn't ya know it, old Leo just got madder! He stood up shaking, pointing at Bob Garner, waving his wattles, blood all but bursting out his skin pores.

"You go screw yourselves!" he spluttered. "You think you can intimidate me!?" Then he turned on Booby, who threw a hand over her tits to protect them from Leo's spittle. "And you can screw yourself, too, Miz Albanese, if this is how you treat the folks up here who've been doing business with you all these years! If I ever was to sell my place—and I for sure won't now—it won't be through you! And I'll fix my will so my kids won't do business with you either. Ever!"

As he marched out, he shot defiant dirty looks at both Henry and Petey, daring them to stop him. Henry did nothing, because, well, he hadn't been told to. He was relieved to find out Bob Garner didn't expect it, either: "Nice going with the Tony Soprano thing there, Henry," was all he said.

Not long after, the door opened again while Henry was getting a drink of water at the sink. Henry turned, saw a tall thin black shadow with a white face, spun around and spat the water back in the sink and bent over it shaking.

Fuck me, it's him!

Creepy old Klaus Bartok, his face like wet, crumbling newspaper, leaning on his wooden stick, tottered into the office as Petey closed the door behind him.

Here comes Mr. Wrinkles, Henry sneered to himself as nausea haunted the back of this throat. This was the closest Henry had never been to Bartok: Thank God, he wore dark glasses to hide his eyes. Henry hated the way old people's eyes looked like monster eyes staring from horrid red caves. Bartok smelled dead, too, as if he'd forgotten he died.

Henry couldn't take it. He excused himself and hurried into the tiny bathroom to dry heave. When he came out, Petey threw him a look, but Bob Garner didn't seem to need the bad-guy-by-the-door act. So Henry stayed in the farthest, darkest corner, over by the sink, pretending to wash his hands, pretending he was thirsty, whatever he could to stay as far from Bartok as possible. Bartok looked like a mouth-shaped sliver of black space that would chomp your hand off if you stuck it in there. Henry pictured the old man laughing his head off while poor Henry ran around screaming, blood squirting from a bloody stump.

So he likes the smell of his own rot does he? I'll give him a smell!

Henry stood at the sink, his back to the room. "Fuck you!" he whispered as he farted another big one in a series of popping, moist, smoky bubbles. He took a deep breath to inhale the aroma he knew would be wafting over to float right up the old man's snobby nose; yeah, let Garner get pissed off.

Instead Henry inhaled the fragrance of roses, moist, fresh, per-fumey, like the roses at his Mama's funeral. He dashed into the bathroom and heaved again.

When he came out, the old man was heading toward the door, his stick thumping softly on the floor. Henry could've sworn the old buzzard winked at him from behind his sunglasses, as if to say: "Yes, go make your farts. I shall make you smell roses!"

Petey slammed his hand on the desk, stopping Henry's train of thought, bringing him back to where he was, in Garner's basement: "Home office will not like this!"

Bob Garner reached for the HeadOn: "Nope."

"What's the problem?" Henry asked. "Durant's out of the way, ain't he?"

Petey hissed at him to shut up, but Bob Garner answered the question.

"I think he was ready to cave. You didn't see it, but I did. The more stubborn sellers sometimes throw a fit before they sell. That way they can tell themselves they fought as hard as they could so they don't feel seller's remorse.

"Now Leo may be gone, but his estate isn't. It's hard enough dealing with one seller, but now we have three heirs to negotiate with. The estate could be in probate for months, years maybe, especially if the heirs start squabbling with each other. Week after next, we'll get the green light from the county commission and we're going to commence construction on that site first, but if we don't have it here"—he jabbed a finger into his right palm— "we can't. Construction on the rest won't be ready to roll for another month or so."

Henry could still smell his rose-tainted farts and how Klaus Bartok had winked at him. The old man owned Alpine Canyon. "What about Count Klaus?" He felt ill at ease, as though saying "Bartok" would conjure him out of thin air, right there in the basement. Henry had heard the old man's name blown like black foul smoke among his Washo relations ever since he was a little boy. Klaus Bar-TOK: an ugly name, like the cocking of a pistol or repeating rifle, that mechanical sound of approaching death heard in a certain kind of movie.

Bob and Petey glanced at each other. Petey gave a knowing laugh.

"No problems there," Bob rolled the HeadOn across his forehead. He pointed at the speech they'd been working on all afternoon. It was getting toward dusk now. Henry felt his nerves grow thirsty. Bob Garner sensed his thirst and laughed, slapping his hand on the pages of Henry's speech:

"Once more, Henry, once more."

....

CHAPTER 20

The Woman in the Corner

Whenever Dave Sutton paid a house call on Chloe Byrne, he always found her waiting in her bedroom, in her bed, in the dark, the shades down.

"You're late," she said with a forgiving smile. He apologized as he turned to close the door behind him. Virginia Byrne stood watching from the hallway, nervously gritting her teeth as though words were damming up in her mouth.

"Can we have a little light in here?" Dave asked, as he always did.

"Oh, if you must," Chloe said with a playfully plaintive sigh, as she always did.

Dave raised the shades to let in the perfect light of another perfect Monitor County day. Miles to the northwest, outside Chloe's bedroom window, Dragon's Ark stood in severe majesty against a sky lightly spread with thin soft clouds. On most days, he stopped to admire it, but this afternoon he was in a hurry. He had an appointment with Leo Durant's kids up at the house on the crest around two o'clock. It was past twelve-thirty.

Chloe Byrne became Dave Sutton's second patient shortly after the Suttons moved to the county. Leo Durant had gone on vacation the day after recommending aspirin, and no alcohol, for some pains Chloe was experiencing "down there." Chloe murmured misgivings to Marissa King who pointed her to that new young doc for whom the Kings had already dumped Leo. The young physician, "So-o handsome, so-o charming!" asked the delicate questions in the most polite way and then called for tests. The tumors turned out benign but Dr. Durant lost another patient anyway.

Chloe looked away and slyly winked: "If this is what it takes to get a man in my bedroom nowadays ..."

Dave laughed then followed up with twenty minutes of questions and polite poking and prodding. At the end, he declared that there wasn't a thing wrong with her that couldn't be explained by ninety-three birthdays. "Still fit as a Stradivarius."

Chloe buttoned her blouse, her chin up: "And fit for battle until those Sierra Future bandits skedaddle out of here." She sneered in the direction of the living room. "If it wasn't for me, she'd sell right out to 'em." She raised her voice, as though hoping Virginia had her ear to the door. "I hear your hands are full these days, young man."

Dave grunted as he wearily folded the stethoscope into his bag. He glimpsed the Korbel bottle and an old jelly jar gleaming side by side under the bedside table, where they always were.

"Poor Leo. Are you taking his practice? No, you can't leave us now. We need you. We need more humans. That lovely wife of yours, too."

He remembered Carla's gymnastics from the other morning ... that thumping shadow spinning down the hallway with impossible speed and strength: "Yeah."

"She was at the meeting Tuesday night."

"Meeting?" He laughed, chagrined. "I haven't had time to think about Sierra Future."

"Is she feeling better? She looked liked she'd been running all day. I so miss that energy!"

Dave shrugged. Since Tuesday, he'd woken up every morning to find her sitting on the bed, humming as dawn rose outside, singing that strange grieving song.

"She almost had a showdown with Edie Ferrand. My, the claws were out! Good thing Sean Temkin took charge. Oh, don't fret if you don't have time. She'll be a fine proxy for you! You're both lucky to have each other. Is she working? It would be so nice to see her take the wheel of the county bus again. She was such a good driver."

As he stood up to leave, he remembered how all those twenty-dollar bills had emerged from Carla's pocket. He'd forgotten to ask her about it. What he said next to Chloe seemed harmless: "She was driving Klaus Bartok around the other day."

"Oh?" Chloe cried out, her face actually flinching as though slapped by an invisible hand. Her healthy pink skin turned dead white. She shook her head and plucked nervously at the coverlet.

"You okay?" Dave put his bag down on the bed and reached out for her.

"I'm fine." She groaned. "I guess someone had to take poor Annie's place." She got out of bed and yanked the window shade down as though a peeper might at the window. She remained there, in the dim light, staring into the shade.

"I don't know about that," Dave shrugged. "I think it was just a one-time favor."

"I don't like the Ark," she murmured. "It reminds me of a ruin. Bartok's castle. He can see—I sometimes think he can see everywhere from up there, even into our souls. That's why I keep the shades pulled. I thought he'd hire another outsider. Not one of us. And not her. Too much spirit for him. Are you religious?"

Dave winced. His policy toward religion was don't ask, don't tell. A patient's faith was none of his business and Dave's own attitude toward the issue was, therefore, none of theirs. He always strove to care for the whole patient, but religion was one place he refused to go.

"Do you believe in anything beyond what you see?"

"I—uh—see what's wrong with my patients. I focus on that."

She shrugged, resigned to his polite evasion: "Your labs, tests and things tell you what you need to know. Here's something they won't tell you: that man is evil. Even the sound of his name makes me shudder, like a gun being cocked, like someone's going to die." Her voice became urgent. "You get Carla away from him right now. I mean it. Completely. If we didn't need you here so much, if I didn't think so much of you, I'd tell you to move away. Right this instant ...but you've fallen too much in love with this place. This land can be like a bad marriage: too beautiful to leave."

"Living here hasn't done you any harm," Dave argued politely, unnerved by how she stood there in the corner by the window, her back to him, her voice sounding flat and disembodied.

"Because I'm a Byrne. I'm stubborn. We were here first: Byrnes, Schumachers, Ferrands, Sulzbergers. We dug the mines, cut the forests, built the towns, the roads, and the dams. The Washoe have their sad story. The Basques, too, but so do we. We poured our blood into this. Many of us died. Then he comes flying in and enjoys the fruits. He didn't sacrifice a thing. Not even his time." Then she said, "I'd like a drink, please."

Dave retrieved the Korbel and the jelly jar from under the bedside table and poured her a finger's worth. Her face in the corner, she took it without looking at him.

"That man will drive you to more than drink. Before I started drinking every night, years ago, he'd—I'd have awful dreams about him, as if something were trying to drive me out of here. You know how hard it is to buy alcohol around here. We hardly have any drug problems. That's his doing. Most communities would be grateful, but it's not for our benefit. It's for his. The further you and Carla stay away from him, the better. He'll hurt her. He'll hurt you."

Dave had never seen Chloe act like this. As he wondered whether dementia was showing its head, he felt impelled to defend Bartok: "I guess he'll be a big ally against Sierra Future."

Chloe waved her hand and snorted: "Some allies are not worth having."

"Look, I'll give you this: I don't like what I've seen of the gentleman either. I promise I'll mention it to Carla, okay? I'm sure it was just a one-time favor."

"One favor too many. Oh dear," she sighed, as though waking up to self-awareness. "I was once called a fool. Now they can call me an old fool."

He left her there, in the dark, facing the corner by the window.

Virginia Byrne appeared at his shoulder as Dave was letting himself out, an old manila folder in her hand. The tab was marked "Chloe" in faded pencil.

"I'm sorry," Virginia stammered tightly. "Dr. Sutton, please don't take what she says seriously. She's been a little off all her life. When I was ten, her brother, my father, had her committed." She blushed and fanned the folder at him. "Here, this explains it. It's not long. It might help you to understand. Do you have some time? Here, have a seat in the living room. Would you like some wine? No? Okay, tea then."

It was past one and Leo's family might be gone already. He'd hoped to gain access to Leo's office to review his files and maybe discuss the family's plans for the practice—this was happening so suddenly, so fast, but he had to jump now.

Still, Chloe's file might clear up a few things. He always enjoyed these house calls—they were much like the future he'd dreamed for himself—but the strange scene in the bedroom made him feel uneasy. Another medical opinion, even a dated one, might offer perspective, an idea of how to help.

The living room was small and cozy: knick-knacks, sepia-toned family photos, flowered prints, small shelves of books, most of them about California pioneers. He sat on a deep, gold-flowered upholstered couch, glanced out the picture window behind him. To the north, he could see across Byrneville Creek and felt an odd relief that from here the Ark was invisible.

The file contained four documents, faded typewritten ditto copies of copies. The first was a one-page, two-paragraph Order of Commitment, dated July 29, 1960, signed by Judge Paul Sulzberger of Monitor County Court. Attached to it was a certified letter signed by a Dr. Harry McGee, M.D. of South Lake Tahoe, recommending the commitment of Chloe Clarisse Byrne, 42, of Byrneville to the California State Institute of Mental Health in Sacramento for a period of not less than six months.

"Miss Byrne is a 42 y.o. white female who appeared in general good health when she appeared in my office on July 23, 1960," McGee's report said. "She was accompanied by her brother John Byrne and his wife, Alma, of Byrneville. They reported that during the previous two weeks, Miss Byrne has been making public accusations against Klaus Bartok Sr., a Monitor County resident aged about 90 years, and his son Klaus Bartok II, age about 50. Miss Byrne had been briefly employed that spring as a personal secretary and chauffeur to the senior Bartok. Said employment was terminated over unpaid wages and what Miss Byrne claimed were unreasonable demands made by Mr. Bartok.

"Starting in early June, Miss Byrne declared to several people in the Byrneville area, including her brother and his wife, that in reality, said Mr. Bartok was, in fact, a 'vampire.' And that Mr. Bartok survived by secretly drinking the blood of various Monitor County citizens and vacationers, including campers, hikers, fishermen, skiers, and hunters. She further asserted that Mr. Bartok and his son, Klaus Bartok II were, in fact, one and the same person.

"Miss Byrne's accusations against the Bartok family have been the source of significant stress and embarrassment to Miss Byrne's family, who are one of Monitor County's most prominent families. At one point, they claimed, Miss Byrne attacked the younger Bartok with a crucifix and holy water late one night when he attended the July 4th county picnic. On another occasion, she was pulled over for speeding while driving to Mr. Bartok Sr.'s residence, located in Alpine Canyon. The arresting officer found the back seat of her car loaded with wooden stakes and various religious accoutrements. She was found to be deeply intoxicated, which led to a year-long suspension of her driver's license.

"One week ago, on July 22, 1960, Miss Byrne was arrested by Monitor County police for attempted assault on the person of Mr. Bartok Sr. in Byrneville. Only the presence of Mr. Bartok Sr.'s chauffeur, a certain Ralph Howard, of Douglas County, Nevada, prevented serious injury. She was, again, determined to be severely impaired by alcohol.

"Extensive questioning of Miss Byrne by the undersigned reveals these delusions regarding the Bartok family to be elaborate and deeply rooted. She states—and her brother and sister agree with this claim—that her heavy drinking only started after the termination of her employment with Mr. Bartok Sr. when she learned that Mr. Bartok would not drink the blood of those who were intoxicated. 'The world would be a lot safer,' she stated, 'if everyone got drunk.'

"Regarding her claim that Bartok Sr. and Jr. were both one and the same person, I asked how Mr. Bartok could be both 50 and 90 years old. Miss Byrne claimed that the alleged disparity in appearance was due to sunlight. Mr. Bartok, 'like all vampires,' was allergic to sunlight, so, during the day, he appeared as an old man. But right at nightfall, the allergic reaction passed, allowing the gentleman to grow young and 'sail among the peaks and the stars as he wished,' in her words 'like a king.' She claimed that Mr. Bartok could turn himself into many kinds of nocturnal animals. 'Even things you didn't know existed,' was one of the more extravagant claims. That he could become 'the night's angel made of fire and water' and no one could stop him 'all through the night.'

"When pressed as to how she knew of this, Miss Byrne exhibited signs of hysteria, screaming 'Because I saw it! He showed me!' She was then forcibly sedated.

"When asked why, if Mr. Bartok was, indeed, drinking human blood, his so-called 'victims' did not also all turn into 'vampires' as elucidated in various myths, Miss Byrne firmly stated that could only happen if Mr. Bartok fed his victims enough of his own blood to 'change them' as she put it. He never allowed them to drink enough to allow this to happen. Mr. Bartok decided who would become a 'vampire' and who would not.

"I also queried if this 'vampire' left any marks on the throats of his victims, as alleged in these myths. Miss Byrne claimed that Mr. Bartok was a 'super intelligent monster' and could drink blood leaving only 'sweet wonderful dreams,' a sore on the arm or throat in the morning, and symptoms of anemia that would pass quickly.

"Miss Byrne then claimed that Bartok had given her a 'taste of his blood' and that it had a powerful stimulating effect on her mind and body. It did not taste like normal blood at all, but like 'chocolaty syrup.' It made her feel lighter and stronger 'like I could fly too.' Miss Byrne stated that, after that taste, the world looked different; she could see at night and 'it's more beautiful than the day. Daylight makes everything look dry, dead, and ugly.'

"She went on to claim that Mr. Bartok made promises that he would teach her to become a 'child of the night' as he was, a process that would take years, if she continued working for him as a personal assistant. But she found the proposal frightening and disgusting and refused the offer. At that point, she terminated her employment, despite his alleged threats that if that she attempted to reveal his true nature, no one would believe her and that she would be labeled insane. (It was at this point that Miss Byrne exhibited what would be the first of several breakdowns requiring sedation as witnessed by the undersigned.)

"Despite the medical consensus that paranoid schizophrenia is the product of neuroses rooted in childhood trauma, Miss Byrne's case shows at least two unique factors:

Her hallucinations are, overall, more highly structured and coherent than is the case with most other episodes of this type; while there are inherent contradictions within the delusions, they lack the element of random association often associated with schizophrenics; there is an internal logic, though it is bizarre and unrooted from reality.

The 'flat affect' consistently noted in extreme schizophrenic personalities is absent here, which would suggest this is an isolated psychotic episode, perhaps brought on by stress factors, such as menopause. Miss Byrne, a spinster, presents as highly articulate, animated and emotional. The affect is one of extreme anger, indignation towards the Bartoks and even shame and embarrassment toward herself. She repeatedly states, "I know it sounds crazy, but it's true.' For someone expressing these delusions, she is unusually self-aware and concerned about her state of mind. This suggests a deep neuroses centering on other issues separate from the old gentleman, perhaps a projection of deep parental conflicts upon the Bartoks.

"Regarding Mr. Bartok, Miss Byrne's brother and sister-in-law both state that while both Bartok Sr. and Jr. are considered eccentrics, they have lived peaceably for many years in Monitor County and, of course, eccentrics are by no means uncommon among country folk.

"Due to the extreme instability of Miss Byrne's emotional state, the intensity of her delusions, her excess indulgence in alcohol, and her apparent capacity for antisocial activity that makes her a danger both to herself and others in the community, it is strongly recommended that Miss Chloe Byrne be committed to a state mental institution for a period of not less than six months. At the end of this period, her case may be reviewed again and a decision on either release or further commitment can be made then."

The other documents included a letter from John and Alma Byrne confirming Dr. McGee's account of the matter and passionately asserting their love and concern for John's sister and a request that the Judge rule in favor of Dr. McGee. There was no letter from Chloe, or any documentation in her defense.

The last document was a letter from Dr. McGee to Judge Sulzberger, dated January 27, 1961, six months after Chloe's commitment. It pronounced the treatment successful and Chloe Byrne to be cured.

"Overall, Chloe responded extremely well to treatment. The combination of tranquilizers and electroshock therapy served to both calm her nerves and, apparently, erase certain delusions from her mind. However, according to the physician in charge of Miss Byrne's case at the asylum, Dr. Herbert Wagner, her analysis sessions were somewhat less successful. While Miss Byrne completely rejected the symptomatic delusions regarding the Bartoks ('I feel so silly! I don't what made me think such ridiculous things!'), she was not forthcoming concerning the true origins of these fantasies. She strenuously denied any history of family abuse, as did other members of her family when interviewed. These denials, of course, are grounds in themselves for suspicion.

"However, once settled in, Miss Byrne proved herself to be a completely cooperative patient who became quite popular among the residents and staff. On this basis, I hereby recommend Miss Chloe Byrne's immediate release into the care of her family and community."

Virginia came into the living room, hopeful and anxious, a torn tissue in her hand. Dave stood up and held the file out to her: "Is this all you have? Is there more?"

"No," Virginia stammered, "that was all." Dave dropped the file on the coffee table next to the cup of cold tea.

"Virginia, those documents are fifty years old and have no bearing, as far as I can see, on the current state of your aunt's health, mental or otherwise." As he let himself out, he turned to take one more shot: "What's more, if I even think you're abusing that woman in any way whatsoever, I'll have you flying out of here so fast, you'll think you've grown feathers. I hope I've made myself clear."

Dave didn't cool down until he was halfway up the hill to the Durants. Maybe he had overreacted, but Virginia's transparent scheme to have her aunt put away was, to put it kindly, grossly premature, and clumsily sinister. He was maybe taking it a little personally, he admitted to himself. His "Male Parent" (as Dave called him) had successfully schemed to have his own mother committed while family and friends helplessly wrung their hands. Dave relished the chance to put a stop to a similar injustice. He pleasurably imagined Virginia toppling back like a tree as he shut the door in her face. Carla would have loved it.

Still, the file provided an interesting, if distorted, peek into Chloe's past and the dark age of psychiatry: the Viennese take on schizophrenia, the ease with which people could be committed to mental institutions, and the nearly blithe application of electroshock therapy. Poor Chloe had known the worst of the old ways.

Delusions aside though, half a century ago, Chloe Byrne had indeed suffered mistreatment by the Bartok clan; cruelly human and explainable. Nowadays, they'd call it sexual harassment. Back then, the term wasn't known, and the accusation disbelieved. It might very well have been that Klaus the Younger had sexually assaulted Chloe, while the late Klaus the Elder stood by. Afterward, post-traumatic stress had kicked in, followed by Chloe's breakdown and that weird tale she'd constructed in her mind to help her cope with the ugly, humiliating reality.

The Bartoks must have known they'd dodged a bullet, which was why they'd hired a male, that Ralph Howard, to draw off suspicion. (And what became of him anyway?) By the time Annie Goodman arrived in the 1990s, time and mortality had promoted Klaus the Younger to Klaus the Last, with his sinister secrets safe.

Even though Klaus Jr. must have been in his eighties when he hired Annie, those perverse urges still smoldered. What hell did Annie suffer through all those years? Whatever it was, Carla wouldn't stand for it. The old bastard would have his hands full for sure. But still, there were better ways to keep money coming in. If she insisted on going back to work—that is, if she were truly capable of working—he had to get her in for more tests, first thing next week; he'd talk to her about it tonight or tomorrow. Maybe they could go for a hike somewhere this weekend, take Sunday off.

The highway suddenly banked steeply to the left. Leo Durant's forlorn mailbox looked like a tiny sliver against a wild purple sky. As Dave drove over the rim, the Sierra appeared below with shocking suddenness, afternoon thunderstorms piling up on its jagged summits. Dragon's Ark towered over the blue crevasse of Alpine Canyon. Dave hit the brakes as he gasped at the vertiginous grandeur before him.

No wonder Leo wouldn't sell, Dave thought, flushing with admiration and envy. I wouldn't sell either.

CHAPTER 21

Song to the Night

As Dave parked in front of the Quonset hut, he growled imprecations at the red Jaguar that sat in front of Leo's house alongside four other family sized vehicles, among them a green SUV. Two men leaned on the railing of the long, pine porch. Even at a distance, he could see Bob Garner's grin, bright as aluminum.

The wind carried the smell of approaching rain. Dave zipped up his jacket, tied his bush hat down, and took in the hallucinatory vista down the slope to his right. Dave loved high places, but the grand sweep to the south made his head swim unpleasantly.

"Doc Sutton!" Bob Garner grinned down, bundled by L.L Bean. Schlesinger leaned on the wall behind him, next to the door, holding up the house with his scowl. Dave glanced at the SUV where someone was dozing behind the wheel, face hidden by a ballcap.

Garner offered his hand. Dave shook it again without thinking and then stuck his hand in his pocket, washing it with the fabric. He stated his business; Garner replied that the Durants were inside "talking some stuff over. Glad you're pickin' up Leo's practice," he drawled unctuously. "We'll need ya." He nodded at the hut: They had plans for that space. "But I'm sure we'll find you a new office. Maybe a bigger one; how 'bout that?" He winked conspiratorially, like he already knew Dave would stay. It felt like everyone knew Dave would stay. Except Dave.

"That's nice." Even that bland reply felt like surrender.

"Glad to hear it," Garner nodded. Dave was about to say he didn't give two good goddamns what Garner was glad to hear when Karl Durant came out of the house in a t-shirt that indicated he'd long forgotten how cold it got up here. The pale skin of his thin arms bristled with goose-bumps, his eyes were swollen and red; Dave had hardly started telling Karl what he wanted when Karl tossed him the keys to the Quonset hut: "I don't see any problems about you taking the practice. None of us are in the medical biz."

So that's how it was: Leo's heirs thought of medicine as a "biz," a road to wealth. He jumped as three kids exploded from around the corner behind him, two giggling redheaded boys chased by an angry blond girl; they looked to be between ten and twelve. Laughing maniacally, the boys tore inside, slamming the door behind them. The girl stopped, baring her teeth: "Dad, are we going soon? It's cold and boring here."

Karl assured her they would. Then he thanked Dave and said they'd be in touch. Dave waved a hurried salute; as he turned away, Garner called out "See ya Tuesday night, Doc! Look forward to working with ya!"

Then Karl said, "We've made a decision."

Dave turned toward the hut to see storm clouds pouring over the Sierra crest, another big, bad beautiful one on its way. But he didn't enjoy the spectacle as much now and it bothered him. After all the trouble and struggles to stay here, he suddenly felt a confusing urge to go.

He wondered if, after thirty years of living at these stormy, lonely heights, day in, day out, Leo's mind had become starved by the thin air. Constant low oxygen levels might have led to hypoxia and the kind of hallucinations that could, for example, turn that black turkey vulture wheeling out of the canyon into a fire-breathing dragon, like Carla's "dragon," though she was only being whimsical. The brain could start firing with bad big ideas. Great heights, it was said, fed a tyrant's fancies. It was unfair say that all mountain lovers were closet fascists, dreaming they were kings, but it wasn't too hard to imagine yourself as Thor, spearing thunderbolts at the midgets below, unsplashed by the rivers of blood you sent flooding through the valleys. It likely was no coincidence that, like his neighbor down in the canyon, Klaus Bartok, Leo was abrasive and arrogant.

The Quonset hut sat at the foot of a park-like knoll of granite boulders that provided some shelter against the weather. A few whitebarks, stubby junipers, and splashes of red paintbrush hugged the base of the boulders on its leeward side.

The hut's interior was divided into a series of cubicles with false ceilings. The reception area was small and neat, desolate and dusty. Sheila Wilson said she only came up once a week or so to straighten up. Dave turned on the Commodore computer with its ancient UNIX system and 5-inch floppies, which contained only a few files.

The hut had been Leo's main office when he started. As Osgood grew and western Monitor County's population declined, he'd cut his office hours here to ski weekends on a contract with the Foxwood resort, Friday through Sunday. Of three other interior doors, the center one led to a small hallway with three small examining rooms and a door to the back. The one on the left opened to a small lab that included an X-ray machine from the 1960s in need of upgrading. The third door on the right led to Leo's private office.

The contents of the reception room filing cabinet revealed the spotty, narrow scope of Leo's practice here. Only the bottom two drawers were full. Most of the files were several years old. The vast majority were single-visit patients with the usual categories of ski injuries. A few were fatalities caused by skiing into a tree, over a cliff, or down a steep and rocky slope; people who had drastically underestimated the environment and overestimated themselves.

Many other patients seemed to share a similar cluster of symptoms: altitude sickness with flu-like symptoms of dizziness, lassitude, and weakness, especially in the morning. Leo's notes, written in a jagged, tight scrawl, indicated that each patient also presented with those localized sores on the throat and forearm that Dave himself had seen at the county clinic, and had suffered from himself from time to time. Some mentioned "bad dreams" but Durant didn't bother with these details and neither would Dave. He remembered how Foxwood advertised itself as a "family resort," which meant no alcohol was served, a wise policy at this altitude.

Durant wrote prescriptions for acetazolamide and antibiotics—too many of the latter because no one had a fever that would indicate an infection. He recommended that patients move to lower elevations as soon as possible to get more oxygen in their red blood cells. There were a couple mentions of "possible anemia." Naturally, since they were all weekenders and tourists, there was little follow-up.

As he closed the bottom drawer, he remembered what Leo had said about Annie Goodman, the last time they spoke: "She hasn't been my patient for years."

There were no files lying around the examining rooms or in the tiny lab closet where most of the equipment looked to be of 1970s vintage. When Dave unlocked the door to the back room and found the light switch, he said "Eureka!" as the fluorescents tinkled and sputtered on. He sneezed as he walked into a cloud of dust.

A big storage area took up the remainder of the hut. A wide side door to the left led outside. The poured-concrete floor, now cracked from the cold air and shifting ground, was mostly buried by dusty midden piles of ski equipment, long forgotten toys, snowmobiles, and at least two ATVs. Under the curved wall to the right stood high rusting metal shelves filled with crutches, bandages, braces, and other medical supplies, the proceeds from the sale of which Leo must have used to supplement his income. He left no nickel unturned.

Five tall gray filing cabinets towered front and center. In the first top drawer on the left, Dave found files that were tightly packed and neatly organized, first by year of the last appointment, then by patient name. Stopping for an occasional sneeze, Dave started with the first year of Leo's practice, then pawed through the subsequent years, looking for three labels marked "Bartok," "Ralph Howard," and "Goodman."

There was no "Bartok" and there was no "Howard," but when he got to 1990, he found the third name: "Goodman, Anne."

Annie Goodman had two files, one thin, one thick, wrapped together in fat, brittle rubber bands. The thin one had more to it than most of the other files, but still only covered three pages. As he took both files into Leo's private office, light shimmered in and a big boom rolled over the hut. He might be here for awhile.

He sat at Leo's desk. On impulse, he pulled open the right bottom drawer: "A-ha." He wasn't a Wild Turkey man, but it would do. Leo also kept a stash of white paper cups in the same drawer. Dave poured himself a finger's worth, then put his feet up and opened Annie's file.

Annie Goodman first presented herself over fifteen years ago to Dr. Leo Durant in this very office. The stamp page of the file gave her address as Dave and Carla's house on Walsh Hot Springs Road.

This twenty-eight-year-old female stood five feet ten and weighed a hundred and twenty pounds, a much thinner woman than the one Dave had seen accompanying Klaus Bartok. Her complexion was pale and her hair was thin, almost missing in places. Anorexic.

Then Dave choked and spat out the whiskey:

"Patient states that she has moved here to 'die surrounded by Nature's beauty.'"

Annie Goodman suffered from breast cancer that had metastasized into her lungs and liver. The second, fatter, file came from Sacramento County General's Cancer Treatment Center. According to the last note in this file, Annie had been given less than three months to live. Leo's course of treatment was to see that she was amply supplied with painkillers: palliative care to the end. She indicated she'd been using marijuana, which brought an angry riposte from Leo—his pen almost went through the paper: "Pointed out serious violation of law to patient, who showed no concern: 'So what? I'm dying anyway.'" "Fair point," Dave murmured. "You go, girl."

The last chart entry from early September of that year noted a phone call from Annie. She stated she was feeling perfectly well and her cancer was actually "in remission!" This time, the pen had actually slashed through. Dave poured himself another.

"Urged patient to come in for exam; brushed off; patient moved to Alpine Canyon Road, working for K.B., replacing Howard (suicide 1 week ago)." The initials "K.B." were circled.

Then: "K.B., don't touch."

That concluded Annie Goodman's relationship with Leo Durant. Dave dropped the file on the desk and sat back with his hands behind his head. Outside, thunder rolled and drummed across the black-purple sky. Rain fell hard, followed by sleet, followed by hail that spattered on the windows and rattled like millions of pebbles across the curved tin roof until he almost couldn't hear himself think as he numbly sipped his whiskey. "Weird!" Annie Goodman, her body riddled with cancer …suddenly it goes into remission …

…right about the time she goes to work for Klaus Bartok.

Then, almost two decades later, along comes Carla, a different disease, but the same result.

Okay, let's get sensible here. This is only coincidence. "Klaus Bartok is not a faith healer!" Dave yelled at the ceiling and poured himself one more.

Of course, there was another explanation. He looked at the mahogany puddle in the white cup: "DNA!" he said aloud. Simple. Somewhere in Annie's DNA, some measurable, observable trigger had been pulled that starved or shrank the tumors and killed off the other cancer cells, a twist invisible to the science and technology of that time. Nowadays, they'd know. Too bad she'd been cremated. They might have been able to better understand what was behind it; or at least the mechanisms, if not the cause; the how, if not the why. Like his blackout of last week, which, he realized, he'd all but forgotten. There was an answer. They just couldn't see the very real, probably banal, completely explainable cause.

Of course, the same explanation applied to Carla, now seemingly fully alive and way more active than any prognosis would have predicted. She'd been right the other morning: she had been seriously misdiagnosed. As soon as he got some time, he'd take her wherever they needed to solve this mystery. He had to break through her denial. They were still deep in the woods with this thing. Again, he promised himself he'd talk to her. Take her hiking on Sunday—they hadn't been out in so long—then he'd confront her.

He poured himself one more and, leaving the files on the desk, went out to the reception area and watched the storm through the windows. Leo's house faded in and out through the racing storm. The vehicles were all gone. Leo's heirs and Sierra Future had fled the fierce spectacle that had enchanted Leo for decades. Therein lay the future.

Dave defiantly enjoyed the storm in Leo's memory. He let its power rumble through his body until his every nerve ending sizzled with electricity and his mind was a disembodied world of rain and thunder. It almost felt like he was the one making it rain. Cracking whips of blue silver lightning crossed the sky, striking Bob Garner and his greedy uncaring crew. "Take that! Yes! I am a destroying god!" he laughed. As the storm sailed east and crumbled away, he felt a grownup's embarrassment and was glad no one had been there to witness his childish behavior. He was an adult after all, his feet rooted on Earth.

Later, as he drove up the slope through silvery shafts of afternoon sun, he glanced in the mirror at Leo's house pulling away behind him and felt a loss. Leo had been all alone in his love for this spot. Now only Klaus Bartok was "master" of these heights. As much as Dave disliked them both—especially Bartok—a tang of sorrow at the eventual passing of both men sounded in him. It wouldn't be a better world rushing in after them.

As Dave drove through Mystic Valley, he saw the sun sinking right behind Dragon's Ark and realized he was driving through the tip of its shadow. He drove faster.

He arrived home during a sugary twilight; for a second, he wondered if he was pulling in at the wrong house because of the giant white SUV that blocked the driveway.

"Just smashed in along the driver's side," Tim had told him. "Torn up a little underneath."

As Dave nervously got out of the truck, he heard a voice humming in a counterpoint with the light evening breeze: a low, measured melody that rose and fell like a lark on the wing. He recognized it; he'd been hearing something like it in the moments before dawn.

He went to the corner of the house to find Carla at the end of the yard, facing west where the Ark pierced the torn red sky. She wore black jeans, a black sweater and held her arms to the sky in supplication. Her voice flew up into the darkening heavens, intense, full of longing, bittersweet and hopeful, wavering between triumph and despair. The notes drew tighter and tighter until they fluttered with a crazed ululating energy.

Then, as the day faded and the first stars appeared, a tiny speck flew up through the scarlet wash, from between the Samsons and the Ark. He watched Carla watching. He couldn't see her eyes, but he knew they were wonderstruck.

The speck seemed to head right for them, unbelievably fast. It grew bigger, blacker, and streaked red and blue flames in its wake. The wind rose and turned colder. The wind lifted his hair as the bird zoomed right overhead and then disappeared, with a sharp crack, as if it had broken the sound barrier. The stars seemed to turn on as it passed.

Carla walked past him. "Hi," he said. She didn't reply, didn't look at him, or even look like herself. Her eyes were two black holes in a white skull, her mouth a small, but frozen smile. It was as if he wasn't there, as if he didn't exist.

The microwave dinged when he entered the house. He found Carla sitting at the kitchen table, gnawing a raw pork chop. She looked at him with her dark, empty eyes, licking the blood from her lips.

Anticipating his question, she answered: "I am hungry."

CHAPTER 22

A Hole in the Dream

All morning, the dream had been a lurking shadow in Dave's mind, in the way his waking life was now strewn with new shadows. It would have been another one of those wonderful dreams, another night-sky adventure over the mountains, floating up and down, a feather riding on waves of air.

But in this one, he was suddenly set down on a familiar patio; he could hear a river roaring somewhere below. Something happened, a detail that he'd been trying to remember all morning. Next, he was flung back into space all the way back to his house, floating down through the roof to land gently on the bed where he awoke to Carla singing her song at the window as daylight fell. How was it that daylight fell? Night was what was supposed to fall. And what was it that happened there, above the river?

Before he had a chance to remember while lying there in his bed, the phone rang. It was Tim King and time to go fishing. Hours later, he was standing in the Carson River. The strong current felt cold and damp through his waders and his fishing rod hung limp in his hand as he watched the orange poppies shimmer on the hill across the river. He felt relief that he couldn't see Dragon's Ark from here, but he saw it in his mind anyway as he struggled to remember that missing scrap of his dream. Tim, standing nearby and fully in his element of fast water, nimbly practiced both the art of fishing and the craft of telling Dave about the latest mess created by Deputy Sam Colbert, his voice rising with both irritation and amusement above the river's muffled roar.

After Tim had wound up his investigation at Leo Durant's house late Tuesday afternoon, he returned to the Byrneville Station: "And guess who I find sitting in the holding cell? Emile de Grasse. Yeah, the DNR biologist.

"So, I go to Sam and I say 'Sam, what the heck is this?' And Sam says, 'I think he's about to confess.' And I go, 'Confess to what?' 'Killing Leo Durant! What else?'"

Tim then slowly, patiently explained to Sam how Emile had stopped by the office the day before and left notice of who he was and where he'd be camping in case of trouble. Tim had checked in with both Barb Albanese, Klaus Bartok's property manager, and the DNR. Emile's story added up.

Sam's murder scenario, meanwhile, had "chewed into his brain like a deer tick. He was a million percent sure that Leo and Emile had some kinda, um, secret gay thing goin' and that Emile had picked up Leo at his house and took him down into Alpine Canyon to, well, whatever, I don't know much about that stuff. Anyhow, he figured Emile and Leo got in some kind of lover's quarrel and Emile hit Leo with a rock or maybe pushed him into the stream."

"Humph." Dave mindlessly waved his pole back and forth. I should find this funny. I don't.

Anyway, Tim went on, he and Sheriff Parker ended up apologizing up and down the county to Emile and now Sam was busted to deskwork down in Osgood—maybe, this time, for good.

"So Monitor County's safe from Barney Fife again."

"Safe as milk." Tim looked up the river. His two sons were up above the falls, Brandon up to his knees with his pole, intensely watching for fish; Timbo sat morosely on the bank, his pole on the ground next to him. The end of Tim's pole shivered. A minute later, he reeled in a twelve-inch golden trout.

Tim carried it ashore, crushed its head with a rock, and dropped it in a pail filled with ice. He baited up, waded back out, and cast his line. Dave sensed that Tim knew something was wrong. Normally, Sam's antics were a reliable spur to laughter, but not this morning. Dave kept passing over the empty spot in his dream, and how it seemed to pull in all the other things that bothered him.

Just as Tim opened his mouth to ask what was wrong, Dave headed him off: "Okay, so Emile de Grasse didn't murder Leo Durant, but how did Leo wind up at the bottom of Alpine Canyon? What did you find at his house?"

"Not a whole heckuva lot." Tim carefully adjusted the reel. "His front door was unlocked; no sign of anyone there, except for Leo. His bed looked slept in. His wristwatch was on his bedroom table and his clothes folded over a chair. His closet door was open, no bathrobe. I figure that's also where he kept the shotgun and maybe his flashlight, too. I found that outside down the slope."

"Any footprints?"

"Just around the leeward side, by the dog kennel. The wind took the rest. It was blowin' hard while I was there. Those poor dogs of his were in bad shape. The Dalmatian was tearin' circles around the fence and the Lab was curled up in their house, like she was scared dead. She'd been gnawin' at her tail. I fed 'em, called Animal Protection, then found the oldest son's phone number in the house and called him.

"I searched down the slope in the back, right to the edge; there are a few old paths down there, most of them made by deer and bear, all of it pretty rocky. Not much track at all. I found an old toy cap pistol, a Gene Autry model, if you can believe it, but nothin' else. All I can say for sure is that Leo wasn't walkin' around down in Alpine Canyon. He fell in from up top."

"But how?"

"Leo was gettin' up there in years. Sheila and Tammy told me he was getting fuzzy and absentminded."

"Sure. I could see it in his patient files, especially the recent ones. The nurses had to fill me in on details that should have been in the charts. Maybe he had early stage dementia, maybe even Alzheimer's."

"Right. He wouldn't be the first senior to mistake night for day and decide to go huntin', even if it was out of season. Even a bear wouldn't get a sensible man out of bed on a cold windy night, especially up there."

"So, he walked off the cliff during an episode of dementia. I'll buy that. What bugs me is how he fell a thousand feet without hitting anything on the way down. His remains should have been all over the canyon floor."

"Freak occurrence." Tim shook his head. "That's the only answer I got."

"I guess. People have been known to survive falls from even greater heights but not many."

Tim's pole jiggled; he hunched his shoulders, peering carefully at the bobber, talking slow: "The canyon rim juts out and drops sheer all the way down at a couple places along that section. You remember how windy it was at the canyon bottom and how windy Emile said it was the night before, enough to take his tent away. A hundred miles an hour, sometimes. A fast enough wind could've carried him just far enough out from the wall and dropped him into a deep part of the river. The current, the rocks, and the scavengers did the rest while he washed down to where we found him. The El Dorado County M.E. says there was hardly any blood left in him, but that's no surprise. He was gouged up enough. The fall killed him for sure."

"I guess so." The explanation still sounded far-fetched and crowded with coincidences. The threads of reasons frayed too soon. Tim's explanations were almost as vague as Dave's regarding his blackout last week and the sudden improvement in Carla's health. Plus, there was what he'd found in Annie Goodman's charts.

"Hey, you got somethin'!"

The fish might've been a thirteen-incher, but it broke free halfway to shore. Dave was too weary to care. "The mid-sized one that got away," Tim joked. Then he asked what he wanted to know before Dave could stop him.

"How's it goin' with your new practice? Guess you can't be leavin' us now huh?"

Dave forced a smile, grateful that the sunglasses hid his weary red eyes. "I'm running my tail off."

"Paul Berman said he saw Carla drivin' around Klaus Bartok the other day, Tuesday I think." He paused. "I thought she wasn't supposed to drive."

Dave fiddled with his reel: "There may have been a misdiagnosis." He hastily added, "That may not be good news. She was definitely sick. I have to get her in for more tests." But when? he thought. There's so little time and she keeps fighting it.

Then he asked a question he had been reluctant to ask: "What do you know about Klaus Bartok anyway?"

Tim answered promptly, as though he'd been asked the question before. "He's not one of our major lawbreakers. The Bartoks were the last of the important families to settle here and he's the last of them. He still carries weight, though I can't say how much. Every community has some cranky old coot livin' alone up in the hills, won't say boo to a soul. I guess he's ours." Tim grinned. "Can't arrest a man for bein' ornery." He winked and tapped the side of his head.

Dave snorted: "No way. He's as sharp as he was when he was twenty. Whatever brain genes he's got, I wish we all had them. What about his father?"

"He passed long before we came here. You sound a little concerned."

"Kinda. Carla seems be taking over Annie Goodman's job." Dave now wished he let it lie. Before long, Tim would think he was losing it; the Kings were churchgoers down in the valley across the state line, but Tim seemed to have no more truck with ghost stories than Dave did. He decided not to mention Annie's cancer. Try to keep it to things he could explain.

"Before Annie, Bartok had a guy named Howard working for him. I found out he committed suicide. Before Howard, there was Chloe Byrne. Bartok abused her so badly she suffered a nervous breakdown and her family hospitalized her. That was almost fifty years ago. Did Annie ever make a complaint to you?"

"I chatted with her now and then. She never let on that anything was wrong. She was a big girl, looked like she could take care of herself, though a bit off in her own world. As for Chloe Byrne, that's way, way before me. Sounds like you don't care much for our old man of the mountain."

Dave mindlessly waved the pole back and forth; he'd lost all interest in fishing. "I've lived up here for two years and I hardly hear a peep about him. He's just someone in the corner of my eye, a name, and a big car that goes by once in awhile. Then suddenly, one day, I pull him out of a wreck. Last night, I come home to find that supertanker of his in my driveway, all fixed up and ready to roll with my wife at the wheel."

"Think she can handle it?"

"She sure thinks so. She thinks she's superwoman. But I don't want her driving up into Alpine Canyon or anywhere else until I know where her disease went to."

He slowed down, tasting every word as though it might poison Tim against him:

"It's not like we'll need his money. If things work out, we'll have plenty of our own. I'd like to find some dirt on him, not to have him arrested, but to persuade Carla to quit and go back to driving the county bus, if she wants to work again. She'd never work for a crook. Maybe there's something on him in the county files, or at the library."

"Good luck. There's nothing before 1965, except maybe some pictures and stuff donated from other places." Tim was referring to the Great Byrneville Fire. "That fire pretty much consumed the history around here. That's why our history museum ain't got much history in it. You might ask the director, Paul Hilliard, about it. He was at the fire, got the scars to prove it. If you see him, you'll get what I mean. The museum's closin' by the way, did you hear?"

The museum had, in fact, missed its traditional opening on Memorial Day weekend. Dave and Carla had only visited once, on their first trip to Byrneville, and found it sad and meager, staffed with a lone, bored volunteer. Neither Paul nor the co-director, Laura Ervin, were anywhere to be seen. Dave had never met them. Like Bartok, they seemed to stay far in the background.

"I think they're packin' up today. Paul and Linda never were able to give it much of a go. They relied on the Washoe Tribal Council for help; they used it more as a community center. They're movin' out like all the old-timers."

"Pretty soon you and me will be the old-timers. Did they sell to Sierra Future?"

"Wouldn't be surprised." Tim sighed and shook his head.

"Speaking of packing, what about that friend of Annie's who stayed with her last fall? She come back for her stuff?"

"Claudia Prentice. I saw her car and a truck draggin' a U-haul up that way the other day, Wednesday. She was too tender for these parts."

They fell quiet again. It grew warmer. The wind died down. As Dave relaxed a little, he thought about how the Sierra Future issue made Tim squirm and decided to press him on it.

"Are we talkin' patient to doctor?" Tim asked.

Dave laughed. "Confidentiality invoked. So, how's your health, Under Sheriff King?"

"Not too good, Dr. Sutton. The same with Sheriff Parker. If the commission votes yes, it'll be a law enforcement nightmare. The more crowded it gets, the more laws there'll be to break and people to break 'em. Until now the only traffic lights we've had were those two down in Osgood. Thank the Lord I don't patrol that bailiwick, but if the lights go up here, it'll be the end of sleep. I'm not even sure the county's gonna fund us like we'll need. Sheriff Parker says he brought it up at a meeting, but Mis-ter Garner piped up and said they'd worry about it later. He's not on the commission, but he acts like he owns it."

"Maybe he does."

"There are other interests at play," Tim responded.

"Like who?"

Tim ignored the question: "It's gonna be like every other place we had to leave. The modern world's been tryin' to corner me my whole life. I'm not up for movin' again."

"Me neither. I'm glad to pick up Leo's practice, but it's not what I was hoping for. I thought I'd be delivering babies, fixing up kids like yours, and dealing with families. Geriatric care wasn't my specialty in med school. If all I wanted was old, rich patients, I could have stayed in the Bay Area."

"You comin' to the commission meeting Tuesday?"

The idea made Dave even more tired. "Almost forgot. I hope so." He talked about the work towering on his desk: not just Leo's patients, but the business and bureaucracy of it all. "There's ten times more stuff to do than there was just working with the county. I gotta go down to the office this afternoon."

Suddenly and sadly, he felt anxious to go. Tim seemed to notice it as he looked up across the river. The shadow of the hill under which they stood almost had reached their knees; the afternoon sun would be on them in minutes and the fish were already gone for the shadows. Tim smiled, the reflection from the river making a weaving gold lace pattern on his face, sunlight sparkling off his big teeth. "Everybody here wants you to stay. Why not stay?"

Then the memory hole in Dave's dream opened up and he saw what it was that he had forgotten:

The patio deck in his dream was Tim's patio, where the Carson River roared below. Tim stood next him, face turned to the night sky, drenched in silver light from a full moon as he said: "Everybody here flies. Why not you?" and looked at Dave, his eyes firing blue sparks. "Watch me!" Then black wings ripped out of his back, blood flying everywhere, but Tim didn't mind, just grinned like a little boy at Halloween as the heavy black wings flapped furiously, lifted him into the air. Then he reached down and took Dave by the arm—

"Yeah, gettin' to be that time. Hello? Hey, Dave! You okay?"

"Huh, yeah, just tired." What was this fishing trip, this conversation, about anyway? There was an odd knowingness lurking behind Tim's smile, as though he'd just tipped him a secret.

Then Tim looked upstream for his sons. Timbo had disappeared. He snorted: "That boy doesn't like fishin' no more. Marissa's parents took him up to Reno for the first time three weeks ago and he hasn't shut up about it. They bought him one of those Xbox things for his birthday. He's probably itchin' for it right now. Says he's gettin' bored up here. I don't get it. Won't even watch old Westerns with me anymore. Whines that they're too slow and all the actors in them are dead so it's like watchin' ghosts. What he's gonna do when the movie stars he likes all die off? He only watches new movies now and only the ones that go ka-bang ka-blooie from the first scene. Somebody oughta get the DNR to breed pistol-packin' fish. If they start shootin' back, he might get interested again. Can't see watchin' John Wayne on my cellphone. Hey Dave!" Tim was already onshore, looking back at him.

Confused, Dave stepped carefully over the rocks on his way back to shore.

"It's good you're stayin'. Everybody wants to stay. Why not you? Hey watch your step! You okay, partner?"

CHAPTER 23

The Torture Chamber

Dave told himself he had time to put off going down to Durant's office. (No, his mind whispered, there is no time, that's why you're not going.) He turned his truck onto Walsh Springs Road, then took the first right up a hill, passing a weatherworn sign whose faded yellow lettering read:

Monitor County Washoe Community Center
AND MUSEUM

The steep corkscrew road topped out onto a small barren plateau. Below, Byrneville lay hidden under green pines and budding cottonwoods. A cold breeze carried the smell of copper. There was little vegetation here. It was possible that the soil had been poisoned by serpentine, but there were no sign of the telltale greenish rock. A mid-size, U-Haul truck sat in front of a single-story, sandstone main building of recent vintage, built flush to a much older red-shingled structure to the left. A light blue, rust-stained Ford hatchback, its trunk open, was parked next to the truck.

Dave found Danny East-of-the-Moon locking up the truck and they fell into easy conversation. According to Danny, the Washoe Tribal Trust had reached an agreement with the new owner, Sierra Future, to move out by June 15. As it turned out they'd be gone tomorrow, two weeks early.

The community center had always been more symbol than reality, the "museum" an afterthought than a genuine historical self-portrait of the county. The 1965 fire had destroyed the original building, leaving the old jail next door scorched but intact. The only exhibits were on loan from other museums and a few minor treasures from family attics. Indeed, the new building, built in the mid-1980s, looked like a strip mall sent up from Osgood. The jail contained a cast-iron cell and a mini-display of an old blacksmith shop.

Danny didn't know Sierra Future's plans for the property: "The trust bought the land from the county after the fire in '65." He leaned on the truck, arms folded, face calm, eyes sad. "We hoped to reestablish the tribe in the west county. Paul and Linda, the caretakers, pleaded with the tribe to keep it." He spread his hands. "Too many fights elsewhere. It wasn't much, but I hate givin' even this inch."

He nodded toward the west, at Dragon Ark's summit. Atmospheric distortion had magnified the peak to a head splitting size. Dave quickly looked away as Danny spoke.

"That was a sacred mountain to us once. We talked about reclaiming it someday, but it might as well be the moon. There's almost no one left who remembers the names of the spirits. Who are we gonna invoke? You notice something funny about the country around here?" he went on. "Some people call this the most beautiful spot in the state, but when you look at it close, there's things missing."

"Like what?"

"Like vegetation. We're like most tribes. We have plants that are sacred to us, because they provide food, plenty enough reason in my book. Lupine, greenleaf Manzanita, Sierra onion, and Pine-Mat Manzanita." He ticked them off his fingers. "All of 'em are Washoe food sources you find all over the Tahoe Basin and elsewhere." He spread his hands, looked around, shrugging in bewilderment. "But not here, not in Monitor County, not since the early 1900s. Somethin' killed them off. Legend says an evil spirit. Whatever it was, that's what finally got us to pick up and go."

"Some change in the environment, probably," Dave said. "The

soil, the water, even a shift in rainfall pattern could do it." He wanted to mention climate change, but he was here for other reasons. "Actually, I came by to find some information about the Bartok family, especially Klaus."

Danny snorted: "Oh yeah. Today's gods. Never laid eyes on him. I have nothing to say for the man." He nodded toward the main building. "You might ask Paul and Laura in there about the history hereabouts. They were here during the 1965 fire. I guess Paul was the first one on the scene. You'll get an idea of how bad it was if he lets you see him. Laura's got a story, too." He leaned in, holding up his hand. "But don't expect them to say much. They don't talk to outsiders, especially Caucasians." He winked. "But don't take it personal."

After Danny drove away. Dave first turned his attention to the pine plaque by the door. It stated the museum had opened in 1986 "with a grant from the Southern Band of the Washoe Tribe and assistance from the Center for Basque Studies." Four horizontal windows lined the front. A bottle of Maker's Mark leaned like a gargoyle against the dusty glass behind one of them. Two cardboard boxes containing the remains of Monitor County's history sat behind the hatchback.

From the first box, Dave pulled out a daguerreotype (taken around 1910 according to its label) of an elderly Washoe woman wrapped in a rabbit skin robe. She looked so snug that it made Dave sleepy, even though he sensed a coiled mistrust in her narrow eyes. He also found photos of beautifully painted, graceful clay pottery, and painstakingly woven baskets filled with pine nuts. The photos were from the 1950s, the objects from the late 1890s and early 1900s. A large exhibit card entitled "The Last Blooming" said:

"For a brief time, the Washoe people's hopes bloomed again, but, in the year 1906 the spirits that had animated the blooming had fled Monitor County never, some said, to return. The sacred plants died out. Starvation and an epidemic halved the native population. The survivors moved down to the Carson Valley where those still alive now tell of an invasion and conquest by 'a mighty ghost spun from the night's cloth, invisible like the wind, fast like the dead, who took the face and form of all creatures, human and wild.' The giants of old could not withstand its power and cunning and it laughed while it spread its terror."

The other box contained daguerreotypes of the nineteenth-century pioneers whom the Washoe had met first—loggers, miners, Hispanic vaqueros, and Basque sheepherders. In one photo, two miners stiffly posed next to a mule-drawn, two-wheeled cart parked at the foot of a trail that had been blasted from the side of a massive cliff. The trail rose up into a flat white eternity. Its caption read: "Silver miners, Alpine Canyon 1895."

In the next photo, a rough 'n' ready crew of cowboys posed in front of a small cabin, looking as stubborn as the great rock wall behind them: "Hispanic vaqueros, Alpine Canyon, 1905."

The last photo: another gang of rowdies in front of the same cabin now remodeled: "Basque sheepherders; Alpine Canyon, 1906 (before Alpine Canyon War.)"

After 1906, there was nothing on the canyon, no further evidence of what the "war" was about or whether it was related to the forces that finally drove out the Washoe.

Dave rose, wiping his hands. Nineteen-oh-six: the year of Klaus Bartok's birth, if his old state ID was correct. Was he a native or an immigrant? Did the Bartoks ignite the "Alpine Canyon War" and take the land for themselves, another wave of racist, high-handed Europeans? No surprise there, based on Dave's impression of the last surviving Bartok. And what had they done with that faraway canyon? Nothing. They didn't even exploit its natural resources. They only wanted to keep its haunted desolation for themselves as a sentimental memory of their *Mitteleuropa* homeland. They were dukes and princes no more, but in Alpine Canyon, they could keep up the pretense.

Dave found one more interesting artifact. It looked like abstract art, a simple drawing of lines in space, no meaning intended: a black sketch on white paper. He let his visual cortex slowly sort it out and realized it was a photo of an etching made on the white bark of a quaking aspen, likely the work of a Basque sheepherder. Dave had seen dozens of these carvings while hiking around Marklee Pass to the east. Basque sheepherders had created thousands of them all over California and Nevada.

The sheepherders made their art with simple sharp tools. To these practical, earthy men, their carvings were mostly graffiti news on such crucial but mundane subjects as weather and grazing conditions. Some cried out with boredom, loneliness, and longing for women or for the Basque homeland. Some showed exquisite artistry—graceful elegant lines and mysterious, beautifully lettered poetry. Some images were crudely and jubilantly obscene: masturbatory self-portraits and pungent, coarse insults aimed at other herders or the bosses who underpaid and mistreated them; some even cursed the land for its heartless beauty.

This tree carving was a singular portrait of something out a stormy nightmare, the kind of thing a herder might have hallucinated after too much wine. It looked like a mountain lion's head, except it had wings, finely cut to the feather, spreading gracefully out from behind the head. It also reminded Dave of an owl, but the carver had made the mouth into a suction cup lined with tiny sharp teeth, like a lamprey's. In the middle of the cup, the artist added what looked like a whirlpool. The eyes were two hungry black holes staring out from under heavy brows. They wore a look of keening joy and cold, murderous passion; like Tim's eyes as he'd seen them in last night's dream. A portrait of a were-lion, or a were-owl or, Dave mused, a "were-whatzit."

The carver had dated his portrait: "Junio 1906." The label read "South Rim, Alpine Canyon, 1906."

"Ghost stories," Dave grumbled as he stuffed the photo back into the box and rose to his feet, his fists clenched. So: the Bartoks conquered Alpine Canyon by dressing up like the characters in the myths that had once haunted their own dreams in the old country—vampires, werewolves, and so on—to terrorize the sheepherders. The sheepherders, mostly uneducated and maybe just superstitious enough to believe they were under supernatural attack, fled. The Bartoks may have even have sent out little Klaus Jr. in costume (though he probably was just an infant then). Any remaining sheepherders who saw through the Bartok's tricks would next face blunt real-world force.

And now, over a century later, the bastard was still playing Halloween. Maybe Carla and everyone else thought it was cute, but not Dave; his father used to play the same goddam mean tricks on him. Dave wanted to rip away the curtain to expose the shriveled little criminal hiding behind it. Sure, Bartok wanted to stop Sierra Future, but maybe only so he could grab the rest of the land around here for himself, that was all—

He heard a breath that was not his. He turned to find a man and woman standing in the doorway to the museum, both watching him with one eye between them.

The man was probably Paul Hilliard. He'd once been handsome. Gray hair rose in a mass from his strangely oblong head and splashed over the collar of a brown corduroy shirt. A heavy dark wood cane grew like a tree branch from his huge gnarled hand. Faded jeans sagged under his belly. A feathered necklace tightly circled his bull neck. He coolly studied Dave with his tawny right eye. His left eye was a drooping slit set in a mass of burn scars. A thick indentation, like another scar, ran from the top of his head down the left side. Another, less visible, indentation showed on the right, as though his head had been nearly crushed.

The woman staring over Paul's left shoulder—probably Laura Ervin—had a round soft face. Where her left eye had once been, there was a black hole, as though the socket had been punched in by a heavy round object. The way she stood behind Paul made them look like a two-headed creature, looking out together through a single eye.

Unnerved, Dave instinctively stepped forward with the same respect he would show a patient, but he felt deeply embarrassed because he couldn't hide his dismay at their ghastly injuries. They saw it, too. Everyone reacted the same way: stare, mumble, run away. Dave at least, would stand his ground and try to treat them as human beings.

"You must be Paul and Laura. I'm Dr. David Sutton. I'm local and was just interested …" He waved at the boxes. "I'm looking for information on Klaus Bartok."

Paul inclined his head slightly in Laura's direction. She shook her head. Though she was on his blind side, he sensed her response and they became still as statues again. They'd heard that one before. His good intentions didn't matter. He'd get nothing from them, only bitter silence.

Dave turned to leave, but then saw the door to the old jail standing open. Would they mind if he looked inside? They didn't answer yes, but didn't say no. Tipping his bush hat, Dave promised he wouldn't be long, nor take anything.

He had to duck his head as he went inside and then bumped it on a beam as he straightened up. His pupils widened until his eyes felt like two huge holes and still they starved for light. The only illumination came from through the door, from a dust-covered window in front and a feeble 40-watt bulb on the wall to the left. The wood plank flooring creaked underneath; dust motes floated in the turbid light, carrying an acrid perfume of mold and rust.

The jail was built back in the days when fear was the only reform anyone believed in. From this prison, a criminal either broke out or broke, and no one broke out of here, ever. The prisoner went mad, curled up on a cold iron floor, staring into the black iron wall with nothing to do but count the rivets.

Dave pulled out his penlight. Having to stoop hurt his spine and made him feel old. He made out an old wood desk, leaning on three legs, all of its varnish gone. The jail cell took up three-quarters of the right rear. In the left rear-corner, the thick shadows hid what seemed to be a bulky workbench set against the wall.

The door to the box cell opened on the left. In a window on the right, an eyeless scarecrow hung, tied to the bars by its gloved hands, a poorly-stitched smile on his otherwise blank burlap face. Somewhere else, the straw man had been a happy mascot. Now sentenced to life in this unjolly corner, he looked like a madman whose mind had been turned into a screaming vacuum by the visions that had visited him in this hole.

A plaque hung to the left of the cell door, a framed sheet of stained onionskin paper, typed on long ago. It told how the custom cast-iron jail was manufactured and brought to Byrneville in mid-1906 in response to a spike in criminal activity that took place in Monitor County. The jail remained in use for only a year and a half during which time criminal activity declined. The jail was disassembled in early 1908 and remained in storage until the completion of the Community Center in 1986.

As Dave stepped inside the cell, the cast-iron box rumbled like thunder. The darkness was near-total. A prisoner would crack-up in no time and the law wouldn't hang around to hear his screams or his fists pounding on the walls until they were smeared with his blood.

Dave quickly backed out, his penlight shaking. He aimed it into the corner room. The solid oak worktable, like the other furniture, had been made for shorter men and only came up to Dave's thigh. Hammers, tongs, pliers, chisels, manual drills, gimlets, a hacksaw, a small scooped shovel, and other tools hung from nails on the wall. Among them was a heavy ladling spoon. Its bowl looked like it would fit neatly in Laura Ervin's eye socket.

More blacksmith tools lay in a careless row across the tabletop. A huge vise grip clung to the right front corner, its jaws open like a hungry beast. Dave brushed his fingers along its teeth and felt dry rust flakes. He twisted the grip's handle. It squeaked a little, but turned easily. As the jaws slowly closed, he remembered the indentations on Paul Hilliard's head.

What did Bartok do to you? What did he make you do? *How could he?*

As he turned to leave, he came to face-to-face with Paul Hilliard blocking the doorway, the ruined side of his face in shadow, the good side wearing an angry smile.

Dave hit his head on the ceiling. "Ow! Excuse me," he laughed nervously. He awkwardly opened his arms to show he hadn't taken anything like he'd promised. He tried to get by, but Hilliard didn't move, as though he meant for Dave to stay here, a prisoner. Then Dave understood: Hilliard wanted Dave to look at his face, see every detail of everything that had had been done to him and understand that it had happened here, in this room. Dave looked at the dusty red flecks on his fingers.

"Yeah, I think I understand," he nodded. "This is no jail. It's a torture chamber."

The anger in Paul Hilliard's gruesome smile faded and he stood aside.

Dave squinted against the blinding afternoon sun and averted his eyes from the Ark's blade-like tower as he walked to his truck. Driving away, he glanced in the rearview mirror. Laura Ervin was pouring the bottle of Maker's Mark around the doorsill, as though she were hanging garlic.

All Dave wanted to do now was bury himself in work for awhile and forget about all this: the museum, the jail, its caretakers, the SUV parked rudely in his driveway, his wife sitting in the dark, waiting for evening so she could go outside and do her thing. He was coming to hate the whole ritual surrounding that bird at sunset and sunrise. At first, it seemed to be harmless whimsy on her part, but now it was like a religion that even made him feel obsessed. He didn't like killing animals, but given the chance, the idea of taking Tim's hunting rifle out the closet and blasting the goddamn thing out of the sky was appealing—but that was crazy thinking.

Work would do him good. Work: the meaning of life. A ton of meaningful things waited for him at Dr. Dur—Dr. Sutton's office.

But when he reached the intersection with Osgood Canyon Road, he took the left instead of the right for Osgood. He made one more left, the one onto Alpine Canyon Road.

....

CHAPTER 24

The Mad Woman of Alpine Canyon Road

Dave stopped at the foot of Annie Goodman's driveway. As he made the wide turn into the driveway, he leaned out the window to find himself less than a foot away from a sheer drop of hundreds of feet down to an emerald carpet of red firs. He felt a hard jolt of fear.

The driveway was steeper than he remembered. The gears choked, the truck lurched, the wheels spit mud against the underside and the tire flaps. A squawking black crow bounced off the windshield. Past the top of the drive, luminous storm clouds sailed east. He dreaded the drive back down and wondered if Annie ever considered it too high a price to pay for beating cancer.

The truck lurched up into a pocket canyon of around half an acre that had once been a mine or quarry. Patches of dead winter grass and a stunted pine struggled for life on the steep sunless slopes of cold, barren granite. It felt like a gray soulless pit.

On the left was a green Mini-Cooper, on the right there was a small cabin built of tough cypress, durable and dry in any weather. The front door, sitting plum center, was made of tightly joined red pine planks. Dingy muslin curtains hung in a large window on the right. There were two more windows to the left, both smaller and both hung with old curtains. Maybe they were a bedroom and the kitchen. It felt like no one lived here. Annie Goodman had lived far off the grid in what appeared to be servant's quarters.

There was no place to go for a hike, and with the car there, someone had to be home. Dave knocked twice. A shadow floated behind the living room curtain, but the door remained closed. He called hello.

The door opened a crack. A woman's face peered through. She wore black sunglasses over a large paisley bandanna that was wrapped around her head, covering her left eye. "Yes?" she whispered in a deep dry croak.

Unnerved, Dave asked if her name was Claudia. When she didn't answer, drawing herself up as though she'd found even that question intrusive, he haltingly introduced himself as Annie's personal physician, hoping the white lie would lower her guard. He said that he'd witnessed the accident and had been the one who pronounced her dead at the scene.

She shook her head. "Annie said she didn't need a doctor," she croaked.

"But there are some questions about the crash."

"I told the under sheriff everything. I don't know anything. I haven't—hadn't seen Annie since October. No, we didn't talk at all after that."

"We're a little worried about, well, foul play or suicide."

"The under sheriff didn't say that. He'd have asked. They can ask again. I'll say it again. I stayed a couple nights, that's all. It didn't mean anything."

The questions struggled to emerge, but Dave's mouth had gone numb, his tongue turning to a limp bag of sand. The blue gray gloom, this half-blind woman and her creepy voice made him uneasy. He felt the weight of this pit pressing down at him.

"I told what I knew. It's none of your business. You have no authority. What do you really want?" Her small mouth pursed up.

"Claudia, my wife took Annie's job."

"What?" Claudia lifted her chin in indignant rage. "I think not!" She threw the door open. She marched out on the porch, driving Dave off the stoop with her anger. He instinctively wrapped his arms around himself.

What was there to fear? Claudia was a frail woman, maybe in her mid-fifties. She wore a shapeless gray knitted sweater that hung on her hunched frame and faded paisley sweatpants that were tied tightly to her thin waist with a worn drawstring. She wore fuzzy, dingy yellow slippers on her small feet. Her gray-streaked dishwater hair splintered out on her rounded shoulders from under the bandanna and her broad white forehead was cracked with worry lines above the huge sunglasses. She wore no makeup, though her lips looked smeared with red. She didn't belong in this lonely mountain hollow but clearly she thought otherwise.

"Excuse me, but I've taken that position. I'm working here. What do you want? Wait—I think I know. You want some of this, don't you?"

She pulled down the neck of her pullover with one hand, as though to expose her breasts, while the other dove to her crotch.

"Is this it? Is this what you want? You're man, aren't you?" Her laugh croaked grotesquely. She licked her lips and the red coloring disappeared. Then she made a slurping noise like Carla did while eating all that meat.

With her sexual offer greeted with silence, she tore on: "I was a vegan when I came here. Then I started eating meat. All meat, all the time and I don't need alcohol anymore. I never drink wine. It kills the taste of the blood. Life kills. That's what keeps everything alive. Life kills. Is that what she wants? What I have? To be here? There's no room for two. I learned that last fall."

She lowered her croak to a whisper and leaned down until her face was all he saw. "Do you know what it's like to lie next to someone who's not there? I bet you do." Her sunglasses and bandanna made her stone-faced ranting even more disturbing. She pointed her finger as though to poke Dave's eye out. "She'll be back with you in your bed before you know it, because I'm here now. I got here first." She straightened up imperiously. "My furniture is here and that makes this mine. I'm wanted here. He wants me here."

"Klaus Bartok?" Dave gasped out. "That's who I'm asking about. Have you met him? What's he done to you? What the matter with your eye?"

She straightened, lifting her chin with weirdly pious pride. "He's teaching me vision. Here. I'll show you."

She whipped off the sunglasses and ripped the bandanna off her head.

"Oh shit." Dave backed away, forgetting his physician's cool.

Claudia's right eye looked to be a normal healthy gray, delicate and round with wounded innocence. Her left eye, however, was a fat ball bulging out of the socket like a giant boiled egg. A sheet of tears spread over her downy cheek.

Dave attempted a quick diagnosis. Thyroid—no, both eyes would be bulging, and he'd never seen a case this extreme. He fought the urge to run, to vomit, to look away, and to fall apart: "Have you had that looked at? You've got an inflammation."

Claudia threw her head back and gave that strange forced laugh again: "Ha! Ha! Ha! I see better than ever! If I close this bad eye," she said gesturing toward the good one, "I can see the mountains on the moon. I can see more stars than any smarty-pants astronomer!"

The damaged eye made a squelching noise in its socket as she rolled it to look over Dave's shoulder: "Mountain Doc 720,'" she read. "There's rust around the edge of the license. I can see bugs at the top of the canyon. Hungry little bugs." The eyeball squelched as it zoomed in on Dave with terrifying precision. "You have 109,423 strands of hair on your head. Is that good enough for you—what did you say your name was? Forget it, names are just arbitrary labels. I don't even need to bother with those anymore. I have everything I need."

"Klaus Bartok did this to you?"

She opened her good eye and tipped her sideways in surprise:

"Not to me. For me. He's giving me vision. It'll be dark soon. If you think I can see now, you should see what I see after dark. It's wonderful!" she cried, her croak touched with joyous weeping. Her tone shifted again, a warning, as though ordering a dog out of the house. "There's been some mistake, you understand? The driveway's dangerous," she snapped. "So is the road and you are blinder at night than you already are. I've got this. Leave it to me. Tell your wife she's not wanted here."

The strange, disjointed interview ended. Claudia's eyes seemed to go empty of life as she walked backward into the cabin and slammed the door shut. The canyon fell into a leaden silence that left Dave feeling as if he'd gone deaf. As he returned to his truck, he rubbed his temples: what happened, what just happened? He couldn't think clearly until he'd made it back down to the road below, until after the valley, now black with afternoon shadow, had passed again under his eyes, as dust and gravel crumbled away from the edge of the road.

Then Dave stopped to think. He'd been planning to finish his investigation by driving into the canyon to confront Bartok, ask him what he wanted and tell him to leave his wife the hell alone! Now he was driving in the opposite direction on a road that was almost impossible to turn around on as the sun was going down behind him …

As he drove, he struggled to organize his thoughts as he'd been trained: Claudia Prentice was ill, both mentally and physically, too sick to be staying alone up there. Someone should intervene, but Dave didn't know who or how. He considered calling Tim to check up on her, but Tim would only say something like: "She isn't bothering anyone." Dave promised himself to press the point anyway. Sometimes, the laissez-faire non-approach wouldn't do. It wasn't right to let someone suffer alone like that.

The afternoon shadow on the valley looked black instead of its usual haunting twilight blue. The dusky sun, behind the Ark's sharp shoulder, was a wan yellow. For the first time ever, since he'd first come here, since Carla's "miraculous recovery" and the "miracle" of inheriting Durant's practice, Dave Sutton asked himself what he was doing here. Two wishes had come true and, in less than two weeks, Monitor County had turned from a heavenly paradise into a weird kind of hell; beauty without the idyll. Every mystery had an answer, simple and measurable, but here no would give him one. He couldn't even ask the right questions, because asking them made him feel like he was losing his hard-won bearings. Where did Carla's ALS go? Why did he have the feeling that Durant's practice had been handed to him, that he was being admitted to a secret inner circle where even the members seemed unaware that they were members?

What was it about Klaus Bartok that made him the center of it all?

He grew angry at this growing sense of paranoia. Bartok was just another old man and Monitor County another place in the physical world, maybe more beautiful than most, but the laws of nature applied here the same as everywhere else. "No time to go medieval," he lectured himself sternly.

As he reached the floor of Mystic Valley, the meadow and forest looked even more desolate, as desolate as Alpine Canyon. What was he thinking? What were all those fantasies about wandering in the woods forever on some boy's adventure? Now, when he imagined getting lost in the woods, he was assaulted with visions of freezing, starving to death, cold and alone, to be eaten while lying under the Ark's unforgiving shadow. He ached with terror, the romance fallen away from nature's lovely face, revealing its ruthless hunger.

He wanted to see lights in the forest, beacons toward home, to civilization, to people. Alone in the forest? No, humans couldn't live like that. We could only live in the world we had made, with its own poisons.

Maybe, just maybe, Sierra Future wouldn't do as much damage as everyone thought. Maybe the opposition's fears were exaggerated. Sometimes these projects did work out for both people and the environment. He laughed—I'll keep that thought to myself! The change wouldn't necessarily be bad. He and Carla didn't have to leave. They could compromise and find a way to stay and live with the world to come.

This shift in his outlook provided him with another reason to not go home, to that white vehicle, to Carla singing to the sunset—no, to the night, to that goddam crazy falcon or whatever it was that shot like a black bullet through the pale salmon sky. That was the worst of all. He had the feeling she loved that bird, that fast, ruthless predator, more than she loved him. Then he'd have to lay there in bed, unable to tell whether he was dreaming or awake, all night long, until her singing awoke him again in the cold morning light, that miserable, mournful song.

They'd never separated before but this was different, an unusual fight over unusual issues. He needed quiet time and space to think it all through and make a plan. Meanwhile, he'd catch up on work at the office. He'd sleep on the big couch in the waiting room or the brand new comfortable examining table in the main exam room.

As he drove out of Osgood Canyon, he felt reassuring gravity once more. His sensible self returned. The lights of Osgood provided the welcome he was looking for. He drove across the state line and returned to his office with a burrito and bottle of Macallan.

By the time he fell into a simple sleep on the couch in the waiting room, he had a plan. He'd go on that hike with Carla tomorrow, to their favorite, secret—very secret—spot. There, he'd tell her exactly what he needed to tell her and she needed to hear. It would work out, too. Carla had had her moods in the past and he'd always been able to bring her back to earth. He'd bring her around again, like always; get her to see things right, see them by the light of day, and then they'd make love by the stream, and become Dave and Carla again.

CHAPTER 25

How the Day Made Her Angry

With her husband away, Carla could sing as loudly as she wanted all through the night, and when daybreak came, she turned her voice into a pure beam of sound that guided the Dragon home ahead of the burning sun. As he dived down behind the green hills, down to his home, inside Dragon's Ark, her song fell with him and sadness rose within.

The day made her angry now. She had to cover herself from head to toe, always wore her big sunglasses, and always ate her raw meat in the dark kitchen. Her every nerve tingled with the power of animal blood (but still, he was right; it wasn't enough!).

The tabby cat sat near the kitchen table like a mantelpiece, watching her eat, its white stomach looking like bare white flesh. It wanted her to feed it! "Stupid beast! Get out!" Its hunger was mindless. It was a thief who wanted to wedge itself between her and her true hero. After she finished eating, she picked the creature up, intending to banish it to the sun-blasted world outside, for good, to let it fend for itself. She put her face to its fur, inhaled its moist and sour body odor, listened to its heart beat and its blood gurgle through its small body. She put it down. "I'll deal with you later," she hissed.

She then sat quietly in the little sunless TV room to wait for the night.

The husband spoiled everything by coming home later that morning. She tried to read his mind, but it was blocked with the draining sludge of the booze he'd obviously been drinking while away. He repeated the message he'd left on the phone last night: He'd stayed at the office, got too drunk and tired to drive, and slept on the waiting room couch. He left out "screwing one of my new nurses," which she couldn't prove, but so what? They were all the same. What if she spied on him and caught him at it? Then she'd be rid of him. What if he'd attempted to drive home, drunk and tired and went off the road and died? She'd be rid of him—now.

She surprised herself by bouncing up to him with a "Hey, sweet-ie!" and an old fashioned kiss devoid of feeling. "It's okay! Lotsa work to do. So long as my stud pie gets home safe!" She would not miss the taste of dead skin flaking off his lips and the smell of his breath and body.

She marveled at her easy hypocrisy. It was as if she were watching her old self from a new room hidden inside her mind. Her old self remained insistently, unpleasantly alive, standing in the doorway to her new life.

As he mentioned the hike again, he avoided looking at her. He had other things in mind, probably sex. She said yes, even though she hated the idea. She wanted to study him through her new eyes, with her new soul.

She said she'd already had breakfast. Thankfully, he didn't ask what. He made himself bacon, eggs, and lots of potatoes, to give himself energy for hiking and the things he wanted to do to her. She looked away in revulsion as he chewed like a dumb bull.

On their way out to his truck, he glanced darkly at the Vampire's carriage as he asked, "You okay?" He was a negative space: He didn't like her huge new sunglasses or giant straw hat, either. "Your eyes bothering you?" He was thinking with his doctor's mind, worried and suspicious.

Her old self said, "I bought these glasses yesterday. Cool, eh? I thought they made me look like the Lone Ranger." She laughed. "Or the Lone Rangeress."

They stopped to buy rabbit food at the village market. Just before they returned to the truck, a reedy voice called from across the road: "Carla! Dave!" She recognized "Carla." But "Dave"?—Oh, yeah. The husband. That was his name.

It was the boy who thought he "loved" her, a delusion she cultivated to keep him on the right path. *I wish this game were over.* Why did people need to be seduced and bribed to do the right thing? Why couldn't they do right for its own sake? There were always calculations, always a price. Where was virtue and its clarity?

The husband and the boy shook hands. The boy tried not make googly eyes at her. She had to pay attention now for the sake of the Cause. She giggled inside. *I'm just like a spy!*

Dave asked the boy—his name was "Sean"—how it was going. The boy eagerly said—like he was supposed to—that they might actually win. There was more support both inside and outside the county than expected. A candidate for the seat in their district, who had opposed the Evil Doers on other issues and looked like a sure bet in the next election, would come Tuesday night. So would a state senator. Real live mucky-mucks. Some of the big tree hugger groups had also been watching the situation. People had been roused to action; maybe this whole pro-development thing had finally gone too far.

Best of all, the boy said, was the dirt his detective friend had dug up on "Bob Garner." The boy didn't know yet what it was, or even if the detective would have his investigation ready to present on Tuesday night, but he was sure they'd present their case before the final vote next week. Once they learned what a slime dog Garner was, it would be over, the nails hammered into "Sierra Future's" coffin.

"They'll carry that tool out in chains!" Sean laughed. Then he beamed adoringly at her. "Tuesday night'll be cookin'! We'll stomp his ass!" She beamed back, turning just enough away from Dave to throw Sean a secret wink, to show the sweet tip of her tongue, her full breasts; the boy swayed as his jeans swelled.

"You-you be sure to tell Mr. B!" he stammered. Then he batted his puppy eyes "Can you drive him down? It would be cool!"

"I doubt it." She wished she could, too. He'd tear them to bloody shreds. Why didn't he just arrange one of his "accidents"? He was sooo good at that!

"Hey, you know, I'd really like to explore his canyon. Did you…?"

"No, we've been busy. But I'll be sure to ask. I'll ask uh… at the realty."

Sean dismissed the idea with a sneer. "Boobs Albanese? No way! She's with Garner now. She's selling Mr. B out. You gotta tell him!"

She winced, though she shouldn't have been surprised by that woman's treachery. Was Dracula aware how vulnerable he was now? How she would stab him in the back?

"Yeah, I'll tell him! He'll appreciate it! And I'll ask if you can come up."

Then I'll talk him out of it. Sean would dirty the place, drag the rest of the world with him. Why do people have to go everywhere? Why can't they leave the world alone, pure and untouched?

She plucked at Dave's sleeve as Sean asked him if he'd come Tuesday night.

"Yeah, I'll sure try. Sorry, I got so much work."

"I'll try …" The future of this paradise was at stake, but the only support he could offer was a liberal's ineffectual mumble. One more reason to leave him.

"We better get going!" Before I lose my temper and kill you both right here!

As Dave drove, she slathered on more SPF 35. He noticed and just had to ask—again—if she was okay. She said fine, and giggled: "It'll make me more gooey and slippery." But he didn't seem to care because he kept on with his questions: How did she feel? How were her reflexes? How was she sleeping? How was her appetite? Her bowel movements, her urine?

"Oh, I quit going to the bathroom! I don't even pee anymore! Not a drop."

He laughed, like he thought she were joking. Then he repeated his stupid idea that the remission of her ALS was like the repeal of gravity or the reversal of death.

"A-HA!" she cackled. "So you've joined the pro-Gravity, pro-Death Party, eh?"

He laughed again, as if that were a joke, too.

By the time they parked at the resort, the husband's name had slipped from her memory again and the redheaded boy's too, but she accepted it calmly because of the starry future awaiting. She was moving on now, becoming someone new, someone incredible.

The air was hot, the sun blinding. They joined dozens of hikers and backpackers on the trudge up into the rocky hills. Now that the big nearby valley had been closed to the public, they all came here, to one of the last tracts of open land in the county. She studied them carefully, wondering which of them would have the privilege of opening their artery to her King after the sun went down. What great dreams would grow from the seeds he planted in their sleeping minds after he drank his cup?

I know what makes your dreams, she thought. I know the secret, the name and the face of the Fabulous Spirit who makes you dream wonders. But you will return to your gray lives in your smoggy light-poisoned world while I stay here, forever free!

Because of their experience on these trails, Carla and the man whose name she no longer remembered quickly marched ahead of everyone. As she walked patiently behind the husband, she imagined herself bounding ahead, springing up the hills to the jagged peaks, flying higher and higher and higher, leaving him below, a confused, lonesome speck.

The forest closed around them, blocking the sun, cooling the air, until it almost felt like night. A couple miles on, they stopped to rest in a sun-bleached meadow. Already, it was mid-afternoon. The world was without color, the boulders like the ruins of a dead, empty city.

The husband pulled out the birding guide. Oh, not this again. He pointed at the gray and white birds that whirled about like fat blobs, looked at them through his binoculars. This was this and that was this. What a nerd. And to think she once thought him so strong and manly.

Then he put away the bird book and whipped out the wildflower guide and started identifying the flower blobs on sticks, with no conception of how the sun burned away real beauty, scorched it out of existence. True Beauty could only be found at night, and only by those who were trained in the Vision as she was being trained.

"I'm horny!" She heard her old self chirp. The husband turned, winked, and laughed, "Well, well, well." At least that shut him up about the birds and the flowers. She coldly studied his buttocks as he walked ahead of her and noticed how they were spreading as he got older. If she didn't figure out a way to get rid of him soon, she'd have to watch him wrinkle and shrivel.

"Here ya go!" They'd reached the turnoff, a narrow slot to the left that cut through a crowded field of giant boulders. He grinned and flexed his eyebrows like some long-dead comedian, trying to act like the devil he was so not.

They had to remove their daypacks to get through the gap. Here and there, they braced themselves with their feet across opposing boulders. Before long, they reached their bed of grass that stretched along a lively roaring creek. On the other side, stood a thick forest of red firs. They were all alone. She remembered their first time, how erotic it all seemed, with its blue solitude and fast water. They'd immediately spread the blanket on the ground and went at it, screaming.

Now it was just another boring place in the sun. She covered a yawn as the husband performed his ritual. He fussed with the blanket until it looked as neat as a postage stamp. He anchored the corners with both their daypacks and a couple of rocks, which had never helped keep the blanket straight. "Like putting up a pup tent in a tornado," she'd once said.

He stretched out on the blanket and smiled up at her. Usually she returned the smile while undressing and asking him those questions for which he always had many answers.

But now all she wanted was to get it over with.

She silently, abruptly, lay on the blanket, facing the husband. His soft belly sagged toward the ground. He sensed she was different, but tried to smile away his unease. He couldn't read her thoughts. He could only lust, blindly.

She undid her blouse. They're just milk glands, she thought as his eyes widened like a horny teenager's. He reached for the zipper on her cargo pants, but she slapped his hand away as if it were a pesky fly and ordered him to turn over, away from her.

"Whatever you say, baby." As if she were an infant.

She reached around and unzipped his pants. As she reached in, she repeated a script that they'd spoken once, among the hundreds of encounters that made up the animal side of their marriage. The words came out of her mechanically, her only passion to finish quickly.

She closed her ears to his cries and looked away, across the creek to where a spider had spun a small web between a tree and a boulder. She felt her eyes swell in her head, bulge out of her sockets. They magnified the spider until it looked like it was only inches away and she could make out every sticky strand of its web. The spider looked like a bumpy brown pebble as it locked each of its feet onto each strand as it marched out to the edge, where a bug struggled fruitlessly to escape. Its eight eyes shone with the thrill of the hunt. I am hungry was its only thought, a glorious, simple idea, unstained by guilt.

As the spider's fangs sank in, she heard a scream and looked down.

The husband had ejected his sperm. His need was satisfied. "Thank you." He kissed her and asked what she wanted. After all, it was she who usually orgasmed first. But she was above all that now. She stuffed him back inside and zipped him up. In a phony sweet voice, she said she would take a rain check, maybe tonight. In her new mind, she laughed: Permanent drought for you, buddy!

He kissed her again and snuggled beside her, facing away. "There's something we have to talk about," he said.

"What?"

"I've been feeling frustrated. I was even thinking we should get out of here and move back to San Francisco, 'cause of the changes happening here. I think Leo's family sold his place to Sierra Future. At least that's what I got from Bob Garner when I talked to him the other day."

"You talked to him?"

"Yeah." He shrugged. Then he sighed and rolled over on his back, using his arm as a pillow, his black hair, now tinged with gray, spilling across the blanket. "Things are going better in one sense. I've got a real practice. That means real money. If we stay, we'll have to adapt to the changes—look, don't get me wrong. I hate what's happening," he shrugged, "but I think they've got it all sewn up. We'll have to live with it or leave it." He wriggled in shame at his surrender. There was something else he wanted to say, something he was afraid to.

"Another thing's that definitely for sure. If we stay, we won't need Klaus Bartok's money."

"Then I'll work for free," she said with a pretend shrug.

"I don't want you working for him at all. I know, he's an elderly man who needs assistance, but I think he's using you somehow. I know he doesn't have your interests at heart. I've been digging into his background. He treats people like garbage. I don't like you driving that SUV around up there and I don't want it in our driveway. Is he paying for the gas? I bet not. Ever since that accident, you haven't been the same. I mean it's other things besides your illness. By the way, I'm making an appointment at the clinic in Sacramento for next week and you're going!"

Now he's getting bossy. Who does he think he is? What gives him the right?

"He can get someone else to take him around." The husband could barely hide his pathetic jealousy. "If Sean wants to go climbing around there, let him do it." He looked sternly at her. "If you really want to work and everything checks out all right, you can go back to driving the county bus. Sierra Future's gonna bring more people up here. They'll want that bus and you liked that job."

She tenderly brushed her lips across his forehead and gently massaged his scalp as though she understood: "Of course, darling. I'll quit tomorrow. It'll be the last time."

This seemed to satisfy him, because he closed his eyes as he snuggled deeper into her uncaring body. Before long, he was asleep.

Carla rose and washed her hand off in a quiet pool in the creek. She watched with satisfaction as the sticky white strands dissolved away until her hands were all clean.

She climbed a nearby rock from where she could see Dragon's Ark, the afternoon sun about to impale itself on its tip. Night was coming. Her anger and impatience rose as one.

So that's how it is, she thought. He's taken their side now. He's one of them.

She looked over at her ignorant, sleeping enemy. Soon, he'd wake up and want to go home, afraid to sleep in the open, under the stars, blind to night's beauty.

She leaped gracefully off the boulder and crept over to her slumbering foe. With a grin, she picked up one of the rocks that held the blanket in place. She hefted it in her hand, thinking, like the Vampire would.

She didn't want to kill him. The Vampire wasn't a scavenger. Because blood started to curdle and decay immediately on death, he needed his prey alive and fresh. She'd only hit the enemy hard enough so it would stay down until nightfall. The Vampire would sense the fresh blood in the night air like that spider felt its web shivering from its victim's struggles. He'd fly from the stars, and again she would see him change from the Dragon to melt through red and blue fire to become a man. Tonight he'd have a full meal as he did with that fat guy and the old man. This time, she'd be serving the sacrifice herself. She laughed. Just like a happy homemaker! They were so close now, the two of them.

Maybe he'd even share with her. And, once they were finished, he would take her to the stars again and this would be the night when it would all change.

No. No, wait. She was getting ahead of herself. What if the change couldn't be finished tonight? He said it took time. What if she still had to walk among the half-living? They would ask questions. She thought some more and altered her plan. After they were done feeding, they'd dump the body in the creek; maybe smash its head on a rock. She'd find her way back, call for help. Through easily faked tears, she'd tell the slow, dumb under sheriff that her husband had slipped and fallen while they were crossing the stream, blah-blah-blah, no problem. They'd find him with his broken head in the water, fractured skull, massive bleeding, easy lie. No one would suspect her. The world saw only a happy couple. Everyone loved them. What fun to be a secret killer and the object of misdirected sympathy!

And, as always, no one would ever suspect him.

As Carla weighed the rock in her right hand, the very same hand that Mr. Bartok had grabbed on that special day, she saw her long shadow stretching across the gray grass. She owed the Dragon this, as she owed him so much else. She imagined the two of them standing together, under the silver light of a full moon, his shadow standing tall alongside hers while he whispered encouragement. She watched her shadow lift the rock in the air as behind her, the stream roared louder.

....

CHAPTER 26

Kill the Sun

The SUV's metal gray interior was cool, and quiet except for the muffled purr of its big engine. It rode up Alpine Canyon Road like an airship, down into the gorge like a boat down a slow river and across the canyon floor like a ship on a calm sea.

The canyon felt a place apart from everything, a land barren but lofty and romantic. A small herd of scrawny deer watched Carla go by and then cautiously followed. A coyote wandered down from the detritus and trotted alongside. Up ahead, vultures circled upward on drafts of smoke-white air.

How lovely it would be under a full moon!

Carla stopped in front of a crooked, fire-blackened tree. She laughed as the tree waved one of its thin branches in greeting. Mr. Bartok had found a new walking stick on the canyon floor.

She was so excited she forgot to reapply sun block before she got out of the SUV. As the sun scorched and shrank her now-pale skin, she crouched, assuming the posture of the sick person she'd once been. The sun was a ruthless all-seeing tyrant, the implacable enemy of night and freedom. Fuck you, Mr. Sun!

"Fuck the fucking sun," she sang in a whisper as she gently took his arm, felt the soft flutter of the feathered coat. She smelled coppery perfume as she lifted him into his safety seat: "I can tell you fed last night."

She didn't feel so bad now about not killing her husband for his sake. But she did apologize for her lateness as she tenderly belted him in. This was her first time driving the SUV. Next time she'd be right there waiting. She'd carry him down from the canyon rim, across the bridge if she had to.

She impulsively took his white hands in hers. "Fuck the sun. Right? Fuck it."

He sighed, grateful that she understood how he felt about things. They stood as one against the scorching sun. There was another side of life against which the sun was the enemy. There were enemies all around.

She had so much to tell, news both good and bad, but by the time she got behind the wheel, he had fallen asleep, his magnificent strength already drained by the sun's evil power. Bad sun!

The drive to the village started out in plush silence until they passed through the notch and Mr. Bartok commenced snoring—huge honking cartoony snores that roared in and out of his cavernous mouth. His breathed smelled of blood. His hairy yellow-white wattles and red lips fluttered. Outside, the world dragged by, a vast dingy crumpled sheet, the mountains like piles of coal. By the time they parked in front of the realty office, Carla felt a strange anxiety and thought, Good thing I only have to do this once a week.

His snoring stopped when she turned off the engine. With a sigh he requested her report, adding, "Sean was inebriated last night—again." His vocal cords scraped like tattered leather and he licked his lips as though he'd been sucking on lemons. "Probably nervous about the meeting tomorrow. He seemed in a good mood, though. I gather he's made progress. Tell me."

As Carla rubbed sun block into her lobster-colored skin, she made her report. The world really did care about this little corner of it after all. She told him about the dirt on Bob Garner, adding, "The shit sounds deep enough to drown him."

"It better be. Garner's an alcoholic himself," Mr. Bartok snorted. "He thinks it helps his migraines. His medications block his mind and his blood tastes like turpentine. What is it with lowlanders nowadays? I used to taste only alcohol and opiates. Now it's like drinking out of a medicine cabinet. Even the blood of the 'clean and sober' runs with the garbage they take to stay on their wagon. Oh, well."

He affectionately patted Carla's arm. "Wait until you taste the real wine, my dear. Clear, fresh, and clean." He kissed his fingertips. Then he grimly shook his head. "Provided, of course we win." He waved his long fingers distastefully at the sun block. "By the way, that fouls up your bloodstream, too. Nasty stuff, not fatal, but why sour the palate?"

"Now for the bad news." She stuffed the tube in her purse and told him about the real estate agent, the one he'd trusted for so many years. Her heart broke for him as he flinched: "What? No!" He shook his head, quaking in disbelief. His naiveté was touching. As a human, Carla could see right through that bitch's glass soul. How funny that Mr. Bartok, great God of the Night, could still be swayed by the ephemeral shimmy of extra big boobs. A man was just a man after all, even if he was centuries old and wielded tremendous supernatural powers.

When she told him what her almost-ex-husband had said about the old doctor's property, he exploded into spectacularly foul curses and shook his stick in the air. She understood. The old doctor's death was intended to stop Sierra Future from taking the land. They'd failed to anticipate the weakness of his greedy heirs.

"They're lying in wait for me in there now. They've picked off one. Now they'll pick off the last. Oh, yes, fuck the goddamn sun. It burns up precious time. I notice my sway over the commissioners has weakened of late. Ferrand and Placido are teetotalers. I can keep their dreams flowing our way as they sleep. As for the rest, I don't know. We'll still fight with what we have." He paused. "I have an idea: I must know the second that Sean and his investigator are ready to present their evidence."

Carla then told of Sean's desire to visit Alpine Canyon. She braced herself for his thunder, and indeed, he looked angry at first, but then thoughtfully sighed:

"Visit?" He nodded. "Well, so long as it is just that. In fact, the more I think about it, if Sean and his associate are willing to share this new information—no, no, my dear," he went on urgently. "I can make this exception. He holds the key to victory and I want to see for myself how it fits the lock. I'll welcome him this once." He sternly wagged his finger like a nagging old grandfather. "So long as he's careful. Best you come along and show him the way, so we won't have to worry!"

Then he shook his head and folded his hands, falling into a rueful mood: "I used to kill any outsider who set foot on my land. As the world becomes more crowded and its shadows vanish, I find I understand what Mr. Darwin was saying: adapt or die. Staying so far in the shadows for so long is actually against my interests. To save my world, I must allow a little of it in, like using a virus to fight a virus. Truth to tell, I wasn't being honest with your or myself about being happy inside that gloomy mountain alone and apart. Sometimes, I wish I were more than an amusing imaginary plaything. Maybe I have to live with the light of that star after all."

"No!" Carla reeled with astonishment. "You're kidding. Get outta here." Maybe Dracula was an unbelievable fantasy, but this sudden turn toward compromise seemed equally unlikely. And dangerous. "You can't be serious."

"No?"

"No!" She took his cold hands in hers. "You're the heart and soul of the night. The king of dreams. You're a unique and wonderful being. I've always been an outsider so I know what you're going through. Now I'm more of an outsider than ever and I'm glad of it. You've made me proud to be different. I'll do everything I can with every ounce of my soul to be part of your world. You can't bring me in and then end it all now. You live a dream and you can't compromise a dream. You can't be half of your true self! You have to be all of it!

"Everybody feels like an outsider sometimes and that's what you are to everyone. That's why they still tell your story. They envy you.

You're the freedom everyone dreams about. You've seen so much of life. You've been places, done, and seen things those losers never will. Who wants to be the one who kills a dream? Who wants the dream to kill itself? Because that's what you'd be doing. You're more than alone and apart. You're above and beyond. You have a right to your place. If I didn't believe it, if I didn't know what I know, I wouldn't be here with you. You gave me back my life and so much more. I believe in you, Mr. Klaus Bartok." She solemnly clenched her right fist over her heart and raised her left. "With all my heart, and to the end."

Amazement showed through Mr. Bartok's wrinkles and he wept in grateful silence. He removed his sunglasses, wiped his eye sockets on his sleeve, and nodded toward the realty office.

"You make me ashamed," he said. "Very well then. Into the breach."

"I'm ready." Carla winked. "Let's go smarten 'em up a bit. What d'ya say?"

Klaus Bartok felt light as air as she lifted him down from the SUV. For a second, she realized that she too had a certain power. He was so frail he would break like Humpty-Dumpty if she dropped him. She felt him tense up: "Careful, careful." he murmured dryly. "Don't drop the precious china."

They hurried together into the shade and as they reached the door, Carla steeled herself for what awaited them inside. But as she reached for the doorknob, Mr. Bartok grabbed her wrist: "No." His face twisted with intense realization. "I'd better go in alone." She protested, but he tapped his head with a wry smile: "Thanks to you, this mighty old brain is ready."

"No." Carla hissed. "You need an advocate with you. Don't be a stubborn male."

He thudded his stick on the ground. "Your sudden presence may arouse suspicion, put them on the defensive. They don't know what you've told me, so the advantage is mine. Remember, you're my spy and a spy works best from the shadows. The weaker they think I am, the more they may let their game slip. I'll tell you everything. Now go. Wait for me. You'll know when I need you."

Mr. Bartok pushed the door open. Inside, the agent and her breasts cast their shadows across her desk; the bearded man leaned on the credenza behind her. "Well, how-dee-do, Mr. B.—" The door closed behind him.

Carla put her ear to the door, but couldn't hear a word. Soon it grew too hot to be outside and she retreated inside the SUV. No stupid vampire I, too dumb to come in out of the sun. The trouble was there was nothing to do but torture herself with worry and fume over the old man's macho stubbornness. It was so funny, how he somehow remained human, almost to the point of self-destruction. Such a vain creature!

Time passed tick by slow tock until she suddenly sensed his mind calling and, sure enough, she found him waiting for her as the door was closing behind him. He looked worse than he did when he went in, smaller and older, his wrinkled face paler than ever, mouth turned downward. He trembled like a dried leaf as she guided him back into the SUV. His eyes shone with rage from behind his sunglasses.

"Did you—?" she asked as she got behind the wheel.

"NO." His shout almost stopped her heart. "Sean was right about Albanese. Ten years. Ten years of loyalty gone," he roared. "At last I can see past her large charms to her betraying heart. They're confident, ohhhhh soooooo confident. They keep sugaring their pot, but as I underestimate them, they underestimate me. They think I'm like Durant, another senile old fool for sale, but I'll not give a millimeter." He whipped off his sunglasses and bared his teeth as huge tears bubbled out and rolled into his cracks of skin like water into dry cracked soil. "Is there no place for me? Where do I live, if not here? Must daylight conquer all? Why can't they let the night be the night?"

They cried together, united in rage, fear and despair, as one against the implacable light. She found the large box of tissue that his last chauffeur kept handy and helped him dry his eyes before drying her own. Then he rattled out a mucosal sigh and asked a surprising question:

"Is Sean working this afternoon?" He put his glasses back on, all business again. "Good. I need to speak with him. He may have some further good news to counter the bad and we can arrange his upcoming visit. His detective friend, too, if possible. Not only that, I'm famished—oh no, Mrs. Sutton, thank you, but I've drunk enough from you for now. Too much, too often, will weaken you, render you less capable, maybe even kill you." He laughed and gently touched her on the arm. "And we don't want you dying, do we? That would defeat our work. I never draw too much from a single well, unless—" and he laughed. "You get my drift." He flexed his eyebrows up and down like that old leering comedian whose name she could no longer recall.

As she drove into resort, she saw the boy's vehicle bristling with his junk in the nearly full parking lot and she thought, It's okay if he wants to talk to him. I don't mind. She shouldn't be jealous when he wanted to confide in others. It wasn't like he was sharing details of their new life together. He needed space. It's not time, she reminded herself. She remembered his wise words: "Rare for a reason."

As she walked arm-in-arm with Mr. Bartok toward the restaurant, crouching against the sun, she imagined how other people saw them and playfully whispered, "We look like an old married couple."

His cracked smile made her feel better. Then he said, "Speaking of couples, there's no need for guilt about not staking your spouse out for me last night. I always get my own dinner. Nor should you kill him for my sake. You wouldn't have escaped detection by the authorities in any case, which would have ended our business together. I've lost enough friends for now. Even if you escaped the law, your conscience would find you. The good doctor may be unimaginative and less inclined to our cause than before, but he'll come around. After Garner is gone, we'll need him alive, almost as much as I need you, Mrs. Sutton."

But she'd made her decision. "I'm leaving him."

He pursed his lips into a horrid, wrinkled pink flower and shrugged his bony shoulders: "Leave him then, if it'll make you happy. But do leave him alive." He laughed at her needy stammering: "Night will rise in an hour or so. I'll talk with Sean, select from the menu, feed, and fly on from there. And of course, I look forward to your song to carry me home—oh, I almost forgot. Nothing comes for free, does it?" He placed a roll of bills in her hand, more money than last time. "Thank you again. The extra is for gas. I hear gas prices are so high, even I can't fly above them." He cackled. "Of course, my fuel will never run out as long as humans walk this planet. Living, breathing gas pumps. If they only knew. Ho-ho!"

When they entered, the proprietress smiled at him in greeting, but ignored Carla. The boy all but bowed and kissed Mr. Bartok's hand, but he seemed to ignore her, too, as though she were a shadow. She left him and the boy in whispered conversation by his table at the window. Later, he would watch the night rise and wait for his evening meal to come for its own supper. She'd see him come the morning as she always did, another special moment that was theirs and theirs alone, moments stretching forever into the future.

CHAPTER 27

The World in His Palm

"Sit up, Henry!" Bob Garner muttered.

Henry sat up, but Petey Schlesinger punched him in the arm anyway, a little payback for having to endure Henry's vile insults. Henry leaned in to whisper: "Is that all you got bitch boy? There's guys in the joint who could push that asshole you call a face out the back of your head."

Henry then yawned, tucked his legs under his folding chair, and tipped his ball cap up on his head. It was 7:30, blue evening outside, and fuck me, I need a fuckin' drink. It had been another long day and late night of his nerves turning raw, but maybe this would be the last. He forced himself to sit still, but once in awhile, he patted the roll of twenties that Mr. Garner had slipped into the left pocket of his clean, pressed blue work shirt. He thought about the ten thousand bonus that Mr. Garner said he'd deposit in Henry's bank account. "If," the Boss had said as he tucked Henry's speech in the other shirt pocket, "you deliver for us."

"If," Petey had sneered from his seat at the computer.

"If I don't," Henry had winked at him, "you can suck my cock like ya been wantin' to ever since our eyes met." Petey flew half out of his chair, but he couldn't pound on Mr. Garner's Golden Boy, not in front of the Boss.

BAM! BAM! BAM!

Gavel time. Fatso Ferrand called the packed library room to order. Henry craned his neck to check out the overflowing crowd, but nausea bubbled up his esophagus and he shrank back down. Thank God, at least I ain't claustrophobic.

Mr. Garner nudged him again and winked: "It's showtime, Henry." Shit, Henry thought as he rubbed his queasy belly and his sphincter tightened. I ain't no fuckin' speechmaker.

Petey took his station at the laptop as the preliminaries started. Before Henry knew it, Mr. Garner was striding through the anti-Sierra crowd, which filled the right half of the room, with his chin up, like he was inviting them all to either take a big swing at his head or give his ass a big sloppy wet one. He took over the podium, turned on his fake farm-boy accent, and made his case for the makeover of Monitor County.

He talked about how isolated Monitor County was; how mired it was in the past and how, despite the excellent health of its citizens, if it didn't change and grow, it would die. "Folks jus' like y'all" saw it as a faraway place where only the "rich elite could pay the freight to come" such as wealthy nature lovers and the like, instead of a place where middle income families could bring their kids without worrying whether they'd fall in the creeks or be attacked by wild animals. "Tourism ain't fallen off jus' 'cause o' the price o' gas. It's also 'cause moms 'n' dads don't feel it's safe for their young 'uns." Then came the whopper about how his little girl almost drowned in Byrneville Creek the other day and he asked how many other kids had fallen in "just 'cause no one had the good sense to put a li'l fence up that woulda solved all that."

Then the PowerPoint show began. Henry kept his eyes on the Boss so he wouldn't throw up at the images that swam across the screen: the computer graphic mockups, scored with New-agey music, of the "The Plan for a Sierra Future."

Sierra Future planned to raze the village of Byrneville and put up that western movie set, lined with "family-friendly" shops and stores—"no liquor bars or nightclubs." There'd be a new family-friendly "green" hotel and vegetarian restaurant up on Dr. Turd-head's place above Alpine Canyon. They'd build five new small "green" winter resorts, all over the county. Mystic Valley would be a special residential section—families only—of ten-acre lots that would be built a hundred percent "green." The Boss used the word 'green' so much, he made it sound like Leprechaun City: green this, green that and all of it "family-friendly," code for "no new booze li-censes." But I'll be the fuck away from here anyway, Henry thought.

The Anti-Sierras booed at almost all of it while the Pro-Sierras oooohed like girls. There were catcalls and counter calls of "Shut up and let the man speak!" Cousin Danny led the Washoe clique in chanting, "NO! NO! to Sierra Future!" Everyone was going to the walls while Henry sat apart from it all, quiet and watchful.

As for the Boss, well, there weren't no flies on him. He kept his moony smile on, kept his words pouring like honey over ice cream. He understood how folks felt. Change was scary, so the boos and hisses bothered him none. It always started out that way, but "folks always came 'round" (code for "I'll wipe my ass with anyone who stands in my way."). He made the Antis look like a bunch of old, grumpy aunties with one hand, while he jerked off the Pros with the other. This motherfucker's good, Henry thought.

Finally, the sickening vistas vanished. Mr. Garner asked for ques-tions and then batted every single one out of the park. When would it start, how long would it take and—a big one—how much would it cost? It would start the minute the County Commission voted yes. It would take three years and be a bargain at $80 million. Where would all the working people live? Down in Osgood, in new "green" housing. How big would Monitor County get? It would grow to a population of six thousand. Mr. Garner added that the tax revenue, plus the profits from the resorts, would pay for new infrastructure. Of course, somebody asked about liquor licenses and Mr. Garner assured them that policy wouldn't change—same number of licenses as before. "Monitor County'll be a family environment. We'll grow without all them other growin' pains."

Sean Clownface, seated four rows ahead to the right, raised his hand: "Yeah, but what about all the other changes?" He stood up. "I don't believe a word of this. You're blowing smoke up—in everybody's ear. What about law enforcement? What about health care?" He went about with his "what-a-abouts" until a commissioner told him to sit his ass down so the Boss could answer.

The Boss blew off the law enforcement question: that was the county government's prerogative and he wouldn't interfere, but he figured with the increased tax base, there would be no problems.

Osgood Memorial would stay open. Everyone seemed to like this, even the Antis, until he delivered a slammer even Henry didn't expect. "The system'll be in the hands of the people it belongs to: individuals and families. We're already hard at work with the county's leadin' physician Doctor Dave Sutton—you saw that picture of us talkin' together in the PowerPoint there—to set up a private system that everybody who lives and works here can contribute to."

The Anti side fell real quiet, like they just had their pants pulled down. "Doc Sutton?" the Boss asked, looking around. "Hmm, guess he couldn't make it! I believe Doctor Dave's negotiatin' with insurance providers for your health. By the by, I wanna thank the doc a whole passel for his support and we both promise you that Monitor County will still be the healthiest county in all of California and the nation."

Everyone reacted as if the president had sold the country out to Al-Qaeda. Even Henry felt bushwhacked. He'd seen the Doc only once in the past couple weeks, up at Durant's, while Henry was crouching in Mr. Garner's vehicle recovering from that sickening drive. Everybody's got their price. Big lesson of the evening.

Meanwhile, the Doc's wife, sitting next to Sean, jumped in her chair like she'd just had a big one hammered up her pretty ass. Clownface blushed so red he lost all his freckles. Carla shook her head, her beautiful raven hair swung, and those fine-boned shoulders sagged as though her heart were falling out. Henry felt for her. However rich he got from this deal, Doc Dumbfuck was an ass-*hole* who'd just lost himself the most beautiful chick in the world.

After that, the questions ended. Mr. Garner said his thanks and walked back on the pro-Sierra side this time, shaking hands, dabbing fists, slapping high-fives. He sat next to Henry, kissed his wife, hugged his kids on the other side, and shook hands with Petey. Then, just when it seemed he would forget, he shook Henry's hand.

They opened the floor to comments. Henry's guts tightened as he started to rise, but Sean Clownface was already charging toward the podium. Henry looked at the Boss who shrugged: "You're next."

Sean was a blast. He made a complete *ass*-hole out of himself! He stumbled through his speech, talking like a rusty saw, while a big black fly started dive-bombing him. He said stupid shit like Monitor County "was one of the last pure, unsullied, untouched places" in the Sierra. (Bullshit. Ten thousand-plus miners were digging in these mountains over 150 years ago; there were more Washoe around then than there were now.) After saying a lot of oozy bullshit about Indians, the stupid dickhead then turns around and says "we all gotta stand up against Sierra Future like John Wayne at the Alamo!" *John Fuck-ing Wayne*! Even the Washoe clique thought this was hilarious.

He did score points about Garner's work for Getgo and how they'd "ruined" other communities, such as the bungee-jumping resort on top of Devil's Tower, Wyoming, and how they'd left ravaged landscapes, empty pockets, and empty houses. He claimed to have paper evidence of other "malfeasances" as he put it, but had no PowerPoint to back it up, just his shit-sorry self and a limp-dick promise to show his "evidence" to the commission before they voted. Sure pal. And I got Santa Claus and his sleigh waitin' up inside my ass.

Meanwhile, that fly kept bouncing on him like he was a fresh turd while everyone laughed as he tried to swat it away until another wiseass yelled: "Someone give this guy a bath!" The Pros broke into hoots and that finished him. Clownface ran back to his seat crying like a baby. Beautiful Carla put her arm around his shoulders, and tenderly kissed his red curly hair as if she loved him. Henry hated him.

"Make 'em love ya, Henry!" Bob Garner nudged him.

Henry was too chicken to walk among the Antis, but walking through the Pros wasn't any easier. The room watched him silently because, all cleaned up and transformed, he was a stranger to them all.

At the podium, he took a deep breath, staring at his speech as he unfolded it with shaking hands and that cloudy nauseous feeling. He paused to remind himself of one simple fact. He didn't want their love and admiration. He wanted to make fools of them. He wanted revenge and he'd get it by persuading them to destroy themselves.

"Good evenin' everyone. You may not recognize me, but my name's Henry West." A murmur passed through the room. "I'm a member of the Washoe Tribe and my people and I have lived here in Monitor County since time began." The Washoe group laughed in nervous confusion. Cousin Danny's wife said "Bullshit" right out loud, but Danny looked like the shit was running out his mouth.

Henry held up his hands: "Now, I know what some are thinkin'. Henry West? The drunken Indian—oops, I mean the pooor o-pressed min-orrr-rity. Henry, the ex-con, the bum sitting outside the Tap n' Grill everyday, his hand out, braggin' about how someday he was gonna do this or that and pull himself out of the gutter he and his people were stuck in …like the second after he gets his welfare check? That guy?

"I got news: that Henry West, he's gone. He's been sent packin'." He paused to let the fake miracle sink in. Sean Clownface's big mouth looked open for another fly; earlier he'd said some bullshit about how well he knew the mountains. Suddenly, this gave Henry white wings of inspiration. He forgot the words in front of him.

"Now, as a Washoe, I also know every mountaintop, every canyon, every ravine and arroyo and trail, every nook and cranny, just like Sean here says he knows 'em. Now, Sean seems like a nice young guy, but I gotta ask myself, where have I seen him before? And I go 'Oh, yeah, that newcomer. He's been up here, maybe a year and now he acts like he's to the mountains born and he already knows what's best for us. He tells a fairy story about how wild and open this country used to be. But the truth is that Indian people lived here already, lived all over America—the Washoe and thousands of other tribes, addin' up to millions of First Americans. We built our own cities. We plowed and planted the land, made and traded goods and hunted game. We were as every bit as civilized—maybe even more so—than any European country. Until the Europeans brought their diseases and took our land without even havin' the decency to pay us a decent price!

"Now I'm not blamin' you all. What happened before we were all born ain't your fault. But what about what's happenin' to my people now? What's Sean here really doin' for us, besides protectin' the mountains so he can play on 'em like a jungle gym? What's he brought besides his climbin' gear, his Birkenstocks, and stories about a place that never was? Does he know my name? The names of any members of my tribe? Or any of the other poor people livin' up here—'cause not all of us poor folks are Indian, y' know. I think Sean's walked past me five or six times in the last year and never even looked at me. Like I wasn't there."

Henry returned to his prepared remarks.

"Now I am here, like I rose from the dead. How in the heck did that happen? How did Henry West, Byrneville's town drunk, suddenly become the man you see now? Did Sean do it? Well, no—it wasn't him. It was someone else. Somebody who stopped, saw my face, and asked my name. A man who held out his hand sayin', 'Henry West, time to get on your feet.'"

Henry gracefully opened his hand toward the back of the room.

"That would be the man in the back there. Mr. Bob Garner."

Henry paused for effect as the room turned around and Mr. Garner bashfully shrugged. Then they turned back around and jumped back into Henry's hand. He slowly closed his fist.

"That Sean fella, what's he brung with him, really? I ain't got the faintest idea. But I can tell you as fact, with my brain, these eyes and—" Henry placed his hand over his chest, over the spot where the money was—"with my heart that Mr. Garner's brought real value and values to the table. A vision of what we can be, and you saw just a glimpse of it. He's buildin' a ladder, openin' a door for me, my people, for all of you. Now I got me a new life. Holdin' down a job, livin' in a real house. I can start a family, too. And you know where my new family's gonna live?" He jabbed his finger at the podium. "Right here in Monitor County. I'm darn proud to be part of it. After a hundred years, the Washoe are back in Monitor County. Not because of some government program or some handout, but because of Sierra Future."

"My dark days are over. Now I stand and walk as a man. The days of the noble long-suffering Indian are over. The days of guilty white liberals feelin' sorry for us and buyin' us off with reservations and welfare checks are done. It's time to walk a different trail and I say 'Thank you! Thank you, Mr. Bob Garner, a real man of the people. And thanks to Sierra Future. Take it from one Indian who knows!"

•

Later that night, Henry lay wrapped in his rabbit skin robe on the bed in the little cottage, gulping the last of the Cuervo Gold while trying to relive his triumph. The Boss was right: Cons are easy. He got half the room cheering for him, the other half booing and it was all great. He didn't even mind when Alvie Simpleton tried to take a poke at him. Sheriff Puker had his dope-i-ties on hand in case the shit-dam broke. Sure enough, it did, though it was a chick fight compared to what Henry saw in Folsom. The jostling made him sick, but Mr. Garner grabbed him by the collar just in time and drew him into a gauntlet he'd made out of his family—no one would attack a woman and her children. Underpants Sheriff King led them outside without a word and Henry got the feeling that his opinion of Henry hadn't changed—Henry was still a shit-bird even with a bath and new clothes. Well, fuck you too, Underpants Sheriff. You'll be bounced out on your pockets, too, right beside me, but I'll be the one laughin'.

As they reached the parking lot, he heard glass breaking. The fools. The cocksuckers were now in the gutter where he'd once been. In the morning they'd awaken to their bruised faces in their mirrors and hate themselves. They got in a fight over their precious treasure and lost it all.

On the way home, Mr. Garner thanked him again and praised him for being "extemporaneous" or something. But once home, the Garners and Schlesinger retreated into their topsy-turvy yellow pyramid and Henry West was alone again. His cottage felt like a dumpy doghouse. "Woof woof," he sighed, looking around the kitchen.

Now he lay wrapped in mama's rabbit skin robe, sucking on the Cuervo like it was a teat, replaying every moment but unable recapture the exact feeling. Who was the party-pooping motherfucker who said "All glory is fleeting"? Why did desolation always roll back in like a runny shit-tide? "Mama, if only you could see," he cried aloud and imagined her face, but it was cold and it wouldn't smile, no matter how hard he tried to tweak it in his mind.

"But, Mama! I didn't screw up this time! I did something right!"

Despite the drink, Henry dreamed that night of his mama's face. She looked like she was cold. He tried to give her back the rabbit skin robe, but it fell through her body into darkness, while her face remained like a still winter morning. Not uncaring but with disappointment, as though at last, he'd destroyed her love for him.

....

CHAPTER 28

The Woman in the Window

Dave felt a confused guilt about missing the meeting as he wrested his truck into the driveway, missing Bartok's gleaming white carriage by inches. With his life now so entwined with the county's, he should have been there to voice his opposition, whatever his pessimism about victory.

He had good enough excuses: a three-hour meeting with Ted Knowland about the sudden resurrection of Osgood Memorial; long e-mails to state medical officials in both Nevada and California; lengthy phone conversations with a medical supply sales rep and reps from three insurance carriers, two of them referred by Garner, referrals he could happily have done without. Just thinking about that made him feel smudged. At least Carla had been there at the meeting.

He groped his way around the SUV, its whiteness turning the night blacker. The house looked empty, but he sensed Carla was home. At the same time though, he shamefully wished she wasn't. They'd hardly spoken since Sunday afternoon, after he woke up from his nap to find her sitting and sobbing by the stream. "Oh, nothing," she stiffly laughed off his question. "I'm just PMS-ing."

He knew she was fibbing and when he tried to press her again about the specialist, she snapped, "You're not hoping I'm still sick, are you?" The music had gone from her humor. Her jokes went over like rocks thrown at birds.

Meanwhile, she'd kept on with her ritual songs, at dusk and at dawn. Both melodies, one exalted, one mournful, had become worms, swirling and streaming through his brain, especially when he looked at the mountains he once so loved without question and in peaceful silence. Now he had a soundtrack in his head he didn't care for.

Kat wasn't at his feet to sweetly greet him as usual. Her sudden absence made Dave feel like a sad sack sitcom husband: Even the cat won't talk to me.

The whole house, in fact, looked empty, felt empty. Yet Dave sensed another presence, an eerie atmosphere, an electric invisible energy. As he walked down the hall toward the kitchen, his shoulder muscles tightened and his hairs bristled all over as his lizard brain murmured "danger danger," as though something was scuttling just out of sight, behind, above on the ceil—oh, stop it. You're just tired. He would not look behind him.

The kitchen light's glare hurt his eyes, the room's dingy air seemed profane and nausea rose like smoke in his mouth when he saw the bloody meringue of Styrofoam and cellophane foaming from the garbage pail. A blood-smeared carving knife lay next to the sink.

Then he turned to call out to Kat again and saw the little striped smudge out on the patio, lying in a square of kitchen light, at the edge of the darkness. He knew the cat was dead before he even picked her up. Her head dangled from a deep bloodless slash in her neck. Her once adoring doll eyes were empty slits now. Dave felt too overwhelmed with shock to wonder what had killed her—an owl, fox, coyote, or hawk. Dave openly sobbed, his grief as terrible as if she'd been human, because Kat, simple and innocent, had died violently, alone and afraid.

"What were you doing outside, little girl? You're not supposed to be out—"

Then the glass door slid closed with a thump and the lock clicked. With Kat in his arms, Dave rose and turned. Carla was standing behind the glass door. She looked like a cut-out doll made from black paper, featureless, faceless, only a bladed shadow.

He clumsily pulled at the door: "Hey! What the hell is this? What happened to Kat?"

Close up now, he could see her cheeks swelling as though she were churning her tongue. She mumbled something but the only word he heard was "hungry." Then she turned and left the kitchen, sweeping her hand over the light switch. The house plunged into total empty darkness, leaving Dave alone in the cold, a beloved friend dead in his arms.

Quaking, Dave banged his shin on the picnic bench as he laid Kat gently on the table. "I'm sorry I wasn't here for you." He stroked her dry stiffening fur.

He fumbled for his penlight but it was nearly out of juice. "Carla!" His nervous shout sounded muffled. "Carla!" he shouted again as he groped along the side of the house. It was so quiet, it was as if she'd left, maybe had come outside, maybe was somewhere nearby. He felt himself growing afraid. It's just the dark, he told himself. It's just the dark.

When he reached the living room window, a familiar but coarse whisper, unseen, floated calmly from inside. "Did you know there's a photo of you and that man shaking hands? Everyone saw it. You must be proud of yourself." The voice laughed bitterly. "Slick."

"What guy? Carla, what are you talking about?"

"Oooooh," the voice teased. "Now he plays innocent."

Dave's fear turned to anger. He wanted to get inside and have it out with her instead of playing kids going "boo!" He felt his way along, stumbling twice, tripping once. His foot missed the stoop and he banged his knee on the top step. The front door was also locked, and as he patted his pockets for the keys, he remembered how they'd chinked as he had thrown them on the hallway table after he walked through the door.

"Carla!" He shook the knob and pounded. "Let me in. Please. Cut it out. This is stupid. We gotta talk. Open the door!"

Her voice floated out coarse, cold and disembodied. "We lost because of you, like you planned. I should have seen it when you took his money. You sold us all out. Me, most of all. I thought you loved me. I get it now, what you were trying to tell me the other day. I get it all."

"I wasn't saying—"

"Oh, stop it." A mature grown-up sigh of weary condescension. "Listen to yourself. I can't stay with you. I just can't."

"Carla, this isn't fair."

"Fair? You mean in the way you swept in on that old doctor's practice? His corpse was hardly cold. Then I saw that picture ...I got the picture alright. Click. Marriage over."

Dave pounded at the door until his fists were sore. "Carla! Please! Let me explain. It's not what you think. Let me in."

He heard a jingling sound. She was shaking the keys and laughing, taunting him.

"Too late. I'm already gone. This is the voice I've left behind, that's all." The keys chinked as they hit the floor. "I'm not here. Just my voice."

Dave panicked as silence fell again. He left the porch, went to his hands and knees, crawled around on the cold wet ground looking for a rock. He would break a lock or a window and get inside where they'd fight this out, settle it, repair the marriage, and become one again. Because everything else was impossible. She couldn't end it like this, in coarse crazy whispers. It was wrong, crazy wrong. She didn't understand. That was all. Just talk to me, just talk to me!

Finally, he found a stone that fit his hand, but when he staggered to his feet, that intense hush had fallen over the house once more, as if it had become a house without doors or windows. The brief flash of terror he'd felt earlier returned, an intense blue flame in his heart, in the windless silence all around.

What will you find if you break that window, if you go inside?

264

Will it be her, waiting there for you? What is it about her voice, cold and coarse in dead darkness? What if it were true …the only thing left, a voice in empty dark air?

The rock fell from his hand and hit the porch with a thump that shocked him back into the freezing present. He hugged himself in shaking despair, the helpless physician with the dying patient, not knowing what do, sensing irrationally that he was safer out here in the night, than inside his house.

The only thing visible was Bartok's vehicle. As he carefully felt his away around it, he mulled over driving to Tim's and asking to spend the night there. It wasn't until he'd reached his truck that he remembered again that he didn't have his keys.

At least he hadn't locked his truck. He could stand one night sleeping in the back. He fumbled around setting up the cot, the sleeping bag, and extra blanket. His frantic mind resembled the aftermath described by accident and assault victims—wide awake, but scattered and incoherent; splintered thoughts, blurred, rushing images swirling in and out. He burst into tears when he couldn't find the scrawny pillow until he reached down behind the driver's seat. His feet hung over the bottom of the cot and when he tried to curl up on his side to conserve heat, his knees lay across the hard, aluminum frame.

He shivered in the pale light from a half moon that gleamed through the windshield. Dogs howled miserably in the distance. His thoughts swirled about in search of clarity and comfort. He tried counting backward from one hundred to calm himself and when that didn't work, he tried thinking like a doctor, seeking a diagnosis, but every theory ended at a locked door.

Finally, he thought about Carla's actual words. He finally remembered the ambush photo Peter Schlesinger had taken that time Garner grabbed his hand. That felt like months ago. Garner had worked it into his campaign so everyone would see it as an endorsement. Indeed, Dave had become an important member of the community, hadn't he? As he went—or more accurately, where he was seen to go—others would follow. Perception over reality equals politics. No matter how much he protested, even if he had the perfect evidence to prove that he—and everyone in Monitor County—had been bushwhacked, the lie triumphed while the truth, homely and nuanced, lay shivering in the dark under a cheap blanket. There was only one thing to do if he hoped to regain a sense of honor: sell the practice and leave under public protest. Go back to San Francisco and start over.

The idea only comforted him briefly. There was Carla to consider. Would she ever believe his story? After the uncanny episode—her disembodied voice stirring around like gravel in the darkness—he wasn't so sure. It was as if something had taken her over. Despite her accusations, she was the one who had changed radically in the last couple of weeks, so much so, she'd become someone else. The Sierra Future argument felt like an excuse, a camouflage for a deeper darker secret.

"But what?" he whispered and then his memory stumbled on that old court-ordered psych evaluation he'd read, about Chloe Byrne. He whispered to himself in its dry objective, but somehow reassuring, language:

"Carla Sutton, lovely 32 y.o. female presented with ALS until almost two weeks ago, when she claims the disease disappeared. Initial examination indicated significant and sudden remission: restoration of muscle tissue, improved reflexes, muscle strength and coordination, as patient performed front flips down the hallway. (Note: patient had only cursory recreational experience as a gymnast.) Further examination impossible due to time constraints and patient's refusal to cooperate. Other symptoms include pale skin and increased sensitivity to sunlight. Also noted are remarkable changes in diet (patient eats only uncooked meat) and personality: Increased energy, increased confidence of already confident personality, accompanied by a detached distracted highly irritable manner; obsessive behaviors, such as getting up in the morning to sing to a bird she identified as an actual, real-life dragon."

He paused for a minute and then muttered: "She didn't call me by my name when we were arguing. She hasn't called me by my name since …I can't remember. I'm not Dave anymore. I'm an object."

"Patient shows possible signs of aphasia in an apparent inability to remember names, especially of those closest to her. Also shows evidence of obsession with new employer."

Yes, that day. Returning to the scene of the accident and there they were, holding hands, Bartok's hand clinging desperately to hers and now that very vehicle was sitting only a foot away, and I wish it had the gone the rest of the way over the cliff.

Abrupt change in patient's condition coincides with….

"Stop it!" he cried, laying his arm over his eyes. "There's no such thing as faith healing!" he announced, violently kicking the thought from his mind. "I will not give in to superstition," he swore. "Ever. He's just a mean stinky old man!"

Back to real-life explanations, like the brain disorders he'd learned about in med school. If she didn't have ALS, then what? Creuzfeldt-Jakob? Maybe, wolfing down raw meat like that. Still, it takes decades before CJ's prions show their dark tracks. Her manner of speaking seemed calm and rational, full of chilly purpose. That was what made her false accusations sting so badly; she'd delivered them in the kind of calm ghostly voice that made fantasy into reality and reality a fantasy. She'd always been glib, but this was insane, the way she'd stood so perfectly still in the kitchen, her face shadowed, her tongue churning in her mouth as he pleaded with her to tell him what had happened to poor Kat, why she was lying out there dead and then—what was it she'd said?

" …hungry …"

Dave sat up as a monstrous image filled itself in—Carla holding Kat in her arms, that bloody knife in her hands, her mouth smeared red.

"I was hungry."

A twig snapped nearby, outside, in the dark.

Dave carefully set his feet down on the cold metal floor.

"Carla?"

"Sweetheart," Carla's graveled whisper floated outside the truck, ethereal, resonant, attractive like a candle, glittering like a star. A silver mote in space, a voice without a mouth, with no one behind it.

He heard a metallic scraping sound along the body of the truck, like a knife being dragged along.

"I'm hungry," she whispered. He heard her tongue churning.

Dave quickly locked the back door. He crashed into medical equipment and hit his head on the ceiling as he scrambled over the front seat, hit the button on the left, then turned to hit the button on the right—

—and there she stood, only the window between them, her face a blank. Next to it, the shadow of a knife in her hand pointed upward—the knife in sink, smeared with Kat's blood—next to her face. Now, she wanted his blood.

Dave calmly pressed the button down, his mouth dry. He spoke slowly and carefully: "I think you should go inside, Carla."

She seemed to sink with disappointment. "Okay," she murmured. "He wants you to live anyway." She stepped back slowly until she faded in the dark. There came one more twig snap. He listened closely to hear if she went in the house, but Bartok's SUV muffled the sound.

Dave crept back onto his cot, his mind clearer now, because, weirdly, he seemed to be faced with something he could understand. The simple fact was that his wife, the woman he loved like no other, had come down with a clinical mental illness, the reasons for which could wait. In the morning, there'd be action. He'd talk to Tim: "My wife killed our cat and threatened me with the same knife." He'd call an attorney specializing in mental health issues. They had to get her into care, fast, before someone really got hurt.

Still, though relieved, his mind clear, he wept anyway, wept for hours.

Then, toward morning, just when at last he was fluttering down into sleep, Carla's voice rose in song again as the air turned morning gray. Dave sat up fast. His fear turned back to the impotent rage he'd fought off hours ago. He threw the pillow to the floor. "Goddamnit it!" he roared at the top of his lungs.

Carla ignored his curse, kept on singing her defiant song in the graying light as Dave rolled out the back door. The backyard was empty. She must have been in the bedroom, her arms raised, her head back, her voice ululating like a serrated blade.

She'd left the front door unlocked this time. Dave tore into the hallway and flung open the closet door. Tim's hunting rifle fell right into his arms as though it had been waiting. It felt as light as balsa wood. The cartridges clicked smoothly in as Carla kept singing her mad mourning song from behind the bedroom door.

Dave ran in a crouch around the corner of the house into the side yard. There it was, racing toward the Ark, against the dawn. It was far out of range. He didn't care. Maybe the shot would scare it off, maybe not, but Carla would know that it was just a goddamn stupid bird, that was all, not a fucking mystical thing about it. One real world gunshot would break the awful spell. She would see its reality and nothing else.

He took aim and sighted through the scope as Carla's voice rose up behind, urging the bird to fly faster. It remained a near-speck through the scope as it flew, swift as a jet, like no bird ever seen, too graceful for a bat, night-black, with tooth-like serrated wings.

The gunshot cracked the air, cutting through Carla's piercing shriek. The rifle stock punched Dave in the shoulder, staggering him, but he sighted on it again as the damned thing flew big and bold across the sky, its great wings beating like a chant.

Then the dragon did an impossible thing: It stopped in mid-air, hung there like a hummingbird, just under where the first shafts of sunlight turned the top of Dragon's Ark a snowy pink. It slowly flapped its wings, like a vulture cooling itself. Tiny blue light sparkled where its eyes would be, as though mocking the small creature's efforts to kill it.

Dave fired again. His feet slipped out from under him and he sat hard on the dewy grass. Carla's voice rose to a screech, a single keening note of fury. The western morning sky stood empty, except for a tiny puff of smoke where the thing had defiantly hovered.

Carla's screams rose to an ear-splitting screech. Dave turned to look but he shouldn't have.

The woman in the window was naked. Her body shimmered, flesh rippling, as though it were changing shape. Her face was all mouth, nothing but white, black, and red mouth, screaming, the rest of her features crushed into deep folds from where shining eyes bulged out like those of a mantis.

The mantis-eyed woman drove her fists through the window.

As glass showered on him, Dave's rational mind finally cracked and rapidly shut down, until only the woman's screams remained, following him down into darkness.

CHAPTER 29

Trespasser

Eight months after she left, Claudia Prentice returned to Annie Goodman's cabin on Alpine Canyon Road to rescue the heirloom settee she'd left behind in her haste. She firmly promised to herself—and the "friend" who brought along her truck—that they'd stay only one night. "Then pack and go."

The "friend" took one trembling look around the bleak cabin in the barren, silent canyon: "I don't see how you could even stay one night." She scrambled back into her truck. "I'll stay in the village tonight and bring the truck back up tomorrow, okay? Promise!" Then her truck disappeared down the steep driveway. Claudia held her breath, wondering if she'd make it without plunging over the cliff below.

The friend never did come back, but, to her surprise, Claudia didn't mind. Though she was alone, she didn't feel lonely here, like she had all her fifty-plus years in the world below, where she'd always been the touchy sort, flinching and taking offense at every affront, no matter how minor or well-intended.

I've gotten away from it all. The thought sounded loudly in the little canyon's silence.

Night, she noticed, did not fall here. It rose from the valley below. She felt herself draw in and felt more solid, sure and centered. That night as she lay in Annie's bed, in a cloak of pitch darkness, she saw clearly how lonely she'd always been and how, in this strange faraway nook in the mountains, she felt lonely no more.

Along with this odd serenity, she felt an anticipation that said this was a first step on a longer greater journey toward the simple, ideal self she'd always yearned for; a self, a soul to be absorbed into the soul of the cosmos. Then, she'd become part of everything.

The cabin had its own quiet soul. Even with her belongings, its simple rooms felt uncluttered like she wanted her mind to be. Meanwhile, while the memory of her life below faded. Soon, the name of the town she where she lived sounded like a foreign word. So did the names of her friends.

Physical changes came, too. Her senses sharpened and magnified. Her fingertips could feel every coarse thread of the settee, even the color variation of its fading dyes. She heard insect feet scratching from behind the walls. She smelled sweet pine air from miles away and the whiff of ozone from passing afternoon storms.

Sometime during the night, she felt her left eye swelling again. At midnight, she grabbed a flashlight, went outside and looked at the half moon overhead. Her swollen eye, instead of being blind, magnified everything so she could see the contours of the moon's mountains. The grains of dirt on the ground from fifty feet away looked like boulders.

The eye also worked microscopically. When she peered closely at her hand, she saw how the tissue cells bound her skin together. Focusing deeper, she gasped with delight that she could see the grand winding staircase of her DNA, as though built for an endless parade of angels and sprites. At this level, flesh seemed mutable, something she could remold by simply saying, "I want. I can. I will."

Also like last time, the sight out of her right eye remained normal. Double vision made navigation difficult but Claudia knew the right eye would soon follow the same evolutionary course. Until then, she'd wear the bandanna over the left eye.

When she returned to bed and turned off the flashlight, it was so dark she had difficulty distinguishing between waking and sleeping.

Annoyed, she tore the old gold watch from her wrist, opened the door, and threw it outside. In this world, natural light would be the only timepiece she would need.

The only other incident that first night was the brief appearance of two blue lights fading in from the ink. They blinked off and on, like a pair of fireflies. She heard something like a sigh and realized that the lights were two eyes. Though there was no face around them, they wore a look of surprise. Before she could rouse herself to even say hello, they drifted away into smoky black air.

She awoke to a morning light that looked to be filtered through an old unwashed stocking. She realized she was missing one more sense: taste. Her mouth felt hollow, a hollowness echoed by the growls from her stomach. The refrigerator was empty. Reluctantly, Claudia tightened the bandanna around her super eye and drove down the precipitous driveway with great care. Down she went, all the way into the valley, to the supermarket in the ugly little town.

Without thinking, she bypassed both the vegetable and fruit sections and the health food section—whose labels she'd once known by heart—and went directly to the giant meat counter. Her mouth sloshed as she looked over the red archipelago of meat. This was a great change, too. She hadn't eaten meat in over forty years and now she was craving it. Something about its pungent aroma unlocked the memory of the path she'd taken to come here.

•

Claudia had been living with her recently widowed mother outside of Carson City when she saw the singles' ad on an online dating service one early September afternoon:

"Women Seeking Women—Untangled Wings. Transforming high country soul, forever alive, needs a companion to make my to-morrow OUR tomorrow, a CLEAN LIVING, PURE THINKING soul for the final breakthrough. Here, a Future beckons, the Great Time is coming and I don't want to rise to it alone. Fly along with me on wings untangled under the light of the moon and stars."

This was vision. Everyone else on the dating board had one flaw or another: Republican; too young; too materialistic; non-vegans; couch potatoes; sports fans; sex addicts; muddled liberals, who maybe weren't bad people, but their "live-and-let-live" philosophy hinted at a tolerance of cruelty and injustice that Claudia found intolerable. No pure souls here, like those back in the day when Sisterhood nearly embraced the world. Where had they all gone?

This ad, simple and enigmatic, with its siren call to purity and a promise of transcendence, proved irresistible. Still, Claudia responded warily. What if the poster turned out to be a man in disguise, a liar laying a dangerous trap? She demanded a photo and nervously sent one of herself. Claudia looked her age, like the serious librarian she'd been most of her life, with her finger to her lips. To Claudia, wearing a smile meant hardening your heart in a violent, unjust world.

Two weeks and two failed dates later, a reply came. The way she looked, Annie Goodman should have been named "Annie Good-Woman." The drugstore photo couldn't hide a full-faced, ruddy wholesomeness and fruity natural goodness; her huge blue eyes twinkled from under silver-frosted curls that barely hid large seashell ears.

A week later, Claudia found those eyes shining at her from a rear table of a darkened coffee house in the sad little town across the state line. As she approached, Annie rose like a bear and swallowed Claudia in a warm hug. Claudia's boyish body flushed as if it had been flooded by golden honeyed sun.

"Hello, mouse," Annie whispered. "It's wonderful to meet you."

Annie wore no makeup, jewelry, perfume or other glitter. Her baggy khakis and earth-brown, hand-woven woolen sweater concealed her healthy womanly curves with becoming modesty. Her voice, though strangely hoarse, sounded ripe with spirit and soul.

Despite Annie's enchanting voice, however, Claudia recalled little of what she said. They agreed about everything as Claudia spilled out her wounded soul like orphaned buttons: "I know exactly what you mean," Annie replied. "I agree completely …That bastard …

Those bastards …Yes, we should always strive to transcend our earthly selves …Yes, I'm very careful about what I eat."

Finally, Claudia woke up from tumbling down love's long winding staircase to ask apologetically what Annie did for a living.

"I'm a caregiver."

Claudia felt a toasty warmth as Annie told how she'd been chauffeuring Mr. Bartok, a wealthy old recluse, around the mountains for "more years than I can count." He paid more than enough for them both to live on. Whoever joined her in her cozy cabin would never have to toil in the world again. Someday very soon, she promised, the old hermit would leave her all his wealth, setting them both free, making them feel truly empowered. "We'll grow wings and fly invisible like angels!"

Much too soon, Annie slipped on a pair of big black-lensed sungoggles. She had to be home before sunset. "Night-rise," as she called it, was the most beautiful time up that way. She'd never missed a mountain sunset and rose every morning to watch the dawn, she said, nodding as though extending an invitation.

The next weekend, Claudia drove into the big, blue mountains, where the Fall leaves shimmered with flaming orange and bright yellow in cool, clear air. The road to Annie's was her most challenging drive ever. She didn't dare peek at the scenery as she patted her little car's dashboard while its engine gasped for air: "C'mon, little car!"

She only saw the mountain when she reached the entrance to Annie's driveway. Its blackness filled her windshield. At first it reminded her of a gigantic old castle. Then she thought it looked more like a phallus, the way it arrogantly, crudely thrust its peak up between pure white clouds into an innocent blue sky.

It's a mountain. It's part of Nature. It's all good, she quickly shushed her disquiet. I'm in Gaia's world. Not man's.

Claudia's car coughed its way up into a small, gray steep-walled canyon where sat the little cabin. Claudia felt lightly pinched by claustrophobia, but told herself it was cozy.

Annie lived simply between bare wood walls, in a bedroom with only one bed and wardrobe; a living room with two plain wood chairs, one rocking, the other not; a kitchen, with a wooden table with two unpainted chairs; no rugs, only plain muslin sheets on the windows. A cracked flaking bathroom mirror was the only sign of vanity. The only appliance was an old refrigerator, run by a small, noisy generator that she didn't need because the cold air kept her food fresh. Annie lived by the glow of candles and lanterns.

"All I need is someone to share it with me, mouse."

"And maybe a little more furniture," Claudia teased and immediately regretted her thoughtless remark. Already, she wanted to stay.

They talked and drank tea for too few hours. A week later, Claudia, ignoring her mother's tears and her "friends'" warnings, met Annie in the sad town, this time pulling along a mid-sized trailer full of books, furniture, and her beloved settee. They hooked the trailer to the SUV and Claudia followed Annie up to the little cabin.

Annie was a superwoman. She toted Claudia's things—including the heavy settee—into the cabin over her head with an inspiring strength that wore Claudia out. Afterward, Claudia rested on her settee and talked while Annie listened silently while rocking in her rocker at the window, still wearing her sungoggles even in this sunless canyon. Claudia fell asleep to the sound of her own voice.

She awoke just before sunset. Annie had gone out. Claudia rushed to make dinner, eager to give her new life partner a taste of nourishing vegan cooking. But just as her hand felt the refrigerator door's greasy handle, Annie's voice, slightly raspy, but rich, warm and strong, floated in through the dusk. She was singing!

Claudia ran outside and found herself the privileged audience for the best vocal recital she'd ever heard. Annie's voice seemed to lift the night into the sky. She sang a wordless sweeping melody that celebrated the waning of the day and welcomed the waxing of the night. With each uplifting note, a star twinkled on, songs and stars playing together across the purple-black sky. Then, for a finale, as the song faded, a great black bird swooped down into the canyon and flew between them, so fast, Claudia saw only a streak of blue and red fire.

A cold puff of wind lifted her hair. Then the bird was gone.

Annie went inside without a word, her eyes shimmering with what looked like tears of joy. Claudia stayed out for awhile, gazing up into the sky, feeling a new magic. The canyon was a bowl filled with a dense throbbing power, and the sky was a well full of stars. She felt so happy, she felt weightless. She'd always wanted to be a bird. She'd never felt so close to being one before.

Then she remembered dinner and hurried inside. She found Annie seated at the kitchen table, a plate piled high with red medallions in front of her, her large blue eyes bulging from her head with fierce childlike absorption, her mouth running red.

"Beets!" Claudia murmured in warm satisfaction. "Yummy!"

Annie threw her head back in a huge red barking laugh. Claudia drew near and smelled a familiar rusty smell: No, not beets. It was a mound of raw sliced beef.

Nausea punched Claudia in her stomach as she covered her mouth with her hand. Annie scowled before realizing she was being rude. She held up a dripping chunk of beef impaled on the tines of her fork:

"I'm sorry! You want some?" She waved at the fridge. "There's a whole cow in there. Go for it! It's not as good as wild blood, among other things."

"Annie. That's not healthy. You said you were—"

"You didn't ask if I was vegetarian, like you—"

"Vegan—"

"Whatever. I said I was careful about what I ate. Haven't been sick a day in years." Annie wiped her mouth on her sleeve.

"The blood is the life, little mouse!" she winked.

Claudia retreated to the living room where she listened in horror as Annie chewed and slurped the flesh of once-sentient creatures with near-pornographic pleasure.

By the time Annie heaved her last sated sigh, Claudia's candle-lit fantasies of making love to this woman had been doused. Annie didn't seem to mind. "It can get lonely up here and I'm just glad to have someone with me," she sighed as she pointed to the side of the big bed next to the window. "You sleep there. Blow out the candle, would you?"

Claudia sat staring out into the dark outside: What have I gotten myself into? She turned to look at Annie who had fallen right asleep, lying on her back, her arms at her side. For the first time, Claudia noticed how huge her eyes were, so big, her eyelids only closed halfway, leaving two eerie white slits.

Claudia blew out the candle. Darkness fell like a trap door. She lay down slowly, afraid the bed wouldn't be there, only a bottomless hole.

In darkness so black, she couldn't be sure if she'd fallen asleep, an ever deeper darkness rolled into the room. She heard a slurping sound as two icy blue eyes faded into view, staring at her over a mouth shaped like a suction cup that had attached itself to her left forearm. Then two fingers reached up and pushed down on her eyelids. "Go to sleep," a voice rumbled. Her mind clicked off.

She woke up to Annie singing in a dreary dawn. Her morning song was, indeed, a mourning song, a slow-falling dirge. Claudia tried to sit up, but her heart buzzed and dizziness overwhelmed her. Later, she was treated to the sight of Annie at breakfast—this time pork chops, ground beef, and a slab of bacon. Again, Claudia retreated to her settee.

When Annie entered the living room in her sungoggles, reeking of animal product, Claudia nervously asked if they might go get some food that she could eat. Annie happily agreed. "Anything to keep my mouse by my side." But they couldn't take the SUV—only Mr. Bartok could ride in that.

They drove down to the village in Claudia's car. The general store had almost no healthy food at all, not even soy products. The shelves were stocked with a foul selection of cold cuts, canned tuna, and fatty, processed, slaughterhouse scraps. The wine selection was poor and Annie grabbed Claudia's arm before she could even touch a bottle: "Fouls your blood," she warned. The obsessed lover couldn't bring herself to argue and settled for bone-white lettuce, freezer-burned peas and corn, and pre-boiled rice.

Afterward, Annie took her to the county library where they watched a movie with a tiny audience of villagers. The movie was *Dracula* (one of the few names that she remembered now). Most of the audience seemed to find it quaint and harmless, but not Claudia. She disliked movies in general and vampire movies in particular with their insidious celebration of women's oppression in the guise of "entertainment."

The presenter was a tall, brunette sex bomb who strutted about in calf-high boots, tight jeans, and a half-buttoned blouse. She clearly had forgotten about the struggles and sacrifices of earlier generations of women as she shamelessly flaunted her *buh-rests* like a casino stripper, defending this junk as "Art" with heartless sophistication. Finally, Claudia stood up and, in a piping quavering voice, put the ugly thing in its place: No matter how old and dated the movie was, it remained harmful propaganda for the subjugation of all women. And what did the audience do? What everyone else always did when confronted with sincerely held beliefs: They laughed that post-modern laugh that said, "It doesn't matter." But, she assured herself, they also laughed because they were nervous and they were nervous because, deep down, they knew she was right.

"Why did you take me to see that?" Claudia seethed on the road back up into the mountains.

"My employer recommended it," Annie mysteriously snickered. "He said I'd find it funny. He was right. It made him look wimpy."

Made who look wimpy? Then Claudia remembered what Annie had said the night before.

"Last night you said that blood was life. Dracula says the same thing in the movie, but if you've never seen it before, how did you know—"

"Have I ever tell you about my cancer?" Annie then told the personal and inspirational story of her near-fatal illness and reawakened the love that Claudia feared was fading. Oddly, she seemed to credit her employer for the cure. As a loyal leftist, Claudia in no way believed that bosses ever cured cancer. They only gave it.

"It's why I stay here," Annie said as they reached the bottom of the driveway. "Coming here brought me back to life. Did you know that cancer tumors are immortal? So long as it has blood to feed on, it'll live forever. This time I'll be the one who lives forever."

Claudia almost went over the cliff trying to make that dangerous turn and had to stop to collect herself. The black face of the mountain crowded her vision as she blurted out the rude nickname she'd bestowed upon it.

The mountain shadowed her mind all evening, especially when Annie sang her song again at sunset. This time, Claudia stayed in and baked a muddy veggie casserole on the wood stove. She supped in the living room, while Annie ate raw lamb chops in the kitchen. No matter how hard Claudia brushed her teeth that night, she still tasted blood. Blood now seemed to mist the very air.

That night came another dream. This one snatched her out of bed by her feet and pulled her up through the bedroom ceiling as though it were made of fog. She saw the cabin below, then the canyon rim, fall away. Air raced over her skin, cold and sharp as a knife. She was flown upside down across the sky, shaken and swung around like a doll. She couldn't wake herself up. Suddenly, she was looking up—down—at a pointed peak underneath. Phallus Mountain. Who or whatever it was that had her by the feet, yo-yoed her up and down so the peak looked like it was thrusting at her face. She vomited and glimpsed her half-digested casserole fly apart into the darkness. Then the stars zipped by and she was dumped carelessly back into bed. "Please let her stay, please. Please let her stay," Annie pleaded. Then she heard a frosty finger snap and slept.

She awoke to the sound of Annie's heartbreaking song, a dull gray light, and a grinding headache that swelled behind her left eye. She curled up under the covers to hide. Just when she fell back to sleep, harsh light flooded in as the covers were thrown back. Something like a salty piece of sponge pried itself between her lips and pushed against her teeth.

"C'mon, mouse. Take it please …it's not so bad. You'll get used to it."

Salty liquid oozed between her teeth and spread over her tongue. She opened her eyes. Annie's huge face was a foot away, distorted with effort as she tried to force a chunk of raw steak into Claudia's mouth as though she were an infant being fed vegetables for the first time.

The impact on Claudia's system—free of animal products for so long—sent her flying out of bed into the grimy bathroom, where she violently dry-heaved. When she was through, she tasted her bile and the flavor of the last night's casserole and remembered the way it had flown out of her mouth in the dream. Then, in the shattered reflection of the mirror, she saw her left eye bulging out.

"Oh God! My eye!" Half-blind, Claudia stumbled out and collapsed at the kitchen table, her face in her arms, humiliated, guilty and, most of all, terribly frightened. She felt Annie's cold shadow fall across her and cried out: "I don't think I can do this."

"I know," Annie croaked, her large eyes looking cold, even while hidden behind her sungoggles. Her face looked split in two, one half of it bigger than the other.

Claudia pushed herself to her feet, trembling, mumbling something about her mother needing her. Something had gone wrong with her eyesight. The vision out her left eye was fantastically magnified. It took time to recognize that gigantic leather loop as her purse strap, but it looked too big to grab hold of. Then she saw her enlarged hand and put the two together. It was only until she covered the "super-eye" with her hand that the world returned to human proportions and became manageable through her tears.

She wanted to leave right then, but too much had happened to go without saying good-bye. Her hand cupped over her bloated eye, she returned to find Annie sobbing at the kitchen table. They exchanged tearful heartfelt apologies, each making excuses for the other, until Claudia finally asked:

"Why don't you move down with me? We can live in ..." Suddenly she couldn't recall where she came from.

"I can't," Annie sighed.

"But why?"

"Because," Annie shrugged and sniffed. "I don't want to die. There are millions of sunrises and sunsets, a million tomorrows to come. I can't let go. He promised it would change and I have to be here when it does."

Claudia stomped her foot: "Promised? What—who promised what?"

Annie shook her head: "He said you wouldn't get it. No one ever gets it."

"Get what? What am I supposed to get?"

"I can't tell you. Words make it stupid and you'll laugh, just like they laughed at the movie. You're only seeing half of what I'm seeing." She gestured at her own eyes. "That's all you'll ever see. You're better off with no vision at all." Annie's big body rose and fell in a sigh. "I'm sorry. You shouldn't have come here. And I wish you could stay, I want you to, but you can't."

"You made me want to come here."

Annie shrugged, her voice suddenly chilly: "Maybe I did but it doesn't matter. You don't matter anymore, okay? This world can only be lived in alone."

Claudia swooned at Annie's sudden cold dismissal. As she went out the door, half-blinded, she missed the step and fell, bruising her elbow. At the car, she looked once more at the cabin where she'd thought she'd be happy forever only the day before. The windows were empty, the cabin silent, as though no one lived there at all, leaving Claudia with a story that no one would believe.

She found a bandanna and wrapped it around her swollen left eye so she could see normally. By the time she reached the world below, long slow hours later, the swelling had disappeared and her eyesight returned to normal. The city lights she'd so hated now looked warm, welcoming, and so colorful compared to what she'd left behind.

She moved back in with her mother. "It didn't work out" was the only explanation she would give. Her shame was enough to keep her silent. Her memories of what happened made her lonelier than ever.

Claudia next chased after another impossible dream: going back to her old life. Her job at the library had been filled and the only available bookstore job was at a rusting link of a big chain that sold mostly junk. She remained alone, haunted by the emptiness that had followed her down from those mountains.

In late May, the Monitor County sheriff's department e-mailed her that Annie had died. Claudia drove only as far as the village. She told the under sheriff just enough so he wouldn't think she was crazy. Turned out he was more concerned about Annie's boss, Mr. Bartok, than with Annie's death. Had Claudia "bothered or interfered" with him at all? It was a ridiculous question, but she responded with "I never even met the man." Though she briefly remembered the dream of being flung through the night sky and remembered a pair of frosty eyes. And that mountain, cruel and forbidding.

She avoided the cabin, but did attend the gloomy memorial service with all those strangers. At the end, thunder drum-rolled across the sky while a blue-eyed bird or bat scratched at the skylight. "Annie's ghost," someone said. Claudia fled. She needed a world without spirits and ghosts, a world with only solid surfaces.

Back home, her mother drunkenly nagged her to retrieve the things she'd left behind at the cabin, most of all the settee. Claudia finally worked up the courage and asked Mr. Bartok's property manager for permission to enter the cabin.

And so she renewed her quest to be alone, once and for all.

Claudia bought twenty pounds of raw meat at the supermarket. That evening she devoured whole slabs of it. After dinner, her muscles felt swollen and her body sizzled with a mild sweet fire. As an experiment, she tried to lift the settee off the floor with one hand. It felt light as a feather. As she set it gracefully back down, she saw a drying blood stain on her now colorless blouse, and understood why her first stay had ended in heartbreaking failure.

It was Annie's fault. Some mysterious power had drawn Claudia all the way here to replace Annie, but Annie wouldn't leave, wouldn't get out of the way with her big body and grande dame manner. She was the one who was wrong for this place, not Claudia, and that's why she died, to make room for Claudia. Claudia had always sensed that she was special and different from everyone, that she was meant to serve a larger purpose. This was it, this lonely cabin, high in the mountains.

And so she waited on her periwinkle settee—which now looked a bland gray—for that next step, relaxed in this still, gray world. Night rose and fell, its rhythm defining everything. She ate meat and never went to the bathroom, another sign that she was approaching transcendence. When, she wondered, would that Mr. Bartok come by? Maybe he would point the way. Maybe he had the key. There was much to discuss: schedules, pay, and benefits. As Mr. Bartok's new chauffeur, she would have many responsibilities and she would take every single one of them with her usual seriousness and dedication, even if her new employer was a male, the oppressor. Because he was the key to it all.

Then, one fish-white afternoon, maybe a few days after she'd moved back to the cabin, someone came to the door.

But it was only a stranger, a tall, bearded and terribly handsome stranger. He made her nervous, like all men did. To Claudia, there were only two kinds of men in the world: bullies and weaklings. She feared one more than the other and despised them both. She wished she could remake herself—as she felt she would be able to one day, ripping apart and putting back together her own DNA at whim—into another creature; either one that would fly away; or one that could devour this stranger as would a praying mantis or a black widow spider.

This man was a weakling, one of those who stammer and mumble whenever the bullies attack. He got off on the wrong foot by claiming he was Annie's physician, a total lie. Annie's health had been perfect ever since she'd come here. There could have been only one other reason for him to be here and that was sex.

He didn't want sex. He'd driven all the way up here to ask about his wife, talk about his problems, not Claudia's. Worst of all, he had the effrontery to claim that his wife had taken Annie's job and was now working for Mr. Bartok.

This implied that the cabin didn't belonged to Claudia. Clearly, someone had entirely the wrong idea. Claudia had that job now. Claudia was the one who lived here. Her belongings were here. Wasn't that enough to prove possession? Raging, she ordered the fake doctor off the property and when he wouldn't go, she showed him her eye and—here, she thought she was being brilliant—started acting like the Crazy Hag in the Mountains, a carving knife nearby, ready to gut this stranger if he took another step closer. That was all it took. He ran like a whipped dog.

Afterward, Claudia celebrated with another generous meal of raw flesh and that night, for the first time, she took center stage in the canyon and raised the night by singing the same song that Annie had sung. Claudia had never been able to carry a note in her life, but now, she sang with exquisite purity. Maybe the bird didn't come and the stars didn't twinkle like before, but it was still a sign that she was becoming someone new.

Then daylight fell, night rose again and she started to squirm with impatience. The shiny butterfly curling in her soul yearned to break free of its sterile cocoon, but no matter how long it took, now or forever, she'd wait, a loyal servant of the world that waited behind the empty air.

Finally, that night came.

She was sitting again on her settee, just after night-rise, when she heard a low faraway noise, rising from the valley below. This is it! she thought. I didn't even have to wait that long! The sound grew to a roar as a powerful beam of light pointed up into the canyon from the darkness below. Her heart pounding, she rose and ran to the window.

Then there was a crunch and a thump, as the light beam rocked up and down and the roar stopped. Tires scrunched over gravel. A shape appeared, white as Ahab's whale, a large vehicle. She felt a little disappointed. She'd hoped for a magical carriage to take her to the next world, not an ordinary pile of metal. Where's my carriage with white horses?

Then she recognized the vehicle: Annie's SUV. Her heart thudded almost to a stop. Annie was supposed to be dead. Had she come back from the dead to take the cabin away from Claudia, to send her away again?

A tall figure passed through the headlight beams, tall like Annie, but thinner, shapely, arms swinging with a confident stride. The world just couldn't stay away, could it? Claudia thought as she grew angry.

Just as Claudia reached the door, it flew open, struck her in the face and knocked her down. The inside of her skull exploded in a painful ball of light. Through the light, hard gray eyes stared down with violent scorn. A strong hand lifted her off the floor while another hard hand repeatedly struck her across the mouth, snapping her head from side to side with each blow. Then she was flung down across her settee.

It was a woman beating her. She looked familiar. Her hair was black and shiny as though with starlight. She held Claudia up by the front of her blouse and stared with her hard eyes, the irises ringed by a red circle. Claudia no longer felt like she belonged here. She wished she'd never come.

"Wha-wha—" Claudia tried to say as the woman silently threw her around the living room. She wore familiar-looking calf-high leathers boots with which she kept kicking Claudia, even as Claudia pleaded that she was sorry, that she didn't know she was trespassing.

Finally, she lifted Claudia off the floor. Claudia felt herself grow weightless as though flying until she slammed and skidded face down across the rocky ground. Something landed with a thunk nearby. The echo of a door slamming shut.

Claudia staggered to her feet, fear her only feeling, escape and survival her only thoughts. She grabbed her purse, which was lying next to her. She ran around the white monster without looking back, to her little car. At first, she couldn't find her keys, but when she did, she couldn't get the right one in the lock. The seconds passed like minutes as she struggled to get the key in the ignition as her feet fumbled for the pedals. The darkness was so heavy it seemed to dim the headlights as she fought her way around the SUV.

Whatever control Claudia had remaining, she lost it once she started down the driveway. The steering wheel spun out of her hands, the car bounced from bumper to bumper on its rush toward the blackness below and the headlight beams waved helplessly about searching for help themselves. Her forehead struck the wheel and her neck muscles snapped.

Then it became still. She knew she'd gone over the cliff, was falling through space into the forest below.

"Hello, little mouse," a calm voice said.

Her passenger had blue eyes and a monstrous face, a mash up of many creatures into one. "Meow," it said with a mouth that was a round red hole, lined with sharp teeth. The mouth closed over her.

Then she was flying again. She saw her car, poor little car, falling like a toy into nothing. She heard a ripple of great wings. Stars glittered all around and her last thought was yes, at last, now I really am away from it all.

....

CHAPTER 30

Waiting for Mr. Bartok

Carla growled with predatory satisfaction as the taillights of the little mouse car disappeared down the driveway. She listened to the vehicle's tiny rattle until it stopped. Well, she thought, that problem's taken care of. She stretched lazily across the old flowery couch. All mine now. All I need to do is wait.

Who was that pathetic woman anyway? Carla knew that unhappy face from somewhere but, like all the other names and faces she had once known, it had faded into irrelevancy. Carla had moved on. She had work to do in the new world awaiting her.

Soon, the couch felt too small for her tall frame. She moved to the rocking chair, stared out the black window, ready for him to come to finish his work, to take her where she wanted to go, to fulfill his promise.

She felt so full of energy, she felt her muscles expanding and wondered if she'd ever sleep again. She couldn't wait for dawn to return, not because she wanted daylight, but because it would be time to sing again, to make her voice a beacon that would guide Mr. Bar—oh, stop being so coy—Dracula, yes Dracula, home to Dragon's Ark. The Dragon to the Dragon's Lair. Maybe he'd stop to share the blood from the night's hunting trip with her. Maybe tonight would be the night he would fulfill his promise of power. Some day, the two of them would raid the sleeping world together. Dreams for blood. Blood for dreams.

With the memories of her old self in her old life fading, Carla found herself running out of things to think about. There was only a future to dream of as she rocked in the chair. As lovely night slowly throbbed toward dull daylight, she went out into the canyon and sang her weeping melody. She cried at the sound of her own voice as she wished each star a sweet goodnight as it disappeared. She looked around the canyon and thought it strange that she couldn't see the Ark, his Holy Mountain, or much of anything from here. That was okay. This was only a station on the journey.

He didn't fly by that morning. He must have been busy. Oh well. He'd come tonight, as sure as the stars. She hurried back inside as her skin and eyes started to burn.

"I am hungry," she murmured and laughed delightedly when she opened the refrigerator to find all that raw meat stuffed into its shelves.

After breakfast, she sat all day waiting for the night to return, at times squirming with vigorous impatience. At sunset, she sang for him again. Still, he didn't come by. The canyon and its cabin felt sterile and empty. "Where did you go?" she asked the stars.

Late that night though, he finally made an appearance, and in the funniest way. After dinner, after Carla had sucked the last morsel of marrow from the last bone, she went to the sink to wash her sticky hands. When she turned on the faucet, the pipes clanked as though taken over by a prankish spirit. Tarry water gushed out. As it filled the sink, the water congealed and shaped itself, rising to the ceiling in a spinning whirlpool. From the center of the black whirlpool, blue eyes shone—suddenly there he was, her black-clad, blue-eyed Genie, forming himself from water as he did from the air.

It was the funniest stunt Carla had ever seen him perform. She crumpled in hysterics onto the crumbling tile floor, laughing until her sides hurt. What a prankster! And he knew it too, because he laughed along with her, a big booming trickster's laugh. The legends often claimed he was secretly sad in his heart. Not true. That idea was the sour grapes of helpless mortals. This Dracula was the happiest man she'd ever met. How could you live forever and not be happy? How could you rule the night with anything but joy?

Dracula drank his pint of Carla's blood as she lay on the floor. She sighed contentedly as her energy drained away. She wondered if the deer and the other animals who offered their blood to him felt the same contentment. Surely, she was special. The point was his need. She watched with pleasure as his smooth white face turned red, and the ruby circles around the irises deepened and the blue eyes turned bluer and sparkled with stars.

Then he was through. Without a word, he bounced up through the ceiling and was gone. He was one thing. Then he was another. Whatever he wanted to be, he became. If it hadn't been for the day—for the fucking sun that took their power—he'd be in a state of constant glorious becoming, a true god.

She slept on the floor and woke up feeling sore and drained as she used to when she was a weak and dying creature. She hurried outside and sang in the moments before the arrival of another dull scorching day. She caught a glimpse of him streaking to the south, racing the edge of dawn's shadow, the stars fading behind him as he flew.

She ate the rest of the meat and felt much much better. Then she drove down to the world of the "dead" and bought pounds and pounds of rich red beef, pork, chicken, mutton, and lamb. The nameless drowsy dull ones, their names forgotten, their faces like clay, said hello to her, asked about "Dave." What was a "Dave?" She shrugged their questions away, aware that her haughtiness inflamed their envy.

She drove home, sang as the white daylight disappeared and the fluid colors of night returned. Then she ate and waited, sang again at dawn, sat and waited, ate, sang again and watched the stars come out. Singing, eating, sitting, singing, eating, sitting. Easiest job she could ever hope to have.

Except for that one night, he didn't come by again. She started becoming bored and began to worry: What had she done to offend him? When will he keep his promise? She wanted to drive into the canyon, hike up to Dragon's Ark again, but rejected the thought as soon as it formed. She knew the rules. She'd go when he called and not before. The last one never visited him up there after the first time either. Carla would stay here and wait for him to call. Those were the rules. Sit still. Be quiet. Wait. He will call. You're going to live forever, Carla. You have more than all the time in the world.

In her growing restlessness, she finally found something to think about. She had forgotten that they were in the middle of a war, the fight to save his Kingdom from rape by the greedy "dead" from the world below. The greedy dead were threatening to destroy everything they loved. Invaders. In fact, the final battle would come soon, if it hadn't already. He'd given her a chore, a simple chore, but what was it? The answer seethed just under the murky glass surface of her memory. If she didn't do it, it might mean the end of them. It would be her fault if they lost everything.

She rocked in the chair, paralyzed with mortification, because she could no longer remember the important thing he said he wanted her to do.

Then she laughed at herself and relief flooded her. Don't be silly, she thought. If there was something she needed to do, wouldn't he remind her? He could have told her the other night, instead of taking off like that. All he had to do was fly by. She was ready for action, ready to sow their enemies' sleep with unbearable nightmares that would leave them screaming in the prison walls of their skulls.

So it was all right after all. Whatever she had forgotten, it probably wasn't important. He would know what to do and tell her. He had all the Magic. She would always count on him to do the right thing. That's why they called it "faith."

CHAPTER 31

Call Of The Canyon

Five days later, Sean Temkin still tasted the warm buttery flavor of Carla's kiss. After the humiliating failure of his speech before the commission, the memory of that kiss, given to him afterward, when they were alone, was the only thing that saved him from despair and kept him in the fight. The way her mouth opened as she pressed her full round curves against him made him feel soft and feathery inside. The message was: "I want this. I want you. You, Sean Temkin, you." Beauty had come to Sean at last.

It was like having a relentless orgasm. After that otherwise dreadful night, Sean drank only clean, crisp mountain water and laid off the alcohol and pot for the first time since his teen years. That was when the dreams started, the ones that others who lived here told him about; wonderful adventure dreams in which he bounded weightlessly from peak to peak and walked straight up moonlit cliff walls toward a starry sky. He awoke from these dreams a little tired, a little weak, his heart racing, but by midday, the "hangover" was gone and he felt as happy as if Sierra Future wasn't there to worry about at all.

Today, Sunday, he had one more thing to feel good about—great news for both Carla, Mr. Bartok, Sierra Future's opponents, and the real future of Monitor County. Sean's buddy, Johnny Pyle, had come through with the evidence that would stop Sierra Future, before the company could even switch on the ignitions of their big shovels; facts that would burn "Boob" Garner's ladder out from under him, maybe even send him falling into the slammer where he belonged.

The key to it all was Sierra Future's big sugar basket, Getgo, a diversified, international company with so many hands in so many pockets, it couldn't diligently supervise them all. Johnny had discovered, through tricks he'd learned while working for U.S. Justice, that Boob Garner and his crew took full advantage of this corporate distraction by keeping not two, but three sets of books: One set they showed to Getgo and one they kept for themselves. (The purpose of the third set remained unknown). They'd sent the extra millions they made with set number two—collected through double-invoicing and other pecuniary gimmicks—to the usual Swiss, Bahamian and other overseas hideaways.

The CD-ROM containing Johnny's evidence had arrived in the mail on Saturday. Sean had no printer, so he took it down to Osgood to print out a hard copy. Johnny said he'd come up late Sunday night for the final commission meeting on Tuesday where, just before the final vote—KA-POW! "The question of legal liability alone should scare them all into voting no," Johnny wrote in an attached note.

Sean called all the commissioners to ask for time for Johnny on Tuesday night; he called Chloe Byrne and his other allies to tell them the good news.

Then there was Carla. He called her repeatedly, afternoon and evening, until it sounded like the answering machine had run out of tape. He was relieved that Doc Sutton didn't answer the phone; that would've been too weird. He used to think the Doc was a hella great guy, until everyone at the meeting saw the photo of him shaking Garner's hand and Garner revealed his role in the project. Too bad he turned like that. No one saw that coming.

As Sunday approached, he grew increasingly worried. Carla had promised she'd take him up to visit Mr. Bartok in Alpine Canyon that day. The documents and CD-ROM were packed carefully in his daypack. He looked forward to the great man's face lighting up with joy when he learned that his wilderness would remain pristine, even after he'd left this life; that he would leave this Holy Earth with a great environmental legacy.

And then he and Carla—well, where would it happen? Where would they consummate their love—by the side of a stream, in the cathedral-like hush of a pine grove, at the top of a cliff under a blue sky and bright sun? His thoughts were constantly interrupted by visions of their naked heaving bodies.

Early Sunday morning, he found the Sutton's driveway empty. When he drove back to the village, he saw the Sheriff's car parked outside the Tap & Grill ("Last Day Tuesday!" according to a sign on the gray shingled wall) and, behind it, Doc Sutton's mud-spattered truck.

He tried to back out the second he saw Under Sheriff King and Doc Sutton at a table for two. He glanced around for Carla, but the men were alone. King saw him and waved him over, as if they'd just been talking about him. Sean felt his body turn to lead and his mouth dry up as he approached.

"Hey guys" and they said "Hey" back, and then suddenly the Doc asked right out, "You seen my wife around lately?"

Sean reeled as he stammered out no, he hadn't. He wondered if the Doc even believed him. He probably already knew about Sean and Carla. Everybody knew. Poor guy. He was probably the last to know. Then he stammered, "Have you?" because really Sean didn't know either. Then he blurted, "I'm supposed to meet up with her today. We're supposed to go up to Alpine Canyon and see Klaus Bartok." He almost said why before he remembered the Doc's treachery. ("Now we both know he's not the good guy we thought he was. He's just another hustler," Carla had said, right before she filled his mouth with her tongue. Wow! I know what his wife's kisses taste like!) He grew dizzy.

"You got an invite?" Tim King growled.

"Carla said she'd take me up there. She's working for him now."

The Doc meanwhile was staring into space, his fork poised in the air. He glanced darkly up at Sean, who thought, Poor guy's jealous. The Doc's dark skin looked sallow, purple shadows spread under his eyes. Was that a touch of white in his beard? His conscience was probably eating at him. After Sierra Future was kicked out, his name would be mud around these parts.

Tim King said, "Don't go up there alone."

"Alpine Canyon's all right if you like sitting in a dungeon," the Doc muttered. "Gets dark and ugly up there."

Tim King shook his head: "Remember, we pulled Leo Durant outta there a couple weeks ago. Don't forget Annie Goodman's accident, either. A lot of folks get in trouble up there. Don't you be one of 'em."

Sean felt resentful. Tim King was okay compared to most other John Laws but, when it came to climbing, Sean defied anyone who told him where to and where not to go. He'd been chased off plenty of cliff faces and busted a few times; he was no amateur. He pretended to be agreeable, the best technique for getting away with shit. He had been considering going up to the canyon without Carla. He knew the answer now. And it wasn't no.

"Don't worry, sheriff. If I don't find her, I'll save it for another time."

Sean backed away, wishing them happy trails. The Doc wished him luck in the battle—he seemed sincere enough. Still, Sean couldn't help feeling they were glad to see him go, if for no other reason than they could talk about him: the stammering boy who failed to stop the destruction of their paradise. Well, you're all about to learn different.

Sean's bitterness returned as he drove through sunny Mystic Valley with its dozens of "No Trespassing" signs. He could hardly wait to see the looks on the faces of those three cows on the commission, fucking Boob Garner, that mean little asswipe Penis Schlesinger, and the traitor Henry West when he and Johnny laid out their shit for the whole world to see.

In the end, Johnny had figured, Sierra Future would be like one of those savings and loan scandals—tens of millions of dollars paid for projects that never got built, or only half-built. The whole thing was a con, right down to the "Coming Soon—Mystic Acres!" signs. Garner and his crew thought that, once it was over, they'd be lounging on their asses on the Riviera, leaving Monitor County scarred forever, its magic destroyed, a wasteland of unfinished projects, the wetlands drained, the streams polluted by runoff from the thousands of acres of golden meadows that had been scraped down to dirt and then abandoned.

He wept as he drove for the first time up Alpine Canyon Road. Why had he waited so long to come here? How could Sierra Future be allowed to destroy this bright blue magic just to make a lazy-ass buck? He stopped again and again to marvel at the gold and green fields below, at the massive hills and towering peaks that protected it. Nature's beauty, he believed, really had been made for people because if it hadn't, no one would love it enough to fight for it. It would all be gone and people would be gone, too. Life would be meaningless, pointless after all. Sean even muttered the name of the only god he had the courage to believe in, the god of these mountains. (Though he kept even that faith a secret, as he would a sexual perversion.)

After a while, he drove past a driveway. Must be where Annie Goodman had lived. Lucky lady, to live and die among these mountains. Who'd be the next Lucky One? He briefly imagined he and Carla living up there, the two of them alone, but for the first time, doubt started to edge around his love. Carla, at least, was too outgoing and social for living so far away. Maybe they could rent the cabin out on weekends …

He stopped once more, to marvel at the cataract falls pouring through the notch high on Mystic Valley's western slope. Dragon Ark's proud peak stood against a blue sky. He waved hello at it. No storm today, it looked like. He thought for a long time about what climbing gear he'd need for this territory. He had it all, right there, in the Jeep. His camping gear, too. He could camp the night …that is, with Mr. Bartok's permission, of course.

The afternoon sun blazed right through a notch in the road up ahead. The shadows had lengthened. By the odometer, he was more than thirty miles from the main road and his watch said 4:30. He felt a strange, mystic loneliness. Maybe he shouldn't have come, but he drove the Jeep through the notch into Alpine Canyon anyway, because he always followed every road and every trail. That was the joy of his life: A hiker never knew what magic lay in wait, over the next hill, around the bend.

The drive down the curlicue road was more fun than a roller coaster. Sean whooped happily as the edge of the road disappeared under his left fender. The canyon walls glittered with silver mica. As he drove onto the canyon floor, he remembered what Doc Sutton had said about the canyon only hours ago and murmured: "Dude, what're you sayin'? You got no eyes."

To call Alpine Canyon a mini-Yosemite did it an injustice. Sure, it was hella smaller than Yosemite, but it had an impact greater than a place ten times bigger thanks to its narrow gauge and the straight-up sheerness of its stark cliffs. The entire energy of the Universe seemed to be pushed together between its two great walls. Sean's eyes teared as he drove the old road between its purple ramparts, under a slash of blue sky. There were potentially great climbs all over, dozens of chimney cracks on both walls. A guy could climb this territory for years on end—but then he stopped this thought and heaved a guilty sigh.

This wasn't his property. This wasn't even a park and it felt profoundly wrong, a mortal sin, to think of it like that. This was virgin territory for climbers and, for the first time ever, Sean felt ashamed to be one, mortified for looking at all this beauty as though it were a playground. It was a cathedral and should be left untouched, unchipped, unscraped, by boots and pitons. He remembered the mess he'd found the last time he'd scaled El Capitan—shit smeared on the walls, turds scattered around the base, garbage all over; even fuckin' graffiti. "Hey lookit me—I'm an asshole who can write on the walls!" He'd seen photos of Everest base camps, completely trashed, even littered with human corpses. How could he even think of bringing that here? In some ways, climbers weren't much better than Sierra Future.

Maybe that's why the Doc called Alpine Canyon a dungeon. To discourage Sean and others like him, dudes who cared even less, from coming here to fuck it up. Maybe he was right to tell his white lie. Maybe there are places in this ruined world that should forever remain a secret, even from well-meaning dudes like Sean.

This should always remain Mr. Bartok's land. Even after he dies. His alone. I won't ever tell anyone what I've found here. I'll always keep your secret, I promise.

It wasn't until he reached the end of the road that he realized he hadn't seen Mr. Bartok's house. Did he live by the blue spot of lake through the trees up ahead? The only visible trail led off toward the south wall, up a slope into a long barren plateau of granite boulders and other detritus. Beyond that a trail rose up the great south wall, which was streaked with big white falls that looked like Rapunzel's hair: "A-ha!"

Sean stuffed a couple of bottles of water into his daypack with the documents. He skipped over the redwood bridge across the fast-running stream and up the hill through the boulders and mats of evergreen. No Mr. Bartok here, only scads and balls of spider webs, the mossy ruins of an old cabin, and the skittering of bugs and spiders.

He trotted down the other side, through a thin grove of pines and followed the wagon rut trail past a few blood-red snow plants that looked deceptively like pinecones. Further out, orange poppies struggled to bloom. The trail intersected with another big stream— or maybe the same one he'd tramped over earlier. He knelt by the stream and cupped his hand into cold, clean water. *Giardia* wouldn't be a problem all the way up here. He cupped it in his hands, saw his smiling face in its reflection. It tasted so cold and sweet, it washed away the creamy taste of Carla's kiss.

His other senses opened up like they never had before. He felt a sparkle in his soul, and, though it was late, and experience told him to be careful, he hiked on. Mr. Bartok had invited him. He had food, water, and camping gear in the Jeep, enough for a night under the stars.

With no sign of a house visible from the canyon floor, Sean pondered taking the trail up the cliff. Maybe he'd see the old man's house from up there. The prospect of another perspective on this secret garden pulled him along. The snowy and black peak of Dragon's Ark seemed to be leaning over, as though watching him from over a rail. He felt like a tiny iron filing drawn toward that giant magnet. When was the last time anyone climbed that one? he wondered.

The south wall grew more complex the closer he came to it. It had exfoliated in several spots in the eons since the last glacier had grounded through here. Several chimneys ran down from the top. All of them seemed to stop at the trail. The most promising of them split the wall a few feet up from the big lower falls, about fifty feet above the canyon floor.

The thunder of the falls as he walked through the cave behind them, sent tremors through him. He covered his ears with his hands against the roar. The rocky, slippery trail made a horseshoe through the cold wet cave. One sharp left turn later, another ten, fifteen feet and there he was, at the foot of the chimney.

He looked up and down the canyon, the floor of which lay in evening shadow. No sign of a dwelling down there, or anywhere. He was high enough to see his Jeep on the other side. He studied the chimney, running his hands inside it. Climbing really was like making love and this chimney was what climbers called a "perfect jam," wide enough at the outside for Sean to brace his whole body across it. It narrowed maybe four feet in, and ran up straight up to the top, ending in a notch of darkening blue sky.

Climb me. Climb me now. Sean laughed at how mountains and cliffs could talk to him. He could spring up there like a monkey. He even had the right shoes on.

Whoa, whoa pardner. He forced himself to think sensibly. Never late, never alone, his first climbing guru had warned him—but fuck, even that guy free-soloed sometimes. When he'd gotten enough experience, Sean himself had danced out on his share of limbs, even ones that were new to him.

Let's make a deal: ten feet or so, then come down and camp the night. Adrenalin pumped through him, demanding action and adventure. The moon would rise early, close to full. How sweet to stand at the top and watch the moonrise over Alpine Canyon under the wild majesty of Dragon's Ark!

Sean tightened his daypack, murmuring, "Ten feet or so. That's all."

His big hands found perfect cracks on both sides. His feet found the right ledges. He pushed his torso up with his muscular hips and thighs. His hands found two more ledges. Like the easiest ladder ever. He could climb all the way to the top, fast. He repeated the motions: one, two, three, four times.

He stopped. High above, the night's first star twinkled right through the center of the notch. Wow! That's art! He looked down. Uh-oh. He'd climbed a bit higher than he'd intended, maybe about twenty feet. He looked up again.

The star was gone. Something was occluding it, something that was pouring down the notch right toward him. Flash flood!

But it didn't move like water. It was liquid and sinuous, smooth and silent, its sides gripping the walls like a living thing. A giant black snake. It had eyes. Laughing blue eyes. And it was coming right for him.

Panicked, Sean shrank into his body, lost his grip and his footing and fell. The world shook and spun crazily. The snake's blue eyes stayed with him as he fell. A bright orange bomb burst in his head.

Sean awoke to the sound of thunder. No thought, only a dull awareness like a black ball of tar. The thunder was made by falling water. He sensed he was lying face down on damp ground. He opened his eyes to the sight of moonlit gravel, a bare white tree log, a little branch stump sticking out—no. The tree log was really his arm; the little stump was broken jagged bone sticking out through the flesh.

Fuck what've I done?

Not much blood, okay, but a piece of red rubber tubing was caught on the jagged bone: his ulnar artery. Fuck. He was lying across something, probably a big branch. He'd probably smashed his ribs. It hurt to breathe.

Then a black cloud floated down and landed softly next to his broken arm. Someone's found me. Saved. Blue eyes twinkled from the middle of the cloud. Help. He waited for a human voice to say: "We gotcha. You're okay. We'll get ya outta here."

The cloud congealed into something definite but still shapeless. The eyes burned with the hunger of someone sitting down to a feast. No vulture ever looked so happy.

He knew those eyes. He'd seen them above on the cliff, snake eyes weaving back and forth down the chimney toward him. They'd scared him and that's how he got here. Got scared, got stupid, fell.

He knew those eyes from somewhere. Who was it? He knew, but his world was rapidly shrinking; he couldn't remember names, even his own.

The black thing's merry blue eyes cast a light across his broken arm. A cold light. There came an odor, musty, sweet and sour. He felt like food. Fuck. We're all food. The thought gave him solace.

He knew the eyes, the mane of silver-streaked black hair, large forehead, large ears, hooked nose, big mustache. It's you. Oh thank God, you're here!

The man must've read his feeble thought, because he laughed and spoke inside his head in a familiar voice: "Save you? I'm the one who made you fall. No. I am only hungry." He laughed and winked. "You are food. You've served yourself up to me."

Its mouth became a red hole ringed by needle-like teeth. What the fuck, this is sick, crazy sick. A Vampire. The mouth wrapped around the exposed artery. Pop! The Vampire closed its eyes, content as a boy sucking soda through a straw.

Sean grew weaker. His shock faded. At least the pain went with it. The world narrowed, until he saw only the Vampire's calm sly face.

He once more tried to remember his own name. If he could remember his name, maybe that would make the Vampire vanish like a gnarly dream. Then he could make it 'til morning when someone would find him, someone whom he loved.

My name my name, who am I? What's my name?

The Vampire beamed its blue eyes at him, lifted its ugly mouth from the punctured spurting artery: "Sean Temkin."

The same sonorous voice that had once said to him, "These mountains are timeless."

Sean became weightless and floated up into the night air. He looked down to see himself lying face down by the stream by the falls, his right foot stuck out over his curly head.

The Vampire sprawled like a iridescent black cloak beside him, drinking the last of Sean's blood. Something miraculous about it. Finally, satiated, the Vampire looked up and saw what was left of Sean, floating there. It winked, as though saying, "You've helped me in ways you don't even know. Some joke, eh?"

Then it flew up at Sean and took what was left.

....

CHAPTER 32

The Dragon's Dream, Interrupted

One lonely dawn, Carla Sutton was out singing when Dracula at last visited again. It was a brief fly-by with him diving down into the canyon in a mix-and-match form of black bat and black bird. As he passed close overhead, drops of blood pattered on Carla's face. The warm beads trickled over her dry white skin like syrup. She caught some of it with her tongue, her first direct taste of human blood other than her own. Not as tasty as she'd expected. She'd get to love it, eventually.

He must have enjoyed a hearty meal last night, maybe a hiker who'd fallen down a gully or off a cliff. The dull law man and the dull doctor would nod in dull agreement as they stood over the lifeless husk and go "Mooooooo."

But Dracula's visit also carried another message: a request that she meet him in Alpine Canyon. She decided to let the blood dry on her face. She would wear it like a chevron, a badge to prove how far she'd go for him. Whatever he did, she was part of it, too.

She arrived in the canyon early. This time, she planned to hike to the top of the rim and guide him safely down into the cool morning shadows. The more time she spent with him, the more she would learn.

When she reached the turnaround, she noted a familiar vehicle parked nearby. So, she snickered, he had called out for last night's meal: "Pizza delivery for Mr.— AHHHHH!" But, she next asked herself, who delivers all the way up here?

Now that Carla was color-blind during the day, she almost missed the body lying in the gray shadows on the other side of the creek, near the base of the cliff. At first she mistook it for another dead deer. Seconds later, wearing a ravenous grin, she plunged into the cold, fast stream and swam to the other side, through a floating field of flat, white objects, like leaves. She snagged one them with her hand. It was an almost-blank sheet of paper, the information on it washed away. As she climbed ashore, her foot snagged on a yellow daypack that was tangled in the shore weeds. She angrily kicked it free into the stream.

She was almost drooling when she reached the body. Did he leave her a sip, some dregs at the bottom of this glass? The dead male lay face down in the mud, close by the stream bank, dressed in shorts and a t-shirt. He'd fallen from the cliff and landed funny, though not ha-ha funny. His right foot stuck out over his head. Jagged bone poked through the white flesh of his right arm. The undersheriff would blame the moist, hungry soil for sucking his blood away, she thought, as she furiously chased off the insects that scuttled over him. She brushed the curly hair back from the face and saw the shrunken, half-closed eye, the half-open mouth, and the tongue sagging out.

She knew this man. She suddenly remembered all the facts about this dead creature who lived in the world below: his freckled face, his name, and his nervous voice. The sour taste of his lips, how his muscles and bones trembled against her body as she held him, her revulsion when she kissed him, and the reason she'd gone to so much trouble, had risked so much, to make him believe that she loved him above all else.

She also remembered the chore she'd forgotten: She was supposed to guide him here, so he would be safe, so this canyon, this grand heaven, would remain forever.

Carla's screams echoed around the canyon as she pounded her fist on the cold ground. When she was hoarse, and her tears had run dry, she rose to find a tall thin man in black waiting on the other side of the stream, leaning on his stick, standing still in the abject gray morning.

She charged back across the creek. Sputtering, she staggered ashore, pushing her sunglasses back on her face to protect her eyes. "I'm sorry, I'm so sorry," she cried and stammered out the terrible news to Dracula: It was poor Sean Temkin lying there, dead. It was her fault, all of it. She'd forgotten that she was supposed to show him the way here, and make sure he made it out safe. Would Dracula ever forgive her? What would they do now that he was gone? What did they have to fight with now?

The Vampire appeared unconcerned. His cracked, cottony face wore the impassive but droll look of someone tolerating a crazy's person ranting. He said nothing until Carla blubbered out a course of action: "Y-you stay here. I'll get the sheriff."

"Stay? Why?" Dracula shrugged and nodded at the body. "Are you worried he'll be lonely?"

He turned and headed toward the moraine. When he noticed that Carla wasn't following him, he turned around. "He died as he would have wished to." Dracula gazed around the canyon. "He died seeing wonderful and strange things. Do you know that shock and fear add a special flavor to human blood? That's what the dreams and nightmares are about. The lower animals dream very little. Humans dream much. That's what makes their blood so worth the pursuit." He kissed his fingertips like a gourmet. He nodded once more at the corpse. "That was a good meal.

"Mrs. Sutton, it is time to think of next things. We live, so the world belongs to us. We have business. You may alert the sheriff or anyone else you like. I will give permission to remove the husk. But first, you will take me to today's appointment. Come. I must meet with my partners. I am always punctual."

And so, on he went, climbing up into the moraine. Carla realized that behind those sunglasses, his irises were rimmed with Sean's blood. He turned back again and nodded curtly. In her confusion, there was nothing she could do but follow him. As they wended through the moraine, she hoped that this was one of the nightmares he'd spoken of; that he'd sprinkled it into her mind as a prank that would wash away in the morning light as she awoke.

She fell as she came down the slope on the other side. Ahead of her, Sean Temkin's Jeep sat by the road, a coldly defiant reality.

Carla numbly guided Dracula into the SUV. She yanked hard on the straps as she buckled him in. He snapped a look at her from behind his sunglasses. She growled and bared her teeth at him and slammed the door as hard as she could.

Before getting in, she stopped to vomit up her meat breakfast. She crawled behind the wheel, shut the door, and saw her blood-streaked face in the rear view mirror: Sean's blood, caked and drying. She tried to wipe it off. It felt dry, flaky and sticky and she began to cry again.

"Mrs. Sutton?"

"What have you done?" Carla shouted, banging her fists on the steering wheel. "This kills us. Sean was carrying the evidence to stop the project. That's what all that paper was. He wanted to show it to us, to you most of all. It's all gone now. We've lost it all because you can't control your hunger." She paused as her rage grew. "What have you done?"

"I have no trouble controlling my hunger. I do, however, always protect my interests. Now, I'm tired and need my nap. Drive."

"No!" She gripped the steering wheel, looking away from him, unable to bear his calm sense of entitlement: "I get it now," she croaked. "You were working for Sierra Future all along."

He snorted: "Pfui. No, act-u-a-lly, I was working for myself. That my interests coincide with theirs is a neat coincidence. It's not much different than the contract between you and me. Now drive."

"This isn't what I," she stammered, "I didn't mean for this—"

"Mrs. Sutton, it's far past time to worry about your fine intentions." His words dripped with disdain, as though delivered from the summit of Dragon's Ark. "The game has not changed, only your awareness of its object and rules. It was helpful to us that there a be credible-seeming public opposition, a delusion of democracy and all that. It was also essential that it fail. Now that it has, the fools can go home, telling themselves they fought the good fight and leave us alone to carry on our work. You did a fine job encouraging the boy, and an even better job sending him my way. His blood was sweet with fear. Thank you," he added sincerely.

"You murdered him."

"That is a long list, going back millennia: the fat man at St. Ives? The old couple in the car, and Dr. Durant on your maiden voyage into the stars? The little trespasser, just a few nights ago? All of them 'murders'"—he wiggled his fingers in irony—"as you put it."

Then Carla realized a detail that he'd forgotten: "But his friend, Palmer the investigator. He still has his copy."

"Not anymore. I scared him off the road and into a ravine last night. Fire and flame, everything burned. If there is any evidence left, it'll come out too late to stop us."

"But you're fouling your own nest. It means thousands of people moving up here. They'll spoil all this. You won't be able to live in it."

"Yes, a few thousand more will come. This time, instead of moving to the abattoir, I'm bringing the abattoir to me, under my terms. My hungry years will at last end and I'll live a happy, healthy eternity. No. This in no way resembles moving to an already-fouled city. I'm building my own community, from the ground up, to my own specifications, and under my rules. There'll be adjustments along the way, yes, but as you might have guessed from certain details in Garner's presentation the other night, it won't be anything I cannot live with. Human blood will be clean and plentiful at last."

"We believed in you and then you stab us all in the back."

Again, he shrugged his insolence: "I'm not responsible for your misplaced faith. What I am is sick of starving, Mrs. Sutton. For too long, I've lived at the edge of oblivion. I am tired of animal blood—

deer, goats, coyotes, bears, and cattle—they're barely enough to keep me breathing. I've spent too many daylight hours shivering and sleepless from starvation in that cave, my life dwindling until I thought I would not live to see the night again. The winters are the worst. Even in hunting season, I have had to settle for campers, hikers, and vacationers, and among that mob only those few who keep themselves clean. Yes, a few thousand will come to live here, but the—I think it's called 'infrastructure' nowadays—is being built for my comfort. I will feed comfortably all year round, forever. I've learned to live with the world. And the world will live for me." He smiled and nodded in genuine gratitude. "You are a useful cat's-paw to me, Mrs. Sutton. Again, my thanks. I think a raise may be in—"

"I don't want your fucking thanks or your fucking money. You lied to me." She felt weak, pathetic, and childish. He didn't see the errors of his ways because he didn't think he'd made any errors to start with.

"What can you do about it?" he sniffed. "Run and tell your es-tranged mate? Fortunately, he is alive, because he is useful too. As you have your job, he'll have his: keep my herd healthy, like a good veterinarian. His stubborn skepticism and lack of imagination make him a good fit for my plans. Not only will he not believe you if you chose to tell him the truth, no one will. They all work for me with-out knowing it. Only you know. Think of yourself as privileged, the only member of my inner Inner Circle.

"No, don't even think of betraying me, because I will punish you. Your disease will return, but it will move more slowly. I will take back most of the gifts I gave you, except for one." He grinned with incandescent joy. "The gift of immortality. You'll still live forever, wide-awake inside a skull inside an empty mute husk, strapped in a wheelchair in permanent despair with only your sore conscience for company. You'll live for eternity helplessly watching everyone around you die." Dracula laughed. "You'll never know these gifts again."

"You can't be serious. You can't do this."

"Mrs. Sutton, it is done. I do because I can. What is power and freedom but the capacity to act without restraint? A negative freedom and happiness is only death, nothing else. Right now, I have the freedom and I have the power." He jabbed his white finger at the road ahead. "And I have you. Drive on and be grateful. You still have more than those you left behind."

He nestled into his seat, wearing a smug grimace.

Carla couldn't think of what else to do, so she drove on through an Alpine Canyon that was now empty of all magic. Its beauty had only been a mask. Her husband had been right. This place really was a dungeon, a prison of emptiness and despair.

At the notch at the top of the road, she stopped to look out over the valley. Once she had looked forward to seeing this view every day, but now, the valley looked like a dismal giant quarry and soon it would be a construction site. Dozens of human dwellings, all of them alike, would be planted along winding lanes and carefully manicured cul-de-sacs, signed with names that reflected what was once there and had been destroyed: Mystic Valley Road, Evergreen Lane, Big Bear Road and so on. It would be nature, manicured and mannered.

Once it was built and the new people hypnotized into moving in, their nights would pass in innocent sleep. Meanwhile, the man—the thing—napping next to her, would each night perch on the western rim of the valley, watching with his cold hawk eyes, while calmly, coldly choosing his meals for the night. Those below would lose both their blood and their right to their own dreams. They'd be forced-fed the dreams of a monster.

Meanwhile, Carla would serve him forever in the dull place he'd made for her. She'd be trapped in the twisted desultory space between him and them, in a lonely, middle world, part of both, part of neither, unless …

She switched off the engine. Dracula awoke grumbling in the ticking silence.

"What—what do you want?" She sensed his eyes blinking sleepily behind his glasses. "Why are we stopped? What are you waiting for?"

"I'm waiting to become like you."

"What?" He waited for her explanation.

"I've betrayed the place I live in and the people in it. I've betrayed my husband. I'm an accessory to murder. One of them was a boy I fooled into thinking that I loved, someone I thought was helping you, helping us. I suppose there'll be more murders coming. I don't care to live with that as I am now, especially forever.

"I'm asking you to please finish what you started with me. You said you would. At least keep one promise, can't you? Make me a vampire like you. You've already infected me with your virus, or whatever, to enslave me. At least finish it. If I've learned anything from this, halfway there is nowhere at all."

He laughed in light amusement. "It took even me centuries to evolve the powers I have now. I had to be patient to reach a state where I don't have to be patient. It would be no different for you."

"I've obeyed you in everything." Her voice quavered. "Now I want payback. You can't expect me to sit forever in that shack, waiting for you to call."

"If I gave you what you asked for, you'd have to leave here, go somewhere else. Even with the arrival of new cattle, there would not be enough for two ravenous creatures. Besides, I do not share my world with anyone. I never have. I never will."

"Okay, then I'll go somewhere else. You can hire—"

"Pfui, you will not," Dracula snorted. "I won't permit it. I own you now, nerve and muscle, bone and blood, from your skin to your soul. Where you would go? This is one of the last places on this moist bit of sand where a creature like me can survive. Human civilization has shined its sterile light into almost every corner, to where fewer and fewer people even dream anymore. Now it's dying in its own poison. You'd die like a dog if you tried to live in the world below, as I nearly did. Don't forget your sentimental attachments here. You would also be my competitor and only want to take what is mine. I'd be driving that proverbial stake through my own heart." He laughed. "If I had a heart, that is!

"You have never been one of those weak, confused fools who wish for death," he went on blandly. "That, more than anything, is why I picked you to serve me. Life, consciousness, awareness, that is the only real gold, the only meaning to all this, nothing else. You live the best of all possible lives. Take my word on this: Stay as you are."

He yawned. "Now, stop complaining and drive." With a snuffle, he returned to his nap.

Carla drove down into the dismal valley while Dracula slept. Soon his mouth fell open and out came a great snoring: raw, wet, honking snores, like a swamp belching out gas, a rank humid odor of rotten flesh, blood, and shit.

So this is my eternity, Carla thought despairingly. Some bastards really get to have all the fun, all the glory, all the joy. They get to lie, cheat, steal, murder, and still fly free among the stars. And I get to chauffeur the biggest of them.

The world became a blurry gray wash as she weaved through monotonous curve after monotonous curve. Finally, she stopped the SUV again at the inner crook of a ravine. Ahead, the road ran straight into empty sky.

Dracula continued snoring. His mouth hung open, huge teeth exposed, needle-like tongue drooping out, his lips wrinkled like an empty balloon, distended, fluttering with every shit-stinking breath and sputtering tiny pink droplets of saliva.

She looked away in disgust at the sand-colored sky ahead. A calmness and clarity came over her. Neither she nor Dracula were immortal, not in the daylight. He'd tricked her into believing there was no world out there, but there was, and it could kill them both in its fashion. They were still at the mercy of the day, its gravity and its own ways of death.

Annie Goodman solved her problem by driving into the sky up ahead to end both her life and his. It'd taken her fifteen years to make this decision, enduring endless waves of hope and disillusion. Maybe she also learned of her monstrous master's real plans, and realized all the waiting had been for nothing. Immortal life on Dracula's terms was not worth living. And the world had had enough of the creature sleeping by her side.

Except, Annie had only half-finished the job. It was up to Carla to finish the rest.

I don't care anymore. I'm not waiting fifteen years. I'm not waiting fifteen seconds.

She stomped on the gas. The big tires spun, then caught. The SUV lurched forward, speeding directly toward the emptiness up ahead.

Dracula sputtered awake as the engine roared and his vehicle picked up speed. The speedometer's hand made its way up the dial. "Huh?" the Vampire King asked. Then he realized what Carla was up to and cried out in fright as he raised his stick to strike her. But the stick was too long and its tip caught on the cab roof. He frantically struggled as he bellowed for Carla to stop.

The road vanished underneath. For long seconds Carla saw only a sand-colored sky and felt the aching sensation of flying. She glimpsed where the slope disappeared over the ridge. No giant stone hand to stop them here. She felt a sudden jolt and the crash bag exploded in her face. The back of her head slammed into the headrest as a ball of fire burst in her brain.

....

CHAPTER 33

With His Back To Beauty

Henry West glimpsed the white car blowing through the gap between his cap bill and his nose and almost had a heart attack. He spun the wheel hard right and BANG down went Mr. Garner's SUV into a shallow ditch, the right fender barely missing the granite hillside. Henry's face hit the steering wheel, but the airbag didn't burst. Henry's stomach however did as he threw open the door and heaved his breakfast. Mr. Garner's SUV, at least, was still clean.

Henry almost fell as he climbed down to the dirt road. He knew he was on Alpine Canyon Road, but he had no idea where exactly and he didn't want to know. He struggled to stay on his feet as he tried to identify the motherfucker who'd nearly hit him.

It was big, it was white ...and it looked like it made those tires tracks that Henry saw as he peeked out from under his cap. He kept his nose to the ground and followed the tracks to where they left the road. Then he took another breath as he slowly raised his eyes, revealing the world inch by eensy-tiny inch. He'd made it all the way the fuck up here by keeping his cap bill down to the left and pretending that the violent yaw of Mystic Valley didn't exist. Now he had to look at it. Or at least a little of it. Slowly, blown rear tires, a bumper, a license plate and then the rest, trembled into view.

Yeah, Bartok's SUV all right, sitting about twenty feet down, right before the edge of the—no, keep your eyes down, asshole. Henry closed his eyes, let the dizziness passed.

Had Bartok made it through this one, too? If so, that fuckin' cat had too many lives. He had to be dead this time. And that'd be great news for Team Sierra. The last obstacle was gone. This shitty job would be nearly over. Henry could take his jack and go live the life he wanted, down in the valley, where he'd never be dizzy. He'd hang a keg over his bed, stick the hose in his mouth, while a bottle of Cuervo dripped straight into his vein.

But if the old man were truly dead, Henry wanted to see it for himself. "I want to see you dead dead dead, you mangy cocksucker," he whispered.

But there was only one way to be sure. Henry slowly turned his back to the valley, got down on his hands and knees, and started to crawl backward down the slope. From time to time, he'd peek between his thighs to keep himself on course. Thank God there was no one around to see him clambering down like a toddler from his high chair. He only saw dirt, gravel, granite, dead yellow grass, an occasional itty-bitty flower, his fat hands, and, the one thing that kept him going, the wad of twenties that peeked out of his shirt pocket. It was another bonus from Garner, the real reason he'd forced himself to drive all the way up here, alone.

•

Henry's drive up Alpine Canyon Road started Sunday afternoon when Mr. Garner called him down into his basement office. With his big speech given, Henry had assumed the worst of his employment with Bob Garner and Sierra Future was drawing to a close, but Mr. Garner had yet another "project" for Henry.

Once he heard what it was, Henry almost quit. First, it required driving on this motherfucking mountain road. The other shitty thing was that it involved Klaus Bartok, another cocksucker Henry prayed he'd never lay eyes on again. As he sat listening to Mr. Garner's instructions, he remembered his last encounter with Bartok, the Monday before, an incident that cut another scar into Henry's blistered soul.

The Monday afternoon before the Big Show, Henry, Mr. Garner, Petey, and Booby Albanese were meeting in Booby's office when Mr. Garner finally decided to pull one more rabbit from his hat. Swearing them all to secrecy, he unrolled a batch of architect drawings out on the conference table by Booby's desk: "This is what Sierra Future's really about."

Until that moment, Henry had never been able to get a real grasp of Sierra Future, but he got it then. Bob Garner's real plans centered on Mystic Valley. All his talk about remaking the valley into a low-density, residential rural/suburb-type neighborhood, of one-to-two-acre "green" ranchettes "for good decent folks like you n' me" wasn't half—shit-fuck, it wasn't even a tenth of what he really had in mind. Mystic Valley was going to be whole new bang-up city, pop. 20,000 to start! Garner and the parent company, Getgo, had spent years scheming with contractors from all over the world, including Europe and Asia, to build this new city right there in the mountains to rival cities like Denver. The city would dominate the Nevada-California region. Shitty old Byrneville'd be left to rot, just another Sierra ghost town.

Bob Garner unrolled another set of secret plans: a topo map of the Alpine Canyon area, twenty miles or so west. He jabbed a long finger at the spot where Dr. Turdhead lived before taking his first and last flying lesson. "Remember how I said we were putting up a five-star hotel there?" The map crinkled as he dragged his finger across and then stabbed a spot right in front of Dragon's Ark. "That's where it'll really go. Best view in all the Sierras by my guess." "Wow!" Petey and Booby chimed, as though Garner had just raised the dead. Then Garner added, "A four-lane highway bridge right across the canyon will provide access."

"But don't old man Bartok live there?"

Garner laughed as though Henry had spewed another filthy insult: "Not for long, Henry."

Schlesinger grinned: "'Dragon's Ark.' That's not exactly a family-friendly name. Maybe uh something like 'Mount Garner'?" And Booby simpered, "Oooooooo, I like that" like she's getting her pussy pounded. And Bob Garner does his bullshit humble jig, but that shit didn't fool Henry: Mr. Garner was just another bigheaded, big-dicked fucker who just lived to slap his name on shit, the big dog peein' on everybody's rock. Not that Henry gave a shit. Bob Garner could write his name on every fuckin' blade of grass in the fuckin' county, for all Henry cared.

"That hotel's going to be the crown jewel, the place everybody's gonna wanna stay. Even if they can't afford it, they'll want to drive over to look and we'll pick their pockets that way." Bob Garner stared at the map. He reminded Henry of some guys he'd known in the joint, buzzing with dreams of being a zillionaire once when they got sprung.

"We could lay a professional grade all-sport ski run down through the Samson Range here and run sightseeing gondolas up and down that canyon, like we're doing in Yosemite. We could blast a big cave—there may already be one—inside that mountain and make a Halloween House of Horrors. On Fourth of July, we'll set off fireworks that can be seen all over the Sierras. Don't forget Christmas. We could mount a giant balloon Santa climbing up the mountain. A six-lane highway over the Sierra Crest, another one through Osgood Canyon from the Nevada side. It'll be a magnet for the world. Wow …I …I think I'm having a vision."

"It *is* a vision." Petey said, buttering the boss's ass. "Wow," whispered Booby. Meanwhile, Henry thought, Seems fuckin' nuts to me. Maybe chronic migraines could give a man some crazy ideas.

"Bartok's old and will probably die soon," Garner said as he put the maps away. "Something has to force him down from his castle, sooner or later, somehow or other. How doesn't matter, but the sooner, the better."

And then, stroking his beard, he smiled and winked mysteriously at Henry. And just when Henry was asking himself, what the fuck did he mean by that? a shadow appeared at the door. Seconds later, in shuffled old Shrivelpuss, looking like a windblown, half-dead stork that had been dipped in a barrel of tar.

Garner gestured for Henry to sit in the chair by the door. Henry smiled his bullshit polite smile, but Mr. Baggy-Face, as usual, ignored him. His old man's skin made him look like a mummy wrapped in spider webs.

Henry took his seat as Bartok sat facing him. Once again, Henry started seeing spiders—those big, black tarantulas that had driven him to this place. Out of Henry's control, his imagination pictured them crawling out of the old man's collar and coat cuffs. They scuttled over his shoulders, stroking his face, while the old man cooed, kissed and stroked them as if they were kittens while winking at Henry with a wicked grin—

Henry angrily shook the vision out his head. Luckily, Bob Garner sat between, a barrier between the two of them, at least for now.

Mr. Garner, Petey, and Booby worked as a team. They spent an hour stroking and nudging Bartok. They drooled forked-tongued thank-yous on the old man for all his help in taking over the county. "It makes me very happy," the old man agreed. "We will both have the world we want." They asked how he'd persuaded reluctant sellers to agree to their terms, but Bartok shrugged, casual and arrogant: "I have my ways. I've had them for many years," he chuckled like some movie Nazi. What a dick, Henry grumbled silently.

Sierra Future slowly tightened its garrote. Laying her tits out on the desk, Booby asked Bartok if he was feeling "lonely up there in that empty windy canyon especially at your age?"

"We're very concerned about that, sir," Petey said softly as Bob Garner added, "Maybe it's time to think about your future. And what's gonna happen to that lovely piece of property of yours, once you're, well …"

But the old fuck was on them like paint. He knew right where they were going and got there first. He nodded at all three of them, one at time, sayin' "No. No. No." Then he leaned to his left, peered around Garner, and stabbed poor, innocent, I'm-just-sittin'-here Henry West right in the brain with his drill-bit eyes: "And no."

Those were the first words he'd ever spoken to Henry West. Bartok knew their game, even why Henry was seated by the door.

Still, the Boss kept on. They put it to him again, varying their attack this way and that, but old Krinkly just kept going no, no, no, he wasn't selling his property, in the canyon or on the mountain. That would remain his, as they'd agreed to from the start. They talked like they were sorry for him and they'd pay him the world to go live anywhere he chose, they'd even buy him his new place, so he could end his days in Monitor County but just not there, okay? Please, Mr. Bartok, pretty please?

"I have no intention of finishing my days anywhere," the old man said with breathtaking confidence. That was when Bob Garner's made his impatience known. He massaged his temples, a sign that a migraine was coming on as the afternoon sun cut a shaft through the dusty air. Time to show the muscle, show this ropy old dick who was boss now. He nodded at Petey, who lunged across the desk right into the old man's face:

"Look, old man! Face it! You're old! You're through! We can force you out of there!"

Then Garner shifted his chair sideways. Henry and Bartok were now eye to eye. Henry charged into gangsta mode: fists clenched on his thighs, shoulders hunched, teeth bared as his eyes squinted with malevolence—

But Bartok was waiting for him: he whipped off his glasses. Twin blue light beams shot out from his eyes straight into Henry's eyes, lighting up the inside of his skull, turning everything a bright night blue. The spider that Henry had imagined crawling on Bartok was now crawling around inside his head, eating chunks of his brain, spattering poison, its eight blue eyes shining hungrily as its eight legs scratched at the inside of his skull: "I. Am. Hungry!"

Henry cried out, covered his eyes, bent over and barfed. Shaking, crushed with shock, fear, and shame, he stared at the acrid puddle between his feet as the room fell dead quiet. Then the old man's walking stick slowly thumped by, and his shadow passed over Henry, cold and oily. He'd put that day-mare in Henry's mind. He knew what scared Henry. He'd been there before—in my mind. He can go in my mind. Then the door closed.

"He made me do that," Henry croaked, as he wiped his mouth. "He made me throw up. He made me see—"

"You stupid dumbfuck!" Petey snapped right in Henry's ear. "What the fuck are you doing? You worthless piece of—"

"Peter! Back off." Bob Garner stepped in. Wiping the sourness from his mouth, Henry looked up to see his boss smiling reassuringly while rubbing his forehead. "Forget it, Henry. Bartok makes me sick, too." Then he bared his teeth. "Sick and pissed off."

Then the meeting was over, and Henry had refused to even think about it with everything else going on, until Sunday afternoon when Bob Garner said, "Henry, I'd like you to mosey up to Alpine Canyon and scout around."

Henry's belly sank: drive …up there? "You been up there yourself, ain't you?"

"Bartok refuses to permit us access, as you might guess from that little dispute last Monday. We tried flying over it in a helicopter a few times, but the winds are too strong. The pilot wouldn't put down. We need a ground-eye view of the area."

"So ya want me to trespass?"

"Does that bother you?" Bob thoughtfully rolled his tube of HeadOn between his fingers. Henry knew what he was insinuating: Henry had been in the joint. Why should he shit his pants about committing a two-bit misdemeanor? What he didn't know was that Henry was such a loser, he'd never be even criminal enough to qualify for a "three strikes" sentence.

"See if you can find exactly where he lives. You don't have to break in or anything, just scope it out. We'll give you a camera to take pictures. He can't do much more than wave his stick and yell at you to get off his lawn. Sooner or later, somehow or other, we're gonna get that property and the more we know sooner, the better."

"Don't you wanna come along?" Henry immediately regretted asking the question. So far, he'd managed to conceal his acrophobia from Garner, even that time they drove up to Durant's. If he, or especially Petey, came along, they might find out the truth about Henry. That would mean the end of the only job that had come close to meaning anything, the only one that ever would.

Garner's big, freckled fist slid across the table toward him: a fat corner of green stuck out between the fingers, yum yum candy. The boss winked and smiled.

"Don't sweat it, Henry. We've got your back if you get caught."

•

Henry's rear end finally collided with the SUV's rear bumper. He shifted left and, moments later, stopped at the passenger door. He crawled up the side to find his reflection staring back from the tinted window, hair sticking out from under his cap, nothing but scary tinted sky behind. He avoided looking down to his right.

The passenger door was locked. Henry found a rock lying at his feet and smashed methodically away at the window until it turned to green pebbles and crumbled away. The SUV shuddered and rolled a bit. Henry braced himself but the vehicle remained still.

There he was: Klaus Bartok looking perfectly dead, his sunglasses hanging off his face, strapped into some weird baby seat. White powder dusted everything and the chemical odor of the gases used to inflate the burst airbags made Henry sneeze. The driver was slumped unconscious against the other door. Henry knew her straightaway. "Well, fuck me and ha ha to you, Mrs. Suck-off," Henry sneered with renewed satisfaction. "Looks like you're the one needin' a pity party."

Henry risked a glance down the slope. The edge of the cliff was almost right there. The SUV didn't feel secure either, as though the undercarriage had caught on a rock before it went over the edge to finish them off for good.

How big a push would it take? Bob Garner had nowhere near said as much, but it was clear that once the old man was out of the way, well, maybe that time was here. Henry would be "adding value" to Sierra Future.

There was only one thing wrong this idea: Henry West had never committed a crime like this ever. (Though he did hint to the Boss that he had, just to impress him.) He hadn't even really done the crime for which he served his time. Still, who would ever know, or even guess that it was Henry West who sent Klaus Bartok to die in the valley below? Accidents happened all over these parts and this would just be another one. Everyone would say, "Tut-tut. Drive careful." And that would be that.

Henry got down to look under the SUV. Sure enough, the rear axle had caught on a point of rock. All it needed was a shove with his feet on the bumper. Or find a piece of lumber and pry it loose. He wouldn't even have to tell Bob Garner if he didn't want to, in case the Boss turned to be more squeamish than expected …but he had to love it. He just had to love it!

Henry got to his feet, his decision made. But as he looked one more time at Klaus Bartok, Bartok lifted his head and opened his eyes, right at Henry. Henry heard a shadowy scuttling inside his head.

Just in time, someone shouted "Henry!" He pulled his eyes away from Bartok to see a big hat sticking up over the side of the road: the Underpants Sheriff, Tim King. Once again, Henry was glad to see that motherfucker, just as he'd been glad the other night when King rescued Henry from that angry mob. Gasping, Henry scrambled up the hill toward him, feeling ashamed at being so glad to see a sheriff.

....

CHAPTER 34

Left to Die

Dave and Tim leaned on the Osgood Memorial rear patio wall, looking east with the Sierra behind them. Dave stared at his hands, flexing them, amazed at the wrinkles, and the white in his beard, that had appeared in just the last few days.

Tim was trying to comfort him: "That Dracula story she told, that was just the shock of the accident and the drugs talkin.'" He was looking in the distance toward downtown Osgood, drumming his fingers on the parapet with a slow rhythm.

"Yeah, right," Dave croaked, "but at least one thing she said is true. Klaus Bartok's been backing Sierra Future all along." Tim shrugged, curling his hands into fists. The same accusations were being made against Dave now, but Dave went on with his anyway.

"And I'd bet my life he murdered Sean Temkin." Tim flinched in response, his nerve struck. "Shoved him off that cliff."

"You have no proof of that, Dave. Even Carla says she didn't see him—"

"Bartok's an old man and Sean trusted him. All Bartok had to do was wait for Sean to turn his back on that trail, maybe when he was right near the edge. Then he takes his stick—"

"Dave, you're not doin' too well yourself right now—"

Dave repeated his accusation. Tim quietly reminded him that he had no evidence, no witnesses. With a warning shake of his head, he reminded Dave that Henry West was a witness—the only witness—to the "incident" on Alpine Canyon Road.

"You believe him?" Dave snorted. "Henry's not my idea of a reliable witness."

"His account matches what we found. That SUV had been going at a high rate of speed when it reached the bend there. It left torn-up tires tracks a couple of hundred feet back. Whoever was drivin' knew what they were doin'. The driver was your wife. No, listen, you know what means? It could mean an attempted murder charge, if Mr. Bartok confirms it after he wakes up—"

"Mr. Bartok this, Mr. Bartok that. Everyone's so respectful around here—"

"Sean had a climbing accident, Dave. There's not a shred of evidence otherwise. We both warned him not to go up there. That's all we can say."

"You sent Sam Colbert up there, instead of investigating the scene yourself. After making that false arrest, Sam's not gonna say 'boo.'"

Tim shrugged and looked behind him at the wing where Carla slept. "Your real problem's in there. That's what you gotta worry about."

Dave raised his hands. They were shaking badly: "She realized that Bartok had murdered Sean, that's why. She discovered his betrayal and …"

He trailed off as he looked at Tim, who wore an impassive, almost indifferent, look behind his aviator glasses.

"Everyone around here plays a role of some kind," Dave said, "and Bartok seems to direct it all. You, your job is to protect him, to cover for him, isn't it?"

Tim stepped back from the parapet, his right fist clenching, his face reddening.

"You're talkin' out of line, Dave." His looked at Dave sideways. "You still haven't told me exactly what happened that night at your place."

It was Dave's turn to wince. All he had told the Kings when he'd shown up at their door last Wednesday was that he and Carla had had a huge fight and decided to separate. Something about her disease and her new job. Nothing about walking down the hallway in the dark with the sense that something was crawling on the ceiling behind him …nothing about Kat dead on the patio with her throat cut …nothing about how Carla looked faceless standing there in the kitchen and what she'd said …nothing about how she seemed to vanish from reality, leaving only an ugly ghost of her voice in the empty house …nothing about how she stalked around the truck in the moonlight, the knife in her hand, full of hunger …nothing about trying to shoot that strange bird out of the sky, or the way it stopped in mid-air and *stared mockingly at him from miles away* …and finally, nothing about what he saw behind his bedroom window …how Carla's flesh rippled, how her face changed, how she shrieked …

Because, he reminded himself, none of it had happened the way he saw it, that's why. He didn't know why he saw these things, but the only possible, acceptable explanation was that he'd been hallucinating. Carla had been undergoing some tremendous stress that was causing a psychic breakdown, maybe brought on by her disease—whatever that was—and for some reason he had been sucked into her delusions.

That had to be it. Any other explanation—that delirious Dracula story—was not only ludicrous and absurd, it was irresponsible, unethical, and immoral, especially to a man of science and medicine like Dave Sutton. No supernatural scenarios necessary or permitted. Sure, Bartok was involved, but only tangentially. As a sociopath, he'd zeroed right in on Carla's vulnerability, hit her buttons like playing the piano, even to the point of taking credit for "healing" Carla, the bastard—

"Like I said," Tim was backing away, his face grim with anger, "You need to look after your wife. She's the one in trouble here."

Dave watched him go. Tim's head was down as though sad. Sudden grief flushed through Dave as he wondered if that friendship was over, too.

Dave went inside a few minutes later. He almost didn't recognize his reflection in the sliding glass doors, his shoulders bowed, hands curved at his sides like a man reduced to his ape origins, hunched against the dangers of a world he believed to be haunted by forces beyond comprehension, superstitious and helpless. He would check himself into a mental health facility, he decided. Scour the nonsense out of his brain. He desperately needed someone to tell him that what he had seen wasn't real.

As he reached the door, a ghost behind the glass walked through Dave's reflection, the two images meshing, then separating. Someone who looked both familiar and strange.

Dave entered the hospital into a blast of cold air to see Henry West walking off to the left, into the geriatric wing. Henry West transformed, cleaned up, new clothes, hair trimmed, maybe even minus a few pounds, walking with businesslike confidence. He turned left again, five doors down. Dave followed him.

The name plate read "Klaus Bartok." Another sign said, "Nothing by Mouth."

The room was sunk in near-darkness, lights out, blinds open only part way.

Klaus Bartok lay mummy-like on his bed, on his back, his eyes closed. In the dim light, he seemed a little younger, though not by much. Bob Garner sat in a chair at the foot of the old man's bed, one cowboy-booted foot on the bed frame, his head back, a tube of ointment in his hand. Peter Schlesinger leaned against the window on the other side, his arms folded. Henry was just settling into another chair in a far corner to make himself invisible.

"Can I help—" Bob Garner began, then broke into his empty white smile. "Oh, hey Doc. What can we do for ya? How's the missus? That was a heckuva tumble they took. I guess the Lord was on their side, right?"

Dave had never heard Garner invoke God before. It had to be the latest branding gimmick.

"My wife's doing fine." He gestured toward the bed. "What about him?"

"The attending just left. Says the old fella'll be flyin' home in no time."

"Is he awake?" Dave asked.

As though answering, Klaus Bartok opened his eyes. No matter how dark or light it was, his eyes always seemed to shine with a light of their own. He smiled thinly as though Dave's presence amused him.

"Yeah, he'll back on his bronc in the shake of a chicken's leg. The airbag and his jet pilot seat saved his life. It's darn lucky my boy Henry happened to mosey by right then."

"I was goin' up to see him myself anyway," Henry rasped.

Schlesinger fired an angry look at Henry: Talking was not Henry's job. Garner kept a tight chain on things, but this one link was still soft and weak.

"So, Henry. How's it hangin'?" Dave asked with a weary smile. "You haven't come by the clinic or my office for awhile."

"I been okay, Doc. Been doin' real well."

Dave leaned in the doorway, hands in his pockets: "So you saw the accident."

Henry grunted: "Ran right in front of me."

"Driving around up there couldn't help your acrophobia none. I've seen you get shaky just sitting down on the barstool."

Henry ummmed around, floating up and down in his chair: "Acro—what did you say?"

"Your fear of heights and open spaces. You can't even climb my front stoop without doing a whirlygig. And now you have a driver's license? As your physician, I wouldn't have approved that. Gonna have to tell the sheriff to keep his eye peeled for you. An alcoholic acrophobic driving these roads? Why, I'd ride my horse over to next Sunday to avoid you."

Henry scrunched around his chair, like he was being dived bombed by mosquitoes: "Oh. You mean my *arachno*phobia, the spider thing. You're mixin' me up with someone else, Doc."

"Oh no, it's you, Henry. In fact, I think you have a major case of vertigo. You oughta come by and have me take another look. No charge this time."

"That's okay, Doc. Don't trouble yourself." Henry said, his face screaming, Please Doc! Shut up!

Meanwhile, Schlesinger squeezed his hands with his armpits to stop them from slapping Henry. Garner put his foot down and jerked his chair around. As Dave guessed, they knew nothing about Henry's little problem, no idea that they'd put the wrong man at the wheel of their pricey car.

"That's the thing about Henry," Dave cheerfully drawled. "If you put a little sugar on his tongue, you'll draw flies."

Garner grinned hugely as he changed the subject: "Comin' to the Commission meetin' tomorrow night? They'll be votin' on the future—"

"Cut the hick talk, all right?" Dave snapped. "The only thing I did wrong was not being awake to your game, but I am now."

Bob Garner stopped grinning and talking like a cowboy: "You overslept your alarm. There's nothing you can do about it. You're tied to this ball, so you might as well roll with it."

"We'll see about that." Before turning to go, Dave nodded over at Bartok who'd remained silent throughout, as though confident it would all go his way without his lifting a finger.

"Have they shown you any of his X-rays, his tests? He's a real curiosity."

Bob Garner was through talking to Dave: "We can handle things from here."

"Knock yourself out."

"Would you mind closing that door?"

Dave left it open and smiled his first smile in over a week as their muttered curses followed him down the hallway. He slowed down at the station desk and looked at the cart full of green binders. What curious information—or lack thereof—did Klaus Bartok's chart contain this time?

He backed away from the cart with a wave of his hand: "I don't care anymore." It would only make him feel crazy again.

He was glad to find Carla was still asleep, as he sat by her bed and took her hand. Her injuries were more serious than Bartok's—a concussion and torn neck and shoulder ligaments, but she'd be alright. Tim was right about thing: once the shock and the drugs wore off, her mind would be clear, and they'd get a better idea what actually happened, get past that vampire story to the gray sordid truth.

Right now though, he had no idea what to say. The weird drama of the last two weeks made words impossible, left his mind in its own bizarre jumble. Never had the world seemed so full of things that couldn't be put into words. It was almost like caring for terminal patients, but worse. Even death was comprehensible compared with what had happened to him and Carla. His father's crooked schemes made more sense than this. He found himself thinking about how Jeff Potter was all but unable to tell what happened the night his father died. But that was only an unspeakable guilt. What had happened to Dave and Carla was like the world turning upside down, then space ripping open. But it had been a semi-shared illusion, that was all.

Dave closed his eyes, listened to Carla's breathing and matched his rhythms to hers, tried to empty his mind, to act as if almost nothing had happened. He wanted them to both wake up together and search for a way to go on, together. Neither of them had been in their right minds, but now they would find their way to sanity again. It wouldn't be the same. Hell, it might even be better, stronger and more enduring, like other relationships that had gone through storms. He still loved her more than anyone and would still love her, no matter what.

Awhile later, he emerged from his fugue to find that Carla was still asleep. For the first time in days, he actually felt hungry. He stopped by the front desk and got permission to spend the night in the other bed in Carla's room. Then he drove across the state line to Gardnerville and bought back two burritos.

It was early evening on the drive back. Up ahead, the mountains look like a gray wall. He remembered the freak weather that had sunk down on Monitor County after Bartok's previous accident. The bad weather was back and this helped Dave make up his mind: when their own weather had cleared a little, he'd find someone to sell the practice to and get them both the hell out of here. Garner could do a lot, but he couldn't make the Suttons stay if they didn't want to.

By the time he returned to the hospital, night had fallen. He glanced at the door to the geriatric wing. Its wire-reinforced windows were two black squares. He mused that maybe the hospital should put armed guards on the blood bank—

But he stopped the thought. It wasn't even funny. Not now. "Dracula," he muttered in disgust. "Sheesh."

He was talking to Jeannie Sally at the nurse's station when the shriek came from Carla's room. He and Jeannie rushed in to find Carla sitting up in bed, staring at her hands, a look of horror on her face. A cup of water lay on the floor, its contents spilled.

"My hands," Carla cried. "My feet! My hands, they're going numb again! No, it's not the drugs. It's back. It's started again!" Then, as Dave took her in his arms, rage rose to mix with the horror. "That sonofabitch!" she cried, her whole body shaking. "That god-damn bastard! That sonofabitch!"

Dave held her close as she cried. Once again, he couldn't think what to say, as new and miserable horror washed over him. The ALS had returned, after all. Maybe that wasn't surprising, but Carla still believed she was under the power of Klaus Bartok. Dave couldn't do anything about that either, but imagine the old man in his hospital bed, smiling at the ceiling, his gimlet eyes glittering.

....

CHAPTER 35

Grab the Spider's Leg

Henry West finally got the beating that Peter Schlesinger been wanting to give him. Peter had strength, stamina, and wasn't nearly the human wreck that Henry was. He'd also been a boxer, Henry guessed, from the way he drilled jab after jab into Henry's midsection like a rapid-fire nail gun before he got tired enough to allow Henry to defend himself.

"Doc Suckoff," Henry declared, each word punctuated by a jabbing finger, was a lying Indian-hating quack who was always misdiagnosing Henry's people with one thing or another so he could boost his billing and scam more government money. Henry knew no such thing, but at least his bosses seemed to accept this.

"I'm Indian!" Henry concluded passionately. "We built the Empire State Building and the Golden Gate Bridge. We're human flies. We walk on ceilings for fun. It's impossible for me to have vertigo."

Because passion equals sincerity which equals truth in the ears of the listener, Garner and Schlesinger swallowed that one too. Petey, however, wouldn't apologize.

Petey showed up at the bungalow the next morning looking dismal, his shoulders bowed under a dreary sky that had moved in yesterday. The dense, vinegary air turned everything brown and drooping and felt like it would stay forever.

"The hospital called," Petey droned. "Bartok's ready for discharge. The commission vote's tonight, construction starts first thing tomorrow, and the boss and I don't have time for this. You take him home. There's another five hundred in it for you."

Petey followed him to the Rav-4, the third car they kept on hand: "Boss says you gotta be nice to him, no matter what he says or does, okay? Don't mess with him. At all. Walk him right to his front door. Try to get inside, got it? Don't fuck this up."

"I haven't fucked anything up. I've done everything you fuckers want."

"You're a fuck-up, West, a shit magnet." Then he turned sad eyes on the soapy sky. "God, this weather sucks. This place is a hole. What are we doing here?"

•

Henry found Klaus Bartok in a wheelchair by the nurse's station, all checked out. The staff was ignoring him, their feathers on fire over some theft that had taken place the night before.

Bartok threw a raving fit when saw the Rav-4 that would take him home, but Henry kept his cool, per the boss's orders: "Sorry, Mr. B. It's all we got. Your fancy carriage is still in the garage."

Bartok bellowed as Henry, his ribs aching from the beating, set him into the front seat. Bartok felt light as a pillow. His burnished feather-and-fur black suit must have made his tailor a rich man. It fit him like it grew right out of his bird-like body. He smelled like cool mountain pine, a perfume that made Henry feel weightless and set off another dizzy spell.

Klaus Bartok was the worst motherfucking backseat driver in the whole fucking universe. No matter how carefully Henry drove, Bartok bitched, raved, and bellowed: "Turn left. Turn right. Stoplight. Slow down. Stop. Go. Too fast. Too slow. Look before you change lanes, you peasant."

A million hours later, they made it to Alpine Canyon Road. Henry stopped at the bottom to pull his cap down extra low to the left.

"Are you going to drive with one eye now? Why don't you tie

your hands behind your back and steer with your face?"

And then, as they rode up the valley, hugging the right side of the road, Old Whiny started bawling like a baby abandoned in a high-speed rollercoaster. Henry had never heard such carrying on from anyone but himself. And they call me a whiner? he thought. It was getting scary, too. Bartok's crying only made the drive more danger-ous.

There was one more thing, though: Henry felt an unwelcome blush of empathy for the old man. They both suffered from the same exact problem: fear of heights. Henry felt ashamed. Real men weren't supposed to be suckers for sad stories. Empathy was a sign that screamed "FUCK ME OVER!" Em-pa-thy helped put Henry in Folsom. People's sweet siren song about the hearts they didn't have.

Nevertheless, Henry couldn't go on like this on these roads, so he stopped again, heaving a patient sigh: "Look, old man, I'm sorry about this. It's just my job, okay? Don't sweat. I'll get ya home safe. Promise."

Henry reached in the back and fumbled for a small navy-blue wool blanket, the kind given out at college football games: "I need ya quiet. Sometimes if you can't see what's scarin' you, you feel better. That's why I wear my cap and sunglasses like this. It works like horse blinders, get it? Here ya go."

He draped the blanket over Bartok's head, fussed with it a little, then tapped the old man on his crown.

"There." Henry chuckled. "Ya look like a blue ghostie. Boooo!"

Bartok sat in stunned silence, but the blanket seemed to do the trick. He stayed quiet for the rest of the way, except for an occasional hoarse sigh. At the entrance into the canyon, Henry, saying he had to pee, got out and dry-heaved. The road down into the canyon weaved like a super-tight stitch but they made it safely.

On the canyon floor, Henry got out to dry heave again As he got back in, mumbling about his bladder, Bartok pulled the blanket off his head and let out an exalted breath, wearing the usual look of the lordly white man. He was back in his world now. Henry's bubble of empathy burst. Once again, he'd wasted tender feelings on another ungrateful shithead.

They drove on in silence. Henry didn't care for the canyon's prison-like walls, but thanks to his cap bill and sun visor, he saw little of them. The road wove and weaved, but was, happily, mostly flat and featureless, and the bridges over the big creek were low above the water. Not the worst drive Henry had made since taking the wheel for Sierra Future.

Finally, as he stopped at the end of the road, Bartok spoke: "No wonder I prefer women drivers. So much more obedient. Minds like clay, eager to be shaped, passive and pliable."

Whatever. Henry started to open his door, but the old man nagged on: "I suppose until I hire someone else, I have you—no, I don't want you even near my other car. You are barely fit to ride a tricycle. This will, thankfully, be temporary employment."

With sudden fury, Henry completely forgot Bob Garner's orders to be nice: "Well then, fuck YOU very much. You can go tongue my hole, ya ugly coot. I shoulda tied you like a deer to the fuckin' roof. You can walk in and outta this shithole by yourself for all I care. I've had enough of you stuck-up scumbags. Just 'cause you're white, rich, and old, you think you can blow your snot around, like some king o' the castle. Look, cocksucker, you started out as a drop of come and you're gonna wind up worm food just like me and don't you forget it. You may have got them dumb bitches to blow you—" Henry leaned in, jabbing his thumb at his chest—"but Henry West don't blow nobody." Which wasn't true, but what the hell, it felt good to say it.

"I'm sure your employers will be cheered to hear about our little talk and your forthright tantrum," Bartok sniffed with a thin smile. "Be sure to tell them I feel less cooperative now. Help me out of this tin coffin."

"Fuck you. Get out yourself."

The old man took off his sunglasses and glared. Henry felt the cold beams shooting from his blue eyes, felt the spider's scrabbling legs, heard its whirring voice, felt its hunger.

Henry bolted from the car. He nearly hyperventilated as he groped his way to the passenger side. He unbuckled Klaus Bartok, lifted him out, and set him on the ground. Bartok gruffly ordered him to fetch him a tree branch lying nearby.

Henry handed Bartok his stick, looking away. The bastard straightened his shoulders and marched proudly away down the path toward the redwood bridge.

Henry hadn't followed him two steps before the old man turned on him.

"What do you think you're doing?"

Henry looked at the ground: "Mr. Garner says I gotta see you home safe and sound—no, please keep your glasses on, please?"

"I am home, and I don't need your help. I'll inform your employers through Miss Albanese when I wish to meet again. And send someone else here with my vehicle."

Henry watched the old man cross the bridge over the stream and wondered if he should throw him over the railing. Then Henry sensed something he hadn't noticed before: the further away the old man was, the less of his weird power he seemed to have. At a certain distance, the old man couldn't send his blue beams into Henry's eyes.

As Bartok climbed the hill to the moraine, Henry dug out a half-quart of Smirnoff he'd stashed deep in the back of the Rav-4. The bosses wouldn't smell that on him. He turned to find the old man staring down from the top of the moraine, angrily waving his stick.

"Go away!" Bartok hollered in his grand voice. "Get!"

"Woof, woof," muttered Henry. "This dog's followin' you home."

Bartok disappeared into the desolate moraine. Henry crossed the bridge and went up the trail. The trail curlicued around, in some places doubling back on itself. Here and there, bedlike mats of whitebark pine lay sunk in the cold, gray barrenness. Looking closer, Henry saw that the white dust that covered them were actually spider webs, homes for thousands of ravenous spiders. Fuck me, what if

I fall in one of those? He quickened his pace, careful not to catch up with Bartok too soon. He passed by the ruins of a cabin where more spider webs shivered in the wind. He could hear their eating noises. Was it true that spiders left their prey alive to snack on later?

Finally, the trail headed down the other side. Henry snuck to the rim at a crouch and stopped behind a man-sized rock. A ways away at the bottom of the slope, Klaus Bartok was seated on a fallen log, looking out over a broad short grass meadow.

"What're you waitin' down there for?" Henry called down.

Startled, Bartok rose to his feet shaking, whipping off his glasses. Henry marveled at how visible those eyes were at this distance, but they were still too far away to make spiders in his head. The old man knew it and shook his head in frustration:

"I …I wait for the sun to set. For night to fall." He looked around, his face lighting up with a surprising joy. "This is all wonderful … beautiful." Then he sneered at Henry. Oh, yes …but it's *you*. What would you know about it, little blind man?

Bartok turned his back and sat back down on his log.

Henry looked around carefully and agreed. It did look pretty and restful: the austere man in black against the bright gold meadow; the meadow against the canyon walls that seemed to rise forever while a snow-bright waterfall thundered down, its tail waving in the afternoon wind. Wild animals wandered everywhere: white-tail deer grazed not ten feet from where Bartok sat. Nutcrackers and iridescent blue mountain jays hopped and squawked. A mountain squirrel scampered right up to the old man and sat down chattering and begging. A hawk gracefully flew onto a dead tree. Somehow, Bartok fit with it all.

The afternoon shadows grew long and inky. What was Bartok waiting for? There was no sign of a dwelling anywhere. Henry's eyes followed the trail up the canyon wall a ways, but he shut his eyes at the first sign of blue sky and the Ark's freezing glare. All of it seemed alive, breathing, knowing, aware.

Oh, cut the spirit crap. Just sit and watch. Henry felt a tickle up the back of his neck. He pawed at it and a tiny brown and white spider fell at his feet. Henry lifted his foot to stomp it, but hesitated long enough for the animal to scuttle away. Scared too, huh? Henry had never before let a spider escape. Then he sighed at the sight of a dew-dappled web that stretched across one of the pine mats a few feet away, glistening and shimmering in the afternoon breeze, sparkling like a diamond-dusted blanket. As the wind moaned like a soft flute, Henry wondered what the power of this place was doing to him.

I could use a drink. What else would help him shake the lonesome beauty of this alien world? The old man seemed content in his seat by the meadow. What, or who, the fuck was he waiting for? Someone to walk him up the cliff? Whatever. Henry would wait to see, then get out of here. He nestled behind the rock. He pulled the Smirnoff from inside his jacket. Mmmmmm, creamy warm. One sip …two sips …three sips …

Henry jerked awake to blue darkness, flapping wings, and a big whoosh as if from a jet. He scrambled up, sickened about falling sleep and waking up at night, in the canyon. As sunlight died its red death behind the western mountains, Henry saw a fire racing up black canyon walls toward a turquoise sky that was rapidly filling with blinking stars.

Henry rushed down the slope, but the old man had gone, leaving his stick behind. Schlesinger was right. Henry was a fuck-up. He'd lost the old man and now he was in the canyon after dark. He forgot everything he'd seen and felt only hours before. Except for the spiders. It was only him and them in the awful blackness of Alpine Canyon.

He was crying by the time he found his way by starlight to the other side of the moraine. He heard the spiders eating with every step of the way and swore they were following him. He could hear their tiny feet, millions of them, clicking over the rocks as they chased him through the night, their fangs waving …

There were cars all over when he got back to Garner's near midnight. He parked down Walsh Hot Springs Road and, again, walked home in the dark. Garner's great pyramid blazed with light like a giant lantern, roared with pop music, raucous voices, and the pop of champagne corks. His crazy project had won, but if Henry walked in, uninvited, they would only look at him and look away.

Henry's house sat dark and empty. He took a hot shower but couldn't wash away that tickling feeling of spider's feet. At least there was beer, tequila, and Mama's rabbit skin robe.

Even so, he felt the spiders dancing over his skin all night long, while Mama watched from a shadow, her face empty.

•

"So what happened, Henry?" Bob Garner asked late the following morning in the bungalow kitchen. The weather was nice again, but the boss's long, red face looked tight, whether from a hangover or another migraine or both, Henry couldn't tell and didn't care. No matter how much success a man had, he still had his pain. Henry told him and Schlesinger what had happened.

"You were drunk!" Petey shouted. "That's why you fell asleep." Punch, punch, punch went Petey again. "Fucking. Useless. Indian." Finally, Garner called off Schlesinger, who then stormed out, no doubt to search the Rav-4 and prove Henry to be a liar again. Luckily, though, Henry had left the Smirnoff in the canyon.

Bob Garner casually poured Henry a Coors while Henry wept ashamedly. "Maybe I shoulda pushed his car off that cliff the other day when I had the chance."

Bob Garner reared back in his chair. What did Henry mean by that? Henry told him. The Boss understood perfectly why Henry couldn't go through with it, with the under sheriff there and all. Then he made Henry tell him about yesterday again, but didn't ask, thank God, about the vodka. He was very interested in the trail to the canyon rim: "Did you see him go up there? Did you see anyone come down?"

"I didn't see nothin'. I woke up—poof—gone." He didn't mention the fire flying up the wall. "I don't see how he could get up there himself, unless he flew, or took an elevator."

Bob sighed: "We had a great day yesterday. But we also got word from Getgo—it's their money that's seeding all this—they're demanding that the hotel on the south rim under the mountain be built and open for business by next spring."

"Garner Mountain," Henry said. Garner laughed a little, but his face turned a little redder with anger.

"We don't know when that evil old man's gonna die. As far as we know, he has no heirs, no will. When he passes, his property could be what's called intestate. Dying without a will means the state gets it all. Fortunately, we've got some friends there" —Bob winked—"so taking that empty land off their hands wouldn't be too hard. But it's gotta be emptied first. The shit that's there has to go. Like, now." He gritted his teeth and slapped his hand hard on the table, leaning forward, speaking urgently.

"Henry, going back to that accident, you hinted to me awhile back that you uh …once fixed a problem you were having."

Henry knew what he meant and regretted his attempt at making himself look macho and more valuable.

"What happened anyway? Don't worry. I won't tell." Garner winked.

Henry looked around for inspiration and found a coffee can label. "There was this Maxwell dude, he was the fourth partner on that drug deal I went up for and well, the three of us figured he was skimmin' us big time, maybe even rattin' us out to the cops. So, I took him on a walk by some cliffs down around Pacifica."

Henry pushed out with both hands and laughed. "He went easy. People fall off them cliffs all the time, so that part I got away with all right. Didn't bother me none. Not even walkin' on the cliffs."

Bob Garner thoughtfully sipped on a beer as his face grew redder: "Mr. Asshole's been hiking that canyon trail all his useless life. That's why he can still do it, even at his age. But now he's old, he tires easily, and his reflexes are slow. Old people fall all the time. A lot of them will never get up." He paused. "Like that one."

BANG went the beer can on the kitchen table. Bob Garner started-ed shouting, his face red with spluttering rage.

"I fucking hate that fucking old man's fucking guts. We both do. After all this fucking work, we now gotta get his greedy ass out of the way, or else every goddamn fucking thing we've done means SHIT." BAM went the can. "The whole fucking deal goes poof. I hate to tell ya Henry, but I might not even be able to pay you what I owe you. Everything will get zeroed out unless we get that fucking property. There's no future here so long as that greedy fucker's sitting on his fucking throne. He's an old ghost that needs putting down. He's over.

"Look at the shitty way he's treated you." Garner waved his finger. "He KICKED your people out of these mountains. Now here's your chance for payback, for redemption. Now," he leaned in as he quieted down to a low, fierce growl, "are you gonna take this chance or not? No, it won't be easy. He's a clever fuck. Who knows what he's gonna do on that trail? There's a rumor he pushed that hippie kid off the cliff the other day. That kid was one of the losers tryin' to stop our good work, but well, it was murder. You'll have to watch your back. He'd push his own mama off just to watch her fall and bounce, like he did to the people who lived there before him. Your people, Henry. It's time to fight for us and for your people."

He broke out the tequila. The gold liquid splashing in the glass made a song with his words: "Barb Albanese will contact him to make an appointment for Thursday. We changed our minds about his property, but we need his help on a new deal that's come up. You meet him, but this time, you go way early, hike that trail to the top. That's gotta be where he lives. And from there you walk him down." He flexed his eyebrows, winked and laughed. Then he frowned: "Stay on your toes. Don't take any shit. You be the boss and see how he likes it. And if he doesn't, there's a twenty-five thousand dollar bonus with this, but *only* if the accident happens. Otherwise, it's back to the sidewalk, buddy, tin cups for both of us. Long walk to the next county, remember?"

●

Just after dawn on Thursday morning, Henry found the Smirnoff right where he left it. He chugged a little of it and, with cap down, eyes to his left, started up the cliff trail, circling behind the thundering falls. He turned his back as he rounded the corner into the cold blue air. He kept his eyes on his feet and hugged the wall all the way up, pretending there was no hungry chasm behind him with its seductive call: C'mon, Henry. Take a peek. Look how high and deep I am! Ooooooo! I'm hungry, Henry! Hungry for you! All the while, a cold wind snaked between him and the rock as though trying to pry them apart.

Henry collapsed at the top, in a shaking cold sweat. He kissed the rocky earth, heaved up the Smirnoff, then wriggled a foot or two away, as wind and gravity still conspired to send him over the edge.

Then after he calmed a little, he rolled over on his back and opened his eyes. A huge white face stared down from the empty blue sky.

"What are you doing here?"

The force of Bartok's booming voice nearly rolled Henry over the cliff. Bartok towered like the jagged mountain behind him, his baggy face twisted in demonic fury. Henry wiped his nose and sniffed. He pushed himself up, crossing his legs.

"Morning, Mr. B."

"Who gave you permission to come up here?"

"Mr. Garner ordered me to make absolutely sure you got down safe. We need ya to stay alive. Says he's sorry about the other day and he needs your help real bad." Then he added, "You're too old to be walkin' around here by yourself. That's fuckin' nuts. Especially the way you carry on in the car—"

Bartok wearily cut him off: "What does he need from me now?"

Henry shrugged: "They don't tell me shit, Mr. B. They say come up here and get you, here I be: A mule don't ask."

"You grovel like one too." Bartok gazed out over the canyon, and his eyebrows arced with pleasure. "Ah, the vote went my way. They wasted no time," he murmured.

Henry didn't dare look, but he could now catch a faint clanging

340

echo of construction equipment and the distant holler of construction workers all the way over from the north rim. The road through Mystic Valley that morning had been jammed with endless convoys of them. It made the old man happy.

Bartok whacked Henry on the head with his walking stick: "Go! No, no, in front of me, you clumsy turd."

Henry started back down the cliff, the air below a dark cool gray pond. The hike up had been grueling terror, but going down was infinitely worse, with only the cold comfort of the granite wall to support him on the right, while a horrible tumbling doom pulled from the left. His head spun, his stomach floated, every muscle shook. Gravity pulled like a ton of acid lead on his calves and knees. He wished he could crawl like a baby. As his body quaked, another feeling lurked in Henry's soul, a lurking rage that slowly widened into an open-fire fury as Bartok snarled behind him, whacked his stick against the wall and drove Henry along as though herding a dumb cow.

Henry knew that if he wanted to live, he had to keep cool, play his stoic Indian side. Lose his head and the rest of him would fall with it. Garner was right: Bartok had killed that hippie, shoved him off this very trail and he'd whack Henry the same way. But Henry was ready for him. Right now, he had to stay ahead of that stick without losing his shaky footing, without allowing the sound of Bartok's footsteps, the scrape and pound of the stick, his gravely growl, drive him over the edge to smash on the talus below.

Things grew quiet. Henry glanced over his right shoulder, up along the wall. The old man had stopped and was gazing out over the canyon. Even with his sunglasses on, he looked like he was enjoying the view. Enjoying the view, fucking two-faced bastard! After all that whining on the drive here the other day.

Bartok looked away from the unspeakable scenery to see Henry staring at him. He bared his giant teeth and shook his stick: "Go on. Move. Hurry."

The roar of anger in Henry's mind grew louder, but when he felt his bones start physically vibrating, he knew something else was happening. Uh-oh, he thought as he looked up from the safe ground so see the waterfall roaring some twenty feet away. He'd been so focused on not falling, so focused on his hatred, he lost track of where they were, near the bottom of the cliff. Soon, it would be too late for the accident. To make it happen here, he'd have to turn and look out over the fucking canyon. Fucking impossible.

Then Henry remembered that right angle turn into the cave behind the falls and knew what to do next.

When he reached the corner, he let Bartok catch up a little, within about five feet. Then he slithered around the corner, scraping his face against the wall. As the falls roared and sprayed coldly on his back, he watched the corner with one eye, waiting, his breathing going faster and faster.

The old man's stick appeared first, reaching out like a spider's leg.

Henry grabbed the spider's leg. In an eye blink, he was holding the end of the stick with both hands. Bartok clung to the other. Henry held him right out over the cliff, deep in the roaring dark of the cave. The old man's eyes glowed through the sunglasses, in the dark. He began to change, in the dark. He began to crawl up the stick toward Henry, in the dark.

Henry screamed, flung the old man on the stick away. Bartok was gone, down into the falls. Crying, Henry turned his face back to the canyon wall.

He slithered, tripped, slipped, fell, and rolled muddy and wet down the trail out into cold daylight. He sprawled on his back next to the falls laughing at the sky. He rolled over and pounded his fists on the muddy ground: "Yes!" He got to his hands and knees, looking into the churning froth that foamed out of the hole in the water made by the falls. The water was doing its righteous work: drowning, churning, pounding Klaus Bartok to bits on the rocks beneath, as relentless as Mama grinding pine nuts with her pestle.

Henry felt the urge to sing a war chant, but the Washoe were not a warring people, so he simply shook his fist, gave the falls the finger, shouting, "Ding-fuckin'-dong you're dead, you fucker!"

Henry strolled away by the stream, his head held high and his arms swinging. Sierra Future had had their great day and now Henry West was having his. He'd just made a breakthrough. He'd fought the monster and won, handily. Easy as beating up a baby, he chortled. Now I'm one of them. Ha ha!

Then, at a spot where the pool flowed into the stream, he stopped to look behind him once more and saw the black thing float out from under the falls.

That's a tree branch, Henry thought.

But no. It wasn't a tree branch. It was Klaus Bartok.

Klaus Bartok, intact, on his back, arms out like Jesus, hair streaming behind like weeds, bobbing along on the silvery surface like a crisp fall leaf, merrily floating downstream, right by Henry West.

Henry ran. He outran his own feet, but couldn't keep up with his fright. Over and over, he slammed face first into the ground. He ran past the floating corpse, watching him out of the corner of his eye, just in case, just in case, just in case.

The wild animals scattered before him; hawks dive-bombed him, knocking him down. All the life in the canyon was coming after Henry, for revenge.

At the spot where the stream parted from the trail, he looked back again. Klaus Bartok was sailing right at him, feet first, as though he'd tip up on his feet and walk out the second he touched shore. Henry prayed for him to snag on the rocks, in the weeds, where the water ran heavy and fast, so all the hungry things that lived there would eat him, until only his bird-bones remained.

Klaus Bartok's feet did indeed hit a rock. The body sprang back into the middle of the stream, spun lazily around once, and floated away with stupefying grace and dignity.

Henry scrambled screaming up into the moraine. He was still screaming as he ran down the other side, scratched to hell, his blood making a glue with the spider webs that had leapt out to snag him. Spider webs gummed up his eyes and filled his mouth like cotton candy.

He stopped halfway across the bridge and leaned against the railing, staring down into the white rushing water. But even there, there was no escape as Klaus Bartok floated under Henry's gaze, on his back, arms out, hair streaming above his head, his shocking blue eyes wide and staring, staring at Henry as if to say, "I'll be back. I'll be hungry."

Henry West remembered nothing of the drive home, only the old man's eyes—a bright, staring blue from a cold mountain stream.

....

CHAPTER 36

Memo to Corporate

GetGo Inc.
MEMORANDUM
July 23, 20—
FROM: Keith Clark: U.S. Project Development
TO: Charles Bermann (Berlin office) & Pat Wu (Beijing office)
Attachments: PDF files.
Subject: Sierra Future City and Entertainment Resort Project

Corporate headquarters has expressed concern at delays in the above matter. I was asked to conduct an inspection and review of our latest resort and residential project, following reports and complaints of various accidents and incidents.

Monitor County is located in Eastern California, USA, along the Nevada border, southeast of South Lake Tahoe (the location of our last and largest development project). The Sierra Future Project ("Project") is intended not only as an expansion of our holdings near Tahoe to handle the overflow of tourists into the Sierra Nevada Mountain Range, but also as a separate urban community profit center in its own right, drawing in new residents and recreational consumers from the Reno/Tahoe Metro area, Las Vegas, and other points east. Construction began in June (a month ago as of this memo) with completion scheduled for August 20—, three years and two months hence.

Project headquarters is centered in the village of Byrneville (pop. 150), located on Monitor County Highway, about thirty miles west from the county seat of Osgood (pop. 2,301). While Osgood is the county's current population center, plans exist for a new city of 20,000 to be constructed in Mystic Valley. Byrneville will be abandoned. The new city, Sierra City, will be close to some of the highest peaks in the Sierras, which makes it both an ideal population center and "jumping off point" for other recreational facilities, including the large hotel/condominium complex planned for the Dragon's Ark area on the south rim of Alpine Canyon (originally scheduled to open next Spring). Dragon's Ark is the major geographical and scenic feature in the area.

Upon my arrival on July 16, I attempted to contact the onsite project developer and manager, Robert Garner. Mr. Garner—who apparently suffers from severe chronic migraines—was indisposed, so a meeting was held with assistant project manager Peter Schlesinger. Mr. Schlesinger related to me that all political and property acquisition issues had recently been settled, including all escrow, allowing the Project to begin on schedule.

However, when I pointed out to Mr. Schlesinger that my visit was concerned with other incidents and issues relating to the actual construction, which is now supposed to be well under way (but is not), Mr. Schlesinger became defensive and so combative that the meeting was cut short, pending an improvement in his outlook. (Note: the proposed promotion of Mr. Schlesinger within the organization should be taken under reconsideration, pending his reappearance.)

I next visited the recently abandoned construction site for the proposed Alpine Canyon Bridge, located in the western part of the county, along the Sierra Crest Highway, on the north rim of the canyon. I was accompanied by construction manager Benjamin Haitink, who had recently been promoted to first construction manager, after the death of construction manager Ms. Liz Soderstrom (see below).

Mr. Haitink, while generally cooperative and professional, was

somewhat less than forthcoming as he related the following incidents:

During a dawn groundbreaking ceremony for Sierra City on June
21, just over a week after the final project approval by the Monitor
County Commission, three of the county commissioners—and the
crucial supporters of the company's project—simultaneously suffered massive fatal heart attacks. Whether a coincidence, or a "freak"
chain reaction brought on by anxiety, all three commissioners were
deceased within a matter of minutes (see autopsy results, attached).
Work commenced without a groundbreaking ceremony.

Mr. Haitink related to me further details surrounding the deaths
of two surveyors, Paul Wenkel and Sarah Walker, sent into Alpine
Canyon to survey the south rim. The two entered the canyon on the
afternoon of June 22 and were not heard from again. Four days later
a search party, led by Monitor County Under Sheriff Timothy King,
launched a search for them.

On June 27, Mr. Wenkel's and Ms. Walker's bodies were found
on the canyon floor, under the north rim. The remains indicated
that both had fallen from the top of the canyon, though they were
found at a great distance from their scheduled destination. The location suggests that they were "flung out" (Mr. Haitink's phrase) from
the top of the canyon's south rim.

Another puzzling detail was that both surveyors' surveying and
camping equipment was found scattered around the canyon floor.
Ms. Walker's notebook was found, with the entries for June 23 and
24 indicating normal sitings and activities along the canyon bottom.
However, the entry for June 25 had only one entry as follows:

"June 25: Top of canyon, south rim. Wenkel wants to fly."

Neither Mr. Haitink, nor Under Sheriff King (see below), was
able to provide any further details regarding this matter. (Note:
make sure flowers have been sent to families of deceased Sierra Fu-
ture/Getgo employees.)

This lack of detail is possibly due to the confusion caused by a
near-simultaneous accident that occurred on June 23, the day after

Mr. Wenkel and Ms. Walker entered Alpine Canyon. While prep-
ping the north rim for the first part of bridge construction, the edge
of the cliff gave way (apparently during an outdoor party being held
right after dusk). A backhoe and four workers fell their deaths (Timothy Stookey, David Ennis, John Borges, Susan Gable; see note in
paragraph above; also, attorneys need to be contacted re liability
issues). Mr. Haitink—who, as noted, has been reluctant to provide
details—witnessed this incident and described it thusly: "The stone
turned to sand and dust right under them." (As a former geology
major, I have never heard of such a phenomenon. More likely, the
granite in that part of the canyon simply exfoliated.)

Construction on this part of the bridge project was halted, pending further investigations by this company, and state and federal officials. Meanwhile prep work for the rest of the bridge project continued for the next two days.

Mr. Haitink stated that he and the other workers disliked working on the north rim of Alpine Canyon because of the huge population of turkey vultures that blanketed the area (I saw no vultures
myself on my visit). Some of the workers claimed they were being
"watched all the time" in Mr. Haitink's words: "They would walk
right up to us and sit and *stare* [his emphasis] at us. They wouldn't go
away even when we threw s—t at them."

Finally, Ms. Soderstrom, the then-manager, in response to her
crew's complaints, fired at one of these birds with a shotgun one evening. Asked about the effect of Ms. Soderstrom's action, Mr. Haitink
snapped his fingers: "Boom. Gone. Not even any feathers. Just disappeared." He could not explain further.

Mr. Haitink went to say that on the night of June 25, he observed
"a strange animal" wandering the property on the north rim. Pressed
again for more details, Mr. Haitink described the animal as "like" a
12-point buck deer, but with twice as many points on its antlers and
that it had "weird eyes." Asked to elaborate, Mr. Haitink described
them as "big, blue, and hungry …it looked like it was hungry. I coulda sworn I heard it say 'I'm hungry.'" Mr. Haitink further swore that

the deer ran to the edge of the canyon "sprouted wings and flew away like f—ing Rudolph!" (Drug and alcohol tests later ordered for Mr. Haitink produced negative results; see attached toxicology reports.)

The next morning, June 26, a road worker, Mark Clinton (see note page 3, para 5, and note above), a backhoe operator, was found deceased outside the Quonset hut, where workers stay overnight. Dr. David Sutton, a private physician practicing in the County, (and with whom I spoke several times) indicated the deceased appeared to have suffered severe abdominal wounds, or, as he put it, was "gored to death" by a deer. Pressed further, Dr. Sutton stated that such incidents, though extremely rare, were known to happen to hunters and hikers when they wandered too close to males during rutting season. However, he had never heard of a victim of one of these incidents being "partially devoured."

At this point, despite Ms. Soderstrom's threats of dismissal, the rest of the construction team demanded alternative lodgings, either in Byrneville, Osgood, or across the Nevada border in Carson Valley. After intense negotiations and phone conferences with our office, it was decided, given the additional cost of lodging and fuel and time lost to commuting, to temporarily close all construction at the bridge site until further notice. (Of this date, it has yet to resume.)

It was decided to concentrate resources and aggressively pursue the Sierra City portion of the Project. These project workers were housed in the village of Byrneville. Problems with this aspect of the Project began almost immediately, when one of the workers, Aaron Seymour, awoke the morning of June 27 (the day the two surveyors were found in Alpine Canyon) complaining of severe abdominal pains. Mr. Seymour related that he had awoken in the middle of the night very hungry and consumed a large can of chili, unheated.

Mr. Seymour collapsed late that morning and was rushed to Osgood Memorial Hospital, where X-rays revealed the presence of over fifty three-inch nails in his digestive tract. The nails had punctured the walls of his stomach.

Mr. Seymour was rushed to a Reno hospital for further treatment, but unfortunately, expired en route (see autopsy report, attached; also note above). It has not been determined how the deceased could mistake a can of nails for a can of chili. A search of his room revealed no evidence of hallucinogenic drugs. Toxicology reports (attached) indicate no presence of illegal substances.

Meanwhile, a rash of sore throats broke out through the entire construction team, with new cases appearing every morning, accompanied by extreme weakness and lassitude. Dr. Sutton initially made a diagnosis of flu accompanied by anemia, though anemia is not contagious. Also, no village residents, or any other county residents seemed to catch this particular bug, though some claim occasional bouts, as, I was told, do various campers and hikers.

Dr. Sutton was not able to offer any treatment beyond routine bed rest and flu medicines. (Note: despite his local reputation as a competent and well-respected physician, Dr. Sutton is prone to inappropriate humor, even jokingly suggesting that we were having a "vampire problem"! (Perhaps the State should review his license. Discuss with attorneys.)

The entire construction team was out of commission, showing only signs of recovery in time for the July 4 holiday, when it was decided they would be permitted to attend a fireworks display in Carson City, Nevada, that evening.

When the project recommenced the morning of July 5, construction supervisor Ms. Soderstrom was discovered missing. She had attended the Carson City fireworks display the evening before and was last seen returning to Byrneville in her private truck.

An immediate search commenced along the Monitor County Highway between Byrneville and Osgood. Ms. Soderstrom's truck was found late that afternoon along the Osgood Canyon "stretch," almost midpoint between the two locations, on the other side of the river from the road, a distance of nearly 200 feet. According to Under Sheriff King, the condition of the trunk and Ms. Soderstrom's remains indicated she had left the road at an extremely high rate of speed, enough to collide with the opposite canyon wall. When asked for a closer estimate, the under sheriff stated, "About as fast as a Peregrine falcon dive-bombing a dove." (Note: rural people tend to be imprecise in their calculations.)

Mr. Haitink was immediately promoted to the position vacated by Ms. Soderstrom's passing (see accident report, attached, and note above). However, despite the personal goodwill expressed toward Mr. Haitink by the entire construction team and Mr. Haitink's own considerable construction and management skills, incidents continued to occur that resulted in further delays.

Relationships between the construction team and Byrneville residents were also growing strained. It was alleged that two construction team members were apprehended, naked, inside the house of one of the village's elder residents, indulging in what I will only call extremely inappropriate and bizarre behavior (see attached Sheriff's Report). Excess alcohol consumption was suspected. All county beer bars and alcohol sales were completely banned, over the strenuous objection of local residents. Employees were subject to arbitrary searches of all their belongings and persons.

Three others workers were arrested in a violent brawl at three in the morning in their hotel room, causing considerable property damage and injury to themselves; however, all three involved claimed to have no memory of the actual brawl, though one alleged he saw one of his roommates "crawling naked across the ceiling like a bug while singing 'Polly-Wolly Doodle.'" When I asked if inappropriate sexual activity had taken place, Mr. Haitink became evasive. He claimed he "didn't remember" the names of the workers involved. All three were found to be suffering from a recurrence of the flu that had swept through the team earlier. Two of them resigned and the third was dismissed.

Mr. Haitink, while clearly wishing to be cooperative during this interview, nevertheless was vague and evasive, often breaking down in tears. He was very distressed at my skepticism regarding many of the events he described. I admit I found it difficult to conceal my frustration regarding various holes and contradictions in his version of events.

At the end of our last interview, one week ago, Mr. Haitink broke down and offered his resignation, which was duly accepted. He is currently a patient at a Bay Area psychiatric institution.

Meanwhile, I attempted to interview the Monitor County Sheriff John Parker, who directed me to aforementioned Under Sheriff Timothy King who is responsible for law enforcement in western Monitor County.

While as polite and professional as one would expect a law-enforcement official to be, Under Sheriff King was also maddeningly evasive, almost dismissive, regarding the incidents of the last month. He could not clarify many of Mr. Haitink's statements and casually claimed that he was as baffled as I was. Aside from his casualness regarding facts and statistics, I would describe his attitude as one of "studied incuriosity" about many matters regarding the Project, probably due to a bias against our plans to completely privatize law enforcement in Monitor County.

Under Sheriff King also pointed out, that, while the Project had initially received majority support in the county, the ban of alcohol sales and consumption, the eviction of some of the residents, and the disruptive behavior of Project employees has caused support to drop and opposition to increase radically. Under Sheriff King strongly indicated that, while Monitor County is among the least-rich California counties, several large outside NGOs have stepped forward to offer assistance with any lawsuits arising from this situation.

When asked what steps he had taken to ascertain what might be responsible for the bizarre string of incidents, Under Sheriff King invoked "common sense": that the two surveyors had been blown off the top of Alpine Canyon by an especially strong wind; that there had been possible safety violations on our part in the death plunge of the four workers; and that Ms. Soderstrom had been speeding in her truck.

When I confronted him concerning the employee gored and partially eaten by the "flying blue-eyed deer," he pointed to the many hallucinations experienced by other members of the construction team. He then suggested that "altitude sickness," common to new-comers at this height, may be the culprit. (I admit to experiencing a touch of it myself. The air up here has an unusual fierce shimmering clarity that intensifies color and encourages various optical and aural illusions, especially in the hours after sunset.) This regrettably may point to human agency in the death of Mr. Clinton. However, as all the workers on the bridge project have been dismissed or trans-ferred, such questions will be difficult to follow up on.

Under Sheriff King suggested another interview with Dr. Sutton might enlighten the situation regarding the various health problems. However, efforts to speak further with Dr. Sutton have been frus-trated, apparently owing to the recent disappearance of his wife.

Finally, as you know from my e-mail messages of yesterday, proj-ect manager Robert Garner, whom I was never able to interview, apparently committed suicide. His assistant and accountant, Peter Schlesinger, has also not reappeared since our last discussion and his whereabouts remain unknown (along with another employee, an in-dependent consultant whose name remains unknown, but who was described to me as "local color"). At my insistence, search parties have been sent out throughout the wilderness surrounding the vil-lage, and results are pending.

After the passing of Robert Garner, a review of records on his computer and elsewhere hints at the existence of a second set of books indicating that Sierra Future was engaged in significant "skimming" activity. Much of the funding that our organization has provided for the numerous government and private land acquisitions preceding the start of construction had been diverted into other accounts.

In conclusion, the cascade of incidents and delays that have com-pletely halted construction, along with the likelihood of subsequent and costly lawsuits and other obstacles, makes it imperative that our organization consider other options, including, I am sad to say, our complete withdrawal from this project and the disposal of the tens of thousands of acres of now useless land acquired by Sierra Future.

Anticipating this action, I had made an appointment with the major local realtor (and major Sierra Future player), a Ms. Barbara Albanese, for yesterday. However, I am shocked to say, that while taking an early morning walk on the main road through the village, I had the misfortune of discovering Ms. Albanese's body floating down Byrneville Creek, right underneath the village bridge. Under Sheriff King later informed me that Ms. Albanese had been mutilated in ways I will not describe. The mutilations obviously came from spending a long period of time in the fast-flowing waters of the creek. As the Under Sheriff puts it, "she must've fallen in quite a ways upstream."

I have just come from a meeting with a Mr. Klaus Bartok, who, I am told, was the previous owner of much of the land that was acquired for the project. Mr. Bartok, a peppy, cheerful centenarian, has offered generous terms for the possible repurchase by him of current Sierra Future properties in the county, albeit at terms that will, at best, only "cut our losses." Unlike other county residents, Mr. Bartok seems to be a clear-minded businessman with whom I recommend opening negotiations as soon as possible (and may we all live to such a healthy old age!)

I will be in the Los Angeles office on Monday and we can further discuss matters then. Frankly, I'm glad to leave this area. The nights here seem to unleash strange urges. I hardly sleep now and, when I do, I experience questionable dreams and wake up thinking I haven't slept at all, but have spent the entire night being flown through the sky. If I spend another night here, I'm afraid I won't return.

Yours,
Keith

CHAPTER 37

Moonbeam Migraine

Usually all it took was an hour or two of rest in a dark room for Bob Garner's migraines to go away. But the latest, this new one, stuck like no other. It felt like a little man had taken up residence in a little round room right behind Bob's left eye, all for the purpose of delivering pain, constant pain, pain that burst like bubbles, like firecrackers, like a long siren scream, that rose and rose and rose, until all the world was burning.

Worst of all, at night, when Bob Garner tried to hide from his pain in the far corner of slumber, this little man took on an actual physical presence. He wore a big cherry-red smile, an iridescent, gaudy clown's suit with fat oversized shoes, sharply spiked on the soles, with which he tap-danced all around inside Bob's brain. He also wore boxing gloves with mitts the texture of sandpaper. He was armed with a jack hammer, a supply of long, thick, sharp knitting needles and many other implements of torture.

With these tools, the night clown created headaches, each with its own visible shape, size, even texture. Most of the time though, the headache took the shape of a fiery throbbing white flower, its petals dripping blue flame like hot wax dribbling and sizzling down his eyelids. When Bob Garner covered his eyes, the white-blue flower actually waved, floating on a fiery molten orange pond, as though brushed by wind. If he moaned, the blue-white petals grew more contrasted and the pain became a bonfire.

At other times, the little clown employed a blacksmith's hammer. Pain bounced off pain in loops of ever-increasing agony.

Whether his eyes were open or closed, Bob Garner was good for nothing. He'd even lost track of time, significant for such a time-bound man. He felt his business, his life, slipping beyond his reach. Beyond the lightshow of pain, time went on without him, but within its throbbing walls, time seemed timeless. His last clear world memory was from two days after construction started, at sundown up at the Alpine Canyon bridge site. He felt so exhilarated while watching the bulldozers churn up the ugly low shrubs. He loved how the gray rocky ground rose and spilled away from the blades, and the flat track that the 'dozer left in its wake. From that dirt path, a road would bloom across the canyon to a new world …and if they wanted to name that regal mountain, Garner Mountain, well …

Just after sunset, the first flower bloomed in his skull, so fast, it looked like time-lapse photography. Sheila had to drive him home, herd the kids away, and put him right to bed. The next morning, he was unable to make it to the groundbreaking for Sierra City. Peter stopped by later and said something about their commissioners, their bought-and-paid for commissioners, suddenly dropping dead, their hearts going pop-pop-pop, right before the ceremony, but screw it, that wouldn't stop anything; at least they died fast. He remembered to ask about Henry West's "little task" and Peter said, "I guess it's done." Before Bob could ask what was done, another bolt of pain shot across his skull, struck behind his right eye, then drilled in with an audible whine.

For the next two weeks, he visited every top specialist and neurologist in the state: his regular one down in L.A., others in Sacramento, San Francisco, and even across the state line in Reno. Bob spent hundreds of miles curled up in planes and cars, his eyes covered, but no one could do a thing, not for this migraine. "Normal," they all declared after reviewing the scans and other useless tests—not even a twinge of nerve inflammation. Maybe it was truly psychosomatic, caused by the pressures of work on this, his most ambitious project ever.

At last, he visited an acupuncturist in San Francisco. As he watched the needles go in, the relentless flower faded away. He quickly felt better and rushed back to Monitor County that night, pain-free, his mind clear.

Until the next morning. This time, it was not a flower. This time, the little brain clown whipped out real-looking acupuncture needles. He made them thrust away like pistons, firing little lightning bolts of pain that became one huge needle-studded ball of white-yellow fire.

After that, Bob went to bed and pretty much stayed there. Sheila urged him to leave Monitor County, check in to a hospital for her sake, the sake of the kids, and the sake of his project. But there was no leaving. He was more than indispensable to Sierra Future. He was the soul of this new world of his. He knew this from the first day he came here, three years ago, and experienced the odd magic of its impossibly clear, light air, the drenching smearing colors of sunset and dawn, and the rich mysterious blue of each canyon, crevasse, and valley, and how both the sun and the moon edged the mountaintops with silver. He knew back then the county would be the home of his next project: the project of projects, the monument to his legacy.

He couldn't leave Peter to run things. Peter was a good enforcer and great with the numbers, but like a lot of numbers guys, he rubbed too many people wrong and didn't have Bob's combination of smooth drawling politics and sweeping vision; the ability to see where all the pieces fit and the skill to keep them all together and moving forward. Without Bob Garner, Sierra Future would crumble and scatter on the first wind.

Soon, he believed, the little clown in his head would tire of his game and the headache would stop. It just had to. It always did. It was only a headache. Come the next minute, he'd feel as fresh and bright as a dewy Monitor County morning, where everything flowered gold and blue, silver and green.

That didn't happen. Every day, pain bonged like a bell and ticked like a clock. One day, he heard Sheila say she was going back to L.A. with the kids, if he insisted on being so stubborn. "It's been getting strange here. I've been having dreams." Something about a "flying old man" telling Little Bob he could walk across the surface of the creek just by "wishing real hard." Little Bob nearly drowned. It was getting bad for the kids. They'd come back when that hotel-amusement park by Garner Mountain was done next spring. Until then, they'd stay in fun, exciting—and un-weird—L.A.

Alcohol made the pain worse, so Bob Garner quit drinking altogether and that was when he started getting weird dreams. In one dream, the little clown floated toward him, its face a gray dusty hole, holding another long thin silver needle in its hand. It made a stabbing motion. Bob felt his eye burst and leak its fluid. He woke up screaming, his head flooding with fresh pain. Under his screams, he thought he heard someone chuckle, as though his pain were funny. Even though awake, he thought he saw a faceless shadow kiss him, felt calm cold lips and something sharp puncturing his skin.

He woke up again later, feeling weak. Weak. Bob Garner hated weakness and hated it most of all within himself. They used to call him "24-hour Bob," "Bench-Press Bob," and "Biz-Master Bob." If this kept up, it'd be "Can't-Do-Shit Bob."

Bob Garner vomited a lot. His mouth always tasted like his stomach, and he was always poised on a soft precipice of nausea. Sometimes he saw Peter Schlesinger standing over his bed or couch, mouthing words in a foreign language. He heard himself grunting back, not even daring to nod in acknowledgment, because that hurt too. Peter was now running things. Not good.

No, things weren't going well. Among Peter's distant murmurs, Bob made out "accidents," "arrests," and "shit going down," but they just bounced off the outside wall of his pain. Clark was here, yeah that front office fucker. What's going on? Clark wanted to know. "I got a fucking headache," Bob heard himself say. That was all the answer he had. That and "You take care of it." Then Peter said something about the "tree nigger. Should I can him?" Bob groaned,

"Yeah, whatever." And Peter said, "I'll close that phony account."
"Yeah."

One night Peter came and said, "He's alive!" Last night? Bob couldn't be sure. Pain had become the clock he lived by. "He's still alive!"

Bob asked, "Who?" and Peter said, "Bartok! Fucking Bartok's walking around!"

"Go take care of it," Bob muttered, anything to make that yappy voice go away.

"Tch-tch-tch," the little clown spoke in a clear, bell-like voice. "You shouldn't leave things undone." Then he fired a nail gun inside Bob's brain.

Then Bob went into another nightmare. In it, the headache was fading a little and he saw the ceiling above his bed bathed white like the moon. Something wet was kissing his forearm. He looked down to see a mane of long, salt-and-pepper hair. Klaus Bartok looked up, looking a thousand years younger, his skin smooth as a translucent crimson-shaded pearl. His cobalt eyes gleamed. He wore a blood-dripping grin. "Yes, you screwed up. Now sleep," Bartok said. Bob Garner obeyed, because now, for the first time in forever, the pain actually eased. Go on, if it makes the pain go away, drink all you want.

When he woke up, the pain was back, and he couldn't get out of bed.

Finally, late on some afternoon, desperate for even a whisper of a miracle, he staggered out to the Hummer and drove to the other side of Byrneville, to the GP's house. Doc Sutton, that righteous pious sucker who didn't know what was good for him, one of those lame non-visionaries.

Bob knew he invited pathos and pity in his state. The humiliation of asking this square for help hurt as bad as the migraine. Of course, the quack said he couldn't do a goddamn thing. If the specialists couldn't help, what could he do, besides dispense aspirin? The so-nofabitch actually had the gall to say that it might help if Bob could learn to his accept his migraines as a sad fact of life. Everyone had some sort of cross, and his was chronic migraines. His worry over his migraines could be "creating a feedback loop." (Putting it like that also showed Sutton to be a stuck-up, know-it-all fuck).

Bob finally lost it. Screaming, he told the Doc that he was full of shit. Bob Garner hadn't risen to the top by accepting fate. He fought fate and forced others to bow to the fact that Bob Garner's way was their fate. Truth was, the punk never wanted to help in the first place. He was against everything Sierra Future was trying to do for this two-bit Hicksville.

Then Bob started to cry, right in front of the Doc. It was like being a manic depressive, the way the pain swung his mind from the heights of rage to the pit of self-pity and despair. As he staggered out, he glimpsed the Doc's wife, Bartok's ex-chauffeur, standing in the hallway, raising her aluminum cane as though defending her husband. A glint of sunlight flashed off the cane's aluminum surface and shot like an arrow into his eye. Bob knocked the cane aside. Outside, the afternoon sun's rays almost knocked him to the ground as he stumbled to the Hummer.

Then he found himself looking at the road into Byrneville. The shadows were long. A black hole flew ahead of the Hummer, right down the middle of the lane. The wind blew around it. No, the wind was blowing toward it. No, wind, leaves, and grass were being sucked into the black hole. He let the Hummer be sucked into the hole.

He popped out the other side of the hole into a place he didn't recognize at first. Day was almost gone. He felt a little better. Could the headache be dying at last? It took a minute to recognize the low, one-story building in front of him: That junky Indian museum that was run by those two deformed freaks. Bob planned to tear that down and the old rotting jail attached to it, too. He would raise 3,000-square-foot homes here, like castles in the air. Castles on every mountain top, a world for all the world's kings.

He felt a long-lost smile growing in him, but when he saw a silver glow washing up into starry dark blue sky above the scrubby eastern hills, he became afraid. The glow spread quickly, and before Bob could even close his eyes, there rose the full Moon, a huge fiery white cannonball that blasted into his right eye, blowing it out before plowing to a stop inside his brain, where it proudly throbbed like the night's sun.

Bob slapped his hands over his face and hit his head on the steering wheel, blasting the horn. The noise drove him out of the Hummer. He sprawled face down on the dirt and lay there sobbing, knowing a loneliness he never knew existed. He got up and fumbled in his vehicle for more aspirin and his HeadOn, but the aspirin bottle was empty and all he felt was the applicator's plastic edges scraping more pain across his forehead.

That goddamn Moon pressed its attack as it rolled fat and triumphant up into the sky, while its reflection rolled thunderously around inside Bob's head. Bob crawled into the shadow of the museum. He felt persecuted, tormented, as the Moon relentlessly hunted him down.

Even in the shadows, though, the Moon's oblique light found his brain, a sponge that soaked up the moonlight like it was water. His skull swelled like a balloon.

The museum was closed. The door was locked and the deformed people no longer lived there, but Bob banged on the door anyway, shouted for help, for a miracle to welcome him into a shelter of pain-free darkness.

Then he groped blindly along the front wall, looking for another way in. The slats give way to splintering logs. The splinters pierced his skin, made his blood run, but he couldn't feel it. Finally, he found the door to the old jail, that depressing piece-of-shit black hole.

Then he remembered: The jail was the darkest place in Monitor County. The Moon wouldn't be able to follow him inside. The cast-iron jail was impermeable to light. He could curl up in its darkest corner and massage his head until he fell asleep.

Bob Garner pulled on the door, but it was locked. He burst into fresh tears. He pulled violently, angrily on the lock, cursed it, cursed

God, and every atom of reality. He hated being teased.

Suddenly, the lock fell open, sagging in its hasp. The door to the jail creaked on its old hinges, each squeak like a little rusty nail in his skull. The darkness looked like soft, black wool. Bob Garner tripped over the sill and fell like a tree. His face slammed on the floor and he lay there not daring to move as every cell of his long, bony body blistered with pain.

When he sat up, his mouth was full of blood. He looked to see a blue-silver block of Moonlight creeping through the door, headed right for him. He crawled deeper into the jail, but the hungry Moonlight followed, determined to get him.

Bob Garner rolled into the back room next to the jail cell. He pulled himself up on the low workbench. As he straightened up, his heart broke. It wasn't perfectly dark here after all. Moonlight craftily snuck through the chinks of the old wooden planks.

He desperately searched for another elusive dark corner. Then he saw something impossible: a long, tiny needle of Moonlight, thinner than a laser beam, slid through a chink in the wall. Its point traveled slowly through the air, as though searching for a target. It stopped at a forty-five-degree angle to Bob Garner and paused. Bob froze, hoping the light would not see him.

But it did. It turned and shot directly into Bob Garner's left eye. His felt his eye burst open and the gel splash down his cheeks. Bob Garner screamed, slapping his left hand over his eye. With his right hand, he swept the workbench tools off the table. His arm hit something hard, solid, and unmovable on the right front corner of the table.

It was a huge vise grip, Bob Garner realized as he blindly ran a free hand inside its jaws. It was solidly locked down and felt big enough to cradle his pain-wracked head, its jaws big and strong enough to squeeze the pain away.

Bob Garner turned the handle on the vise grip to open it all the way. The throbbing in his head grew with every frantic spin of the handle. He fell to his knees and inserted his head face down inside the jaws.

The Moon intensified its attack. Bob Garner frantically spun the handle of the vise grip and wept with frustration as his sweaty hand slipped. He kept turning and turning. The jaws slowly closed on his aching head. Still not enough. More! Tighter! He spun the handle again and again, but he didn't feel anything, so he twisted it some more.

Something popped. The fire burst. The world went away. His body went away. Everything about Bob Garner went away. Except his pain. The pain stayed very much alive, a blue silver ball of pain that rose upward to join other orbs floating through the silver Moon's blue sky.

....

CHAPTER 38

Spider's Moon

Henry reclined in Petey's Jag and peacefully watched the blank fog that flowed outside the windshield. I oughta be poopin' my pants, he thought, as the car rocked back and forth and side to side over the dirt road. After all, they were all way the fuck up on Alpine Canyon Road. So long as he didn't look out the side windows at the gray cliffs racing by, it was almost like riding through a calm sea. He didn't feel sick at all.

Nevertheless, Petey had no business taking his precious sports car here. Petey was a good driver and the Jag handled the curves well enough, but it ran too low to the road. The bottom occasionally scraped over the surface. Henry was waiting for that inevitable crunch that would mean they were stranded miles from nowhere.

"Better take the Rav-4, better take the Hummer, if you wanna go up there," Henry had warned, but Petey wouldn't do a fucking thing that Henry suggested or drive anything but his precious Jag. Now that the world had gone so weird, the Jag had become Petey's only anchor.

Henry stuck his fingers under his cap to tenderly stroke the bump on his head. Henry had woken up this morning to Petey beating him with a wooden stick as he lay in bed. From there, Petey chased him outside where Henry oofed face-down in the sandy, pine-needled dirt, wearing only shorts and t-shirt. Schlesinger kicked him in the side a few times, then got down on his hands and knees and stuck his angry tight face into Henry's:

"Where is he?"

"What the fuck—where's who?" Henry replied, though he could guess who Petey was talking about. Henry sat up as Petey snarled some more, his scowl reminding Henry of the crazy screaming faces he'd seen in prison.

"I saw him!"

"You mean Bartok." Henry hadn't seen anything, but rumors of disaster had been flitting all around the last couple weeks. All this time, the boss and Schlesinger had left him alone in the bungalow, didn't even stop by once.

Peter slapped him. "You didn't go through with it, did you? You chickened out."

"Yeah, I did it. I pushed him off the cliff into the falls."

Now we're both seeing shit, Henry realized, but he wasn't about to share any of it with this asshole: like how the old man crawled up the walking stick and how he floated away downstream like a duck and how he looked at Henry as he floated under the bridge.

Bartok fell under the falls. The water pressure pounded him to pieces. Say nothing that requires further explanation.

"So, you didn't see the body?"

"Where did you see him?"

Petey now sat cross-legged, digging a hole in the dirt with his stick, his little eyes sinking into his head.

"You must've seen someone else."

"No!" Petey hit him again and pointed two fingers at his eyes. "Right here, two inches away. He walked right through me like one of us was a ghost. It happened at night. He looked different, younger, but it was him."

"Maybe he's got an evil twin nephew somewhere."

"It was Bartok. He was telling me he's alive." Petey hugged himself, shivering. "He felt like cold water inside me. I stink inside. Here, smell this." He breathed in Henry's face and boy, it sure as shit smelled sulfurous, like the worst fart in history. "Then I'm lying in bed a couple nights ago, I can't sleep and I see me, myself, my body, float right through the wall, across the room, out through the other wall. I smiled and waved at myself …something's really fucked up." Petey wept.

"That was a fuckin' dream. You oughta take a little alcohol." Henry didn't like where this was going. He had enough problems with seeing things.

"I don't dream. I don't believe in fucking ghosts." Peter bared his caked yellow teeth—he hadn't brushed in awhile—and pointed a quivering finger in Henry's face. "You let him live."

"You talk to the boss?"

"Headaches." Petey nodded up at the big house. The Hummer was gone. Henry had last seen it yesterday afternoon when it was driven away and then Henry snuck into the house to steal more of Bob's booze. "I'm doing everything now," Petey murmured to himself. "Project's gone to shit. Nothing adds up anymore, not even the spreadsheets. I ran cost numbers the other day. I love spreadsheets, man," he babbled, "how everything adds up so square and neat and you know what's coming. I ran the labor costs for the last pay period and at the end, I find we owe $10.18. That's mathematically impossible. Maybe there's a virus in the software, so I do it on paper and pencil, takes me hours and I get the same fucking number. Ten dollars and eighteen cents! I can't even find where I made the error. My own brain's fucking with me!"

Then Petey struggled to his feet: "We gotta go up there."

"Up where?"

"To the canyon. You're gonna show me where he fell and we're gonna look. We'll swim those fucking falls if we have to, but we gotta find that body."

"So," Henry said. "We find the body and then your numbers will add up—ow!"

Henry felt unusually alarmed at his lack of fear about returning to Alpine Canyon. For a couple weeks now, he'd been in a boozy dreamless bubble, untouched by the weirdness whirling all around. He'd just as soon things stay that way. Sierra Future hadn't let him go, but he knew he wasn't needed anymore. He was just waiting for them give him his bit and let him go. He had more than enough to drink himself to death. Wasn't that really all he ever wanted? He wasn't simply an alcoholic anymore. He was truly afraid not to be drunk now, especially when he went to sleep. He didn't want to dream anymore, especially after being in Alpine Canyon, because that's where those dreams all came from.

They drove into the village behind a pickup that they both recognized as Doc Sutton's. While the truck parked by the general store—the last business open in Byrneville—Petey parked across the road and muttered: "The Doc's wife used to drive Bartok around. Maybe she's seen him."

Henry trailed behind. Petey reached out and touched Mrs. Sutton's arm as the couple reached the sidewalk. The Doc spun around, startled. The Missus turned slower, using an aluminum cane for support. Their eyes were hard, like prison eyes. Henry stayed back and even Petey looked away as he asked, "Have you seen old man Bartok?"

Carla Sutton's skin used to be a rich tan, but now it was white, drawn, and haggard, almost like an old sick lady's. She shook her head.

Doc Sutton shrugged, "I thought he was your problem now."

It was clear the Suttons wouldn't answer any more questions, not from them. Henry lingered as Petey hurried away. Henry wanted to stay with the Suttons. The way they were still together made him feel something. Made him think of himself, his life, in a way he never had before. He wanted to reach out, tell them he was sorry for acting like such a righteous asshole all the time. I'm so sorry. So this is what happens when you do all the shitty things you've always dreamed of doing …

"Fuckheads," Petey spat as they drove out of the village. He ranted and cursed everyone who had opposed or turned against Sierra

Future. They'd conspired to destroy the project, destroy their own future, a real future of prosperity and ease. There'd be an investigation, they'd find out who exactly was behind the sabotage.

"And then we'll get them. Bartok was the leader, I bet. He pretended to be on our side, but he was working undercover against us. He made it all fail. Now, he's walking around like Mr. Fuck You, all because you were too yellow to do your job."

"I pushed him off the cliff into the falls." Henry repeated the facts.

"There has to be some body parts floating around and if there isn't …!"

They rode through Mystic Valley at the edge of a massive fog bank. Evidence of construction lay everywhere, idle, forgotten. The few roads they'd plowed wound away into the fog. The summit of Dragon's Ark peeked above the gray fog under a soft blue sky.

Petey stopped ranting, but remained edgy as he concentrated on driving Alpine Canyon Road, swearing occasionally and blasting his horn at passing shadows. The bumpier and curvier it got, the madder he got. His beloved wheels were built for straight paved roads and highways, not for this unpaved pretzel. Sooner or later, the road was going to come up a little too high …

"How far is it?" Petey spoke softly, hoping for an encouraging answer. Henry started feeling as though he were behind the wheel of this expedition now.

"Quite a ways. Even in daylight, it's a piece. Canyon's probably fogged in too."

Finally, Petey stopped. The "Trespassers W" sign was barely visible through the fog. The road disappeared up into windblown blankness. Petey stared at Henry as though saying, Are we there? Please say we're there.

Smiling, Henry waved for him to go on.

The Jaguar's bottom scraped over the top of the notch, but made it. The road down into the canyon looked different than last time, more curves in different places.

Petey took the bottom too fast. The Jag's front fender dug into the ground. The rear end tipped up. As they slammed back down, Petey panicked, hit the gas, and the car leapt forward. Henry covered his face with his hands and his vertigo kicked in. They landed hard and bounced once. There was a crunching sound. The bags didn't explode, but Henry could smell gasoline. His stomach pushed up into his chest. Seconds later, he was on his face in damp sandy earth, violently heaving.

Cursing, Henry slowly sat up, wiping his mouth. Gasoline ran from under the car like blood. Peter stumbled around the front.

"Nice drivin', Lone Ranger."

Peter spewed out a string of lame obscenities, as Henry rose gingerly to his feet. When he looked again, Peter was holding up his .45 like some movie gangsta.

"Like you're gonna shoot your way out with that?"

Peter sneered as tucked the pistol in his belt and nodded at where the road twisted away into the silent fog.

"Dipshit, you don't get it. That road goes for five miles. It's fuckin' three o'clock. It'll be past five, six o'clock when we get there. Then it's another mile or two after that. We'll be here after dark."

"I'm not a baby," Petey sneered, rising up on his toes. Henry was getting mad to the point where he felt suicidal. He imagined trying to grab the gun, forcing Petey to shoot him and end this cold dread. Compared to the dream horrors lurking in this canyon, it'd be the easy way out.

But Henry was too chickenshit for suicide-by-crazy-guy-with-a-gun, and he was enjoying Petey's suffering in this lonesome faraway world. He wanted to see how Petey acted when the things in Alpine Canyon started moving into the corner of his eyes.

"Whatever. Got a flashlight in the car? Bring it."

A minute later, Henry glanced back and saw the fog had swallowed the Jaguar. The canyon walls were invisible, too. Under the roar of the nearby stream lay a dead silence. Suddenly, something huge and black flapped close by. Petey shouted, pulled out his gun and dropped it. By the time he picked it up, the shadow had flown away. Petey asked what it was. Henry was tempted to say he didn't know, just to scare the cocksucker even more, but right now, it was dangerous to mess with his head.

"It's a turkey vulture. They're all over."

"Will they attack us?"

Henry twirled a finger in the air: "Nope. They just fly circles around ya sayin' 'Die, asshole, die.'"

Petey stuck close to Henry the rest of the way. Henry smelled the odor that had been left inside him, and tried to stay a little ahead.

At the end of the road, Petey looked at his watch. It had stopped working and he burst into tears. The fog was darker now. Petey yelled that it was Henry's fault they'd be stuck here after dark. Henry shrugged; an hour, half hour, made no difference. The canyon owned them now.

They walked silently across the redwood bridge toward the moraine. At the top of the bank, Henry shined the flashlight onto the trail. Pockets of spider webs shined everywhere, dew-beaded like millions of strands of pearls. Henry struggled to keep his cool as he picked up a stick and handed it along with the flashlight to Petey. He waved Petey to go ahead of him: "You don't want to be left behind here."

Finally, they heard a distant roar and the trail sank away into the fog. The Smirnoff still lay by the rock. There was a little bit left. Henry suddenly realized how late it was. By now, his whole system should have been screaming, but it wasn't, shit-fucking scared as he was. So he let the bottle lie there.

Henry led the way down the embankment and pointed out where the old man had sat as though waiting for sunset. They followed the trail to the stream. Up ahead, the waterfall roared down like an invisible giant. Slowly, the great cliffs emerged ominously from the fog. At the bottom, where the trail disappeared up behind the falls, Henry stopped and sat down on a large rock.

Petey shivered in the clammy cold: "Well?"

Henry pointed up the other side. The spot where the trail

emerged from behind the falls was barely visible. "Pushed him from right up there."

Petey waved the flashlight: "That's only maybe twenty feet. He might've survived. Why'd you wait so long? You could've pushed him before that."

"I was concentratin' on gettin' down safe. I didn't want Bartok pullin' me with him. Y'know, Doc Sutton was right about my vertigo."

Now Petey drew his gun on Henry and stepped back.

"So you were fucking lying to us!"

"Oooooo, like you fucks think that's a bad thing? Sure, I'm an Indian, but only half." He laughed. "Man, you guys don't look close enough at shit, that's your problem. Go fuck yourself. I've gone far enough."

Peter spread his legs like a gunfighter and aimed the gun at Henry, his eyes squeezed shut. Henry shrugged and spread his hands.

"You ain't gonna shoot me, butt breath. You're a pussy. Otherwise, you'd have done the old man yourself. Oh, here's one more lie for ya. Until old Mr. Bartok, I never even tried to kill anybody. Guess I'm a tougher man than you now, cocksucker."

Petey lowered the gun, seething. Right again, Henry thought. Shit, I coulda run this operation.

"I'll go look." Petey stumbled and slipped up the boulder-strewn trail behind the falls, the flashlight beam feebly lighting the way.

The fog began to lift. The light turned silver. Canyon night was almost here. Henry glanced up the gleaming walls past the falls and froze: A black stream of water was pouring down from the foggy sky. It weaved back and forth with reptilian purpose as two tiny blue dots glowed from its head.

Henry stood up shaking as the blue-eyed black snake slipped smoothly around the corner of the cliff, behind the falls. He wished he had his own flashlight to find his way out, but then he felt something cold and his skin turned silver white. Behind him the fog was rising over Alpine Canyon and the edge of the full moon showed above the rim. It would light the way home.

But it wouldn't be enough. Whatever slithered into the cave after Petey would catch up with Henry in no time.

A long scream pierced through the thunder of the falls, stretching on like a high thin song of terror and suffering that sent shivers down Henry's spine.

"Put me down! Put me down!"

Petey flew out from the cave through the falls, straight over the pond, about twenty feet in the air. He stopped in front of Henry, dripping wet and dangling, clutching the flashlight and pistol. Whatever was holding him up in the air—he sure wasn't flying by himself—violently shook him. Pistol and flashlight fell into the water below as Petey flailed and screamed, "Let me go! Lemme go!"

The big, strong, invisible hand lowered Petey and dunked him in the pool, dunked him again and again. Henry briefly recalled the time he saw a great blue heron nail a fat vole with its sword-like beak, then flew its catch over to a shallow pond where it dunked and stabbed, and stabbed and dunked, until the vole was dead enough for the great blue bird to tip back its long head and suck the rodent down its gullet.

This flying invisible thing was no blue heron. It knew its pleasure. It was putting on a show for itself and for Henry West, who grew sick with disgust as he watched. Whatever he thought of Petey Schlesinger, the brazen sadism of this monster was too much to bear: "Stop it!" Henry yelled. "Cut it out."

The creature stopped its torment as if in reply. Petey hung limply in the air, half-conscious. "Put him down. Don't hurt him no more," Henry yelled. The flying invisible monster responded by taking Petey down to a huge rock near the base of the falls. It laid him down in the shallow water face up, his head tucked right against the base of the rock.

Petey spluttered and struggled. Henry rushed to help him up but as he got there, the big rock tilted upward a foot or two. The invisible monster shoved Petey's head under the rock and let it fall, slowly, so both Henry, and especially Petey, would know what it was doing, and that it didn't care what they thought.

Under the roar of the falls, Petey's cries were cut off. There came a sickening crunch. Henry's legs crumpled. He looked away. There came a wet, tearing sound, like a cooked chicken being torn apart, then a gulping sound, like someone drinking out of a bottle. Henry looked just long enough to glimpse Petey's headless body floating upside down in the foggy moonlight, legs askew.

"Oh stop it!" Henry wept. "Stop it! That's enough, stop it."

The invisible monster dropped Petey's body in the stream like an empty bottle. Henry struggled to his feet, watching as the wind blew and the fog gathered together into a pearl-colored ball, high above the other side of the stream. The flying invisible monster was spinning itself into a visible monster out of the moonlight and fog. It took the shape of a silver white bird. The bird spread its wings to slow itself as it glided down, it legs stretching to the ground. Its feathers turned to a black satin sheen; its savage-looking head turned into a man's.

It was, of course, Klaus Bartok. Very alive, just as Henry knew he would be, and very well. Night and moonlight had smoothed away his wrinkles, turned his long hair black, and made him a very big and strong man who could command the moon's rays. His fierce eyes nailed Henry to the ground.

"I am hungry," Klaus Bartok's voice boomed in Henry's ears.

At first, Henry thought Bartok was making a bow, until he planted his hands on the ground and immediately two more sets of limbs sprung from his side to make eight. His butt expanded behind him and his two shining blue eyes split apart to become eight eyes, each with their own bloody circle.

"I am hungry!" Klaus Bartok's voice pealed like a bell.

Shoulda known …shit, I always knew. Henry West turned to run as the giant, silver-black spider sprung across the stream and landed with a big skidding thud, kicking up clods of dirt.

"I am hungry."

It immediately caught up with Henry and knocked him down

with a big, spiny foreleg. Then it stood back and watched as Henry got up and ran, again.

Henry fully understood what the creature was doing: playing with its food.

Despite its huge body, the vampire spider danced lightly along in pursuit of Henry, like a happy hunter, while Klaus Bartok's voice chortled in Henry's mind. "Fear makes the blood sweet," he whispered. Whenever Henry looked behind him, it rushed forward and shoved its awful face at Henry. Henry saw his screaming face reflected in all eight of its blue eyes.

"I am hungry!" the spider boomed. "Run, West. Run."

The vampire spider allowed Henry to stumble on, just out of reach. Once it fell back, letting Henry get a little bit ahead, tricking him into thinking it was letting him go. Then it leapt after him, laughing, its feet clicking over the rocks.

"I am hungry. Feed me, Henry. Feed me."

Finally, Henry thought he'd found a place to hide: a narrow slot in the canyon wall. He squeezed himself inside, then looked back to see the full moon shining impossibly from the black sky. Bartok's vulpine human face faded in, slyly grinning, eyes glowing. Then it turned back into the spider-face.

The giant spider now had Henry where it wanted him and finally tired of its game. Henry closed his eyes, but the spider's powerful mind made his eyelids perfectly transparent so Henry was forced to see it all: its greedy eyes, its eager drooling and panting as it reached in and grabbed Henry with strong hairy legs, dragged him out through the slot, and rolled him toward its black mouth as it waved and clicked its fangs.

The spider's mouth closed over his head, wet, cold, smelling of shit. Henry watched the starlit tip of a black fang slowly puncture his exposed belly. Henry saw his face reflected in the funhouse mirror of the shiny fang, his mouth a distorted screaming slit.

"I am hungry ...!"

....

CHAPTER 39

I Ask You Again

A couple of days after Bob Garner was found dead in the old jail, Dave left for Osgood at eight-thirty, promising like a Boy Scout that he'd have them both back in San Francisco by mid-August. Carla gave him a light peck and said, "See you soon."

Then she spent a slow half hour clumsily fingering the keyboard in Dave's office. "Darlng: Im so sorry, but what I told you wen I woke up in he hosptal is true, as sure as you'r readin this, as sure as Im gone from you. Look in cnyon"

When she'd finished the message, she left it there glowing on the screen and picked up the cane Sean had given her, put a bottle of water and a bag of gorp into a small day pack, and walked out to the garage.

She hadn't driven since the "accident" (as it was now officially known). The gas and brake pedals once again felt soft, almost invisible under her feet. She also thought herself invisible and focused entirely on her hands, her feet, and the road ahead.

A short ways up Alpine Canyon Road, she stopped to take a flickering nap. She passed the driveway down which she'd sailed with such pluck and skill only weeks before, eyes closed. She fought to keep the coughing Volvo out of the ditch to the right and away from the cliffs to the left. She had to think in complete sentences, ahead of every move, as the signals from her brain struggled through dying nerves to carry out her commands. It was like driving on a thread while drunk.

She rested repeatedly, napped again once, woke up fighting off cramps, almost choking on saliva. She carefully ate tiny mouthfuls of gorp. Her withering muscles trembled with exhaustion. But she couldn't die now. She would die at a certain time and at a particular place, after a specific request was made and responded to. The request would, of course, be denied, but then he'd have to answer for her good-bye, after she slipped over the edge of the cliff.

Once she made it through the notch, the drive down into the canyon became somewhat easier, with the walls acting as a solid guide. She encountered another big obstacle at the bottom when she had to steer around the dusty red Jaguar. Schlesinger and, likely, poor hapless Henry West were somewhere in the canyon. She'd seen them together only yesterday. She laughed in bemused wonder: What weird cruelties, what attacks on their bodies and souls, had Dracula subjected them to? What bizarre, wacky, peculiar magic did he spin to exact his revenge and sweeten his meal? He never killed simply. He always made his victims grateful for death.

She nearly drove into the stream trying to drive around the Jaguar. Then she rested. At the end of the road, she stopped facing the mountains. There'd be no return trip. She pushed the seat back and fell right asleep without even a glance at the landscape she had once so loved. She was no longer color-blind and Alpine Canyon's colors were brighter and more varied than ever, like fresh paint, neatly but exuberantly applied, dotted here, splashed there.

She awoke in the late afternoon, in blue shadows, as a puffy-white storm rumbled away over the sunny cliffs to the southeast. She pulled herself out slowly and closely watched her feet and the tip of Sean's cane as she walked carefully and steadily toward the south rim.

She rested again on the other side of the moraine. She fell for the first time shortly after she started up the cliff, just up the trail from where Sean was pushed. His gift slipped from her hand and spun away, making a soft chink as it land in the scree below. She felt a pang of hiker's guilt: My last hike ever and I litter up the place.

Awhile later, she felt the daypack weighing her down and shucked it off, leaving more evidence that she'd passed this way. Her feet dragged as she pulled herself along the granite wall, remembering times when she could see her face reflected in tiny mirrors of crystal. Finally, exhausted in the last stretch, she fell to her hands and knees. Then, she was wriggling, slithering, and shoving her numbing body over the rocky soil, gasping for every breath.

Why not end it now? Just roll over the edge. Hardly enough of her was left to feel much pain, only enough awareness for a surge of terror as strong as the surge of life she felt that day when Dracula took her hand in his.

He'll say no, refuse me anyway, like last time. Shrug, give a dismissive wave of his hand. "Why should I give you anything more?"

Dracula had led her to the door of his kingdom of ecstatic, heedless being and no further. He led her to the entrance of his great dark house and, just when things had gone too far for her to turn away, he said, "Far enough for you." All the while, with her unwitting help, he'd been casting his sly spell of lies and committing his evil deeds, while closing off any path to redemption, leaving her a ghost forever bound by undying flesh.

Maybe this time, he wouldn't be able to shrug it off after she'd rolled herself over the cliff. Dave would find the letter on his computer and they'd come looking. They'd find the car, the daypack, and then they'd find her, shattered on the rocks below, right beneath his hideaway. Maybe, just maybe, they'd get it. They wouldn't be able to explain the story she'd left behind, but they might understand that there had been one accident too many in Alpine Canyon, and that the old man wasn't harmless at all. Maybe they wouldn't kill him, but they'd drag him out into the sunlight, maybe hold him there just long enough to see who and what he was.

And what he became after the sun went down.

She reached the top of the trail at twilight and curled up on her side to watch the evening fade, the sky over the crest turning from yellow to crimson, then burnt orange, a flash of green, then sky blue, finally dark blue.

She could make out the bright wreckage and dim scars left by Sierra Future over on the north rim. How did Dracula feel when he—so confident of his power—realized that he'd also been played for a fool? He may believe himself god of the night, but he was blinded by the day and lived tangled up with time and space even as he was able to bend and twist it. The Superman of Evil could be snookered, be as blind to his own hubris as he was to mercy. He thought he could let in the noisy night-destroying modern world under his terms and his control.

Wrong. He'd misread his coconspirators and failed to see when they'd become his enemies and, for that, he'd nearly paid for his pride with his ancient precious life, the thing he valued most. Death would not happen for him, he believed. It was something that only happened to *those* people, the people whom he thought he was completely free and apart from, but in reality, desperately needed.

Did Dracula feel chastened, embarrassed, humiliated? If so, his regret probably lasted mere seconds. He would conveniently praise himself as the savior of the land he'd almost destroyed. Besides, tomorrow would be another night.

That is, unless the discovery of Carla's body, practically at his doorstep, sent the message she hoped it would.

One other thought gave her exhausted mind some satisfaction: After all his efforts, Dracula was back to feeding off what he'd been living on for the past century—tourists; cooperative, agreeably sober residents; and the wild creatures who worshipped him (and whose extinction from these mountains he had so blithely consented to). He was back to long hungry winters in this barren land. Maybe that would be punishment enough.

The first star appeared and she wished on it: that he would come soon and give her the answer she wanted. Night hawks and falcons cut across the sky. She wriggled her husk around to face Dragon's Ark, that craggy Gothic rock reaching proudly for the stars.

She gave some last thoughts to Dave. Her only gift to him was a negative one: He wouldn't be burdened with watching her fade without dying. He wouldn't have to wrestle with the unscientific mystery of how she could live so long with her heartbeat and brain leaving only soft blips; with having to age and die himself while wondering how it could be that she still lived.

With her gone, Dave wouldn't have to move back to the city, though, of course, he wouldn't want to stay here, not in this kingdom of shadows, working for Dracula, tending to his small but unnaturally healthy herd. From the first, he'd been right about the old man's moral qualities—or lack of them—and her refusal to listen to him shamed her.

She wished for him to find another paradise, like this one, except there'd be no demons or ghosts like the one who ruled here. Fly away, Dave, fly away where you can be the doctor you want to be, tend to people who really need you. They'll love you better than I did …

She ran out of thoughts. Her tears fell on the hard rock and cold soil. She felt a steady force pushing at her and realized it was the wind. She couldn't even feel its cold.

Then she saw black wings leaping up from the base of the mountain, through the light of a rising full moon to make a graceful curve toward the summit of the Ark.

She'd imagined her defiant, angry speech, passionate in her demands, eloquent in her outrage: "You can't leave me like this. If you do, I'll end my life right here and this time they'll look at you and ask those questions you don't want asked. No, that wouldn't be in your interest would it, to be suspected, to be known as anything but the harmless little old mountain recluse?"

He flew robustly over the canyon, greeting another night of freedom to sow dreams and reap blood. The hawks and falcons swirled after him and she heard the footpads in the brush as the night world emerged to greet him. Happy vicious ghost, joyful demon, taker of blood and freedom, grand wizard of nightmares!

She saw the blue flash of his eyes and knew that he'd at last seen her lying at the edge of the cliff. As he swooped lazily down, she felt a flash of that old childlike wonder. He erupted in red fire, which then turned to hot blue flame. He lengthened and stretched his body as his wings fluttered up behind him. He folded them in neatly as he landed right on point, a few away, wearing his capering grin, the moon shining behind him.

"Fucking showboat," she mumbled into the dirt.

His eyes lit up the hard planes of his face. The wind whipped his cloak sideways and lifted his hair, silvery black in the moonlight. He looked down at Carla with smug cruelty, at this worm that lay at his feet begging for what he would not give.

Suddenly, Carla felt herself leave the ground and found his eyes staring into hers from inches away, like she had that first night when he'd swept her up into his grand, heartless world. Now he held her by the collar, as though holding a kitten by its scruff: to drown or not to drown?

As she felt her body sway in the wind, she realized what he was really saying with his smile and his eyes—that she was as helpless as ever, and that extortion and blackmail were fruitless. Coming here had been a bad idea, a fruitless climb. He knew why she'd come and, no, he didn't need her alive, either. Dave wouldn't believe the story she'd left on the computer. It would only reconfirm his own view of reality. Dracula could simply dump her among the rocks and crevices where she'd remain unfound and alive forever and they'd no more suspect him then than they did now.

"Tch-tch. Foolish," his voice echoed in her mind.

Dracula tossed Carla Sutton away, over the cliff, down into the darkness.

Carla felt perfectly weightless as she fell. The stars streamed by and then they were gone as she sped down into the chasm, the wind screaming in her ears. The hum of her nervous system faded like light filament. She felt herself bounce, as though she'd fallen onto a spider's web, had found not the oblivion she sought, but only another hell she didn't know would be there, waiting.

·····················

Uncertain Mercies

Dave's truck skirted the edge of the road all the way down into Alpine Canyon. He almost crashed into the Jag, and took a minor pleasure in sideswiping it. It was almost dark when he parked in front of the Volvo at the end of the road. He jumped out of the truck into a sudden, powerful wind that almost knocked him down. He shouted Carla's name over the fast-rising wind, even though he knew she wouldn't hear him, even if she were standing inches away. He raced across the redwood bridge, waving his flashlight around. He tripped and fell twice, getting up quickly both times so he wouldn't give in to the temptation to collapse in fear and despair.

He called out to Carla again when he came across the abandoned cabin in the moraine. His flashlight revealed only the wind-tattered remains of spider webs.

The wind had done its work, erasing all trace of footprints. The only sign of recent humanity was a near-empty vodka bottle lying by a rock. As he crossed the wind-blasted meadow, he thought he heard a long thin screech from the west. He saw a black bird dive down through the fading orange strip of daylight, down the south wall. He started toward it, but was blocked by the stream. Following the stream bank would only take him around back to where he started.

As he backtracked, the wind almost lifting him off his feet, he heard a distant car horn from the other side of the moraine. Next to his truck, he found Tim King parked in his Explorer.

Dave and Tim had spoken to each other for the first time in a month when they found Bob Garner in the old jail two days before. He'd told Tim about Garner's surprise visit to his home office the afternoon before. Garner's migraines had pushed him to the brink of violence and, apparently, drove him here where he found the relief he'd sought—though how he'd stayed conscious long enough to crush his own skull to the point of avulsion no one knew. No evidence existed to indicate that he'd been anything but alone when he died.

Tim shook Dave's hand again, glad to find him alive in Alpine Canyon. The moonlight highlighted the new furrows that had been plowed across his brow by the events of the last few weeks.

Dave told Tim that he'd called home once at noon, got no answer, and figured Carla was either napping or couldn't get to the phone fast enough. He called again just after three and this time became alarmed. His concern was confirmed when he pulled in the driveway and saw the Volvo was gone. No, no note, not even on the computer (which had crashed), but he sensed right away where she'd gone.

By the time Dave finished his story, the wind was nearing hurricane force, making it too dangerous for a thorough, safe search in the dark. Still, Dave managed to persuade Tim to follow him back to the foot of the falls where they found nothing, except some unusual spoor that looked too large to have been left by a deer or bear. "Somethin' big's been stompin' around here," said Tim shaking his head.

Tim persuaded Dave to wait until the morning to launch a full search. "She knows enough to stay safe for at least one night." Tired, Dave fell behind on the way back over the moraine. When he reached the other side, he found Tim crouched by the stream, next to the bridge, shining his flashlight down the bank.

It was a body, but thankfully, not the one Dave feared it would be. The deceased was a male whose feet had been jammed into the rocks.

His ankles had been broken by the current's efforts to pull the body back into the stream. The arms waved over its shoulders, back and forth like algae. Immediate visual identification was impossible. This was because the head had been torn—violently—from the shoulders.

They pulled the corpse out. The deceased wore khaki slacks and an Izod shirt over a white muscular body. Since the red Jag at the other end of the canyon belonged to Peter Schlesinger, this had to be him, the last of Sierra Future: "I'd say he went in by the falls," said Tim, "given the damage. Like with Barb Albanese."

There was no sign of anyone else—like Henry West—around. They wrapped the body in a yellow plastic sheet from the Explorer for pickup the following day.

That night, Dave called a couple of physicians he knew up in Tahoe to fill in for him. The trouble that had swept through the county in the last month had abruptly stopped, but there were still regular patients to care for.

The next morning, Dave and Tim made the hours-long drive back to Alpine Canyon, this time with a search party. Toward midafternoon, while searching along the foot of the canyon's southwest wall not far from where they found Sean Temkin, Deputy Colbert shouted "Hey!" and jumped up and down waving Carla's cane. As Tim chewed him out for tampering with a potential crime scene, Dave hiked up the trail. There, he found Carla's daypack.

He shouted down to Tim, pointing to his feet. Tim hollered back up, maybe for Dave to wait for him, but Dave marched on up anyway, all the way to the top, out of the canyon's cool gray shadow onto the grand plateau that lay under the stern tower of Dragon's Ark. The mountain's presence was so strong, even the sunshine seemed muted.

While waiting for Tim to catch up, Dave searched along the rim and scanned the canyon floor with his binoculars. Carla had come here to end it, he was sure. He couldn't blame her for wanting to get it over with, for not wanting to die trapped inside four walls, strapped to a chair or a bed. But, why come all the way to this grim canyon?

He glanced behind him and, irritated, waved away the mountain, as though it were a sneering interference. He scanned the canyon floor once more but saw no sign of her. Maybe she had fallen down out of sight into some crevice, or had rolled down under some boulders.

When Tim caught up, they rested awhile, then took the mining trail across the plateau toward the mountain, searching among the matted trees, in the jumbles of rocks, in deep pockets of soil, and bowls of crusted snow. They took time to gape at the head-spinning vistas surrounding them, speculating whether Sierra Future had made a grab for this spot. At least they had left before they could do any more damage. "Though we coulda done without all that death," Tim said.

Soon, they found themselves shivering in the Ark's chilly shadow. Dozens of birds flew about. Vultures sailed up from the canyon on updrafts. Clark's nutcrackers churred and black crows cackled about. Eagles and falcons screeched as they circled the summit of the peak. Tim and Dave ducked as a Red-tailed hawk swooshed right over their heads and snatched a plump marmot from the top of a boulder a few feet away. The hawk carried its frantically struggling prey, tipping its sleek wings to keep its balance. It landed on another nearby boulder and began to stabbed its beak into the rodent with disturbing enthusiasm.

Dave and Tim walked by a vulture who was seated at the foot of a wind-battered juniper. It would do them no harm, but they walked warily by anyway, avoiding its fixed stare—

"Good afternoon, Dr. Sutton," a familiar voice called. "Under Sheriff King! There must be some emergency afoot, as this is hardly a spot for an afternoon stroll, is it?"

The vulture unfolded its wings. It's lined, bony face grinned as the creature stretched its head up from between its shoulders on its long neck. Dave and Tim exchanged looks and slowly approached Klaus Bartok who reclined against the juniper as though it were a favorite chair, his sunglasses on, his stick at his side.

"I think you know why we're here," Dave began, then told Bartok anyway. He was in no mood for guessing games.

"I'm very sorry." Bartok unctuously shook his head. "No, I've not laid my old eyes on Mrs. Sutton, not since she resigned. You say other fools have gotten lost too. Another accident? No, the mountains, the cliffs, the weather all guard me. My responsibility ends with that sign at the entrance. What would you have me do? Put up those security cameras that are all the rage in the all-day world? My canyon is hard on strangers and should remain so."

"Carla was no stranger," Dave snapped. "She came up here because of you."

"She didn't find me, doctor. Not even a knock at the door."

Dave noticed where the mine trail disappeared into the base of Dragon's Ark: "So you live inside the mountain?"

Bartok gestured with his stick: "Yes. An abandoned mine. My father and I fixed it up nicely."

Tim said, "We'll need a warrant and probable cause."

Bartok laughed softly and insolently: "No, go on in. Search, if my word isn't good enough. Though why she would visit me now, only she'd know. I have nothing to hide, but watch your step in there. It's dark!"

Indeed, it was pitch dark inside the cave. Klaus Bartok occupied one large hollowed-out granite room with a well-laid, black flagstone floor, a secondhand Mahogany bed, many rows of bookshelves, and a black-leather easy chair that was almost completely camouflaged by the darkness. They didn't see a single window anywhere, and the walls were bare. Tim and Dave pointed their flashlights ceilingward to see the beams diffuse into smoky nothingness. Bartok seemed to live completely off the electric grid, in monkish luxury with not a speck of dust anywhere. Dave felt a repressed power about the place as though he were caught within a closed fist of rock.

Dave searched all the way past the bookcases to the back wall. There were a dozen or so cracks in the wall, some big enough to be passageways, but every one of them narrowed to a dead end. Even so, someone could hide back here or hide a body. As he carefully sniffed the cold still air Tim called out from somewhere up front:

"Dave. She's not here. Never been here at all, I'd say."

As he walked back to the front, he flashed his light across the book spines. The bindings of many volumes had split and flaked away. What titles he could read were in Latin or referred to the occult—words like *Maleficium* and "magick." He wondered if Bartok had used these volumes of infantalia to fool Carla into thinking he'd cured her.

Dave and Tim exited the cave. Even though they were still within the mountain's afternoon shadow, the light blinded them and everything around looked hugely out of proportion.

"Imagine seeing this every morning you wake up," Tim's said reverently, but Dave ignored him as he strode angrily across the rocky plain right toward Bartok, who still lounged at the foot of the juniper that grew in the gloomy shade of his home.

"I hope you find her, Dr. Sutton." Bartok's ugly grin masked his indifference. "You may keep searching the canyon as long as your heart calls you there." He sighed wistfully. "Deadly as it can be, the canyon's beauty always calls."

Dave clenched his fists deep in his jacket pockets. His foot found a large pointed rock, half-buried in the earth, and nudged it loose. A rumble of thunder rose as he reached down. But just as his hand wrapped around the weapon, Tim grabbed his arm from behind.

"Storm's comin'. Let's go. Better get inside yourself, Mr. Bartok."

Dave let go of the rock to see Bartok staring at him with a look of complete fear. They stared at each other for a long moment. It was Bartok who blinked, though, waving his stick toward the darkening western sky as though he controlled the weather, a gesture more infuriating than funny. Dave leaned down and put his face right in the old man's.

"When I graduated from med school, I swore an oath that I'd never turn a patient away, ever. You're my first exception. You ever need help, you get yourself another doctor, got that? If I ever find you on my doorstep, I'll let you die right there."

"Don't worry, Dr. Sutton." Bartok shrugged, though his large teeth were bared in anger. "My shadow will never darken your office door."

Dave spun on his heel and marched away across the plateau.

"But I'm glad to hear you're staying among us!"

Just before they headed down, Dave looked back one more time. Bartok had sunk back to being a dozing black vulture again, sitting at the foot of the juniper, while purple storm clouds gathered overhead.

"Funny," Tim said, "but I didn't see a kitchen anywhere. I wonder how he eats."

•

Two more weeks of daily searches passed without finding any further trace of Carla in Alpine Canyon. Even afterward, though, Dave went out searching every free day both in Alpine Canyon and throughout the rest of the county. He refused to give up.

Later that August, Chloe Byrne passed away. Before her death, she changed her will to leave Dave Sutton the bulk of her cash assets "to help ensure his continuing presence in Monitor County." Virginia Byrne got the house and some stocks and bonds. She also got mad anyway, as only a loyal niece would. One day, she drove over the mountains to Sacramento to meet with an attorney to discuss a challenge to the will.

She never made it home. That night, her car left a straight stretch of the Sierra Pass Highway, just a couple of miles down from Leo Durant's place.

Dave now regretted the brusque way he'd treated Virginia that day in June. The morning after the accident, he dropped by the hospital observation room to find that she was dying from massive internal injuries. There was nothing left for her except palliative care.

Virginia's green eyes were staring at the ceiling when Dave leaned over her bed. Her eyes shivered and her mouth fell open as she saw Dave. She mumbled something about a "wife."

"I'm sorry. What did you say?" Dave put his ear to her lips.

"Big wife spider," he thought he heard her whisper.

Dave stood up, shaking his head, not understanding.

"I saw it!" she cried. Then she turned her face to the wall and died.

•

Getgo Corporation unloaded the tens of thousands of acres surreptitiously purchased by Bob Garner at dirt floor prices, creating a mini-land rush. Several land trusts and conservancy groups collaborated to buy Mystic Valley while the Southern Washoe bought back the old museum-jail and the Durant property. Their neighbor across Alpine Canyon, Klaus Bartok, appeared to get most of the rest to much muttering from certain quarters in Monitor County.

Dave Sutton used the money Chloe left him to buy Bob Garner's property on Walsh Hot Springs Road, cheap. After he closed the deal on the phone, he cracked the cap on a bottle of Macallen with a satisfied grin: Carla would laugh her head off if she knew. He made immediate arrangements to knock down Garner's monstrosity and build something more companionable with the surrounding wilderness. He'd stay in the little bungalow out back in the meantime and later make that into the office where he'd serve west county residents. A rabbit skin robe he'd found in the back room was threadbare and smelly, but he had it cleaned anyway and donated it to the re-established Washoe center.

But what he liked most about the property was its location far down the valley floor out of the sight of Dragon's Ark.

•

"So you're stayin' for sure now?" Tim asked one night, when they were on Tim's back patio above the Carson River.

"I won't leave until I find Carla." Dave was leaning on the patio rail, watching the river below. "That's all there is to it."

"We may never find her. If we do, it'll be by chance."

"Another thing: If I were to leave," Dave nodded toward a far ridge to the northwest, toward unseen Dragon's Ark, "it would be like giving it over to him, running away. So long as he's alive, some-one has to be here to stand against him."

"You mean Mr. Bartok."

Dave nodded: "Besides, it's still special here, like it was when I first came. I can still feel the stars on my shoulders. I won't ever find a more beautiful spot than this one. Not anywhere."

Then Dave heard a dark fluttering in the darkness behind him. He looked quickly, his heart pounding, but Tim was still in his chair, his face hidden by the night.

•

One Monday afternoon, Dave drove into Byrneville to meet Tim for lunch before heading down to Osgood. As he parked next to the Tap & Grill, he saw a familiar but unsettling sight: a large, white, smoke-windowed SUV sitting across the road in front of the realty office.

What lost, sick soul had been seduced by the false dream of making an easy living and getting away from it all? Dave wondered as he ap-proached the vehicle, thirsting with curiosity. There was a shadow be-hind the wheel, its head forward as though asleep. Dave rapped softly. The shadow snapped up straight and the window hummed down.

"Hi there! I'm—well, I'll be damned! Henry West!"

Henry West looked equally caught by surprise, even confused, as if he didn't recognize Dave. "It's me, Doc Sutton." Henry's face brightened in recognition: "Oh sure, Doc. Caught me nappin'. How are ya?"

Dave slowly offered his hand and Henry slowly took it. Henry's hand felt strong but cold, as though it'd been in an icebox. Hen-ry looked well: His complexion no longer presented as sallow and baggy, but was rich, dark, and filled out. His eyes looked bright and clear, though a little distant. While he no longer bristled with hostil-ity, his wariness remained. As it had been with both Annie and Carla, the change in him was nearly absolute and inexplicable.

Dave asked some doctor questions. Henry answered them promptly. He'd been dry for over a month now, with no withdrawal problems; and best of all, his vertigo had disappeared. "Here I am, steerin' Mr. B.'s carriage around. I can almost drive her blindfolded and backward. It must have gone into—what do they call that?"

"Remission," Dave said doubtfully. "Are you living up on the canyon road?"

"Nah," Henry shook his head. "There's another old cabin inside Alpine Canyon." He jabbed a thumb at the back of the SUV where cords of lumber were stacked to the ceiling. "I'm restoring that. Gonna build it all on my own."

This surprised Dave, as he'd seen no sign of Henry at all while searching for Carla in the canyon. "Yeah, I know that spot, from when we were searching for my wife. Say, you haven't seen anything?" He tensed up as he remembered the speculation that Henry had been somewhere in the canyon that night.

"No, sorry, Doc. Tim King already talked to me. I haven't seen a sign of her. Be sure to let you know, though." He sounded a little indifferent now, as though, like so much of the world, he'd moved on from old sufferings and maybe Dave should move on from his.

"Guess your boss likes having you close by. If I recall right, whole lot of spiders live in those moraine mats. Are you sure that—?"

"Them?" Henry laughed, finding the idea preposterous. "They don't bother me no more." He stretched exuberantly. "I sleep good in them mats."

Then Henry West winked: "My life's good now, Doc. I've found my home."

"Henry, if you ever find yourself in trouble—say with your boss— you can call me."

Henry didn't reply, and as Dave offered his hand again, the little man's eyes suddenly widened and he reached for door handle.

As Dave heard the door to Sierra Realty open, he mumbled a quick goodbye and hurried back across the road while a familiar pursuing shadow spread coldly behind him.

•

On his last morning in the old bungalow, Dave woke up on Carla's side of the bed. At first, he thought that the Ark was right inside the bedroom, but he realized it was only a trick of the first dawn light mixing with a fleeting dream.

He rose to find himself looking out the window. He'd never seen the mountain like this. It had always been Carla's thing, and he'd meant to leave it that way. This last time though, he would allow himself to see the spectacle as she saw it, dawn falling over the distant mountains.

The bird sailed into view, from the south, when the first stars began to disappear, heading straight for Dragon's Ark. It flew with calm purpose, a grace and simplicity that Dave found moving, a sense of ancient greatness that stretched across valleys of time. He grabbed Carla's binoculars from under her bedside table. As he focused, the speck became a big black dot, but still remained elusive, unnamed, unknown.

He stayed on it for a moment and then, with a start, lowered the binoculars, shook his head, wiped the glue from his eyes and looked again. The focus was correct and he wasn't seeing double. There was another bird, another mysterious species, struggling alongside to keep up with that big hawk as though in a race against the dawn.

Dave lowered his binoculars and closed his eyes, fighting off his tears. If only Carla were here to see this, he thought. How happy she'd be to know that the old dragon no longer flew alone.

The End

ACKNOWLEDGMENTS

....

While *Dragon's Ark* is an imaginative novel, it does have its roots in the real world. First among those seeds, of course, is Bram Stoker's original *Dracula*, a novel that still casts a grand shadow. I further wish to thank the people of beautiful Alpine County, California, where the idea for this book took wing one summer evening, for their help and hospitality. I wish to thank Ellen Martin of the Alpine County Museum; Dr. Richard Harvey, director of Alpine County Health and Human Services, and staffers Liz McGeein, Regina Britschgi and Gail Day; Beverly Caldera and Hector Caldera of the Washoe Tribe Southern Band Headquarters, plus contributors to the Washoe Tribe website at www.washoe.us; Christine Branscombe, support services coordinator at the Alpine County Sheriff's Department, and Tom Linder, sheriff's deputy and coordinator of Search and Rescue. You are all so lucky to live in one of the most beautiful spots on Earth.

I also wish to thank to Jamie M. Kneitel, assistant professor at California State University, Sacramento, for pointing me to resources documenting the flora and fauna of the Sierra. Many thanks to early readers who kindly wandered into the murky thicket of confusion that marked earlier drafts of this book: John-Ivan Palmer, Don Herron, Margaret Wheeler Clark, Toni Lee Gould, Alan Beatts, and Tim Stookey.

During the run-up to publication, I was happily stunned by Cathi Stevenson's superbly threatening cover. With only my summary to go on, she seemed to have read my mind. Thanks also to the copyediting of Bonnie Britt and the excellent interior design of Joel

Friedlander. Special thanks are also due to the California Writers Club-Berkeley Branch.

I would also like to mention A. Roger Ekirch's wonderful book *At Day's Close: Night in Times Past*, a treasure I unearthed just when work on *Dragon's Ark* was drawing to a close. Mr. Ekirch's work helped to clarify themes that had only been shadows in my subconscious.

A scratch behind the ears to our calico cat Flo, who, as the days wore on, would wander by my desk and gaze up at me with her button eyes as though reassuring me that no matter how hard things got, the whole world was still wonderful. We will miss you always!

And most of all, I owe everything to my patient wife, Elizabeth Wheeler Burchfield, who lived with this project for much too long and inspired me with her love. As we walked along a busy Sierra mountain highway one summer evening, it was she who mistook my jumpiness at the huge trucks that were thundering close by for something else and joked: "What's the matter with you? You look like we're about be attacked by Dracula!" I then looked at the burnt umber sky above the black forested hills and the shadowy peaks around us, as a grand colorful nightmare fluttered to life.

www.ingramcontent.com/pod-product-compliance
Lightning Source LLC
Chambersburg PA
CBHW070159120726
47909CB00001B/181